Elia Kazan's

THE ASSAS

"The tone of the book is extremely striking, for it really does not seem to depend on anything that we think of as a literary tradition, but on something older than that: the tale being told by a member of the tribe."

—James Baldwin,
New York Review of Books

"BEAUTIFULLY WRITTEN . . . AN OUTCRY FOR UNDERSTANDING, A PLEA FOR TOLERANCE . . . THE BEST THAT KAZAN HAS WRITTEN."

—*Hartford Courier*

"It is impossible, in a short space, to give a work so rich, complex and subtle, its due; here is one of the finest novels out for a long time."

—*New Republic*

"THE NARRATIVE IS CHARGED WITH LIGHTNING."

—*San Francisco Chronicle*

"A novel for those who rejoice in the rare experience these days of getting hooked by a master storyteller. A novel to change your life by."

—*Life*

ARE THERE FAWCETT PAPERBACK BOOKS
YOU WANT BUT CANNOT FIND IN YOUR LOCAL STORES?

You can get any title in print in Fawcett Crest, Fawcett Premier, or Fawcett Gold Medal editions. Simply send
title and retail price, plus 15¢ to cover mailing and handling
costs for each book wanted, to:

MAIL ORDER DEPARTMENT,
FAWCETT PUBLICATIONS,
FAWCETT BUILDING,
GREENWICH, CONN. 06830

Books are available at discounts in quantity lots for in-
dustrial or sales-promotional use. For details write FAW-
CETT WORLD LIBRARY, CIRCULATION MANAGER,
FAWCETT BLDG., GREENWICH, CONN. 06830

ELIA KAZAN

THE ASSASSINS

A FAWCETT CREST BOOK

Fawcett Publications, Inc., Greenwich, Conn.

THE ASSASSINS

THIS BOOK CONTAINS THE COMPLETE TEXT OF THE
ORIGINAL HARDCOVER EDITION.

A Fawcett Crest Book reprinted by arrangement with Stein and
Day.

Copyright © 1972 by Elia Kazan.

All rights reserved, including the right to reproduce this book or
portions thereof in any form.

Library of Congress Catalog Card Number: 70-164684

Alternate Selection of the Book-of-the-Month Club, June 1972
Selection of the Playboy Book Club, Spring 1972

Fiction is fiction; it's not fact. The persons and events in this book
are creatures and incidents only of my imagination. Any reference
to living persons and actual events is coincidental.

Printed in the United States of America
March 1973

TO MY CHILDREN
FOR THEIR FAVOR

THE ASSASSINS

CHAPTER ONE

They were flying out the next morning, and Master Sergeant Cesario Flores had a farewell word to say. He did this correctly, as he did everything else, saying neither too much nor too little, singling out no one for praise or for censure. He allowed they were a good troop and if he heard some day that they were really doing a job, he wouldn't be surprised. He reminded them for the hundredth time that the men flying the planes could be no better than the maintenance on the ground. Then he said the word, "Goodbye," paused, seemed to be thinking, pushed his slightly tinted glasses up to a more comfortable rest. His last joke was a postscript; he didn't expect to hear from any of them personally, but if he did, please no more dirty oriental postcards, he'd had enough from the last gang he'd trained. When he smiled you could see he was Mexican, de las Flores.

The men laughed and whispered; then they saw he was waiting for them to be silent. When they were, he said, "You're representing a great country, don't forget that!" He seemed about to add something caustic, didn't. That was it. He walked up to the men, twenty-seven of them, shook hands with each, calling him by name and rank. It was as close as Sergeant Flores could come to giving them his blessing.

The bulky body turned, correctly and in place, the sergeant picked up his hat and walked out of the shop, down the clapboard-lined corridor to the exit, out and under a sign which read, THROUGH THESE PORTALS PASS THE PRETTIEST ME-

CHANICS IN THE WORLD, past another the sergeant himself had ordered, P R I D E, and so to the first parking slot at the side of the building, the one with his name painted on the macadam. His car was a Dodge, GI brown, and belonged to the air force. Sergeant Flores checked the rearview mirror to see that it was correctly angled, cinched his seat belt though he was only going three hundred yards to the office of his commanding officer, Colonel Francis Dowd.

"For chrissake, you didn't have to finish this today," Colonel Dowd said when Flores handed him his report on the embarking squad. "I won't look at it till the weekend."

"Yes, sir," Sergeant Flores smiled. He liked Colonel Dowd; when he was with him, a sly Latino humor showed and he looked like what he'd been, a kid from Sonora, smiling, half mocking, half envious of the wealthy American tourists.

"You're a freak, you know that, don't you?" Colonel Dowd said, looking at Flores sternly, which was part of their affection game.

"Yes, sir?" The sergeant said, looking equally severe.

Colonel Dowd had seen action overseas, and he often observed to his wife that there was only one man on that goddamn base who seemed to be aware that there was a major war on, so put out top effort at all times. "The man's a pro!" he'd said to his wife, "there aren't many, not alive. The good ones buy it, the goof-offs come home."

"Master Sergeant Flores!" Dowd cracked out.

"Yes, sir?" The sergeant straightened for orders.

"Take your wife and kids, for chrissake, and go fishing. Your new troop doesn't get here till Monday, which means Tuesday, which means you don't get them till they've been processed, which means Wednesday, so take one hell of a weekend. That's an order."

"I like it on the base, sir, thank you, sir," Flores replied.

Collins Air Force Base is in New Mexico, on the edge of a city in the great desert south of Albuquerque. It is a world. When you stand in the middle of the area, all you can see is air force installations. Behind in every direction are mountains like paper cutouts, remote, abstract. A visitor gets the impression in which the lifer who lives on the base is confirmed: There is nothing else.

Actually the base has it all: a ball field, a golf course, a bowling alley, a movie theater, a library, a supermarket, a drugstore, a filling station, two banks, two bars, three chapels, and a barber shop. There is no reason to go off. Every once in a while the Flores family would make the mistake, take a vacation trip. They were always relieved when they turned back through the main gate, past the sign, PEACE IS OUR PROFESSION. Home!

The base commissary is one-third cheaper than those in town, and it has piped-in music. Everyone there knew that Cesario, not his wife, Elsa, did the family's food buy. Up and down the aisles he talked bargains with the women regulars, recipes, too. Thanks to the air force, Cesario had been able to collect recipes from Germany, France, Belgium, and from Panama, where he'd also done a short tour.

When people asked Flores how come he prepared the family meals, he'd answer he liked his own cooking best. The fact was that Cesario liked to eat well, and Mrs. Flores, Elsa, seldom ate a full meal. Beer was her thing, and with it she nibbled, particularly when she could get a neighbor to nibble-gab with her.

Mrs. Flores was German-born, Elsa Matz. Cesario had met her after V-E Day at a USO dance in Bad Tölz, Bavaria. A lot of the fräuleins were quick-marrying GIs in those days. For a time Cesario actually believed Elsa had fallen in love with him because he petted before intercourse, which German men, so he'd been told, did not. But the fact was that Elsa appreciated Cesario's ways in courtship for more vital reasons.

Munich, where Elsa was born, had been badly hit. Her mother, a soprano in the state operetta's chorus, had died at home in a collapse of old brick. It happened while Herr Matz, the head hall porter of the Vier Jahreszeiten Hotel, was at work, so he didn't learn of the disaster till he got home at daybreak and found his daughter standing at the side of the collapsed building, miraculously spared but in a state of uncontrollable trembling.

That raid came back in nightmares; it left a scar on the girl's courage. She was ready to sacrifice anything for safety.

In his concern for the girl, Herr Matz began to spoil her. He influenced the management of the Vier Jahreszeiten Hotel to make available a small chamber under their eaves, used by chauffeurs and valets. Elsa slept on a cot across the foot of his bed. He saw to it that a kindly old waiter brought her every meal. The chambermaids dressed her, kept her fresh. In the servant society of that hotel, Elsa was treated like a guest.

The victorious army of Yanks set up a large base at Bad Tölz, an hour's drive south. Herr Matz knew what he was doing when he arranged for Elsa, eighteen and in blossom, to spend the summer in Bad Tölz at the home of an aunt. Herr Matz had learned the lesson of history: the vanquished survive by bedding the conquerors.

With the no-fraternization rules relaxed, USO scouts recruited dancing partners for the boys from nearby towns. Elsa was discovered. Plump as a dumpling, she showed a perfect retroussé nose; her mother's hair of white gold; her mother's aura: the fairy princess; her mother's way with clothes: pastels and frills; her mother's laugh: trills running up a scale.

At eighteen this piece of ornamental china had never been chipped. Cesario saw in her everything he could have found in a Mexican maiden—suet in all the right places, but white as a church candle.

Elsa noticed how everyone in his group looked up to Cesario. At twenty-two, he was an experienced noncom, an *Übermensch* compared to the nineteen-year-olds in his charge. Attractive, too; he had lovely brown skin, exceptional manners, sang beautifully, was hell on "Las Mananitas," it brought tears to his eyes and to hers. He was quite a dancer, too; just to be in the clasp of his great bear body was safety itself.

Herr Matz died two weeks after their wedding, a testament to his absolute confidence in his son-in-law.

For many years they didn't have children, though Cesario wanted them and they certainly tried. Elsa defended her failure: The air force kept moving them around, she needed a settled home, what kind of places were those? Korea? Okinawa?

Finally Command moved Cesario back to Germany, to the base at Wiesbaden. Two months later, Elsa was proved right; she conceived, a girl, Juana. Playing their luck while it was running, they immediately had another, Elizabeth. Then the brass gods shipped them out again, to California. This was the limit, Cesario did not re-enlist.

His years in private industry, working maintenance for a major airline, were miserable. He missed the order of the air force, had fits of temper and melancholy, took to drink and quarrel. The arrival of still another girl, Linda, did not help. He wanted a son.

It was Elsa who suggested he re-enlist, become a lifer, enjoy that security. As soon as he did, she conceived again, and this one was a boy, Diego. The day he was born, Cesario swore off drink.

Three things here bewildered Elsa. When she married Cesario in Bavaria he was an American. In America he was Mexican. In Bavaria, Cesario was rich, servants fought for his dollar. In America, the family just got by, couldn't afford servants. In Bavaria, Cesario was a hero. In America, he was a member of a minority.

Rapture dies; it needs no reason. These discoveries hastened what would have happened in any case. Her practical goals gained, Elsa had years before stopped pretending ecstasy. Raised to respect power, she did not conceal her disappointment with her shrunken man.

Like the rest of us, they lost what had brought them together. There wasn't anything else.

She determined that her girls would grow up ladies, desirable to men of position and power, marry better than she had. Her models were the daughters of the massive Junker industrialists she'd observed in the Vier Jahreszeiten. Those girls did not wash dishes; they were not required to master the vacuum cleaner.

She began to assume many of the imperious ways of Herr Matz. Raised to expect her dinner served her, Elsa was quick to accept that service from her husband.

Her daughters accepted it, too.

All this was okay with Cesario. He had discovered that in America, without inexpensive domestics at hand to pick up after them, his lady and her belles left more work when they were through cooking or cleaning up than they saved by going through those motions.

So breakfast was pickup, lunch was pickup, and dinner was waiting for daddy.

Elsa had very definite ideas about how she and her girls should look in public. Early each season, she went out and bought what was "suitable," usually fussy, frilly things for ladies of quality and leisure. Nor was she satisfied with what was available in the shops of that part of the world. Finding a seamstress on the base, the wife of a grease monkey, she put the woman to work on patterns of her own styling, elaborate perishables.

So when Elsa dressed up, she did. But when she didn't, she lay around the house all day in her gown and looked like a "pretty tough tomato," to quote Sergeant Jack Jones, their neighbor. Elsa had two ways to face the world, one as a little girl living in privileged leisure and the other a "heinie stone crusher," to again quote the sergeant next door.

Now in their forties, Cesario and Elsa had made their adjustment to the world and to each other. She could scold him by the hour, and he would respond with an attentive face, but hear nothing. From not being a talker, he'd become not a listener. Her talk was all the same anyway; she found the brown marks on the inside of everyone's underdrawers. Rather than listen to her stream of put-down, Cesario would hum to himself and cook the meal. Or he'd turn up the TV to where Elsa's soprano couldn't buck the level, so get through till it was time for bed. There he might put one into her or he might not; it didn't matter.

What of passion? Cesario had one, the only one that took more of him than his work, his eldest daughter, Juana. Whereas the other children looked like throwbacks to Herr Matz or his frau—with a pinch of brown added--Juana, by some genetic accident, was pure Aztec. She had the most beautiful eyes, almost black, a little close-set, true, but that made them more intense. And a nose that somewhere way back took its contour from the Indian women profiled on the pyramids of Chichén Itzá. She looked exactly like snapshots Cesario had of his mother when she was a girl, taken against a white plaster wall in Sonora.

Elsa, of course, complained that Cesario hopelessly spoiled their eldest. At seventeen, Juana still sat on her father's knee, there got anything she wanted, an Indian princess stranded on an air base in the middle of a desert in a foreign land.

For Cesario, Juana was the only part of Mexico left to him. He couldn't stop fussing with her. In town he'd walk up to a complete stranger and ask where she'd bought something she was wearing, a blouse, a skirt, an ornament. The woman might, at first, think he was getting fresh, but then she'd look at Cesario's earnest face, the heavy anxious eyes behind the tinted glasses, that bulk of innocence, and she'd listen while he explained why what she had on would look good on his daughter and please, no offense, where had she bought it? That night the item would be on Juana.

So Juana became a point of contention between them. Often when Cesario came home, Elsa would be waiting with a complaint, and it was usually about Juana. On this night, she was waiting for him to get home, ready to fire.

"I've got something important to talk to you about," she said as he cleared the kitchen table of the pickup breakfast and the pickup lunch. "Are you listening, please?"

Cesario was looking at the large frying pan still plastered with the curds of that morning's eggs.

"I was so upset, I didn't have concentration to do that pan. Cesario, listen this time."

He nodded, scraped the pan with the back of a knife. "Go ahead. Talk."

"I will not discuss something intimate while you are doing that!" She looked toward the other room.

The common room of the house was dominated by a large color TV, which was never off. Before it now were two of their three girls and the boy, Diego.

"I thought they were only going to watch one hour a day," Cesario said. "Have they done their homework?"

"They start killing each other when I turn it off." She took the pan out of his hand and slammed it down on the sideboard, then led him into the girls' bedroom and closed the door. She walked into the closet, stooped in the dark corner, and from the bottom of a pile of laundry on the floor pulled a pair of girl's slacks and held them up.

They were purple and flared at the bottom.

"Take a look if you please," she said.

"Whose are they?"

"You know whose."

"What's the matter with them?"

"You're not looking." She held the slacks up close to his face.

On the front, half way up, were white drops, now dry.

Cesario took the purple bells and walked to the window.

The stains were what he thought.

"I told you to forbid her to work at that place. But with you, no. With you, whatever that girl wants, she gets."

Juana was working night-shift carhop at Bennie's Big Boy Hamburger Joynt.

"You must learn to listen to me, Cesario, at last. So? *Dummkopf!*"

He didn't speak.

"She's going to be a whore in the Reeperbahn, your daughter."

"Don't talk that way about her, Elsa."

"I'm warning you, you'll find her on the floor of freight elevators, your madonna, with taxi drivers—"

"She's a good girl."

"I'm telling you, last time, don't wait for two-thirty, go down to that filthy place for hamburgers and order her out!"

"I'll go there at two-thirty."

Bennie of Bennie's Big Boy Hamburger Joynt was talking to a pair of cops in a prowl car when Cesario drove up. Bennie had been burglarized a few nights before. Although the cops hadn't found a scrap of evidence, they'd been dropping by every night for appearances. Bennie was always ready with a double-decker, and his was as good a place as any to unbutton for a smoke.

The presence of the police hadn't kept anyone away. At two-thirty in the morning, Bennie's was the live place on the west side.

"Sergeant Flores!" Bennie was walking up to him.

"Hey, Bennie, *qué tal?*"

"Oh, business is good. The robbery helped, though that kind of help I can do without. I'd look after my kid if I were you." He pointed.

Cesario saw Juana and another carhop just going off work. They were being pressed by some boys, longhairs.

"What are they, students?"

"Students, former students, dropouts, pushers, dealers, faggots, how do you tell? You got a nice kid there, if I had her I'd sure keep her away from that pack."

"Thanks," Cesario said and walked toward the gang around his daughter. The boys were coming on with her, all except one who leaned against the side of a car with an air of consummate indifference.

He was the one Juana was looking at.

Cesario walked into the group and put his arm around Juana's shoulder before she realized he was there.

"Time to go, kid," he said.

"Oh, daddy!" She looked around at the boys. They'd gone silent. Juana either didn't know their names or chose not to introduce them to her father. "You know Marcie?" She indicated the other carhop.

"Hello, Marcie," Cesario nodded, then, "let's go, baby."

"They're going to drive me home." She looked at the boys.

"Like hell they are."

Sergeant Flores was trembling. Everyone could feel it. No one looked at him. No one spoke.

They waited.

"Get in the car," the soldier said to his daughter in a voice barely audible. Juana went to the car without a word.

Cesario stayed where he was, surrounded by the freaks. Then the pressure in his head dropped, and he walked away.

Riding home, Cesario felt—why the hell should he? —that he'd done something wrong. Was it because Juana wasn't talking to him, was it because she sat at the other end of the seat looking out the black window?

The instant of murder had left him with a headache. Once he'd lost control of himself that way and almost killed one of his close friends, slamming his head again and again on the concrete floor of the shop. They had to pull him off that man.

He looked at Juana. He didn't mind when Elsa didn't talk to him, but he couldn't take it when this damn little kid locked her mouth. Well, the hell with it, this time let her talk first!

"Was I mean to those kids?"

She didn't answer.

"I'm sorry if I was, but I got worried about you."

No answer.

"I mean, Juanie—you know how to protect yourself?"

Nothing.

"I mean, baby, don't rely on any boy. He'll tell you, sure, sure, leave it to him, know what I mean? That's the thing men say when they get excited. But don't believe them, know what I'm talking about?"

"Is that what she thinks?"

"Who?"

"Mom."

"Your mother is upset because—"

Juana was laughing. "I've never been with anybody, daddy."

"Well, okay, okay, I'm glad."

"So you thought that, too?" She was laughing, and her eyes had the black Indian look that only she—and he—had. "I'm saving it for you, daddy."

"Don't talk that way," he said. "Juanita!" But then he laughed, grabbed her arm, and pulled her up against him.

They drove home in silence, turning in the main gate, through the installations of the silent base, through the streets of the little community of identical white homes known as Vinson Village.

He was just climbing into bed when Juana slammed open the door to their bedroom and held up the purple bells.

"Who hacked these up?" She came around to Elsa's side of the bed. "Did you rip these up?"

Elsa turned over.

"They're my best bells!"

"I'll buy you a clean pair," Cesario said.

"Go back to bed," Elsa said. "Immediately."

"I don't want a clean pair! I want you to leave my clothes alone!"

Elsa was awake now. "As long as you live in my house, I'm going to look after you properly, never forget that."

"Properly!"

"Yes! And don't come into my room yelling at me that way!" Elsa, breathing hard, turned to Cesario. "You allow her to talk to me," she demanded. "That way? Cesario?"

"Shsh," he tried to quiet his wife, remembering that an officer is supposed to keep his house in order.

"And when is she going back to school?"

"I'll go back when I'm ready."

Elsa turned to her husband. "You hear that? What are you going to do about that? Nothing? Not a—"

At this instant Juana began to scream, "I don't want to live with you! I don't want to live here any more!"

Elsa grabbed her and began to shake her, and Cesario had to get between, put his arms around the girl, and walk her out of the room. "Shsh," he whispered, "she's a good woman, she's worried because she loves you."

They could still hear Elsa: "They suck my life out, those

girls. I can't fight any more. She's yours, you take care of her."

Six weeks later, Master Sergeant Cesario Flores went in to see his commanding officer, Colonel Dowd, and asked for a transfer.

"Transfer! To where?"

"I don't care, sir. Spain. Germany. Japan. First opening."

Colonel Dowd looked at Sergeant Jack Jones, whose desk was in an alcove off the colonel's office and who was leaning forward to listen. Jones knew what was eating Flores.

"Are you unhappy here?" Colonel Dowd asked.

"Not on the base, sir."

"Then—?"

"It's a family matter."

Colonel Dowd looked at Sergeant Jones again and then back to Master Sergeant Flores.

"That it, sir? Thank you, sir." He turned to go.

"Wait a minute. You can't come in and ask for a transfer like that. There's a form. What's the matter with you all of a sudden?"

Cesario tightened his mouth.

Colonel Dowd made up his mind to stall. The operating procedures of the air force would help. "First thing, you go out to Corporal Fenton and get the form. She'll help you fill it. Then I'll sign it, and we'll begin processing."

"Thank you, sir." Flores turned and walked out of the office.

"What's eating him?" Colonel Dowd asked Jones.

"I don't know."

"Don't give me that. Come in here, Sergeant Jones!" Jones walked up to his desk. "Jack, I don't intend to lose that man!"

"His daughter left home three weeks ago."

"Where's she now?"

"He can't find her."

"Get him back in here."

"Don't tell him I said anything."

"Why the hell not, what is this? Bring that man to me!"

When Jack Jones was out of sight of the colonel, he made a little gesture of apology to Cesario, then the sign that he was to go back in.

"Sergeant Jones tells me your daughter ran away."

"Yes, sir." Flores had his head down.

"Well, that happens—to everybody! Sergeant Flores, I'm speaking to you!"

"Yes, sir."

"If she's disappeared, why do you want to move away?"

"Yes, sir. I mean, I want a transfer."

"Sergeant Flores, look at me! If there's a problem, the air force might be able to help you with it."

"Yes, sir."

"I'm bothering with you because I value you and don't want to lose you. You appreciate that?"

"Yes, sir."

"Now, then, answer my question. If she left home, why do you want to transfer to Spain?"

"I want to get her away from here."

"There are boys everywhere."

"It's not the boys."

"What then?"

"It's none of your business, sir."

"Flores, I'm asking you as a friend."

"I think she's in with—drugs, you know?"

"Three quarters of that college down there—"

"But she's my daughter." Suddenly he turned on Sergeant Jones, his voice trembling. "What are you laughing at?"

"He's only smiling in sympathy. What the hell's the matter with you, Cesario? He wants to help you."

"It's my problem."

"I want you to tell me what happened, Cesario."

"We woke up one morning, and her bed was empty. That's the last we seen of her."

"How do you know she's taking drugs?"

"I've been talking to—whatever they are—students. I'm sorry, sir, I'm supposed to keep my house in order. And I will." He turned to go.

"Flores, I'm going to find out where your daughter is. I'll put Base Intelligence on it."

"I'd rather you didn't, sir. I'll find her myself." He stood there, head down, breathing with difficulty. He looked heavier to Dowd, puffy, and very ashamed. Colonel Dowd felt sorry for him.

"I'll bring the form back for your signature," Cesario said with half his voice. And he walked out of the office.

"Goddamnit, I don't want to lose that man," the colonel

muttered. "Where the hell am I going to find a maintenance man as good as—"

"You're not," said Sergeant Jones.

"Get that damned intelligence officer in here."

Cesario hadn't had a good night's sleep in the twenty since Juana's disappearance. He'd go to bed, then, without the jolt of the alarm, wake at ten after two, get in his car, and drive off the base.

First stop was Bennie's. Bennie knew some of the other hangouts, had suggested where else Cesario might look. But he was pessimistic about the chances of finding the girl. "They're like deer, sleep all day, move at night, might be around here a few days, then way over to Tucson or Nogales where the marijuana comes in, or to L.A. for acid. Now it's warm and I understand they go to the side of Father Felipe Pass, there are places in the desert there where they stay. In the open, like animals. There's really no way to look for them, just wait and hope."

Bennie had promised to put him in touch with a friend of his, maybe this fellow, an Italian from out of town, could help. "The family don't like these kids dealing drugs," he said. "It gives the traffic a bad name."

But the Italian didn't show. "He maybe thinks you're a narc," Bennie said. "But I'll be talking to him. He plays golf where I play. I'm going to lock up now."

"I'll stay a while, just sit in the car."

Bennie gave him a container of coffee, the last strong stuff from the bottom of the vat.

Cesario sat there sipping it for another fifteen, twenty minutes. Then he drove slowly through the streets of the sleeping city, out to the top of Father Felipe Pass about five miles north. The sun was coming up, glancing across the tubes of the saguaro.

Then it was morning, and Cesario went home.

There was a letter from Juana, a short one, just to tell them she was all right, living with a girl friend, they could write her if they felt like it, she gave the girl's address, sorry if she'd caused them any worry, but she wasn't a kid any more, had to find her own way, which she was doing, so take care!

As Cesario shaved, he studied the address on the back of the envelope. "Where is this?" he asked.

"South Side," Elsa said from the doorway. "Where all the Chicano whores stay."

"She's got nice handwriting," Cesario said. Finished, he walked into the bedroom, put on his blouse, looked at himself in the mirror.

"Muy macho!" Elsa observed.

Cesario let this pass too. Carefully, he combed his hair.

"You know what my father would have done by now? You have any idea?"

"I have my own way." He walked out on the porch.

"It's already got to Elizabeth, your way. She's talking about leaving school."

Cesario nodded.

"Why are you nodding? That's the first step, when they leave school."

Sergeant and Mrs. Jones were sitting on the porch of their house. "They're watching us," he whispered to Elsa as she walked down the porch stairs.

"They're not watching, *Liebchen*, they're laughing at you."

He got into his car. "Call the shop, tell 'em I'll be late."

"You realize the whole base is laughing at you, not only your friend Jack Jones and his wife, everybody?"

"I realize," Cesario said.

Over the windshield hung two white baby shoes, a compass taken from a scrapped fighter plane, and a medallion of the *madrecita*.

He had trouble finding the house. When he finally did, it was noon.

In front of the house was a fat man with tiny feet and Italian blood, most of it in his face, the owner. On the lawn had been piled everything that had been in the house. Inside, painters were at work. A dump truck arrived.

A policeman was standing by. "They were two months behind in the rent," he said, "so they just walked out and left all that." He pointed. "Look at it. Did you ever?"

In the warm sunlight, it looked particularly dank. There was a three-legged table, a big mattress with a corner eaten out by fire, months of beer empties, half-eaten packs of Fritos, cheese gone green, health magazines, a tattered copy of the

Whole Earth Catalogue. Flies buzzed over what looked like a pile of baby's diapers.

"Where'd they move to?" Cesario asked.

"Who knows? There are places like this all over town. We found the usual, weed and twig ends. They were dealing."

"Then why you don't do something?"

The owner had overheard. "They ruin my place. I have to paint everything! Cats under the floor! Dead! Stink! Dealing! Why you don't run them out of town? Police! Bullshit!"

The cop didn't take offense. "A couple of our fellows picked up one of these creeps last month," he said to Cesario. "His place was worse than this. Turned out he was a state senator's son! Who needs that kind of trouble? They're all through the university out there, sell the stuff in the classrooms. One professor, his class got bigger and bigger, he couldn't figure it out!"

He noticed Cesario wasn't listening. "You looking for someone in particular?" he asked.

"No, nobody," Cesario said. He thanked the officer and left.

The next day was Saturday, and he stayed in the house. He didn't speak to anyone, didn't really move—but once. Elsa said something he didn't like, and he hit her. Then he was quiet, and everyone was careful.

He didn't eat dinner. He didn't cook for them.

The next day, Sunday, Cesario got up before dawn and made coffee. He sat in the kitchen and slowly emptied the six-cup perker. Then he went into the bathroom and shaved with meticulous care. He put on his dress uniform, and, just as the sun was coming up, walked out on the porch and sat, tensed forward in his chair, as if in the moment before a departure.

When Elsa got out of bed, she saw him. "Where are you going, *Liebchen?*"

"Church."

"What church is six o'clock?" He didn't answer. "Look what you did to my eye! Now was that nice?" He didn't look.

When Elsa woke the children, she put her girls in their best Sunday frocks, frilly pastels, trimmed with machine-punched lace; the boy in his little blue suit, his shirt with French cuffs and his clip-on blue tie. People who watched

Master Sergeant Flores and his family walk down the aisle of the base chapel that morning were impressed with their clean, cohesive look. A veil covered Elsa's discolored eye.

At the head of the aisle, Elsa noticed, Cesario did not kneel and make the sign of the cross as he usually did.

The first hymn was an old Anglican exhortation:

> *Awake my soul, stretch every nerve*
> *And press with vigor ah-un*
> *A heavenly race demands thy zeal*
> *And an immortal crown.*

In the space between this verse and the next, Elsa heard Cesario muttering something, she wasn't sure what, the words were—Spanish? Indian? She couldn't make them out.

Cesario was in some sort of trance. People were beginning to notice. Elsa reached across her daughter Elizabeth and shook his shoulder. "Shshsh," she whispered.

"Excuse me," Cesario said. He slid past Elizabeth, then past Elsa. As he walked up the aisle the congregation sang:

> *A cloud of witnesses around,*
> *Hold thee in full survey-ay.*
> *Forget the steps already trod*
> *And onward wend thy way.*

At the door Cesario became aware that he was still holding the open hymnal. He laid it on the little wooden box with the money slot which stood across the exit. Then he left the chapel.

He got in his car and drove off the base, south along the fence, past the graveyard of planes, through the slum flats on the other side of the federal preserve. He drove slowly, stopping longer at intersections than he needed to. Free to talk to himself, he did.

That day he needed magic, not religion.

To the south was Chicano town. He was at home in the environment, that of his youth. Though he had only been there once before, he found what he was looking for almost immediately.

The church, except for one small shrine and the altar itself, was bare of ornament. Bare of humanity, too, except for two old women in black remembering their dead. Cesario walked slowly down the uncarpeted aisle, turned at the nave, and approached the shrine of the Madonna. Before her figure, he fell on his knees and in the Spanish of Sonora made a deal with the Mother of Jesus.

He offered that if she would help in his crisis, as he knew she could, if she would lead him to where his daughter was, as it was in her power to do, if she would have pity on him now, intercede with her mystery, bring his daughter home again, he would pay her back with a demonstration of faith that would amaze all who saw it or heard of it, he would walk on his knees from the base through the town of the poor to this neglected church, down the aisle on his knees to the place at her feet where he now was. So would he manifest his thanks and proclaim his renewed faith for all to know.

When he got home, Colonel Dowd was on the porch waiting for him, an honor.

Dowd had decided to have a talk with his maintenance chief. He believed in getting into a problem early; he was late on this one. When he found Cesario was not home, he looked for a quick excuse to get away, remembering how Sergeant Jones had characterized Wife Flores. But Elsa insisted he have coffee, showed off her pretty daughters and Diego, who saluted as his father had taught him. They gathered at his feet with sugar and cream and coffee cake and looked up at him with the kind of attention he did not enjoy at home.

"Cesario is such a good person," Mrs. Flores said. "Such a big heart! He was a little wild when I met him, *borracho,* you know Mexican? But we corrected that, we control it. But now, I'm worried. There's only one person—" Elsa fixed Colonel Dowd with a look that embarrassed him. "He worships you!"

"I think I can help him," Dowd said, turning his attention to Cesario's car, which was driving up.

He took Cesario for a walk. As they passed Jack Jones's house, they spotted Jones in his doorway. When the colonel waved, Jones saluted. On the next porch, man, wife, mother-in-law were speculating why the base commander was there and what he was saying.

"The population of Vinson Village will have something to talk about over Sunday dinner," Colonel Dowd observed. "Where have you been?"

"Church."

"I don't go to church, leave that to my wife."

"Yes, sir."

"Sometimes on Sunday mornings I read books I like. This morning I was rereading Jack London, and I thought of you."

"Thank you, sir. What's that, Jack London?"

"I don't think the young bright ones in this country favor Jack London—he's a writer—but I understand the Russians think highly of him. They would, being a realistic people. Jack London looked at the society of wolves and understood brother man."

"Not a bad idea."

"He made this point. There's an uphill to life and there's a downhill, and unless you protect yourself—man or nation—you find you're on the down, a lot sooner than you need to be. You've got to protect what's yours. Wolves do it with tooth and fang. But the principle is the same. If you let them take it away from you, they're going to take it away from you."

"I see what you mean."

"London described the young males who live on the periphery of the pack. Every once in a while they rush in and grab one off."

"One what?"

"A bitch wolf. I was making reference to your daughter, no offense intended."

"Sure."

"Did you see your friend Jack Jones standing in his doorway and those others all down the line?"

"They can go to hell. Excuse me."

"They're judging you. The fact is—no matter how civilization tries to cover it up—everyone is on trial all the time. You Mexicans built a whole culture on the absolutely basic proposition that your balls is who you are. *Macho* or *pendejo,* right?"

"You got it!" Cesario laughed.

Colonel Dowd reached into his pocket, pulled out a filing card, folded and held together with a strip of scotch tape. "First time my goddamn G2 came through for me. Here's where your daughter is."

Cesario took the card.

"My opinion is you've been remarkably restrained. That's the opinion of every man on this base."

They'd reached the car. Dowd offered his hand. "You know," he said. "I liked your wife. And those girls— *wunderbar!*"

And he drove off.

Cesario opened the card. The house was on Queen Street.

———————————————————————

Cesario had a favorite picture of himself, taken in Panama City twenty-six years earlier by an army staff photographer. It made front page on the post paper, had showed the winner of that Friday night's fight, not in the ring, but out of it, being restrained by four M.P.s. There was a big hole in his face—his grinning mouth, from which blood roiled like tomato soup. Cesario had won that night like he'd won other nights, by catching everything his opponent could throw for the first five, six rounds, taking it all till the other man thought he had the Mexican ready for the kill in a matter of seconds, another flurry or two.

That's what he was most proud of in those days, his ability to take punishment. When his opponent finally punched himself out, couldn't hold his arms up, Cesario began to come on. Having eaten more fist than any normal man could, "Loco" walked out for *número siete,* crossing himself, and bit by bit paid his opponent back in leather for what he'd whispered in the clinches, and for what his twin brother and bunk buddies in the front row had never stopped shouting from the rail underfoot.

It wasn't a matter of race—well, that was part of it—but mostly because they all had their pay riding on the other guy and were watching it go.

Cesario enjoyed the last round most. He had his man staggering every which way, one eye closed, the other fluttering. Every time he was about to fall, Cesario would let up so he could recover enough for Cesario to begin to punish him again. The end of the fight was perfect, and Cesario recalled it now as he drove to the address on Queen Street that Colonel Dowd had given him. Just as the final bell rang, the man fell on his face, out! At this, his partisans in the front row decided to climb into the ring themselves. But they didn't have to because Cesario was over the ropes and among them like a badger, going for their vitals with foot and fist, in any direction there was belly and balls.

It had taken four M.P.s to break it up. When they were finally holding him back, that's when the picture was taken.

As he drove up to the house on Queen Street, Cesario was primed for that kind of encounter, himself alone against a houseful of the freaks he'd seen around Juana that night at Bennie's.

The single-story house, windows to the floor, a lawn with pepper trees, didn't look bad.

When he got out of his car, he left the curbside door open for a quick getaway. With his heart pounding the inside of his ribs like a baby's fist, he hopped on the porch, ready for anything.

He tapped on the door, waited, got no answer. He hit the door a solid shot, waited. He heard music, but no one came.

He tried the handle. It wasn't locked. He opened it a little and called in, "Anybody home?"

The music was that stuff Juana liked.

Now someone was coming.

The door opened farther, and a boy, not over fifteen, inspected him—and his uniform—for a few seconds.

"I'm looking for Juana Flores," Cesario said.

The boy called back into the house, "Michael, somebody's looking for Juana."

There was an answer Cesario couldn't make out, but the boy turned to Cesario and said, "She's not here."

"Are you sure?"

The boy called back into the house. "He wants to know if I'm sure."

Again he got an answer, again turned to Cesario and said, "Yeah, I'm sure." Then he closed the door on Cesario.

The hell with this, Cesario thought and walked into the place.

The room was dark. The only light was from the Joan Crawford oldie on the tube. Cesario saw Garfield and Crawford's lips moving, but what he heard was rock. When the film cut from a night scene to sunrise over the city, Cesario was able to distinguish two people, a girl lying on the floor, not looking at the movie, the top buttons of her jeans unbuttoned, held together with a ribbon. Pregnant?

The other person was a boy in his late teens, sitting at the

end of a long sofa. He wore trousers only. The upper half
of his body was so thin his ribs showed. He smiled up at
Cesario, a gentle offer of welcome, then turned back to the
old movie.

They were smoking a twisted cigarette. Cesario knew what
it was. The boy pulled on it, passed it to the girl lying at his
feet. She held it at the very end, drew in, passed it back to
him. The exchange was unhurried and did not interrupt their
preoccupation, his with the screen, hers with her thoughts.

The music was reaching a climax. When it was done, the
thin boy looked up and smiled at Cesario again. There was
something about this welcome that threw Cesario off.

A quick look around the room showed there was no one
else there, no gang of freaks. The boy who'd come to the
door was not in sight.

"I'm Juana's father," Cesario said.

The girl looked up at him, then dropped her head back on
the floor.

The record stopped, the arm swung out of the way of the
disc about to drop, and in that silence Cesario repeated, "I'm
Juana's father. Where is she?"

"Out in the desert," the boy on the sofa said.

Garfield began to play the violin, but what they heard
was Jim Morrison singing. The thin one nodded his head
in rhythm.

"Where abouts?" Cesario asked. "Can you tell me where?"

"Sure," the thin boy said. "It's hard to describe. In the hills
back of Saint Ignacio Mission, know where that is? At the
rear end of the reservation? You know where Father Felipe
Pass is?"

"Yeah. Near there?"

"Back of there. It's not on a road, though."

He's being evasive, Cesario thought.

"We're going up there in a little while," the boy said, "if
you want to come with us."

There was something about this young person that deflated
Cesario's anger. He smiled at Cesario; nothing mocking about
the smile. Metal-rimmed glasses added to his innocence.

"When you going?" Cesario asked.

"Soon as she decides something," he indicated the girl
lying on the floor at his feet. "I want her to come with me,
she's making up her mind."

He fussed with a small brass pipe, filling it with crumble, lighting it. He took a couple of pulls, then offered it to Cesario. "Want some?"

Cesario shook his head. "I thought Juana lived here," he said.

"She does. But sometimes she goes out there."

"Where's her—boyfriend?"

"Vinnie? Had to go to San Francisco. So when some of the kids decided to go out to the desert, she went, too."

"Where does she stay when she's here?"

"Like to see?"

"Is it all right?"

"Come on." He got up. "You sure you don't want to try this?" He offered the pipe again. "It's really good."

"No, thanks. Thanks, though." Cesario followed around to the hall at the back of the house. A naked man, just about awake, was coming through. He looked at Cesario without surprise, then went to the refrigerator and looked in.

"Michael," he complained, "no more beer?"

"Guess we're out," Michael said. He touched Cesario gently on the elbow, led him down the hall to where two rooms, doors open, faced each other.

In one of them the boy who'd come to the door was sitting on the floor busy at something Cesario couldn't make out.

Michael pointed to the room opposite. "She stays in there."

The entire floor space in this small bedroom was taken up by two large mattresses, neither of which was covered with a sheet. Crumpled at the head of one of them was a Basque striped blouse that Cesario had first seen in a store window and bought for his daughter.

He looked at the other mattress. Someone, boy or girl, was asleep, almost entirely covered by a blanket. The man who'd gone for the beer came back and, lifting the blanket, got in next to the sleeping person.

Cesario felt he was intruding, turned and looked for Michael. He wasn't there. The people under the blanket rustled around, then fitted together spoon-style and were still.

Cesario backed out.

His eyes, now opened to the dark, could see what the boy on the floor of the room opposite was doing. He had a pile of dried weed in front of him and was breaking off twigs, then crumbling the leaves onto a flat sieve that was propped across two cinder blocks.

The fifteen-year-old dealer looked up at him, lifted a leg, kicked the door closed.

"He thinks you're a narc," Michael laughed. He was kneeling on the floor close to the girl, whispering to her.

Cesario heard her say, "Right, right, I don't own him."

Michael stood up. "We're going, Mr. Flores," he said.

"I'll leave this here." The girl shut what looked like a home-stitched leather satchel.

"How you all going out?" Cesario asked.

"You won't need it out there," Michael said to her. He was putting on a long-tail shirt of thin white cotton. "We'll get a ride," he answered Cesario, "sooner or later."

"I got my car," Cesario said.

Michael smiled. "Then we can take some stuff out." He turned to the girl. "You got any money?"

The girl shook her head.

Michael nodded a few times as though her answer was the one he wanted. "This is Rosalie," he said to Cesario. "She used to be with Vinnie—before Juana."

As they left the city, Cesario stopped at a supermarket. "How many people out there?" he asked Michael.

"I don't know," Michael said, as if that was a helpful answer. "Get a lot of beer and some Fritos and cheese, you know. And some oranges." Then he turned and looked at Rosalie lying across the back seat. "She's asleep," he said, looking at her fondly.

"Whose kid is that she's going to have?"

"I didn't ask her. I suppose it's from Vinnie."

The shock pulled Cesario back to what he was there for. He'd begun to enjoy the experience; it had become an adventure! Now he was burning.

He stayed in the store till he had control of himself again, buying enough for a dozen people. He had to keep up the friendly front until he got hold of Juana.

When he finally came out, a full bag in the crook of each elbow and one between, he saw a policeman bent into the car, questioning Michael, who was looking at the policeman with utter friendliness.

"That's all right, officer," Cesario said, coming up.

The officer straightened, took in the air force sergeant, then looked back at Michael smiling at him from the front seat of the official car. It occurred to Cesario, now that he was back in the world of straights, that Michael was a pretty weird sight, sitting in the front seat of an air force car, his long hair falling over his shoulders in heavy curls, his face emaciated to where his cheekbones shone through the skin like amber, his soft, dark beard setting off his teeth as he laughed at the cop's bewilderment. For the first time, Cesario noticed a small aqua stone in one earlobe. And his voice—!

"He wants to know whose car this is, whose is it?"

"U.S. Air Force. I'm Sergeant Flores. Want to see my I.D.?" To his astonishment he found himself protective of Michael.

"I guess not," the cop said.

"Open the door, will you?" Cesario said, half an order.

The policeman obliged, then walked away.

As soon as they were in traffic, Cesario asked, "Does what's his name, Vinnie, know it's his?" He was whispering, but it wasn't necessary; Rosalie had slept through the encounter with the cop.

"You never know what Vinnie knows."

"Because maybe if he did, he wouldn't leave her like this."

"He didn't leave her, exactly. Your daughter's a very aggressive person, did you know that? She made up her mind to take Vinnie away from"—he indicated the sleeping girl—"and she did. Rosalie told him, any time you want to go, go. But her feelings were hurt. That's why she didn't want to move back."

"I don't believe that—about Juana being all that goddamn aggressive!"

"Well, okay," Michael laughed.

"She'd never even been with a man before."

"Okay," Michael laughed.

"What the hell are you laughing?"

"If you say so. Anyway, it's no put-down."

"Well, she hadn't. Don't you believe me?"

"If you want me to, sure."

Cesario, on the verge again, again held back.

They had come to the last cluster of stores before the climb up to Father Felipe Pass. Cesario stopped the car in front of the liquor store and went in for a fifth.

"That stuff's no good for you," Michael advised. "It'll rot you out."

Cesario didn't answer. Look who's talking! he thought. He felt better with the bottle in the car.

———————————————————

Cesario drove up the long, winding roads that were the way to the top. He wanted to change the subject, and Michael was very ready to talk about himself.

"I was in chemistry, can you believe it? The University of Pennsylvania, I was becoming an industrial chemist!" He laughed. "How to make new synthetics. For a while I was good, too. Straight Bs. But I could see most of what we were working on had to do with killing, insects or men or the earth, anything for big profits. I used to sit through those classes in a daze. People thought I was cracking up, talking to myself out loud, I couldn't hassle that scene. Because I was asking myself, is this the way I'm supposed to be? Like these people?

"So I began to read, not what the teachers told us to, but the hidden histories, the beliefs and ways of savage tribes. I found out it hadn't always been this way. What we are is recent as time goes. Other ways men live, that was what I wanted to learn more about. So I transferred out here, to this university. I began to study anthropology, that's their specialty, they got Indian ruins all around. The point of anthropology is that ours is not the only possible way. But the teachers were all apologizing for the old ones, calling them primitive, like you had to get into their houses by climbing down smoke holes and all like that. But they didn't seem primitive to me because they were what it's all about, and ours is about money, right?

"So I quit here, too. I sure have quit a lot of places!" he laughed. "I just decided to sit real still, live inside myself instead of inside a house, you know what I mean? No? Anyway. I sold my books and my clothes, let my hair grow out, like saying I was not for sale, and I began to look for my own way. I didn't do a thing except I believed in it, which means I didn't do much, right?"

"What did your father say?"

"I never found out how to talk to him. I wrote him a letter, thanks, goodbye, that was all."

"What did you do about the draft?"

"Oh, that was funny!" Michael laughed. "When they finally found out where I'd moved to, they invited me to come visit. So I did. They took one look at me—one good listen—I got this high voice, you hear, though I'm not a faggot, though I wouldn't care. Anyway, they took one look, and they could see I was telling them the truth. I told them I'd never shoot a gun at anything, not a man, not an animal, not a bird, nothing. If they sent me over there, I told them, I'd sit down between those armies and do my postures and my yoga breathing and my *asanas*. They asked me what that was. So I got down on the floor and I was standing on my head"— he couldn't control his laughter any more—"and they were all around looking at me and calling other soldiers in to look at me. This is a posture of relaxation, I told them, I can stay up here for fifteen, twenty minutes. They declared that wasn't necessary and that I'd be hearing from them, which I never did."

Michael laughed without end, and finally Cesario couldn't help joining in.

"You're Mexican, right?" Michael asked.

"Mexamerican, Chicano."

"Part Indian?"

"Who isn't?"

"Why don't you come with us?"

"Are you kidding?"

"Maybe we have the same path, how do you know?"

"Are you kidding?" Cesario threw him a scornful look. "I was born in Sonora, but we moved—ever hear of McAllen, Texas?"

"No. I wish I were Mexican. Do you know this one?" He began to sing in a thin sweet voice.

"Sure—my father used to sing it. 'Adelita.'"

They sang together all the way to the top. Different songs, the first time Cesario had sung since he got married.

The place called Father Felipe Pass is a saddle. On each side is a hump of reddish-brown rock, covered with the thorny growth of the area and a scattering of old, soft boul-

ders. The prominences rise perhaps five hundred feet above
the plain, and between them is the pass, discovered by an
intrepid churchman, where the wagon traffic used to move.
Now it's a place to park for a view of the desert below.

"It used to be a lake," Michael said, "you can tell! See?
The bottom of a lake?"

"A lake? When?"

"What would you say to two hundred million years ago?"

"That was a lake?"

"You know Kansas? That was a sea!"

They walked down off the top of the rise and stretched
out, and Michael told Cesario about the life that was once
on the hot muck of this earth, about the Diplodocus and the
Brontosaurus as high as a three-story building, about the
dinosaurs who fed on vegetation and were so big they had
to eat all day without stopping just to stay alive, and the
Tyrannosaurus Rex who fed on them.

"You hear that silence?" he asked. "That comes after
something has disappeared forever. They were here and
they're gone and now there's silence!" Cesario noticed his
eyes, how soft and kind they were, and he stared at them
till Michael had to ask, "Why you looking at me?"

Cesario had brought his fifth, opened it and had a long
drink, and then for no reason that he understood he thought,
My wife's trying to kill me. This made him feel even closer
to Michael, and that was puzzling, that he could be fond of
someone like this boy.

They rode over the flat, through the thorn bushes and
past the saguaro. "Those things are full of water," Michael
said, "and those—their fruit is good. You could survive here
without food and water, if you needed to."

Then Rosalie woke and leaned forward in the seat and
put her arms around Michael's shoulders, and Michael kissed
her hands. Cesario couldn't remember when he'd last been
the object of any such tenderness. Except from Juana, before
all this.

"You ought to buy her a gift," Michael said. Cesario was
startled. Did the boy know whom he was thinking of?

"You know what she'd like?" Rosalie said. "A rabbit."

"Where the hell am I going to buy her a rabbit?" Cesario
asked.

A few miles later, Michael told him to turn off past a sign

that read McIvers, and they went back to a clump of feathery Australian pines, and down under them was a little house and a big barn, and there they bought a small white rabbit. While Cesario was paying for it, Michael washed Rosalie's face in the water that flowed out of a length of pipe. There was no pump in sight.

Cesario didn't know how to hold the animal, so the girl did.

As they were getting into the car, a pair of fighter-bombers, wings almost touching, passed low over their heads, and the sound following made the earth quiver. They watched them disappear, then got into the car.

"You see," Michael said, "since our civilization is a failure, we're looking for another model."

"Who says it's a failure?"

"We all know that," Michael said gently. "You, too." Then he reached into his pocket and pulled out a little earthenware object. "Here," he said, "I want to give you this."

Cesario took it. "What is it?" he asked, turning it over.

"I found it out where we're going. It's an Indian whistle. Blow in there." Michael took it from him and blew into an opening, and there was a thin, plaintive sound.

"There used to be birds nestling under the roof of the house where I was born," Cesario said.

They had turned off the road and onto a dirt trail. Then that came to an end, and Michael told him to stop. There was another car standing there, an old Chevy without a top.

"We walk the rest of the way," Michael said. "It's the other side of that rise."

It was very hot now, and Michael took off his shirt and Cesario started to take his off, too, but decided not to. He had plumped through the middle and didn't look as firm as he'd like people to see.

There were a couple of hours of sun left, the hottest part of the day with the wind down to nothing. Michael, carrying two of the bags, led the way, then Rosalie, then Cesario with the ice-cold beer, now warm as broth.

When they trudged over the dirt rise—it wasn't sand, it looked like it had once been the bottom of a lake—they saw the house. It was something that had grown in stages, a stone cabin, added to in dobe, then finished with a wooden addition. There was no door, no window frames in the openings, but that side of the hill was already in shadow and it was very dark inside, so dark that at first they couldn't see the single person there, a girl sitting in a corner at the end of an old automobile's front seat. Michael put his packages down on the floor, greeted her as "Sandy." She seemed barely aware of him, stared through him, still held out her hand. When Michael took it, she squeezed, but didn't say a word.

From somewhere they could hear sporadic rifle fire.

Cesario put the beer down. He could see more now, but there wasn't much to see; the place was unfurnished. There was a large fireplace with a grill in it and some pots alongside, including a large enamel coffeepot.

The rifle fire stopped, and they could hear distant voices in dispute. Cesario walked out into the heat again, and in a minute, Michael followed, stood next to him.

"Where's Juana?" Cesario asked him.

"We'll find her." Michael began to walk in the direction of the rifle fire, which had resumed. Cesario followed, sweating. "Why don't you take off your shirt?" Michael asked.

In the next hollow there were four young men firing carbines at beer cans. The one with jump boots waved to Michael, then he saw Cesario and stared at him as if he recognized him.

Cesario had never seen the man before. He was black, his hair grown out Afro-style, and he wore glasses. As Michael approached him he turned his back to Cesario and whispered to Michael. The other men, laughing and fussing, paid no attention.

Rosalie, who had changed to shorts, came up to Cesario.

"What are they doing?" he asked her.

"Learning how a gun works."

"But there's no dangerous animals around here," he said, "are there?"

"Come on," said Michael trotting up, "we'll find Juana. Isn't it great here?"

They walked along the ridge into the glare of the sun.

On the last high point they came on a man entirely covered by a heavy, coarse blanket except for his head, which protruded from a small hole in the center. He was staring into the setting sun. Michael and Rosalie didn't speak to him, and he didn't take his attention off whatever it was fixed on.

The shooting began again.

Cesario, for some reason, perhaps the candor with which Michael had answered any question he'd put to him, decided to ask again, "What are they doing?"

"Learning to hit a target. They have the idea it may be necessary."

"For what?"

"Self-defense," Michael smiled and nodded a few times.

They walked up to an enormous cactus. Its main organ was twenty or twenty-five feet high. "Some of these hold as much as two tons of water," Michael said. "And their roots run off, just under the ground, sometimes for half a mile. A big one like this sucks up all the moisture round here. You notice there aren't any others around it. Survival in the vegetable jungle!"

"Hey, I think there's Juana." Rosalie pointed to a bra and dungarees on a bush. "Juanie," she called.

Juana raised up. She must have been sunning herself; she was naked.

"Your father is here," Rosalie ran and sat next to her on the ground and embraced her.

She's telling her it's okay what happened, thought Cesario. What the hell kind of people are these?

The whispering and embracing over, Juana looked around at Cesario and waved. She was putting on her pants, back turned to him. Michael was standing right over her. Juana grabbed her shirt, and, holding it in front of her breasts, ran to her father and embraced him, kissed him. Cesario hadn't held her so unclothed since she was an infant.

Without another word, he and Juana walked away from Rosalie and Michael.

"He bought us some food," Rosalie called out after her.

Juana held on to his arm and looked at him. She's really glad to see me, he marveled.

"You're sweating," Juana said. "Why don't you take some of all this off?" She led him to a declivity, a cup in the hill. He sat in the shade, she in the clear.

The sun was beginning to set. "Isn't it beautiful here?" she said.

"Who owns this place?"

"I don't think anybody does. Michael says some man bought it because he thought the city was going to grow out this way. Then it didn't, so he just forgot about it. Michael fixed the roof, and now they come out even in the rainy season."

"How do they—I don't see any wires."

"There's no electricity," she said. "Candles."

"How do they cook?"

"There's a fireplace—we make out. How are the kids?"

"They're okay. They miss you."

"I miss them, too. But these people—they're like a family, too. Don't you like them? Michael?"

"Yeah! You know I like him!" Cesario didn't control the surprise in his voice.

"And Rosalie?"

"She's pregnant—you know that?"

"I know. It's wonderful!"

Cesario decided to lay it on her. "She's got your boyfriend's kid in her."

Juana lay out flat in the dirt and looked up at the sky.

There wasn't a sound. In the distance, Cesario saw the men who'd been at target practice walk slowly up the hill, their carbines pointed to the ground, then down into the shadow and out of sight toward the house.

He wished he hadn't said it, not that abrupt way. "You didn't know?"

"No." Whatever Juana was feeling, she didn't let show. "I don't care," she said.

Cesario couldn't think of anything else to say. He watched the sun go down.

A man dressed in a suit without a shirt under the jacket was walking toward them. Cesario watched him approach. Juana must have heard his footsteps, but didn't move. The man, Cesario could now see, was an Indian. He carried something wrapped in newspaper, blood-stained. "Hello," he said. "Where's Vinnie?"

Juana shaded her eyes and looked at him. "Oh, hello, Arthur." She was still flat on the ground. The man squatted on his heels next to her.

"We killed a deer yesterday, and I brought him a side. It's a young one, tender."

Juana didn't speak. The man asked, "Where's Vinnie?" again.

"He had to go somewhere."

"I know he likes venison. He be back soon?"

"He went out of town."

"Didn't say where?"

"No."

"I brought him something else." He held up a little brown paper sack, the kind used to hold bits of candy or items of hardware in a general store. Juana took it.

"You gonna see him again?"

"Yeah, sure."

"Give him those. He knows what they are."

Juana nodded. He made a sign and walked away.

Juana covered her eyes with her hand. "That's the way Vinnie is," she said.

"Michael says he went to San Francisco."

"He has to go there sometimes."

"You know he deals in drugs? You know that?"

Juana didn't answer.

"Juana?"

Juana didn't speak.

"That's how he makes a living."

"I don't care," she said and got up. "Let's go back to the house. It gets cold pretty quick here, and you're sweating."

"Not any more, we can stay a while if you want."

She looked at him and he seemed so kind. "You're a sweet man, damn fool daddy." Then she embraced him.

Cesario held her in his arms. "I can't stand for anyone to hurt you."

"He's not hurting me, daddy, what's the matter with you? He's helping me. I didn't know anything before him. About anything. He's teaching me who I am, daddy. Come on, let's go down—"

But Cesario wouldn't let her out of his arms. "I'll kill him if he hurts my girl," he said.

"Don't talk that way, daddy."

"I mean it."

"You probably would. You're a wild man."

She was standing in his arms and looking at him with everything in her face that he could ask for. He thought of the Virgin in the old church and thanked her.

"You see," Juana was saying, "you're really like these people here, but you've forgotten what you are, which is a goddamn Mexican and not made to act so G.I. all the time."

"What do you know about anything?"

But she was saying what he'd been thinking.

———————————————————

Everybody in the house was turning on to grass. There was a stack of Rolling Stones on the portable, nothing else, and everyone was turning on to the Stones.

Cesario was turning on, too, halfway down his fifth, remembering the days when he was young in Sonora, before his family was pushed out by the then Mexican government. "The goddamn Mexicans!" he said.

Juana was standing, holding her arms out. He was proud of her, the way she stood waiting for him with her arms out. "Get up, daddy," she demanded. She was the best girl there.

He did what she said, got up, held her close, began to move. He hadn't danced like that in years, not since he was in Panama and had his big strength, took it all, and was still starved for it after. He held her against his body now and he moved, holding her and moving, not far or much, mostly in place, like a bear in his heavy rhythm.

Everyone watched, even the black boy half-hidden in the corner.

"They teach you to dance like that in the air force, daddy, that where you learned to—?"

"Hell, no, hell, hell no!" Cesario said. He bent over her and laughed and held her harder and moved sideways, then forward, then sideways, and back and—

Sandy, the girl they'd met when they first arrived, was sobbing uncontrollably. Everyone looked at her, but there wasn't much you could do about the pain she was in. Rosalie went over to her.

"What's the matter with her?" Cesario asked Juana.

Michael walked over to Sandy, and the girl rose and embraced him and began to sob. "Michael," she said, "Michael?"

Cesario didn't want to watch any more. It frightened him, not only because some time or other Juana might have been in that condition but because the anguish of the girl was so awesome, so uncontrolled.

Outside he crouched against the wall of the house, sitting on his heels, his back to the dry dobe, and he prayed.

"What are you doing here?"

Cesario raised his head. It was the black boy in the paratroop boots.

"You CIA or something?"

"No."

Michael came out of the house. "He's Juana's father," he said. "He's a friend of mine."

"I want him to know," the young black said, "if he's CIA or something, he's not jiving me—maybe you, not me." He turned and went into the house.

"Don't mind him." Michael squatted next to Cesario. "He's been hiding out here for five weeks, and he's beginning to freak out—when he saw your uniform, you know?"

"He doesn't bother me," Cesario said. "How's the girl, the one who's busting up in there?"

"She's on a real bummer, a lot to work off."

"Who is she?"

"You heard of the—?" he stopped. "Oh, what's to hide?" he said. "She's the daughter of—" Again he stopped. "What's the difference? She's rich. Her family. See what good it did her? She's out there all alone like everybody else." He laughed. "Her grandfather, that old man don't know it, but he's been supporting the revolution in this state, like for those carbines. And he's always good for bail. 'Call Sandy for bail!' She's way into all that—like the guns. All right, this," he touched the stripes of Cesario's sleeve, "that has to go, I mean all of it, there has to be a silence again. Like we heard on Father Felipe Pass, then a new thing has to come to be, right! But for me—what happens outside— I'll just watch that. I decided I'm going to explore my own space, inside me. Like that shooting. I was into it, too, but now I look at things different. I got to go someplace and listen to myself. You know? Instead of hating other people, I got to like myself. It's a whole different route, right? You see the difference there? No? Well, you will. I want to say something to you."

Cesario nodded.

"About Juana. Get her away from him. Vinnie, he don't stay with anybody. Never has, can't, he's way out, like in orbit, alone, that's the way he is, moving out, way out—"

"Food, daddy! Want something to eat?" Juana looked frightened. The girl inside could still be heard.

The venison was from a young animal, and there was a lot of it because Michael and the older man whose meditation they'd come on didn't eat meat. It was mostly knuckles and joints, but the meat between was sweet and good, and Cesario enjoyed it. Besides, he could see it was happening; Juana was going to come back with him. He chewed at the ribs, and he sucked the meat from between, and he washed it down with the rest of the whiskey. He didn't even mind the young black—what was he, a deserter?—staring at him.

"What are you looking at?" he finally asked.

The black didn't answer, just kept looking at him.

"What the hell you looking at?" Cesario asked again, now laughing.

I'm going to pick me a fight with this fucking black boy, he thought. He felt like he used to feel when he was a young man, before he joined the air force, when he was just a Pfc. in Panama and used to fight for the hell of it when there was no other entertainment, like he used to before he got married and learned control. He could feel the strings loosening, the knots becoming undone.

"You black shit-head," he said, "what are you looking at?" Then he took the bones that were on his plate and shoveled them on the boy's plate.

"Daddy, don't do that!"

"Well, he keeps looking at me, that's not polite. You trying to ruin my meal? I'm enjoying it. What the hell you looking?"

"I'm looking at who's helping the Man kill his own people."

"My own people!"

"Black people."

"I'm an American, fellow."

"You're a murderer, fink!"

"Let's cool it," Michael said.

"Cool what? I told him I don't want to eat with a murderer." Juana was holding his arm.

He smiled at her. She's with me, he thought, and he didn't care to fight the boy. "Okay," he said, "you don't want to eat with me, don't eat with me."

The boy got up and walked to the fire and lay down near Sandy. She looked at him, then took his hand and held it over her chest. Her eyes were out like a frog's.

"The U.S. Army and the U.S. Air Force and the U.S. Navy and all the U.S. people in U.S. Washington," the black boy said, "they're racist murderers, all of them, and you've got your brown tongue up their brown assholes, so that's what you are, too. So I don't eat with you, see?"

"Good," Sandy mumbled, "that's good." She tried to get up, fell back.

Cesario, full of flit and very ready, felt Juana's hand on his arm and tried to say what he had to say in as controlled a way as he could. "You can talk all that about the air force and the navy and Washington because we protect you. We protect you so you can curse us and do your let's-pretend target practice. You can peddle your drugs and live like this in someone else's house and eat the food and drink the beer someone else bought because you know when you get into trouble there's always grandpappy to come running with the bail money and pull the pig off your ass. Revolutionists! You ain't gonna revolution shit, and you ain't gonna shoot shit either because this country's strong enough to let you play your games, so go ahead!"

Cesario walked over to where the boy lay with his hand on Sandy's chest and said, "Don't worry, buck, I won't tell anybody about you, because nobody's worrying about you, boy, no one's scared of a nigger who—"

The black jumped to his feet and began to flail at him like a faggot—Cesario saw that right away—and Cesario crossed himself quickly like he used to before every round, then moved in and laughed and laughed, he was so exhilarated, picked off a couple, then stepped inside, then back, then in again so that the black boy's arms went around him, and Cesario was laughing all the time, which made his assailant all the more frantic to kill him. Cesario felt like in his younger days, when he thought for a bit he might really become a pro, he had some kind of gift and took a hell of a punch, people who knew fighters said that little Mexican cock sucker, he could be another Carmen Basilio. Oh, God, it felt good! He muscled and shouldered and blocked and slipped and when he was inside the boy was hitting him everywhere except where it might hurt and Cesario himself didn't throw a punch,

he knew he could take the boy out any time he wanted, but
let him punch himself out, he was beginning to hang his arms
and Cesario decided to finish it a different way. Being inside,
he said to the boy, "You better quit, nigger, you gonna get
hurt!" But the boy was out of control, had to kill or be killed,
only way he could stop. Cesario feinted with his hands and
the boy stepped back off balance and Cesario put his right
foot behind his left foot and gave the boy a quick shove,
with one hand, that's all it took since he was off balance, and
the boy fell over backward, his head hitting the floor just
hard enough to stun him and stop the fight.

Cesario looked down at him, then at the others, and he
said, "Revolution! You can't even put me away, twenty years
older than any of you, it would take every man in this place,
no, not all of you together, want to try?"

Michael was sitting with his back to the wall, petting the
rabbit Cesario had bought for Juana. He held it up now and
said, "Look at this, Mr. Sergeant Flores, come over here,
please, and look at this animal. Because there's something
I'm wondering."

For a reason Cesario didn't understand, he did what
Michael asked.

"Here, take it," Michael suddenly put the rabbit in Cesario's
hands. "Look in its face," Michael said. "Could you kill it?
Then how come you kill human beings? Because you don't
have to look in their faces?"

The rabbit moved, and Cesario had to look at it.

"You're right about this country being strong," Michael
said, "so why do we fear everybody? And you're right some
of us come from money, so we had everything, right? And
didn't want it."

"You're all sick!" Cesario said.

"Maybe. But since you're healthy, answer me this. Has
there been a year since your Christ died that somewhere on
this earth Christians haven't used their best knowledge and
their best sons to kill other Christians? And now we've re-
fined the art, we don't even have to look at them, press a
button, that's it! Like you! Can you look that rabbit in the
eye? Cross yourself, Christian, like I saw you do before,
then break its neck? With your hands? Looking at it, can
you do that?"

Cesario couldn't look at the animal.

Now Michael's voice was so quiet that Juana had to come close to her father to hear it. "Tomorrow, go sit in the desert, sergeant, like the saints, the saints started as murderers. Go where there's nothing around you but the cactus and the snake and ask yourself, Mr. Sergeant Flores, aren't you what he said, a murderer?"

"No, he isn't!" Juana stood up. "I know him," she said.

"All right, Juana," Michael said.

"He's my father, don't talk to him that way!"

"All right, Juana, all right."

That was when Cesario knew for sure that Juana was coming with him.

In the desert the stars still have their fire. Juana and Cesario lay out in the sand, side by side. They heard a coyote. The wind was right, and the lean animal soon passed just above them and looked down at the house, smelling the smoke and the meat in the smoke.

Cesario took Juana's hand so she wouldn't move and wouldn't be afraid, and they watched the animal trip nervously back and forth, take a few quick steps toward the house, then change its mind and lie down, then get up and trot back into the darkness.

"I've got a transfer. To Spain, I think."

"Spain!"

"You're a grown girl, and you can do what you want, but I wish you'd come with us."

"I love you, daddy. Don't mind what Michael said."

"I mean what happened with you and—Vinnie. Well. Maybe you made a mistake, that's part of life, that happens."

Juana didn't say anything.

"I know what you're worried about. Your mother."

Juana nodded.

"She's just a worried woman, and she gets frightened. Can you blame her? I don't want you like that girl in there. I want you to have children. I'd like to be a regular damn fool grandfather, anything wrong with that?"

"No."

"So, I say, try it. Then—do what you want."

"All right."

"Did you say all right?" Juana nodded. "Well, then, we'll go back in the morning, okay?"

"Okay, only tell her—tell her—"

"I know what to tell her," Cesario said. "Where'll we sleep, it's cold out here." He got up.

When they went back into the dobe house, Cesario let Juana find their way to a spot on the floor. He rolled his coat up and put it under his head. Juana slept with her head on his shoulder. Cesario was as happy as he had ever been.

In the middle of the night, he guessed it must have been two-thirty because he had the habit of waking at two-thirty, he heard a rhythmic sound from close by and turned his head. Michael was on his back, and over him, Rosalie. Her breasts touched his chest, her belly curved to meet his. She was riding. There was longing on their faces, not diminished by the fact they were with each other.

Cesario turned away, remembering the way he and Elsa had been before they married. Long gone, he thought, and not about to come back.

Against the side of his body he could feel Juana's belly filling with breath, then emptying. He'd had that with Elsa, too.

He could hear them moving again, this time faster. Rosalie moving, Michael absolutely still.

Cesario looked again. Rosalie was holding Michael frantically, in that way that Cesario also remembered. Then it was over and she lay down on top of Michael and they were still.

Cesario now watched them without embarrassment.

In time she turned her head and looked at Michael, and there was something there that told him Michael was still distended.

I'm no killer, Cesario told himself. But I need what they have, I've got to have that because if I don't—

The life was still in him, he felt it now as hard as it ever was, and he turned away from Juana so she wouldn't by some chance move and become aware of what he had.

He turned his head, and there was Michael, looking right into his eyes. What he saw was a look of friendship, more than a look, an offer.

But it was too late. And it was too early. Cesario, when he looked at Michael now could think of only one thing— that Michael, he and that other one, Vinnie, had taken his daughter away.

So he stared at Michael, without giving. "I've got her back," his look said.

In San Francisco, Vinnie went straight from the airport to his friendly pharmacist. He had money to put down for two hundred tabs of acid. The man said it might take a few days, and Vinnie made a slight gesture of one hand that gave permission. Then he hit the street.

He strolled along, his head elegantly tilted, a prime boy who didn't know the pinch of obligation or the press of competition. His hair, heavily curled, fell on his shoulders, neither combed nor brushed, hand-parted, naturally ordered. His beard was the best on the street, burnished, regal. Every street he passed through belonged to him, a visitor from a superior time and place, an eighteenth-century noble, a swell.

Although he only had two dollars and change in his pocket (along with the return plane ticket), he was not looking for favor, shelter, or hospitality, least of all for companionship. He would nod at old acquaintances, stop for no one. Whoever wanted to talk to him had to walk alongside. Vinnie did not change his pace.

From a street booth, he made a call. The girl said, "What'll I tell my husband?"

Vinnie didn't know she'd married, but showed no surprise. Five months ago, she explained, she'd made the move; the time had come for her to look after herself.

She hoped he'd be upset, but he didn't even ask who. In fact the impression she had was that he preferred it this way— so long as when he came to town and did call, she'd be with him.

The girl had the courage to complain that he had been in a couple of times and hadn't tried to reach her. Vinnie said, Yes, that was so, he'd been with a dancer he met on the plane the last time, and the time before with someone he couldn't remember, but now he was calling her.

Vinnie waited, lowering the phone, watching the life on the street.

She was trying to think, but with that pressing silence, who could think? She felt she was being tested, didn't know for what, but didn't want to fail the test.

Finally the girl made a sound, "Vinnie?" and he raised the earpiece. She said she couldn't meet him in the place where they used to meet, with all those people coming in and out all the time, so why didn't he get a hotel room? He told her she should do that and let him know where it was, he'd call later. Also she should bring money, he'd given what he had to the pharmacist.

She never did tell him what she said to her husband to explain her absence, and he didn't inquire. That was her problem.

After a round or two it came back to him, the thing about her he couldn't stand. It was that she kept touching him. It was okay when they were making it, he didn't mind it so much then, but it was like her fingers were always on him, his hair, his chest, the back of his neck, an ear—he finally had to tell her not to touch him so much.

When she went home at night, he didn't express regret. In the morning she returned with coffee-and.

It was cold in San Francisco that month and damp. Vinnie didn't even have a sweater, so she bought him a present, a handsome lined raincoat. He wore it once, the day she gave it to him. They never went out together—she couldn't chance that. When he was alone, he preferred to stay in and watch TV.

He'd had a dream that disturbed him, a premonitory vision. Juana had left him, and though he pleaded with her in a way he never had with anyone in his life, she wouldn't come back.

He put the light on and wrote Juana a letter. He'd never written a girl a letter before. He wanted to tell her how much he missed her, but somehow he couldn't get that down. He figured if he wrote, she'd know he was thinking about her and realize he missed her. His handwriting was that of an eight-year-old child.

The sex act had long ago become a sister-brother affair for Vinnie, even at its accidental best, even the surprise happenings. He had, at one time or other, been with every girl who lived in the house on Queen Street, but he couldn't have said which or when or under what circumstances, how it had come about, and what they were like. He knew, for instance, that he had balled Sandy—well, who hadn't—that she had come into his room one night when Rosalie was—had Rosalie gone out that night? Or was she in the front room? Did Rosalie know about it? Yes? No? Well, if she did, it hadn't made any difference.

With Juana he didn't even mind that she had been the aggressor. With her he'd liked that.

So what was there, he wondered, sitting in that cold room in that damp Bay City—what was there about that chick?

It sure wasn't a matter of looks. Vinnie would have had trouble describing Juana, remembering a single feature clearly. Yes, she was chubby. What else? She really had tits, right, a lot of girls didn't. And? Her eyes, they were warm. But what color? Black? No one had eyes that dark. She does. No. Then what? What got him?

It wasn't a matter of how they did it. He and Juana always did it exactly the same way, which was the way he liked it. And it wasn't what she did for him.

It was what he did for her, that was it!

In the first place, when they were starting out, Juana looked up at him like she was scared, or like she couldn't believe it was happening to her. He couldn't remember any other girl who'd had that look.

Then when it happened, a lot of girls pretended and were a hell of a lot noisier about it; but this chick, her whole body quivered and her chest, like it broke out in a rash and her tit ends were hard as marbles, her eyes locked into his till the last minute, then they'd turn up and slowly close, *Oh Jesus!* Like she'd survived, like she'd come around the dark side of the moon, communication restored.

Then she didn't recover directly, chattering and toweling. She waited for him, held on and waited, her whole body sending that message, "More!" Juana was too damn dumb to know it couldn't happen again, not right away.

It was routine for Vinnie to walk away from a girl a few days after he'd first balled her. It was a declaration, one they understood very well, of undependence. Even this time, with Juana, he'd suddenly left for San Francisco without warning or explanation. He'd felt he should lay down those old conditions.

Now he was worried he'd lost her. That's why he turned on the light and wrote her a letter in his child's hand, telling her the goddamn pharmacist was holding him up, but he'd be there soon and—well, the rest, between the lines, was "Wait!"

But he knew girls didn't wait any more than boys did.

The next morning he went to the pharmacist and made his

pickup. He didn't call the airport to see when there was a plane; there'd be one waiting.

He left the raincoat in the room and, in place of a note, the last of his grass.

When Vinnie walked into the house on Queen Street, it hit him in the eye, his envelope, unopened.

Juana wasn't in her room; she wasn't anywhere in the house!

Sandy was there, as usual, not seeing, not hearing. And Rosalie'd moved back. He saw her come out of the room where Michael stayed. Vinnie didn't care, he liked Michael, he liked Rosalie as a person, and he didn't expect a woman to be faithful but—

Where the hell was Juana?

Rosalie started to tell him what had happened, but he told her he didn't give a shit so shut up!

He sat down, lit a joint, listened to the Doors.

He'd trusted her so he had himself to blame. A woman won't stay put, he was born knowing that; you can't leave them alone. Well, fuck Juana!

The Doors. "The End." His favorite side. And right in the best part there was this tick, tick, tick off, tick, tick off, tick, tick off! "Goddamnit," Vinnie was yelling, "who dropped the fucking arm on my record? Who scratched my side? Listen to it!!! Rosalie! Rosalie, come out here! Listen to that! Who did that to my record? I don't want anyone playing my records. I only dig a few, leave 'em alone!"

He lifted the disc off the spindle, found his other Doors and Stones, scattering the rest of the garbage all over the floor, took what was his into his room, and stowed them top shelf of the closet. He lifted his foot and kicked the door. Slam! Bang! That was it! He lay on the bed, waiting.

When Michael came home, he saw Vinnie looking mean. But Michael didn't back off. He told Vinnie what he knew would blow his mind, that he and Rosalie had driven out with Juana's old man, at which Vinnie yelled, but then heard it out because he knew Michael was his friend.

That night Vinnie didn't talk to anyone, sat in a corner, put three roaches together and turned on, listened to his records from up close to the player. He had a way of sitting, the top half of his body turned one way, the bottom half the other, an S curve out of an older time. The toe of the leg that was crossed over pointed naturally, and his head was thrown back. He shared his joint with no one.

The whole family was there that night, and a lot of outcasts and dropouts, students, too, maybe half were students, but many irregulars, some from far away. They'd come for the action at the university gym Saturday to protest—from what Vinnie could make out—that the other team didn't let spades play, or not enough of them, or something, scholarships maybe, anyway something. They bickered about tactics, couldn't agree, then asked Michael's advice. Vinnie noticed they had a lot of respect for Michael, who wasn't even in the damned school any more and not into all that political bullshit either, not like he used to be. But they sucked at him, got him going, because he was the one planning when they should rush the gym, when break out on the floor and grab the ball and who'd do that, then they'd sit in the jump circle, lock arms, and say their piece. Michael had it all figured out in steps and signals.

Fat Freddie Povich, one of those from out of town, got into a hassle with Michael. Freddie was a patchy redhead with more hair in his beard than on top of his head. He wore a shirt of old strings, and he walked in cracked sneakers. You couldn't tell any more what his pants were made of, they were that far gone. Vinnie guessed he weighed maybe two-seventy-five. He looked soft, but had a history of famous fights, was known that way, and everybody was scared of him—except Michael.

Freddie wanted they should throw rocks through the big gym windows from the outside at the same time the action inside was happening, but Michael wouldn't go for it.

"You running scared?" Freddie said without antagonism. You could see he liked Michael.

"We want all those kids and teachers with us inside," Michael explained patiently, "not running for the exits."

"Your turf," Freddie said. He must have seen the kids were with Michael, not him.

Vinnie himself didn't say a word until one of the out-of-towners asked him if he was showing up.

"You jiving?" he said, and since he was talking anyway, he let on he didn't go for all that social action shit, he wanted to listen to the music now, so if they were going to hassle, they should split.

It got quiter then, a little, for a while.

Somewhere in all the gabble, Michael came over close to Vinnie and suggested he write Juana a letter and tell her he wanted to talk to her, she should come to a certain place in the fence around the base.

Which Vinnie did. Michael and he, again close, went down to the main P.O. at four in the morning and dropped the letter.

Vinnie got through the next day okay, dealt some of the new acid and put money in his pocket.

Late the next afternoon, Friday, he borrowed a car from one of the fellows who'd come in for the gym action and drove out to the base, around its southwest corner, which is a great bay of desert filled with row after row of discarded planes, models from only three or four years back, abandoned to the weather.

Vinnie found the place at the fence where he could look down a long corridor of the killer junk, and there he waited. At the time he'd set, he saw Juana walking toward him. Now he remembered what she looked like.

He didn't waste breath to scold, told her to walk to the gate, now, come out, he had a car and would be waiting for her.

She looked frightened, said tomorrow.

"Why tomorrow?"

She didn't say.

"You seeing one of those dudes in there tonight?"

"I'm not seeing anyone, Vinnie."

"Then why did you say tomorrow?"

"I don't have any clothes with me, Vinnie."

"What the hell, clothes? I'll get you clothes, just tell me what you need and we'll go get 'em."

"Nothing, just—"

"You get your ass to that gate and walk out, now, or I'll come over this fence, you better believe me."

"I believe you."

"So I'll be waiting for you." He turned and walked to his car.

When she came out the base gate, Vinnie saw she'd gotten

over her fear and her hesitation; she rocked in that old way, her body chugging along, tits this way, then that, her ass swiveling up and down in halves, he could just feel it. She walked past the guards and smiled at them, then, without a glance at him, got into his car.

When he'd made his U and straightened out, she slid over next to him. Once he had the car in high, he dropped his hand, lifting her skirt. She parted her legs.

All he said on the ride was, "I thought you were with me." She didn't protest the reproach.

When they got to the house on Queen Street, she knew what was coming. He walked in, she following, into their room, and when she was in, he closed the door. Then he beat all resistance out of her.

She did not defend herself. She tried not to cry out, waited for it to be over.

In the front room, the others could hear, knew what was happening.

When he was through and feeling much better, he said, "You belong to me, and when I go somewhere, if I go for a week, you stay here and wait. A month, you wait a month."

He made her swear it again and again, and at the end, he told her he didn't believe her.

No one went into their room that night. Vinnie reclaimed her, and it was like he remembered it. Juana knew why she was on earth.

When he was tired, he put his arms around her belly, his head between her tits, and let her mother him. Before he fell asleep, he told her things he'd never told anyone. He enlisted her in the struggle of his life.

He didn't know who his father was, he told her, but he did know his mother, Irene. She'd given him away when he was seven years old to her older sister. She wanted him out of the way when she brought boyfriends home; no man wants another man's kid around. When Vinnie used to ask her when he could come home and live with her again, she used to say, "Soon, Vinnie, real soon." When he asked his aunt the same question, she'd play dumb. But his aunt's husband told him the truth. "Forget her," he said. "She doesn't want you around."

A few days after his thirteenth birthday, Vinnie left; no one chased after him.

His mother was right here in town, he told Juana; she tended bar at a hotel downtown. He'd gone in once and looked her over from a distance; she was just what he'd heard.

It was from her he'd learned never to trust anyone, a woman, that is. "I was beginning to trust you," he said, "but I'm straightened out now."

And as he was snarling at her that she'd proved herself no good, just like the others, he fell asleep in her arms.

—————————————————————

The next morning was Saturday, and Vinnie slept till noon. Juana got up before him and went out and talked with Rosalie a while. They made coffee and oatmeal.

Juana told of her father's promise that things would be different; she supposed he had done his best. But he was a different man when he was with Elsa. In a couple of days, her mother was back treating her like a twelve-year-old, scolding and telling her how to be.

"I got so I was reading all night and sleeping all day," Juana told her, "just so I'd have nothing to do with her. Well, one night I heard them talking through the wall. She was coming on strong, all I could hear from him was this lousy mumble, 'Yes, Elsa, you're right, Elsa—' Like you say, he's a good-hearted man, but he's given it all to her."

Vinnie came out and had some coffee and appeared not to notice the two girls talking. He said, "Get me a beer." Which she did. Juana was glad to be taking care of him again.

She went into the bathroom, filled the tub with the hottest water she could stand, and lay in it. She wasn't going to look ahead or worry or question anything; she was just going to be with Vinnie. That was it. She reached down, parted her lips, and eased the soreness there. Then she lay back with her hair all over the top of the water, closed her eyes, and enjoyed the end of struggle.

"I have no clothes," she said, walking into the room, naked except for her bikini panties. She held up the dress her mother had given her, the one she'd worn yesterday. "I don't want to wear this any more."

"Wear it for now," Vinnie said. "We'll get some clothes later."

Then he told the girls what to do. Rosalie put on a blue dress with a little white collar, and Sandy looked as rich as she really was, and Juana was just as beautiful as her mother had hoped when she had the seamstress make her that frock of dotted swiss.

Through the end of that spring day's light they walked down Queen Street, left on Piermont to the campus, between the stone buildings to the gym.

Rosalie was worried about Michael, inside; she pointed to the two black buses with small, barred windows. "Somebody must have tipped them off," she said to Vinnie. "You think I ought to try to find Michael and tell him?"

"Hell, they want the cops here," Vinnie said. "They want arrests!"

They heard the commotion inside the gym at the same time the police did. The cops came tumbling out of their black vans like *bocce* balls dumped out of a sack. The girls looked back, but not Vinnie, it was all shit to Vinnie. He made a sound, and the girls came to heel.

This was a good time for what he'd planned. First he had to have a nice-looking car. He found one, with the key in it, and they drove to the other end of the city. On the way out they passed police cage-cars coming in.

Vinnie was exhilarated, even talkative for a change. As they drove, he explained to the girls that any department store as big as Connally's puts up with a certain amount of shoplifting. Much better than for a store to get a reputation it's full of detectives and its customers being watched all the time. That would sure kill the fun-of-shopping atmosphere, he said. A write-off for stealing, he told the girls, can go as high as ten percent and no sweat!

And if a woman is well-dressed and Anglo, she has one hell of a head start. And a pregnant woman? All right! Juana's Aztec schnozz was against her, but she was in good company and the dress from Elsa was a perfect front.

Vinnie told the girls to pay for a couple of inexpensive items to start. This would throw off any tails and provide them shopping bags with the store's label.

It was such fun, so simple to do, Juana wondered why anyone ever paid for anything. They breezed out to where Vinnie was waiting, drove off without incident. Juana was delighted. She had a beautiful new pair of bells.

That night there was celebration in the house on Queen Street. The basketball game had been halted for almost twenty-five minutes. The bleachers had joined in the shouting; the police came in swinging. Of the three members of the student council arrested, one was the president; another, the daughter of a prominent businessman, had been roughed up more than a girl should be; and the third, the lone freshman, had a concussion. The papers were going to be full of it, thoroughly illustrated.

One kid wasn't happy: Michael.

Michael was taking on three of them, Fat Freddie Povich, his buddy Jeff Wilson the deserter, and Lennie Weil, who was called "Che" because of his get-up.

"We said it right here," Michael told them. "No rocks, we agreed, through those windows."

"He changed his mind, man," Che said.

Fat Freddie was riding a big high. "Yeah!" he shouted. "I changed my mind."

"And somebody told the pigs," Michael said. "Half the force was outside waiting."

Che was insulted for Freddie. "Don't say that, Michael, because I'm going to have to break your bones."

Freddie hit Che on his forehead with the heel of his hand, turned to Michael, and laughed. "You saying I did that?"

"I thought you might know who did that, yes."

Vinnie saw Freddie go for Michael, got across the room fast. But what Freddie did was throw his arms around the boy and embrace him. "I really like you," he said. "You're some kind of out-of-sight reefer-weight champ. I really like this mother, Jeff."

"He ain't smartened yet," Jeff said.

"Cool it, Freddie." Vinnie didn't like the man playing grizzly bear with his best friend. "It's over, Michael, cool it."

"That's what it ain't," Freddie said, "over. All those elite daddies are down in pigsville right now with their bondsmen paying off their kids' Anglo asses. And when they get their darlings back home, they're going to have a real heavy heart-to-heart on this whole subject, which is when those kids are going to first discover where their daddies' heads are at. That's why I say it's just beginning. The only trouble tonight, there wasn't enough."

"That's bullshit, Freddie," Michael said.

"You'll learn," Freddie said, "like everybody else, with a little running blood."

Michael and Rosalie were in one bed, Vinnie and Juana in the one opposite, the girls dozing.

"I thought you weren't going to get into all that movement hassle again," Vinnie said to Michael.

Through the closed door, they could hear the fat boy laughing.

"That son of a bitch," Vinnie said.

"I like him," Michael said.

"That stupid—"

"That he's not. He reads, he's into some heavy books. And all that confrontation stuff, he may be right."

Juana turned to Vinnie. "Go to sleep," she said, and her eyes closed.

They didn't speak for a while.

"Vinnie!" Michael said.

"Yeah?"

"Did you ever think we don't have to live here? We could split—I mean like altogether?"

Juana's eyes opened again.

Around four in the morning, when even Fat Freddie was asleep, half-bricks came crashing through every first-floor window of the house on Queen Street. The straight community was hitting back.

In the morning, the bikers moved in, six of them. No one had sent for these angels, but everybody knew why they were there.

The bikers are the police force of that world, move when it grabs them, enforce their unwritten laws. They could be seen in front of the house now, fussing with their cycles. In the afternoon, they decided to take a ride through the desert. They returned just after nightfall with the carcasses of some thirty rabbits they'd shot. They threw the animals on the ground in front of the house, then sat on the porch and watched the traffic react.

Passers-by spread the news: The place on Queen Street was under security guard.

The next morning, Master Sergeant Cesario Flores was summoned to the office of his commanding officer. He was asked
to bring his wife.

When the harassed man and Elsa entered the office, they
found Chief of Police Burns waiting there.

Introductions were made, their tone funereal.

Only then did Cesario notice that the chief was holding
a large manila envelope.

"Let him see them," Colonel Dowd said. Elsa leaned over
to look first.

The photographs were blow-ups of single frames of a film
taken by the concealed camera at Connally's Department
Store.

Elsa took a quick look at Cesario.

"That your daughter, Sergeant Flores?" Chief Burns
pointed.

Cesario nodded.

Burns turned to Colonel Dowd. "I'll have to do something about it, of course," he said. "I mean respectable
housewives are doing it, women with the money to pay for
anything they want. It's become sort of a sport. Connally's
has had it up to here!"

"I don't blame them," Colonel Dowd said. Then he looked
at Cesario.

The man sat with his head between his knees.

"Don't wait for him to do anything," Elsa said.

"Thank you, Mrs. Flores," Colonel Dowd said, "I don't
think we need keep you any longer."

Elsa stood up. "What are you going to do?" she asked her
husband. "Nothing?"

She turned to Colonel Dowd. "You see," she said.

"Thank you, Mrs. Flores," Colonel Dowd nodded to
Sergeant Jones, who escorted Elsa from the room.

As she left, she burst into bitter, angry tears.

Colonel Dowd waited till the silence had settled. He
looked at the man who'd been, a few months before, the
pride of his operation. Then he turned to the chief.

"I want to tell you," he said, "his daughter Juana, the
one with those pants in her hands, I've watched her since
I came on this base, she was the sweetest girl, gentle, neat.

I would have been proud to have one of my sons marry her. Once."

He stopped and looked at Cesario, who was staring at the floor as if there was an instruction there.

"Is there anything you want to say?" Colonel Dowd asked Flores.

Chief Burns was surprised how kind the base commander was, how patient.

Cesario raised his head and looked at Dowd, his eyes rheumy, his face puffed like a white mushroom. He had put on close to twenty pounds.

"Chief Burns," Dowd said, "if we could lock these photos away for a while? Take my personal word that some sort of restitution will be made."

"Well, sure," Burns stood up. "I mean I don't know, I'll have to talk to the people at the store. The security chief there used to work for me. Maybe I can hold him back on this for a while—maybe not."

"I assure you," Colonel Dowd said, "it will not happen again."

Chief Burns nodded but seemed doubtful. "This country's going to hell, they're killing cops like quail," he said to Sergeant Jones, who was showing him out the door.

Jones came back with a suggestion. "Colonel Dowd," he said, "I'd like to go down to the barracks, get me maybe a dozen guys, go down to that place on Queen Street, and tear it apart. Sir?"

"Jones get out of here and close the door," Dowd ordered. Then he put his hand on Cesario's back.

"Sir," Cesario said, "will you listen to something?" His voice sounded strangled; he cleared it.

Dowd sat close to him.

"When Juanie first disappeared, remember?" Cesario said, "and I couldn't find her, I went to the *madrecita,* in the little Mex church and I promised her I'd do something for her if she helped me get my daughter back."

"Who? If who helped who?"

"The Virgin. And she helped me. I found Juanie, she came home, and we were happy. But then I didn't pay the Virgin—"

"Pay her what?"

"I can't tell you. You see afterward, when Juana was back with me, it seemed silly what I had promised."

"Which was what, what?"

"So I put it out of my mind, what I'd promised I'd do. So now she—"

Colonel Dowd had had it. "That's why I always distrusted the Catholic religion," he said, "forgive me saying so. My father was a deeply religious man, but he never went to any church. He taught us God helps those who help themselves. Do you understand that?"

"I'm going to show you. I've made up my mind now."

"I'll believe it when I see it."

"Oh, you can believe it, you can believe—" Cesario was standing now.

"I was on the Yangtze River, Flores, and let me tell you, force! Sometimes it's necessary! That's how civilization works. Some change is necessary, sure, social progress, all right, there's a wave of protests and demonstrations. But then it gets to riots and God knows what, assassinations. And ordinary good people, like us, we have to think. How much are we ready to give up? If we let things slide too far, something basic gets lost. Then we get angry. Almost too late, we act! And order is restored. I've seen it, I know what I'm talking about. It's our anger, when it comes, that finally saves us—"

Colonel Dowd stood up. He was riding a wave of feeling that he always held in. "Now get the hell out of here!" he said suddenly.

Cesario came up to him. He seemed exhilarated, if not by Dowd's words, by his feeling.

"I don't want to hear another goddamn word about all this, Flores, I haven't got time for it."

Cesario was extending his hand.

Dowd didn't take it.

"And what I said to you here, you're to forget that. I never spoke to you this way, right?"

"Will you shake my hand, sir?"

"I only did because I remember that once I had a whole lot of respect for you."

"You will again, sir." Cesario still had his hand out. "Please, sir," he said.

Colonel Dowd reached out, took his hand, shook it.

Cesario woke in a calm like that of a man who has, by

a miracle of healing, come safely through a long and serious illness. It was the first night for many weeks he had not been wakened by the compulsion to get down to Bennie's, the first night since his troubles began he hadn't stewed in terrible dreams, the first morning his body and pajamas were not soaked in the perspiration of anxiety.

He lay back and listened to the Sunday sounds of his home and the silence of the base on its quiet day.

Having made up his mind, Cesario was in no hurry.

This was the day of the family's big spring event, the double birthday. Elizabeth and Diego were born seven years and one day apart, and it was the family's custom to make one occasion of the two celebrations.

It was also one of two days in the year—the other was Christmas—when Elsa obliged with her specialty, potato dumplings. She made them ceremoniously, and they were as good as she thought, prepared from her grandmother's recipe which she'd never given to anyone, at least not accurately.

Elsa also helped with the cakes, Elizabeth's favorite, orange icing with shredded-coconut filling, and Diego's double chocolate. Elizabeth's was to be illuminated by fifteen little white candles. On Diego's six kitchen candles would provide a conflagration to challenge his wind.

All Cesario did that Sunday morning was sit in a corner on a high stool and enjoy his family and a cigar. They couldn't remember when they had seen him more at peace.

By two everything was ready. It was little Diego who suggested they go get Juana. Cesario told him his sister could not come and then, when he saw the boy's disappointed face, suggested they cut into both cakes and take her a piece of each.

He didn't go into the house on Queen Street. Elizabeth took the boy in and Cesario waited, smoking his second cigar.

He seemed surprised when Juana came out with her sister and brother and asked if it would be all right if she came to dinner. He nodded and kissed her.

Juana ran in again and in a couple of minutes, a boy followed her to the door, staying in the dark just back of the opening. Juana called out to him that she'd be back right after dinner.

The boy didn't answer.

Juana got in the back with Diego, and they gabbed all the way home.

Juana even kissed her mother. Then she went back into her room, and Cesario saw her preparing a little bundle of clothing to take with her later.

When he said grace, he did it formally, thanking a cool Anglo deity for bringing the family together. He made no requests of that God. The meal that followed was harmonious. No one noticed that Cesario was not listening to what was being said. He sat among them enjoying the echoes the occasion produced, not turning his head from one speaker to the next, savoring the whole, the fact that it was happening.

He knew without question that this harmony was worth sacrificing his life for.

Once Juana slipped, said that roast beef was Vinnie's favorite, too.

But no one picked up on it, least of all Cesario.

At the end of the meal, they all got up to clear the table. For a few minutes Cesario was alone in the dining room. He could hear them, far away, laughing as they lit the candles on the cakes, as they spooned the half gallon of ice cream into the biggest dish in the house. There was a slight smile on his lips now, the one immortalized by certain Mexican terra-cotta masks, the smile in stone. He was in that world of self-hypnosis necessary for ritual.

Cesario turned his head and looked at the black *madrecita* on the wall, the holy image he had taken from the wall of his mother's bedroom in Sonora the morning after she died. He crossed himself.

Elizabeth and Diego returned to their places in the dining room. Elsa followed them into the room, pulled the shades down, and turned off the lights. Then Linda carried in Elizabeth's cake, the fifteen white candles burning. Juana followed with Diego's aflame, a sparkler in its heart.

Cesario told Elizabeth to make a wish, and she did. Her sisters asked what it was; she giggled and looked at Juana as if she would be the only one there who might understand her desire. Then she blew all the candles out with one big breath. The candles smoked; the family applauded.

It was Diego's turn. The boy said, "I wish my sister Juana would never leave the house again."

And Cesario immediately added, "Don't worry, she's not going to."

Diego blew out his six candles and smiled at Juana. Everyone was looking at her now. She said, "Diggie, I'm living somewhere else now, but whenever you want, I'll come see you."

"I want you to live here," Diego said, cutting his cake.

"She's going to live here," Cesario said.

No one said anything.

The phone rang. Cesario lifted the receiver just off the cradle, as if that was a part of the ritual. They could all hear the distant male voice. Cesario dropped the receiver back, and there was silence.

In silence, they ate the cake and the ice cream. Only Diego was unaware, only his appetite uninhibited.

Juana looked up from her plate. Her father's lips were moving. Then he saw her watching him and said, "We all love you, Juana, you must remember that, whatever happens," and he looked at her like a man who didn't expect to obtain the understanding for which he was asking, "you'll know today, how much I love you. I will prove it to you today."

For the first time it occurred to Juana that her father might be cracking up. She looked at the phone, hoped it wouldn't ring.

When they'd had their seconds, Cesario, keyed up now, stood and said to them all, "Clear the table!" He was not concealing anything any longer. He walked to the television, yanked the plug out of the wall, and wheeled the stand into the girls' bedroom. "You can listen to it in there," he said, and then to Diego, "no curfew tonight." All the children sensed something strange; they went into the other room obediently.

Elsa continued to clear the table and stack the dishes in the sink. Juana wanted to help her, but Elsa waved her off, told her to sit. She did, and Cesario moved, leaning toward her.

"He's the only one you've ever been with, isn't he?"

Juana nodded.

"The good Lord gives us another life if we ask for it," he said, "by the act of true contrition we start again. It needs only that we be ready to sacrifice for it, our lives if that is necessary. As He did. For us."

There were shouts of anger from the TV in the other room.

Juana stared at her father, who was changing his glasses, substituting a pair with a tint. "What happened to that rabbit?" he said.

"It died," Juana said. She could see her father's lips moving again, she heard "Michael, how's that boy, Michael?"

"Fine," Juana said.

Cesario knew he would have to do it that way, without looking at the person.

The phone rang.

Cesario nodded at Juana, giving her permission to answer. Juana walked slowly to pick it up.

At the sink, Elsa stopped stacking the dishes.

"Hello," Juana said. "No, this is not"—she listened—"I think you have the wrong number." They could all hear the angry boy's voice at the other end. Then Juana said, "Yes, this is me." When he was through, she said, "No, don't come out here." Cesario could hear the fury at the other end. Then Juana said, "I'll be back in about an hour. But don't come out here—"

That was all she got out because Cesario had taken the phone from her and was speaking as a life in the service had taught him. "She's not coming back to that house. Those are my orders. Not tonight. Not tomorrow. Not ever."

Juana, screaming, tried to take the phone away from her father. Before he put it down, he hit her with his open hand.

She dropped into the chair by the phone, rubbing her cheek.

"Good. You deserved that," Elsa said.

"You shut up," Cesario told his wife. Now both women could see the murder in his face. "Wash the dishes and shut up!" Then he sat very close to Juana and spoke more gently, but no less intently.

"Are you pregnant?"

Juana didn't look at him. "No," she said.

"You're not going back there if I have to kill him, I've taken all I can of him harming you."

"He didn't harm—"

"Look what he made you into. Look what he did to you!"

He closed the door to the girls' bedroom so they could not hear. His eyes were those of an animal in the woods at night who is cornered and knows it must kill to save its life. "He's not going to put his dirty body into you again," he said.

Through the closed doors, from the TV in the other room, Juana could hear the shouts of the convicts as they broke out and the deadly rifle fire of the guards. The heavy labor of her father's breathing sounded louder.

"I've made up my mind," Cesario said. "God knows the reasons of my life. He knows what I have to do."

The phone rang. Each waited for the other to pick it up. It rang again. Cesario picked it up.

"Come out here," he commanded the stranger. "I want to talk to you. I came to your place, now you come here."

Juana made a sudden move and, pulling the phone out of his hand, knelt with it pressed between her breasts, talked into it like she was talking into her own body, pleading, "Vinnie, listen, Vinnie, don't do what he says, don't come out here!"

Cesario was trying to get the phone, but Juana kept turning her back to him each time he reached, protecting the phone with her arched back, begging, "Don't come out, don't—"

Cesario grabbed her neck in his two hands and began to squeeze, shaking her till she dropped the phone.

The phone, on the floor, was saying, "Juanie, Juanie, what's he doing, what's he doing?"

Cesario picked it up, and when he spoke into it, his voice was seductive. "What do you say, boy, will you come out here and talk to me?"

"Don't tell me you're going to hassle that spook out there," Michael said.

Vinnie held the dead receiver.

"Vinnie, listen, we'll take in a movie. By the time we get back, she'll be home."

Vinnie put the receiver on its cradle and walked into the bedroom. Then he was back in the doorway, pulling on a tank shirt. "Jeff, can I take your wheels?"

"Help yourself, man," Jeff said, missing Michael's signal.

Vinnie closed the bedroom door.

Michael knew he didn't have long.

When he opened the door he saw Vinnie on the closet floor.

"Close the fucking door," Vinnie said.

He had pulled a month's laundry back off the floor boards

and pried up a plank, reaching in and under for the carbine he kept there, for protection, he'd said, just in case, he'd said.

Michael closed the door.

Vinnie flipped a pair of printed pants off a hook, shoved the carbine in one leg, and wrapped the rest of the garment around the stock.

Michael was casual, lay on the bed next to Rosalie—she hadn't caught on to anything—put his head against her big belly, said, "Man, this has got to be the longest day, I'm sleepy," yawned and said, "want me to go out with you?"

Vinnie looked at Rosalie, so Michael told her to go out of the room, then put it to him. "You looking for an excuse, Vinnie? They don't need one, but if you want to give them one, you're doing it."

"He said I wasn't man enough to go out there and talk to him, that's what he said."

"Well, you know you are, any time, any place. But if you go out there with that piece, they'll powder you."

"If I don't, he'll think—"

"I didn't say don't. I'll go out with you. We'll all go listen to what he's got to say, give him that yes-sir-no-sir-shit-for-straights, then come back, and tomorrow she'll be here—"

"I don't trust her. You trust her?"

"Well—"

"I know where her head's at. That goddamn base is full of those glamour dude pilots all looking like Steve McQueen with that hardware all over their chests and plenty bread, which is what her father's parading her up and down in front of—"

"So why do you bother with her?"

"Like she was a prime two-year-old filly. I can hear her laughing, too, eating it up."

"Put it away, Vinnie, will you, come on."

Vinnie looked at his friend, then he nodded, sort of, and said, "All right, I'll do like you said, I'll go out and I'll listen—"

"Listen, just listen, that's all."

"Okay," Vinnie sighed. He unwrapped the carbine and slid it back under the floor. Michael helped him put the plank in place. Then they sat on the closet floor like two kids without toys.

"Thanks," Vinnie said after a while.

"For what?"

"You're the only friend I got, Michael."

"Well, then, why don't we stay home, she'll be back to-morrow."

"I got to go, Michael, I got to."

"Okay."

Michael took Rosalie along to give them a respectable look and Freddie because he was the only one who could handle Vinnie in case, and Jeff because he knew the old Chevy Bel-Air, an uncertain machine that car, you could hear it groan and cough when he turned it over.

When Cesario ordered Juana to go into the bedroom and watch TV with the other children, she obeyed.

But Juana didn't watch the movie. She had to find a way to keep Vinnie out of the house, she had to think of something quick. Her father would never let her out, that she knew.

So she leaned down to where Elizabeth was sitting on the floor watching a convict burning down guards with a blow-torch, and she whispered to her, through the screams of the victim, to go catch Vinnie and tell him he mustn't come into the house.

When Elizabeth came out of the bedroom into the parlor, Cesario was not in sight. She went to the door of her parents' bedroom, and there he was, sitting in front of his footlocker, holding a pistol. He lowered it when he noticed her.

"I'm going over to Marjorie's," Elizabeth said. Marjorie was Sergeant Jones's fifteen-year-old. Cesario nodded and Elizabeth left. "Just stay in her house," he called after her, "don't come back here. I've got some business to attend to here."

Cesario locked the door after Elizabeth. Then he loaded six .22 longs into his target-practice pistol, put it in his belt, and pulled his sport shirt out and over the butt, *Cubano* style.

At the sink, he washed his hands in heavy lather, slowly, around and around each other. He decided to wash his green-tinted glasses, which had fogged. He did this carefully, rinsing them in the hottest water he could run and blotting them gently with toilet paper.

Then he walked over to the black Madonna, a painting in oil on a crudely cut square of wood, and put his head on the wall next to it. He remembered the room in his father's home where the black Madonna had hung; he could smell the wick of the candle that had burned in that room night and day. He remembered the miracle: Drops of moisture had appeared through the fibers of the board precisely where the Lady's eyes were painted. People had come from nearby villages to marvel at the miracle of the tears. Yes, she was living magic, not like those cold glass saints in the windows of the base chapel. This Madonna was dark like him, and she was living. She had cried once, and if his gift pleased her, she would cry still another time in understanding. He could feel the warmth of love that flowed from her to him. Now, he told her, he was about to pay her back, not by walking on his knees to her shrine in Chicano town, but with the richest gift he had to give.

It was half an hour from Queen Street to the base, so he had time. Cesario sat in his chair, glad to be alone, hearing only the sound of the movie from the other room. Juana and the other girls would not in all their years forget how much their father loved them.

He picked up a comic book and began to read it, forgetting time and circumstance in the adventures of Spider Man. When the phone rang, he didn't jump. When he answered, his tone was as even as ever; he felt nothing, he was proud to note, except what an experienced noncom officer should feel under stress—control.

It was the main gate calling.

"You got a pass?" The air police at the main gate had only to look at Jeff's car and the people in it to know what the answer was going to be.

Michael insisted they'd been invited in. The A.P. called his superior; that line was busy.

Michael, grateful for the stall, walked back to the car and told Vinnie they were being processed.

"It'll be a while," he said. Vinnie jumped out of the car and started toward the gatehouse, Michael alongside. Very little would be needed, he knew, to throw his friend out of control. And once they busted him, it wouldn't take any kind of effort to prove Vinnie dealt drugs.

Then Michael got a surprise. Vinnie reversed, headed away from the gatehouse, and as they walked side by side, he threw his arm around Michael's shoulder, hugged his neck. He seemed about to say something.

"What?" Michael said.

"I've been thinking," Vinnie started, "about what you said—"

"Yeah?" Michael encouraged.

"Do they have trees in Mexico?"

"I don't know. I think so."

"If we could get a place in the desert, maybe—a place where there's mountains and trees and I can keep some animals, like that Indian, Arthur. He hasn't got a thing. I don't need any more than he needs. I don't want to be anywhere *near* a city. I get loco here. And dealing drugs, that's no life. Live by the sun, the Indians say. I talked to Juana about it once, and she said she'd like it. I don't like cold, so maybe Mexico. Jesus, Michael, Mexico! What?"

He looked at Michael as if he sought some reassurance.

"Oh, yeah," Michael said, "we'll get some money and—"

"I got better than money. I got a mayonnaise jar under the floor in my closet full of H. My life's savings, you could say. I could get maybe a thousand dollars for what's in that jar, it's fine really, fine—"

"What's wrong with the place we got, the place in the desert?"

"I'd like further out, maybe Mexico."

"Oh, yeah, yeah, I'll start out tomorrow with you, Vinnie."

Vinnie nodded slowly. "It's what I want."

Michael was elated. "Then we'll do it! Okay?"

Vinnie looked down at Michael and smiled the most unguarded, untwisted smile he'd ever put on anyone and said with more feeling than he'd ever before allowed himself to show, "I love you, Michael."

So Michael tried for it. "Let's start now, Vinnie. This minute. Let's walk away from this. That could be a bad scene in there."

"You mean not go in?" Vinnie pointed to the gate.

Michael nodded.

"I don't run scared," Vinnie said. Then he looked at his friend, his eyes narrowing. "You meant it, didn't you? About tomorrow? You weren't just saying that to get me to—?"

"I meant it." Michael, frightened by the sudden change in his friend, persisted. "*You* know you're not scared."

Vinnie didn't answer.

"I don't want you to go in there, Vinnie," he said. "Vinnie!" There was suddenly a lot of distance between them.

The A.P. came out of the gatehouse, found them and shouted, "One of you a Vin somebody?"

Vinnie waved and turned back to Michael. "Okay," he said, "I meant what I said and you meant what you said. Tomorrow. Soon as we get up. This is my last day here."

Jeff had trouble starting the old car, but he did, and the A.P. waved them in.

——————————————————————

Sergeant and Mrs. Jones were in their TV nook watching the Giants-Dodgers game being played at Chavez Ravine. The score was tied, but the Giants had a chance to break the game open; Lanier on second, Dietz on third, Bobby Bond up, one out.

"That son of a bitch'll strike out," Jones said, putting reverse English on it. He was a Giant fan.

Mrs. Jones, her head in a turban towel, her belly in a sweat shirt, challenged him. "Dollar says they don't score."

"You got a bet!" said Jones.

A ray of light swept the room. Jones looked through the window, saw that Cesario had opened his front door, reangling the beam reflected from the overhead streetlight. "Elizabeth," Cesario whispered across the space to where his daughter was talking to Jones's daughter on their porch. "Get in that house. Now!"

Elizabeth heard the car drive up, its muffler corroded to rust lace.

The boy she knew to be Vinnie was low in the back seat talking to another boy. In the front seat a black boy was lighting up, Elizabeth knew what.

Now was the time to warn Vinnie.

"Want me to go in with you?" Michael asked.

Vinnie shook his head.

There was a stir in the doorway of the house before which they'd parked. In the dark they could make out a girl trying to come toward them and a man holding her, finally pulling her back where they couldn't see anything more. Then it was quiet. The man stood in the doorway, just behind the fall of light; they couldn't see his face, and he didn't move. Whatever the girl was trying to call out through the screened window, the fans in Chavez Ravine covered.

Not anxious now, his heart slowed to the beat of a trance, Cesario Flores watched the blur of the Chevy through the black screen. The car, he knew, contained the boy he'd never seen; the perverter was one of those sitting at ease there, chatting casually, not hurrying any more than Cesario what could no longer be avoided.

The moment for the break had come. Most of the prisoners had joined the diversionary riot, an act of solidarity with the three scaling the wall. Elsa, lying tight up against Juana on the bed, told the girl how precious she was to Cesario and to herself, stroked her heavy brown hair as she whispered love.

Juana didn't respond. I'm not going to spend another night in this house, she vowed. She pulled herself away, sat up to watch the screen as sirens drilled the air. Guards rushed to the break along the rim of the wall. The odds were hopeless. The Flores kids, eyes locked to the slaughter were learning that crime doesn't pay.

Fat Freddie reached back with a small pair of electrician's pliers that held a roach. Vinnie sucked it twice, handed it off to Michael, climbed out of the car, and began to walk to the house where Juana's father was waiting for him.

It was Elizabeth's last chance to get to Vinnie. But when she started around Sergeant Jones, he shifted his weight to plug the doorway. "Whatever the hell," he said to his wife, "made Mr. Horace Stoneham believe a so-so relief pitcher named Clyde King would make a great manager?" Then, without taking his eyes off Vinnie, who was strolling into his neighbor's front yard, the sergeant said to Elizabeth, "There's a coke in the icebox."

As Vinnie mounted the porch steps Cesario turned his head to avoid looking at him. But there was an impression on the periphery of his sight: How white the bastard's skin is! And another: There's something missing from his face. He looked quickly to see what wasn't there; the boy's eyes were invisible behind his dark shades. "Are you Vinnie?" he asked, looking away again. "I'm the one," he heard Vinnie say. Through the space between his cheek and the edge of his own glasses, Cesario could see Sergeant Jones moving up to the screen door. "Your friends want to come in, too?" Cesario asked, he didn't know why.

"He's got a pistol," Elizabeth whispered behind Jones's shoulder.

"Be quiet," Jones told her, "and get me a brew."

Overhead a tandem of F-4's flung themselves at the sky, their roar following.

"You Flores children stay up too late," Mrs. Jones observed.

Michael had heard Cesario's invitation, waited to see if his friend might change his mind. Michael saw Vinnie shake his head, walk up the last step, and stand in front of the sergeant.

Rosalie pulled at Michael's shoulder anxiously.

"We're splitting tomorrow, in the morning," Michael said to her. "If you want to come—"

Cesario, perspiring heavily, turned his head and looked squarely at his antagonist. Except for the eyes, covered by the dark green shades, Vinnie looked like a figure Cesario remembered from an old religious lithograph, one of those around Christ. Paul, Peter, John, which was the fisherman? Cesario remembered the sea in that litho and the ascetic figures in their drapes; he remembered the parchment white of their faces and how the cheekbones shone through the skin. There'd been a chaplain who'd preached that Christ's first disciples were the wandering hobos of that day, possessing no more than the rags on their backs, their faces and frames purified by hunger, their eyes shining with the certainty of right.

Cesario was glad he couldn't see the boy's eyes.

"I saw the pistol," Elizabeth insisted to Sergeant Jones.

"This is between them," Jones told her. "Go get yourself that coke."

"Naturally, your father has faults, *Liebchen,* he's quite unreasonable at times. But I can assure you of one thing, you're his life, Juana, Juaná—!" Elsa had lost her daughter's attention. Juana was watching the last of the escapees, cornered, all hope gone, pulling the trigger of the pistol he'd put against his head. At the sound, guards lumbered around the corner and, seeing some movement still in the dead body, pumped in round after round. Even after it was still, it twitched as the heavy slugs plopped into the soft muscle and chipped the bones. Then there was an instant of silence, and the family could hear the little squeak their screen door made when it opened.

Vinnie walked in. Cesario closed the screen door, then the front door. He turned and looked at his guest again, his hair, his face, his chest, making a cop's identification, then lower, the bulge where the trousers met, extra large it seemed to Cesario, he'd broken into his daughter with what was there. Cesario thought of his own, how it looked as if it had been in cold water too long. He lifted his head now, couldn't see the boy's eyes, did see the hatred in the other features, the mouth, the way it twisted down, the lower lip, how it protruded past the hard-drawn upper lip. This boy was no saint—the pallor had fooled Cesario—or if he was, it was the saint who'd betrayed Jesus.

"First thing he ought to do with that McDaniels," Jones declared, "is trade him for two ushers and a sod man, I mean get rid of him!" His wife laughed as three big Dodger runs crossed the plate and still only one out. Elizabeth came back holding a beer and nursing a coke.

Standing in place, waiting for the thing to happen over which they had no control now, they spoke their words as if they'd been rehearsed.

"You're taking her over my dead body!" Cesario said,

remembering the phrase from a TV program he'd seen, speaking in a voice audible to no one but Vinnie and in a tone that had no threat in it. It was simply something he said.

The prisoners knew it was over. Glad they were still living, that there would be another day for them if not for the three who'd been killed, they marched back to their cells in long lines. The exaggerated sound of their footfalls, too many in unison too perfect, stopped abruptly, the men had reached their cells, the doors clanged shut and—

Vinnie and Cesario could hear the locks, the rows of metal teeth biting together.

"Then that's the way it's going to have to be," Vinnie said.

"Holy Cow! Now they got firecrackers over there," Mrs. Jones said. She turned to Elizabeth and complained, "You Flores kids really are a trial to a person's nerves. Firecrackers."

Later that night, a pathologist was to establish that no one of those first four shots killed Vincent Connor. His report detailed that one slug entered the chest and lodged in the left lung, another creased a rib, splitting the bone, and two entered the lower abdominal region below the line of the pubic hair.

Sergeant Jones knew what the sound was; he'd been expecting it. Michael knew, too. He was out of the car, running, Rosalie calling after him, "Michael, don't go in there. Michael!" In Chavez Ravine the crowd roared. McCovey had struck out to end the game.

Cesario felt wonderful. All those years he had behaved with that hard-reined control he'd thought necessary. But now he felt joyous and wild and without inhibition. He wished he could have done it with his hands, instead of with that dinky .22, or that he had a machine gun to spray the neighborhood, including the home of his shit-head buddy, Sergeant Jones, who the hell was he to stand there judging him? Yes, including the base commander, his majesty, right in his office, yes, who always acted so goddamn superior. But first finish those dirty little bastards sitting out there in that black Chevy without a top. Then to the officers' club, where he'd never set foot, and show them what a Mexican was, speak his mind to them at last. He wished they were all watching him now, wished his daughter was there to see him, where was she? "Juana! Juana!" he called, "Juana!" He could hear them trying to start the black car, but it wouldn't fire for them, while overhead his F-4s pounded the drum of the sky with the power he'd given them. "Juana!" he called. "Juana!"

Michael stopped. The demented man had come out on the porch, gun in hand, shouting, "Juana!" One step down, then another—Michael turned and ran toward the nearest house.

Look at them running, ducking into their houses, covering their heads, those white sons of bitches, scattering like birds, burrowing like animals, who said they're smarter, stronger, braver? Finish with that! Now everyone can see who's boss round here. No one fucks the daughter of Cesario de las Flores like she was common dirt, because, *mira!* I'm danger, right, not so damn reliable, right? Ha? Maybe now they understand who is Cesario de las Flores, a blood, a brave, a true Indio, bronze in my skin, they never forget that again, kiddo, ha? *Mira,* how they run. Flat on the ground! Hugging the porch. Mama! Mama! The *maricóns!* Look, they can't even start up a damn Chevy motor!

"Choke her, Jeff," Freddie cried. "Get it going! The son of a bitch has a gun!" Jeff, who usually tried to park the Bel-Air on a hill so he could roll and start it that way, was on the flat now. Rosalie, one hand under her belly, was out and running for shelter.

Running for his life, Michael leapt up on the nearest porch. As his hand touched the handle of the screen door, the wooden door behind was slammed shut by Sergeant Jones and the lock turned.

They wrestled down the hall from the bedroom to the front door. Juana, struggling to get out of her mother's grip, finally struck her with her fist across the nose, and Elsa fell to the floor. Juana did not see Vinnie where he lay half-hidden by the sofa, thought he had run out of the house, her father following. From the porch she could see Cesario running toward the car, then saw it start forward and—

"Run him down!" Freddie shouted. From a hole in the dashboard he pulled a ten-inch length of broom handle which had been sharpened to a point—all he had to meet the emergency.

From a window, Elizabeth saw her father raise his pistol; she saw the impact, the bits flying off the windshield, and the spider-web tracings in the glass. She saw the boy driving, the black boy, and the fat boy next to him duck down to avoid the bullets, and, when they did, the car swerve out of control and pile into a little white compact parked a ways down the street. The hood buckled, and the car stopped, throwing the two boys forward—

When the car crashed, Fat Freddie, stunned, saw the man coming toward them, pistol first. Freddie tried to shake Jeff, thought to run, but it was too late, he knew, it would make him the target. So he stayed where he was, playing dead. Out of the corner of one eye he witnessed the man he'd never seen before lean into the car and put a service pistol against the side of the unconscious boy's head and demand, "Where's Juana?" Getting no answer, the man grabbed the boy's Afro and pulled his face up. "Oh, you!" he said with a kind of laugh. "So it's you."

Through his window, Sergeant Jones watched Cesario with the fascination violence has for men who've known it but not seen it for a long time. "He's flipped!" he thought. "He's off his fucking trolley!" The pistol, he saw, was up against the driver's black head—the dumb nigger didn't even move—and Jones heard the two shots fired into the skull. Then he saw the demented man turn and look straight at him. "Jesus! He's not coming here!" But he was. Sergeant Jones ran for the phone.

On the Joneses' porch, Michael found out it happens; he pissed his pants.

Cesario turned. His pistol was empty. He had to reload and quick. He was running to his house—where was Juana? He seemed to remember now, he'd seen her running—but when? Where? "Juana!" Juana was loose again! "Juana!" he shouted as he entered. On the floor he found his wife, clothes disarrayed, nose bleeding, crying hysterically. "Where's Juana?" Elsa didn't even lift her head. "Where's Juana?" he demanded of Vinnie, writhing in pain and still alive, the son of a bitch!

The Joneses' door, locked against Michael, was thrown open, and Michael saw Elizabeth charging down the steps and across the space to her house.

"Last rubber!" Colonel Dowd said. "Hate to quit when we're ahead, don't you, partner?" Colonel Dowd and his daughter, Marian, were generally considered to be the best team on the base.

"Phone for you, father," Mrs. Dowd called from upstairs.

Juana saw Rosalie running out of the dark.

"Where's Vinnie?" she asked her.

"He's in your house," Rosalie said. "Didn't you see him?"

Elizabeth saw her mother sprawled on the floor, then her father stuffing bullets into his pistol, looking at Vinnie who was on the floor behind the sofa, clutching his abdomen where the pain was killing him.

"Where's Juana? Goddammit, where's Juana?" Cesario yelled.

"I don't know," Elizabeth answered. Then she saw her father walk to where Vinnie was and do the unbelievable thing.

"Don't, daddy, don't!"

Cesario was over the body, bending at the waist. "Putting the animal out of its misery," the caption might have read.

Mrs. Jones turned the set off; the game was over; the Dodgers had won, six to three. From the TV nook, she hadn't seen her husband lock the door. Only now, when she heard him say, "Get me the air police," did she realize something had happened. Then she heard another firecracker, realizing it wasn't.

The pathologist was to say that death came as a result of a single shot fired full into the boy's face from one foot away; there were powder-burn marks to indicate this. The tiny slug had passed through the top of the mouth and lodged in the cerebellum.

It was easy, Cesario thought, I never saw his eyes.

Cautiously, fearfully, Michael rose to his feet. There was the sound of a second shot; Michael cursed his innocence. "I let him come here like that. I let him walk in there unprotected."

Fat Freddie stopped playing dead. Sitting upright next to him, his head thrown back, Jeff was dead as hell.

Cesario stood over Vinnie, satisfied now, at ease. Elizabeth was looking at him as if he was insane; he had nothing to say to her. He walked out on the porch as Juana rushed up.
"Thank God you're safe," he said, smiling at her lovingly, as if to say, "Now you know how much I care for you." But he didn't speak those words. When she ran into the house, he sat in his chair and waited for what was coming. Someone else ran by him, a boy, one of them. Good! Let him see too, let them all see!

Juana saw the blood, thick as gravy, leaking out of the corner of her lover's mouth, into his hair and down, soaking his beard.
She turned and walked out on the porch. Her father was sitting in his chair, looking straight ahead, waiting, the pistol held loosely in his lap. "I wish that was you on the floor!" she screamed.
Cesario turned his head again and smiled at his daughter, softly, mysteriously. "I did it for you, *mi corazón.*" Later Juana was unable to remember whether he said that or if it was just what she read in his soft smile.
Michael crouched over his friend, trying to reach him, "Vinnie, Vinnie!" then again, "Vinnie!"

————————————————————

An A.P. car had driven up. Two police, one of them a black, leading, were walking to the Chevrolet. The black lifted Jeff's head and examined the holes in his temple. "He put the piece right against him," he said to his mate. Then he looked where Rosalie and Freddie were looking and saw Cesario on the porch, pistol in hand. The black A.P. lifted the flap of his holster and took out his own pistol. Cautiously he approached the murderer.

"What are you going to do?" Freddie asked the other A.P.

"Don't touch that body," he answered. He walked back to his prowl car, pulled a microphone off an overhead clasp, and said something into it.

When Mrs. Flores saw the black air policeman come up the steps, she began to weep again and started out to him. "Stay where you are," the man said. He saw Juana come into the doorway, "Everybody stay right where they are."

Juana heard him say something to her father which might have been, "Did you do it?" because Cesario answered, "Yes, sir."

Cesario started to get up, but the A.P. told him to sit where he was. At the door he stopped, then he kneeled. He had discovered some drops of blood in the doorway. More drops led to the chair where Cesario sat.

"Who shot you?" the A.P. asked.

Cesario looked where the man was pointing and was aware for the first time that there was a bullet in his leg. He took his glasses off, cleaned them against his shirt, and looked at his leg.

"Get up," the A.P. ordered.

Cesario did.

"Drop the pistol on the ground and put your hands against the wall."

Cesario did. The A.P. searched him. Cesario must have thought the black man was patting his body more forcefully than necessary, because he jerked his head around and muttered something.

Juana heard the A.P. say, "Go on, make a bad move, man, because I'd really like to waste you, you son of a bitch!"

At this, Cesario turned and looked at the black. There was no fear in his smile, that of the misunderstood martyr who is sure time will vindicate him.

Suddenly Mrs. Flores burst out of the house, ran down the steps and up to a car which had just driven up. But Colonel Dowd, followed by a subordinate, walked right on past Mrs. Flores who was pointing at the black A.P., making an accusation in a low voice.

"All right, corporal, I'll take care of him," Dowd said.

The A.P. stepped back.

Cesario, released, sat, ripped open the trouser leg, and found the place where the bullet had entered his leg.

"Who shot you?" Colonel Dowd asked.

"I don't know," Cesario said, "don't know how it happened."

"He didn't have a gun," Michael called out from where he was over Vinnie's body. "Vinnie didn't have a weapon," Michael repeated, coming out on the porch.

"He shot himself," Elizabeth said, pointing at her father, "I saw him do it right after he killed Vinnie."

The other A.P., a Pfc., came up and reported to the base commander. "Ambulance on the way, sir."

"Vinnie didn't have a weapon," Michael said again.

Colonel Dowd ignored him, turning to the A.P. "Search them all," he ordered, indicating Michael with his eyes. "Search their car, too." Then he turned to the lieutenant with him. "Get the city police here. I want statements taken from all witnesses tonight."

Michael felt the A.P.'s hand on his elbow. "Let's go," the A.P. said, pushing Michael in the direction of the Chevy.

Michael could see Freddie and Rosalie with their hands on the hood of the car. Other A.P.s had come up. Freddie was being searched. Michael shook off the A.P.'s hand and turned to Colonel Dowd. "What's going to happen here?" he demanded.

"Let's go, let's go," the A.P. said, taking Michael by the elbow again. But Michael wouldn't move. "He shot him in cold blood," he shouted at the colonel. "Vinnie was unarmed."

"Complete statements before they forget details." the colonel continued to the lieutenant, "before they have a chance to make up anything." Then he walked into the house.

"He was unarmed," Michael said to the A.P., who was moving him toward the Chevy.

"That's for us to determine," the lieutenant said.

Oblivious to everything going on around him, Cesario was probing with his pocketknife the hole where the .22 slug had entered his leg.

The people of the base were cautiously coming out of their homes. Some of them had gathered around the car where Rosalie and Freddie were being searched. As Michael was brought up, he heard one of them say, "She's pregnant!"

The woman was looking at Rosalie's bare feet, which were very dirty.

In the house, Colonel Dowd was inspecting Vinnie's body. Elsa was all over him. "He told me he was going to kill my husband," she said. "He came out here to kill him."

"She's lying," Juana said. Then, to her mother, "I hope you rot in hell."

The colonel didn't look at either woman.

"She's a liar," Juana said to him. "There wasn't even an argument. Vinnie came in here and Daddy killed him."

Colonel Dowd walked out of the house, found Sergeant Jones on his knees inspecting the small wound in Cesario's leg. The lieutenant came up and whispered something to the base commander, who nodded. "Sergeant Jones," he ordered, "take all of them down to the main gate. The city police will pick them up there. You go down to police headquarters with them and see that their statements are taken tonight."

"Yes, sir," Jones said.

The base ambulance drove up, and two medics opened the back.

"You won't need that," Cesario said, meaning the stretcher.

"I want you to go down to the police station now," Colonel Dowd told the girls, "and I want you to tell exactly what happened, every detail, the precise truth as you saw it. Do you understand?"

The girls nodded.

"You are not to speak to each other again until after you've made your statements. And signed them!" He made a sign to Jones.

Jones led them off the porch.

Michael's hands were up against the hood of the car. He was being slapped all along his body.

Cesario got to his feet, arched his back, stretching it. Then he limped to the ambulance, feeling the wound now. As he was about to pass by his commanding officer, he stopped, seemed about to say something.

"Go to the hospital," Colonel Dowd ordered. "Have the wound dressed. Then stay put. I'll be coming down."

As Cesario walked to the ambulance, he passed the car into which Sergeant Jones had put his daughters. He looked at the girls, but they wouldn't turn to him. Then he said to

Jones, "I couldn't let him go on doing that to her, could I, Jack?"

The girls heard Jones's answer, "I'm surprised you took as long as you did."

———————————————————————

At the base hospital, the doctor, a plump Jewish kid named Leibman, had trouble with the .22 slug. He had to dig around with long tweezers, into the muscle controlling the knee, but this appeared to cause Flores little discomfort; the man was self-anesthetized.

Finally Dr. Leibman held up the little pellet and asked, "Want it for a souvenir?"

"You better save it," Cesario said. "They'll want it as evidence."

At Sergeant Flores's request, they'd sent out for ice cream, a pint of strawberry. Cesario was laying it over his tongue, spoonside down. Dr. Leibman was puzzled over the way the man was taking it, as if it had happened to someone else.

"Who shot you?" he asked.

"Guess I did, didn't Elizabeth say that?"

"What the hell did you do that for?"

"Damned if I know."

"You can get off the examination table now," Leibman suggested. But Cesario didn't move. He sat enjoying the ice cream and reflecting.

"You do know both of them died," the doctor said.

Cesario thought that one over, too, a spoonful of strawberry halfway to his mouth. "Yeah," he said, "I saw them." He noticed the doctor's bewilderment. "I'm glad I did it," he said, trying to help him out.

Some of the ice cream dripped on the sheet covering the examination table. "Now look what I did!" Cesario said, quickly mouthing the rest of what was on his spoon and reaching into his back pocket for a handkerchief. He dabbed at a pink stain on the white sheet. "I'm sorry," he said.

"Oh, that's all right," Leibman said.

At police headquarters, Juana and Elizabeth were taken to a room furnished for questioning. Rosalie, out of respect for her condition, was shown to a small lounge next to the ladies' room. Freddie and Michael were dropped into the tank. "Oh, you're the ones he missed," said the cop who locked the steel-barred door.

A detective, having advised Juana of her right to remain silent, proceeded to take her "true and voluntary" statement, given not only voluntarily, the detective thought, but eagerly. The girl, he found, had an extraordinary memory for detail, spilling it all out in great chunks that came so fast the police stenographer had to hold her back again and again.

These statements were later corrected in ink and the whole presented to Juana to read. She didn't seem in the least disturbed at what she'd described—a series of actions starting with her father taunting Vinnie over the phone, challenging him to come out to the base, and, when the boys arrived at the gate, shaming him into coming to his house, where he waited with a pistol. This and everything that followed, particularly the absence of any sounds of dissension preceding the killing, made her father appear to have planned and carried out a deliberate act of murder.

After Juana had read her statement over, she initialed the places where it had been corrected for spelling and signed it in front of the witnesses, Sergeant and Mrs. Jones. A tough little tomato, the detective thought her. Off the record he asked her a question he shouldn't have, "Do you hate your father?"

Juana thought about it and answered the truth, "I don't know."

Jack Jones, shocked by what Juana had given the police, contradicted her. "She sure as hell does," he said.

Then it was Elizabeth's turn. She had fallen asleep, had to be awakened. As soon as she realized where she was—and why—she began to cry like a child.

Colonel Dowd did not want to interview Sergeant Flores until Police Chief Burns was with him. He had to obtain the chief's concurrence on something, and it would be easier if they examined Flores together.

The chief, known even among the kids as a patient and fair-minded man, was uncharacteristically disgruntled as he and Dowd walked over to the base hospital.

"Those kids been asking for it," he said. "I saw the condition that man was in. They drove him out of his mind."

"Could you testify to that in court?" Colonel Dowd asked.

"Well, I can't quite say what I just said. Not in court. I only saw the man once. Besides, I'm not so worried about the addict he killed. It's the other one, the black kid. He was just sitting there in his car. You know you can't kill a black like that any more. It's no different than killing a white man now."

When they arrived at the hospital, they found the murderer sitting with two ranking officers of the base air police, watching the Johnny Carson show.

As the colonel came in, the A.P.s jumped to their feet, but Cesario was slow to get up; the events of the night had reinforced his confidence and even his status on the base. He smiled at Colonel Dowd in the manner of a host welcoming a guest to his home, a visitor who had suffered a tragic loss and whom he, Cesario, hoped to comfort.

He saw to it that they were seated as comfortably as the accommodations permitted, then started speaking as if he, not Dowd, was in charge of the meeting. "I want to say straight out, I killed that person. I'm glad I did it, and I expect to pay for it."

"Wait a minute," Chief Burns interrupted. "You saw this young man who'd been regularly violating your daughter walk into your home and suddenly you went——"

"No. I planned it just the way it happened."

"What about the black kid in the car? You plan that, too?"

They could see Cesario trip up. "I don't know why I did that," he said, "but it was indefensible."

"Sergeant Flores," Colonel Dowd started, "I intend to help you——"

"No, you're not!" Cesario's voice lashed out, and they could see he was capable of what he'd done. Then he controlled himself again, smiled his host smile, and said, "Excuse me, sir, but you can't help me because I'm not going to help myself. The law is right, you know; when people do what I did, they should pay for it, right, Chief Burns?"

Chief Burns did not answer.

Outside, later, he told Colonel Dowd to give it a couple of days. "I never met a man yet who didn't hold on with his teeth and nails when it got right down to it," he said.

"Here's what I want to ask you." The colonel hesitated,

then, "Can I keep Flores on the base? House arrest, you understand? That way I can control the situation."

"What situation?"

"The situation where some wise-ass newspaperman will talk to him, and the damn fool will tell him what he just told us."

"You like the guy, don't you?"

"I don't like him or dislike him. I'm here to protect the air force and on this one I want advice, I want orders, I got to go pretty near to the goddamn top on this one."

Sergeant Jones whispered to the detective questioning Elizabeth that it might be kind to stop; the girl, crying throughout her statement, was hysterical, Jones said, so her testimony was unreliable. But the detective, accustomed to sobbers, had had more frequent cause to doubt the calm and collected.

Elizabeth resented Jones's whispering. She had come to the place in her story where daddy bent over the boy on the floor and shot him in the face. Looking straight at Jones, she asserted that Vinnie was still groaning and clutching his belly and moving his legs like he was trying to get rid of something. "That last shot killed him."

The detective knew this was critical evidence, he wanted to make sure he had it right. "Do you remember exactly where your father shot him?" he asked.

"He shot him in the mouth."

The stenographer had it; the detective nodded to Elizabeth to go on.

"I'll remember it as long as I live because when Daddy fired, Vinnie's mouth moved, but he didn't say anything."

The detective nodded, then, concluding the interview, asked, "Is this a true and voluntary statement given by you without promise or reward, threat or duress, so that the true facts in this case may be known?"

Elizabeth answered, "Yes, sir."

Mrs. Jones whispered to her husband, "I told you those kids were no goddamn good."

Jones, who an hour before couldn't see how his friend could possibly be convicted, now wasn't so sure.

"You mean you're not going to get statements from us?"

Michael asked when they pulled him out of the tank and told him he could go home.

"Let's split," Freddie said.

"We're going to get to you, but not tonight," the detective lied. "Meantime, we don't want you to leave town."

"Till when?" Freddie asked.

"Till when we tell you when," the detective said.

"Fuck that."

"What'd you say?" the detective turned to the fat one.

"I said fuck that. If you want anything out of me, ask me now because I'm splitting, I've had you dudes—"

"Don't make us come get you," the detective said very quietly. "I'm telling you nice, don't do it."

"Why aren't you taking statements from us?" Michael asked the officer.

"Why do you think?" The detective was gathering his papers.

"Freddie was in the car when Flores shot the black brother. Like, he'd know more about that than anyone."

"So why do you think we're not taking your stories?"

"Maybe because we're Vinnie's friends?"

"That's what you think?"

"That's what I think."

"Okay. Just don't leave the city."

"You can tell them one thing for me," said Fat Freddie.

"Tell who?"

"Tell 'em if Flores gets away with this we're gonna pull this town down around their ears, you tell 'em that."

"I'll remember." The detective put on his coat.

"Where's his body?" Michael asked.

"Listen, you little joker," the detective had had it, "when you ask me something say please, understand, say sir, because I'll lock your ass up so goddamn quick—"

"You're not locking me up because you have no warrant to hold me, and all I did was ask you a question, and I'm not required by law to say please, but you are required to answer my questions, right? Now, where's Vinnie's body?"

The detective thought that one over, then said, "In the morgue," and walked out of the room.

When Queen Street got to the morgue, Vinnie's mother was

there. At the side of Irene Connor was her best friend, Hal, who did the windows at Connally's department store.

When Irene saw the body she'd collapsed.

Vinnie was naked on a stone slab. The drain beneath was still moist. On the slab next to him was a young black boy.

Irene had to be helped to a chair in the corner of the room.

"Now, now, baby," Hal was soothing her, "you'll stain your best blue." He gave her the gray handkerchief he always sported in the breast pocket of his gray suit.

Michael, Juana, Freddie, Rosalie, Elizabeth could hear the woman crying through the half-open door.

"Now, baby, you have a tiny decision to make," Hal was saying. "The boys and girls he was living with have come to pay their respects. They're outside, and they are a sorry-looking crew, I must say, but really sort of sweet. The fellow in charge here, I can't remember his name or office, though he told me twice, he says he has orders to exclude them, but my dear, it does seem to me—and I said this to him— if they're his friends, they're his friends, and I suggest that you simply insist they be admitted."

Irene flipped. "No! No! They killed him! They're the ones who corrupted him. Tell them to go away, Hal—"

"Now, now, baby, just wait a little minute, because it's certainly up to you, but they're just kids, and the very fact they've come to this godforsaken—"

"No!"

"Why don't you just see them and—"

"I saw them. The one and only time the bastard ever came out to see his mother, he had them all in the car, they were filthy, those girls, no bras, holes in their pants, their hair matted like someone had spilt a pot of glue over them and none of them washed in weeks and weeks, they sat there in the car laughing and smoking that stuff, I know the smell, no, No, NO!"

The five friends consulted. "I'll get to her when she comes out," Michael said. "I'm going to talk to her."

They went outside. It wasn't long before they saw Irene and her companion, the thin, graceful man in the gray suit, leaving the building.

"You're Vinnie's mother, aren't you?" Michael said.

Irene didn't answer.

"Please, listen to me. Your son was our brother—don't turn away—" Michael shifted around so she was facing him again. "I think he figured something like this could happen because he used to tell us how it should be, his burial, like a party for his friends, he'd say, and we'd like to bury him like he—"

"I don't want you near him!" Irene seemed ready to strike Michael. "Stay away from him! Filthy addicts! I blame you for what happened to him. He could have been a good boy, but you—" Hal had to support her to where he had parked the car.

It was twenty after three, a cool night. They stood at the side of the road opposite the faceless building, exhausted, dispirited, waiting for a pickup back to the center of town.

One of the men who worked the morgue came out, got into his car. Michael held up his thumb, but the man drove past.

At the front door of the morgue, the other man was locking up. This man had seen bodies by the hundreds lying on his slabs, the unclaimed dead. He was impressed that these five bedraggled kids had come out in the middle of the night and without transportation. He had also heard Irene's diatribe, and it had disgusted him. He kept hoping that somebody someday would show some kindness to somebody. He had noticed that the kids didn't hit back at the woman and liked them for that, too. So he stopped for them.

"Where you going?" the boy who seemed to be their leader asked.

"Right through town."

"Can you take us all?" Michael asked the man. "Five?"

The man took them right to the house on Queen Street. As he let them off, he said, "I'm sorry about not letting you in to see the body, but those were my orders."

"Whose?" Michael asked.

"My chief."

"Who ordered him?"

"I don't know."

The kids looked to Michael, who didn't speak.

"Well," the man said, "maybe you can get to see him tomorrow, he's being moved to a funeral home."

"Which one?" Michael asked.

"Bryant's. They'll fix him up. The poor kid—his jaw was—you're lucky you didn't see him."

"Bryant's? That's expensive."

"It's what his mother wanted. They do a good job. She's bringing out a suit, and they'll clean him up, give him a shave and a haircut—"

"But he wouldn't want that, a haircut," Michael said. "You mean cut his beard? They can't do that."

"That's not yours to say," the man reminded him. "Don't you want him to look decent?"

"No! I want him to look like shit, like us!"

"That's for his mother to say, kid, how he looks."

Suddenly the five young people looked threatening, even dangerous. He put his car into gear. "Who are you people anyway?" he asked.

"His family," Michael said.

"Now, kid, that's a damn fool thing to say," the man released his safety brake. "In the first place, he's dead, so what does it matter? In the second place, you're not next of kin, so there isn't a thing in the world you can do about it. So take my advice and—"

Michael turned and walked away. The kids followed him into the house.

Juana wanted to heave, couldn't, felt something sour in her mouth lifting the trigger at the top of her throat. She had a headache behind her eyeballs; it throbbed as the blood pumped.

Michael placed a cool palm on her forehead. "Just lie down," he ordered.

Michael was in charge of the family now, nothing he had chosen, just what had happened. There were some pillows on the floor, and he put one under her head.

"Turn the light off," Juana said, "it hurts."

The house was quiet, even the record player, for once. The room was dark except for light reflected from the street-lamp on the corner. Juana heard Michael moving. "Don't go away," she said.

"I'm not going anywhere," Michael said. "Okay if I take a piss?"

"Take one for me." Juana began to laugh, and then she was crying.

Michael got down on the floor, his body along hers and

his arms around her. Rosalie, from the other side, put her arms over Juana and around Michael's back. She could feel the girl trembling, then becoming rigid, then trembling again.

Suddenly Juana turned so she was facing Michael instead of Rosalie. She put her arms under Michael's and around his waist, and she clung to him. Her trembling stopped; her whole body tensed once again, then relaxed, and she was asleep.

Elizabeth said, "I ought to call home," then fell asleep.

Michael looked past Juana at Rosalie. She took his hand, then closed her eyes and was still.

Fat Freddie was on his back, looking at the pattern of light on the ceiling. "Michael," he whispered, "I got to go to St. Louis and tell Jeff's mother. What the hell am I going to say to her?"

"Tell her the guy's not going to get away with it."

"I got the same feeling," Freddie said, "that he will."

CHAPTER TWO

————————————————————

In the air force, malcontents wear masks.

When Colonel Dowd came down to breakfast the next morning, his daughter Marian was there, and with her, his son-in-law, Alan Kidd. Lieutenant Kidd was on the judge advocate's staff, the base's legal department. He was dressed for tennis.

The way Dowd looked at the young man made Mrs. Dowd feel a defense was called for.

"We were having blueberry pancakes," she said to her husband, "and I remembered Alan particularly enjoys—"

"You playing tennis this morning, Alan?" the colonel asked.

"Try to every morning, sir," Alan was coating the last of his griddle-cakes with soft sweet butter. Dowd watched him. Alan noticed his hesitation, said, "Join us, sir." A gesture offered a chair.

"Have you read the newspapers?" the colonel asked.

"Try not to before I play. Does something to my concentration on the court. I did hear we had some violence on the base—"

"Are you trying to kid me, Alan?"

"I am. Yes, sir." Alan arched his back. He was a perfect six-foot, one-hundred-and-eighty-five-pound specimen, a Yankee classic, at twenty-five distinguished not because of anything he'd done but because of what he was, a man aloof, protected by his passivity. He had made no concessions to

94

the new full fashion in hair. His was blond, parted in the middle and falling just to the top of each temple. President William H. Taft wore his hair in this style; so had Secretary of War Henry L. Stimson.

"I heard you were in the base hospital last night," Colonel Dowd said, "just before me."

"Yes, sir, I heard all the commotion, took a stroll, and I did drop in there."

"It was you who brought Flores the ice cream—"

"Yes sir, that's right, strawberry he wanted. Curious."

Colonel Dowd looked at his watch. Alan refilled his coffee cup. "Only be able to play a couple of sets this morning."

The colonel gave up. To his wife he said, "I told you not to let me eat those frozen Mexican shrimps last night."

"They weren't Mexican."

"They were Mexican, and they were frozen, and they froze again in my stomach."

"He's quite right, Mrs. Dowd," Alan gently set her straight. "The Mexican variety, you should remember, have the larger fantails." Then Alan turned to the colonel and threw the largess of his approval from the other side of the royal carriage. "But I must say, sir, I find them delicious."

Muriel twinkled. Alan had a knack of making everyone grateful for his approval.

"Take a bromo, sir," Alan offered. "You seem a bit over-wrought this morning."

The cook hadn't heard the news about the colonel's stomach, put pancakes in front of him.

"Not today, Mary," the Colonel said, "tomato juice today."

"I'll just relieve you of those, sir," Alan said, and did.

"How the hell can you play tennis with six blueberry pancakes decomposing in your stomach?"

"He does very well," Alan's wife, Marian, defended him. She was reading the morning paper, all about it.

"A full stomach never bothers me," Alan said. "That's one of those myths, sir." Having carefully buttered the six sides of the newfound cakes, he reached for the honey. It was Heidi-Heather, a great favorite of the base commander's, a delicacy which his brother, Bank of America in Holland, sent him from there. Alan spooned into it twice, scraping bottom.

"There's plenty of maple syrup," Colonel Dowd observed.

"Your Green Mountain Boy Maple Syrup, Colonel, under

some pressure from the federal government, has admitted in the smallest possible type that it is composed nearly altogether of chemicals, sweetening, color, and flavor. Read the label when you have time, it's instructive."

Colonel Dowd had to laugh. Actually he liked Alan. On days when base H.Q. business was light, he often went out of his way to seek him out. On such days his son-in-law never stopped gabbing, overturning old mossy stones. But his jibes and jeremiads were gentle, passed for entertainment. And after a few late drinks, Alan needed only a nod from Dowd to sit down at the piano and sing in his modest tenor the good old tunes the colonel loved, "Drink to Me Only" and "The Blue Bells of Scotland."

Colonel Dowd felt very close to his son-in-law at those times. He had lived long enough in different societies to be suspicious of ambition when it was the central force in a man's life. In fact, Dowd had a streak of hedonism in him, now dead from neglect and the rigors of propriety. It had left a trail of memories. For no reason, now, he remembered the young mistress he had in Tokyo during the Occupation; he remembered her as he often did when he was unhappy, her silky, straight, and very black pubic hair; he recalled the stinging hot baths they'd taken together and how she'd ask, "Have I pleased you?" after they made love. He looked at his wife, Muriel, and his daughter, Marian, each a very handsome woman, each with a sizable piece of aristocratic flint in the middle of her face, past which they were now scanning him, trying to read his thoughts.

"I want to talk to you," Marian said. She put the newspaper down.

Alan finished what was on his plate.

Dowd said, "What about?"

"About what's on your mind," Marian said.

"How the hell, daughter, do you know what's on my mind?"

The cook hurried in. "Omaha on the phone!"

Colonel Dowd ran for the stairs.

"Get your breath before you talk to them," his wife called after him. Then she turned to her daughter. "Marian, leave him alone! You know he's in a bad mood."

"Mother, I am not in the air force, and I do not adapt my behavior to what his mood happens to be."

Alan stood up. "Think I'll run along," he said.

"Alan," Marian complained, "I want you to be here when I talk to him."

"Thank you for breakfast, Mrs. Dowd," Alan said, "I enjoyed it." He walked to the door, picked up his racket and a cable-knit white sweater.

"Alan! Please!"

He turned and looked at her. "Would you come here a moment," he said, "and excuse me, Mrs. Dowd?"

Marian walked to him like a child about to get a scolding she deserves. He looked down at her for an instant, smiled his Apollo smile, patronizing yet protective, then suddenly bounced the flat of his racket ever so lightly off her hairdo and, as the gut twanged, said, "I really don't want to be mixed up in this case. Let's not burden the base with my indifference this time, let's leave this opportunity for honor and achievement to hungrier men?" He looked at her, nodded agreement for her, then inclined his head gracefully as he did everything gracefully, kissed her lightly on the lips, and sauntered out, leaving her in love with him.

Nevertheless, she waited for her father to come down.

Upstairs in the bedroom, Colonel Dowd was lying on his bed, prepared for what he thought would be an extended conversation. But when he told his superior the news, all he got back was "Chu-ryst!!"

"What does that mean?" Dowd asked.

"We'll have to meet on it and call you back. Don't do anything till we have a chance to consult here. Meantime I want you to tell the automated recorder exactly what happened and what the considerations are as you see them. Try to essentialize, Frank. Now—when you hear the signal."

Beep. Colonel Dowd talked a précis of the night's events into the phone, laid down the facts, then summarized. "We can't win on this one," he said. "If Master Sergeant Flores, with our help, gets off, we will be reinforcing the impression general in our society that the air force, the navy, and even the army are privileged. On the other hand, if the man is penalized—and remember this is clearly a case of murder in the first degree—we will be outraging the community. They are fed up with those kids—hippies, I mean. There is another consideration on this side, even more serious. Either way—and this is why I say we can't win—we are leaving the impression that our highly trained personnel have been highly trained to solve their problems by the use of a gun. We are, are we not, trying to create the impression that our services are made up of decent, law-abiding citizens, repeat citizens, civilians! You can see the problem is complex, correct?

"I need immediate, specific instructions. How do you want me to proceed? I will be under considerable pressure here from the media and the community, and this pressure is sure to increase. Please make every effort to get back to me with an early answer. Waiting. Over." He spoke his name, rank, and station and hung up, repeating, just before he did, "Urgent!"

Downstairs Muriel had cornflakes waiting for her husband. Also waiting was the judge advocate on the base, Lieutenant Colonel Earl McCord. He had brought the late morning edition.

"What does it say?" Dowd asked. "Good morning, Earl."

"Could have been worse. Good morning."

"Have some coffee," Dowd said, asking for silence.

"Had some." McCord nodded thanks at Mrs. Dowd. Then he ventured, "I thought you might want to talk to me, colonel, before I go to the office." His eyes slid over to Marian, then back to Muriel. "I mean after you read these."

Well-trained Muriel got up. "I wonder if you'd excuse me," she said. "I'm leaving." She looked at Marian.

"I'm not," Marian said.

"I didn't mean—" McCord started.

"I know what you meant," Marian said to him. "Now if you will let me say what I have to say and pay proper attention, you'll be rid of me within a couple of minutes."

Dowd had taken in the front-page stories with a glance down, a glance up, and turned to the sports page.

"Daddy, pay attention, please."

"Marian, I have a crisis this morning."

"On the sports page?"

McCord chuckled to cover his embarrassment. He was glad he didn't have to handle women like these, especially the daughter. Lieutenant Colonel McCord had trained his wife not to talk in the morning. "Perhaps I'd better move along now," McCord volunteered, looking at his chief for instruction.

"Sit where you are," Marian said. "What I have to say involves you, too. Daddy!"

Dowd put his paper down. "Yes, Marian."

"I want you to give Alan a chance on this. I think you're misled, both of you, by his easygoing ways, and you haven't allowed yourselves to discover that Alan is an exceptionally—"

"Now, Marian, did I ever say he wasn't intelligent?"

"Daddy, Alan has never had a chance—don't look at me that way, Colonel McCord. I know I'm being personal. I'm his wife." She took an instant to quiet down. "Daddy, I know you're going to see to it that Sergeant Flores has every bit of protection the air force can give him—"

"My dear," Dowd said, "the air force doesn't yet know—"

"Daddy, that's pure bull. This could mean a lot to Alan."

"All right, Marian, we'll talk about it later."

"He has two more years to do. I should think you'd want him to go out of here with some sort of reputation, some sort of professional standing—listen to me!"

Lieutenant Colonel McCord reached for his cap.

"Colonel McCord, you've always treated my husband as a playboy when the fact is that he's really got a brilliant mind, far more interesting and original than your own, if you'll forgive me saying so—"

Dowd blew. "Marian, get the hell out of here!!"

"This is the first time I have ever asked you for anything, daddy," she said. "I know I'm making a fool of myself, but goddamn it—"

"I appreciate your loyalty, girl."

"This is going to get in all the papers and on television, and it's a chance for Alan. He's too proud to ask for it, so I'm doing you a favor, I'm giving you a chance to be a decent father."

After Marian had left the room, Dowd asked McCord, "Why don't you like my son-in-law?"

"Well sir, every time I assign him, he acts like he's doing me a favor to accept."

Dowd smiled.

"I like your daughter, though. I like it when a woman sticks up for her husband that way."

"You didn't answer my question," Dowd said.

"Well—are you serious?"

Dowd nodded.

"He's just not a soldier," McCord said.

"He wears a uniform."

"With moccasins."

"They're black. That's within limits. What do you mean, he's not a soldier? What's a soldier?"

"Well, I was raised on a post, Frank, and I suppose I'm as blind as any other lifer. Lieutenant Kidd's got all the civilian virtues. He's gentle, kind, amusing, agreeable, companionable, clean, tolerant, understanding, intelligent, I didn't mean to leave anything out. And he looks great. Okay. Now! How has he earned the right to behave so condescendingly?"

"He's the son of a famous judge. You've heard of Judge Nicholas Kidd?"

"I certainly have."

"And, well, he was brilliant in college and law school—"

"We are still preparing for the eventuality of a full-scale war, are we not? Can you imagine an air force of tennis players? Someday someone may have to stand up again and mean what he says again and die to make it stick. Lieutenant Kidd is above it all or—I don't know. Do you?"

Muriel found her daughter sitting at the window of the room she used to occupy before she married. Muriel was a sensitive woman, trained to accommodate herself to the moods of others. She went to a chair, the mate of Marian's, sat, and looked out the window, too.

They sat for a minute without talking.

"Alan," Marian started slowly, "is suddenly, totally without ambition. I don't know what to do." She waited for her mother's response.

"Apparently," Muriel said, "he has everything in the world he wants."

"Well, that's dangerous. He's in the air force for one tour, he has two years to go. What's going to happen to him when he gets out?"

Muriel thought a moment. "Men have stages," she said. "When your father came back from Japan, I thought he'd never need me again. But in time—"

"I keep wondering, is it my fault? He's like a car that's had a sudden loss of power."

"Well, he was always—"

"No, he wasn't!" Marian said. "Jesus, mother, he was 'most' everything in college, most likely to succeed, hardest worker, Phi Bete! Sometimes I think I understand what's tuned him out, but if I'm right, I'm part of it! It's like he was dying of some gentle but fatal disease, one he enjoys. Suddenly he's decided to quit on everything. That's why I thought if Daddy—"

"Does he still love you—physically?"

"Nothing like he used to. You notice how he was down-stairs—detached, a little mocking, you can't quite touch him, godammit mother, he makes love to me like he's doing me a favor!" Marian picked at the hem of her skirt. She made up her mind to raise it an inch and a half.

"I'll talk to your father," Muriel said.

Marian leaned over and kissed her.

Downstairs, Colonel Dowd had told McCord about the call from Omaha. "For the moment," he said, "there's nothing to do but wait to hear. Meantime, avoid the press. I've closed the base to visitors. How the hell did those hippies get through the gate last night?"

"Sergeant Flores passed them through."

"Apparently he was waiting for them. With a gun."

"Apparently."

"What's your judgment on this?"

"I've been trained all my life to do one thing."

"Enforce the law?"

"*Uphold* the law. The subtleties of public relations, I sup-pose they're involved here, not my field." The pipe had gone out, and he put a flame to it.

"But dealing with your field, upholding the law—?"

"There's only one answer. First degree. Deliberate and un-equivocal. He's guilty."

"That's his opinion, too."

"He was in a position to know."

"You don't think he stands a chance?"

"That's not my point."

"What is your point?"

"I don't think we should defend him," said McCord. "I don't think we can—and be what we're supposed to be. Not really. We have to uphold a certain standard. We know what happened. And we know the law."

"But aren't there human considerations that—?"

"The law is what we have."

"You mean, you'd ask for his life for killing a couple of drug addicts?"

"I want you to know," McCord said, "I like Flores. He's a damned good soldier from what I've been able to observe—"

"But you'd—"

" 'Fraid so. Have to."

They were silent for a moment, then Colonel Dowd slid off with, "Well, let's see what they say in Omaha."

He got no help from Omaha. "The only instruction we feel sure about giving you is that it must be a civilian trial, no display of privilege. If he's guilty, he must be punished, just like any other citizen. Incidentally, how does he intend to plead?"

"Guilty. Says he wants to pay for his crime, seems eager to, in fact."

"What's the matter with him?"

"Religion, I think."

"Well, here's our feeling. You are there to protect the United States Air Force, and the services in general. You must bear in mind that at this time we are on trial with the American public; we have to watch every move we make."

"Peace is our ever-loving profession, right?"

"Frank, you have to look at this killing as if it happened on Okinawa. One of our men got drunk and killed a native. Remember how we bent over backwards there—?"

"Sergeant Flores is a good soldier."

"No privilege. Don't throw our weight around. You're head of an occupation army. If the soldier did it, he did it. Incidentally, who did he shoot?"

"Two longhairs."

"Well, could be worse."

"One was black."

"Oh God, I thought you said long-haired."

"You know, Afro, electric, something."

"What the hell did he go and do that for?" There was a silence, then, "There's nothing in our instructions, Frank, to prevent you from getting the best lawyer in that community and charging him with defending your man."

Colonel Dowd didn't answer.

"How's the weather out there?" Omaha asked.

"Oh, you know, it's the desert. That hot wind blows up from Mexico and we fry."

"Well, keep in touch." The phone went dead.

Mr. Don Wheeler, first partner of the biggest law firm in that world, rearranged his morning so he could sit down with the colonel immediately. He asked only that the base commander come out to his home. "We'll be able to talk without anyone informing themselves that you've consulted me. I can guess what it's about. The murders last night?"

Colonel Dowd made a sound for yes.

"I don't think I can help you," Wheeler said, "but perhaps I'll make a few suggestions. You remember how to get here?"

Two years earlier when Dowd had been brought back from Asia and put in command of the base, he had been introduced to the substance of that desert motoropolis at a series of social gatherings. The most important as well as the most convivial of these took place on Don Wheeler's hilltop, where his home, Points o' the Compass, extended its paws over four terraces. The party centered around an ox roast served from a reproduction of a chuck wagon. It started late in the afternoon so that Mr. and Mrs. Wheeler's guests could have margaritas on the west terrace and enjoy the sun setting to the music of mariachis. The party stopped rather early so that the male guests in ranch clothes, broad cowboy belts with heavily ornamented buckles cinched over desk-chair bellies, would be in good shape the next morning when, dressed for what they were, insurance executives, bankers, real estate developers, department store owners, mine owners, they redevoted themselves to the business of life and the life of business. Dowd remembered the occasion and the house very well. He pointed out the hill to his driver and told him to go to the top.

Dowd got a surprise. The house was full of packing cases. Three Mexican servants were packing up Mr. and Mrs. Wheeler, who were leaving for good.

"I'm going back to my cows," Don Wheeler explained.

"Ten years late." Mrs. Wheeler smiled and shook hands with the colonel. When Dowd had seen her last, she had looked to be maybe ninety-five pounds soaking wet. In the two-year interval, she'd lost weight, now looked twenty years older than her husband, a tiny, gracious crone.

Wheeler, on the other hand, had a "western" build, a solid six feet, broad across the shoulders, thick through the chest, tight in the waist and thighs, very long legs, longer for the boots he pulled on every morning. A slight swagger was inevitable. "Yes," he said, "Hope's right. I promised her—"

"You promised yourself," Mrs. Wheeler corrected gently.

"So I did. That when I was fifty I'd live out my life the way Hope and I like to live."

"He was sixty yesterday," his wife looked up at him as if he was a son of whom she was very proud. "He doesn't look it, does he? Give him a couple of months on a horse, and he'll look just like all the other hands." She patted his belly, ever so lightly. When she raised up on her tiptoes and stretched her neck and head to him, he kissed her, called her darling, and she left.

"No one knows exactly what she has," Wheeler said, "but it seems to be progressive. We've seen a lot of doctors."

The colonel didn't know what to say. "Where you moving to?" he asked.

"Two hundred thirty-nine miles due north. Got a couple of sections, half a mountain, one real pretty stream, full of trout, ranch house, out-buildings, bunkhouse for the hands, run a lot of cattle. But it's not a business. Like Hope says, how do you want to live? I propose to get on a horse every day. I do not propose to hear cars, sirens, typewriters, telephones, complaining, bargaining, bluffing, all the sounds of humanity at business. I don't understand the world now. What I do understand, I don't like. I'd rather see a rattler in the morning than most of my clients. A coyote sounds more brotherly than anything I hear in that city. And I don't know a friendlier sound than the one my cows make when they come in at the end of a day. Now air traffic is a problem. TWA goes over four flights a day, but they're at six miles and I can take that. You people fly one pattern over me that's a noisy bugger! But I figure you're protecting me from—what the hell are you protecting me from, please, sir? What? Huh?" He laughed and said, "You look worried."

Turning away from his guest, Wheeler slung his feet upon the arm of the chair next to him and began to shake out the base commander's memory. He demanded the precise sequence of events, time and geography, the smallest details, the contradictory versions. He seemed not to be listening to Colonel Dowd; often his questions did not link up to the answer he'd just received. Like all good lawyers, Wheeler had the knack of making the most innocent man feel a little guilty. Just when Dowd began to resent this, Wheeler turned and apologized. "I know I'm doing this like you were the fellow who shot him. Force of habit. I'm sorry." Then he looked at his guest and smiled.

But Dowd was not so much angry as fussed. Wheeler turned away, noting this, stretched his arms and yawned. Then he decided to satisfy his curiosity.

"I must admit there is one thing that puzzles me, and it hasn't a thing in the world to do with the case."

By God, Dowd thought, the son of a bitch wants to chew on me some more. "What's that?"

"I can't help wondering why you're so worked up over this." Wheeler let the question hang. The moment became uncomfortable. "You must be very close to this man," Wheeler continued. "He doesn't sound your sort at all. But here you are, and——"

"I rather dislike him, to tell you the truth," Colonel Dowd said.

"Then what?" Wheeler persisted. "It's irrelevant, of course, but this kind of trip is well outside your line of duty, isn't it?"

"Well, he's always been a valuable man at his job."

"So you're protecting a good soldier?"

"I can't imagine anything else. How did we get into this?"

Wheeler recognized that something he knew a lot about, his instinct for the jugular, was loose again. "I'm sorry," he said, then asked, as if Dowd had started it, "may we please just drop this? I feel I've embarrassed you."

"Oh, that's okay," Dowd said. "I'm just surprised you found me to be so—involved, so exceptionally——"

"It means your instincts are in the right place. I don't imagine there are many bits of brass who'd take the trouble to personally set up a defense for—what did they say in Omaha when you spoke to them this morning?"

"How did you know I spoke to them?"

"I didn't."

"They were—cautious."

"Look after the air force first, its reputation, its public standing?"

"More or less."

"But how do you best do that?"

"That's the question." Wheeler smiled at him, and Dowd tried again, feeling his way. "I'm still surprised by what you asked me," he said.

"There's a mystery in most human behavior. That's always been my interest in the law. Most of our work is for industrialists and real estate people, and to tell you the truth, I despise it. But this stirring around in people, I'll miss."

Wheeler smiled at him again, and now Dowd went with it. "How about some lunch?" Wheeler asked. "Huevos rancheros, some guacamole, we might even dip into an early margarita."

Dowd found that despite Wheeler's questioning, he was enjoying the man's company. Wheeler insisted that his wife make the margaritas herself, and she even brought them out herself, setting them down carefully so the salt around the rims did not shake loose. Then she kissed her husband's forehead—they were always saying goodbye, it seemed—and left. He watched her go, pausing to bend over some border flowers, pulling out three dead stalks with three quick plucks. Then she straightened up and didn't just then remember what destination she had chosen for her next trip, said, "Oh!" and set off purposefully into the house, light as a bag of feathers.

Wheeler found the eggs too bland and added chili till he liked them enough to order another set of twins. While he ate these he informed Dowd, "You don't have anything to worry about."

"I really don't know why I'm so wrought up over this," Dowd replied.

Wheeler was looking down into the valley where the city was laid out under a blanket of mustard smoke. "Would you believe it, when I first settled up here, the air was as clear as a mountain brook in the spring? Now I don't dare draw a breath when I go down there, wait till I get back up here to get my oxygen. The irony, of course, is that what you see down there comes mostly from copper mines, some as far away as one hundred miles, and they are our clients, I work for them."

"What's the solution?"

"I'm leaving the battleground in disorderly retreat. It's every man for himself now."

"Still—the rest of us—we haven't got a place two-hundred-odd miles north of here to go to."

"I'll take you with me. I got a couple of cabins up there, one five miles from my house, you have to get there on a horse. In the winter you can watch the antelope come down off the mountain, they go right by the front door; and any time you're liable to see wolves in packs or a puma alone, and eagles, they're still there, but you better hurry, they're going—"

"What did you mean I have nothing to worry about?"

"The air force is not going to have a damned thing to say about this. It's a community matter, and the community is going to protect itself."

"The murderer was air force."

"This community is not going to let your man pay with his life for something every single one of them would have done."

"But justice—"

"Fuck justice! You would have done the same thing if it had been your daughter, right or wrong?"

"Well—"

"Answer my question!"

"No, I don't think so."

"You would and you know it. I'll tell you something. If it had been one of my boys who'd shot one of those long-haired freaks, I wouldn't be worrying over it, no, sir, nor feeling as guilty as you—or I guess as he does."

"He doesn't feel guilty. He says he's ready to pay."

"I don't care what he says, it's out of his hands. This is frontier. We protect our homes, and we protect our women, the damned fools. I'll tell it to you plain. Your man did right."

"Well, perhaps he did—"

"No perhaps about it. My grandfather came out here, Bible and gun, from the state of Maine, and a meaner-looking son of a bitch you won't find even in the movies. He put four markers down, and that was it. No deeds, no grants, no favors. And brother, I'm telling you, if someone had fooled around with the sorriest of my five aunts—" He burst into laughter. "And if he'd been away, my grandmother would have taken care of it and without a whole lot of soul searching; she'd just put her pistol down on whoever. What the hell is going on—I'm going to be candid, sir—when you, the commander of Collins Air Force Base, are uncertain where the values in this thing are?"

He got up. "Come on, let's go down to my office. Ride with me, your driver can follow."

Just before they passed into the smog, Wheeler stopped the car. "There's one now," he pointed to a bird circling about a mile down range.

"Hawk?"

"That's an eagle. Don't know what the hell he's doing down here, looks like he don't either. Poor son of a bitch can't see through this soup to get himself a meal. Wish I could communicate with him. I'd tell him I got a couple of his cousins for neighbors up north, and he ought to come on up."

"Beautiful, the way he floats."

"He can drop like a big red rock! There isn't a damned thing man has ever made that's as beautiful as that bird. I'll tell you a story. When I was a kid I thought I'd get me a young eagle to train. So a buddy of mine—he's dead, went down over Bremen—we climbed a mountain, made fast a rope, and dropped me to the ledge where the nest was. Well, sir, the mother of that brood spotted me. I had looked around carefully before I went down and hadn't seen her. But I sure as hell saw her coming at me, and I'm telling you I was lucky to get out of there with my life. I never forgot how that lady defended her kids, I mean those are fundamentals. Mister, what happened to the fundamentals?"

Dowd had no answer.

"You wonder and quibble and consult about a man who finds his daughter's been corrupted by a worthless drug-consuming son of a bitch and does something about it. What the hell has this society lost when that bearded bastard whose picture I saw in this morning's paper is flushed down the toilet? Tell me that?"

"Not much, I guess."

"Tell me the truth, don't you admire your man for doing what he did?"

"Well—"

"That man has done us a service, Colonel Dowd, and while your mind won't let you admit it, your feelings, which are truer, they know it. And that's why you're here on an errand that a second lieutenant should be chasing out. You're paying the man respect by coming up here. You're thanking him. And believe me, the community will, too. Because whatever bad I say about this city and this area, I still know these are right-thinking people here, and they're not going to let your man die. So relax."

As they turned into the parking lot next to Wheeler's office building, he said, "I'll take the case. I mean my office will. I won't be around much, but I'll put a good man on it, and I'll be looking over his shoulder to make damned sure he does right. Okay?"

In Wheeler's office there was a saddletree between the two large windows and on it an elaborately worked Mexican saddle of golden-hued leather with brass fittings. Dowd admired it.

"It's been there fifteen years, lest I forget my cows." Wheeler leaned over the intercom, "Tell Gavin McAndrews to come in here." Then at Dowd, "You look like you got one thing more to say."

"Just this. The air force is extremely desirous of preventing any and all impressions that its members are privileged. When I spoke to Omaha this morning—"

"They'd rather see the man dead. I know."

"Oh, now, come on, they've got a point. We just can't be prominently involved in seeing to it that our man is let off easy."

There was a soft knock on the door, and Wheeler bellowed, "Come in here, Gavin!"

When Dowd saw the way Wheeler looked at young Gavin McAndrews, he remembered the moment on the terrace when Hope appeared in the doorway holding the two goblets of linda margaritas up in front of where her breasts had been, and Don Wheeler leaned over to him, whispering, "We have no children."

"Sit down, boy!" Wheeler said with surprising roughness, pointing to a chair. "But before you do, shake hands with Colonel Francis Dowd, you heard of him!"

"I certainly have, proud to meet you, sir."

Dowd noticed that Gavin had a slight limp.

"Read the papers this morning?" Wheeler asked the young man once he was seated.

"Yes, sir."

He's too young, Dowd thought.

"What I was referring to," Wheeler said, "and why the base commander is here—is the murder on the base last night."

"Yes, sir?"

Wheeler put Gavin on the spot. "What did you think?"

"I think," Gavin began slowly and thoughtfully, "well, I haven't met the man, but I'd certainly believe that he'd have an awful lot of sympathy behind him in this community. He certainly has mine. I hope to have kids and—well, what do I think? It looks like an open and shut case of first degree, but if the case is presented right, which means in its human context—the law, when you get down to it, colonel, is the most human of the professions—I believe your man might get off with manslaughter two." He turned to Wheeler. "Are we going to handle it?"

"You are."

Gavin looked at the colonel. "Is that all right with you, sir?"

"You're handling it for this office," Wheeler said. "Colonel Dowd is leaving it up to me, and that's my decision."

Then he looked right at Dowd and waited. If he was going to object, now was the time.

Dowd let it pass.

Wheeler didn't camouflage that the pause and the silence amounted to an acceptance of Gavin by Dowd. "Okay," he said. "Now Gavin, tell the colonel what manslaughter two means in terms of penalty."

"Five to seven, he might have to serve that much. Depends. Might get off with less. It's flexible. I'd say five."

Maybe it's good he's so young, Dowd thought, won't look like entrenched power at play.

"I'll do my best," Gavin said. "I surely will!"

"You better do better than that," Wheeler said sourly. Then he laughed, and they all joined in.

Gavin looked at his watch. "Well then," he said, "I think I'll high-tail it down to the jail and meet the man."

"He's not in jail," Colonel Dowd said.

"Where is he?" Gavin asked.

"He's on the base. House arrest. I spoke to the chief about it, and he said—"

"What the hell did you do that for?" Wheeler demanded.

"Jesus, I thought you were so concerned about public—" Wheeler stopped. "I'm sorry," he said. There he was again, treating Colonel Dowd as a subordinate.

"I know," Dowd said. "It does seem wrong, but—"

"You did say you didn't want to create the impression air force personnel were privileged?"

"Now, calm down, sir, calm down," Gavin said. He often had a way of scolding his chief, a treatment that Wheeler loved. "I agree it was a wrong move, but we'll straighten it out. We'll have him in a nice comfortable cell for his supper —and—"

Any doubts Colonel Dowd had had about the young man were gone, not only because he saw the boy had poise but because it was clear that he could hold his own with Don Wheeler, something Colonel Dowd had not yet done.

"Mr. Wheeler," Gavin said, "what would you say if we wait for the county prosecutor's office to act on this one? Let them be the ones who throw our man in jail. Make them the guys with the big black hats straight off? Let's lose the first round, what do you say?"

Wheeler looked at him with the purest admiration. *"Muy inteligente,"* he said. Then, to Dowd, "Ain't he the shrewdest little son of a bitch?"

Gavin, a local boy, was said to be a creation of Don Wheeler's. He had seen him playing football on his high school team, had liked what he saw enough so that he chose him for one of the college scholarships that the office maintained. Two years later Gavin was being declared the best one-hundred-and-fifty-five-pound quarterback in the Southwest conference and that was a quote. The next season no one mentioned his weight when praising him. He was the toughest, the most resourceful, the most surprising, the meanest when that was necessary—yet so soft-spoken off the field that no one believed it was the same boy. Then, instead of trying to defer his service, he volunteered into the Marine Corps, once there volunteered for combat duty, was wounded, so that he walked ever after with a slight limp, a kind of distinction. Once back, he worked days, went to law school nights, didn't ask for help from Wheeler, accepted it reluctantly when it came, modestly—just the opposite, Wheeler had often observed, of the young men you read about who thought the world owed them a living. Gavin clearly believed in effort, not subsidy, respected his elders and their traditions. Wheeler had never told anyone, but he had made up his mind long ago that when he left, Gavin would take over his office, the corner room that looked out over the city to the mountains in the north.

But he had a problem with Gavin. Their best-paying clients were not yet ready to accept him, preferred older men with a lot of experience. One reason Wheeler had suddenly decided to take on the case for the office was that it had occurred to him he could assign it to Gavin. Win, lose, or draw, it would enlist the sympathies of every decent-thinking person in the area for the defendant and so for the lawyer defending. The industrialists developing that area were certainly decent-thinking.

Even if Gavin lost, they would still have to be impressed with Gavin's appearance, his demeanor in court, how well-prepared he was and how well-organized—Wheeler would see to that—and how sincere. Gavin needed no help there.

As Wheeler had watched the boy talking to Colonel Dowd, he noticed for the first time that his close-cut hair was thinning, there was a gleam of scalp as he bent over, elbows to knees, that habitual posture which combined deference with intensity. Hell, I've got to stop thinking of him as a boy, Wheeler thought, he's a man and his time has come.

_____

On the lawn of Bryant's Funeral Home, a perfect piece of sod, they all waited for Michael, silent, not stirring.

Inside, Mr. Ernest Bryant and his lemon-complected daughter Ernestine, who kept the books and was to inherit the business, hurried into the doorway of the room where Vinnie and Jeff Wilson were laid out.

Vinnie's beard had been shaved and his hair well-trimmed. Irene's friend Hal had contributed a dark suit with a shadow-striping, a white shirt with a cellophane-stiffened tab collar, and a tie Hal had bought to wear to one of his boss's parties. Mr. and Miss Bryant thought Vinnie looked wonderful. Rouge had endowed his sallow cheeks with a TV glow. The sun had rarely touched that boy's face, and never so effectively.

But Mr. and Miss Bryant had not rushed in just to take

another look at the handiwork of their mortuary's beautician. The man at the desk guarding the entrance to their establishment had summoned them over the inter-office phone, and he'd sounded frightened. What the Bryants saw was an extremely thin boy, dressed in Lee's and a faded sport shirt, kneeling at the feet of Mrs. Irene Connor. His head, the hair long and curled, chin softly bearded, was tilted close, and he was whispering to her urgently. Mrs. Connor's face was white. She shook her head, looked away, unwilling to listen to what was being said to her. Now she made a violent motion with her body, shaking the boy off.

He got up and, without looking at the body, walked past the Bryants and out of the room.

Relieved of Michael's pressure, Irene dropped her head and began to sob quietly. When she felt a light tap on her shoulder, she looked up at Mr. Ernest Bryant. "Why don't you come have a cup of coffee with us?" Irene nodded her head, a child allowing comfort from an adult.

Upstairs, while Irene told Mr. Bryant about Michael's threat, Ernestine watched the group on the lawn through a window. Michael had gone over to where Juana waited; the others gathered around, a compact group, debating.

"Are they still out there, Ernie?" Mr. Bryant asked.

Ernestine nodded and walked over to the sofa before which coffee and brownies had been placed. Her father nodded toward Irene's cup, and the daughter refilled it.

"I'd call the police as you suggest, Mrs. Connor, if I wasn't absolutely convinced by thirty-four years' experience that this will ease off. Death is a time of hysteria, not always quiet, but temporary, always. The experience of all our law-enforcement agencies has been that the introduction of police into a situation of this kind serves only to aggravate."

"You didn't hear what he said for chrissake."

Mr. Bryant knew then he had a nut on his hands. It also occurred to him she'd been drinking. "That boy threatened that he and the others would dig up the body if Mrs. Connor buries him as she's planned," he informed his daughter.

Ernestine made a sound of disgust.

"The boy is dead," she said, "why don't they honor that?"

"We go in there now, look at the body, make like it's goodbye, and split," Fat Freddie was urging. "Then we drive away. But we watch the place. Like Sandy, if she fixes herself up, looks very straight. So she watches just to make sure. Then tonight, maybe three, four in the morning, we break in, man, and before the police wake up the shit's on, we get Vinnie and we get Jeff and we head north to the reservation, and by eleven o'clock they're in the ground."

"I have an idea," Ernest Bryant was saying, "but I offer it with considerable hesitation. In fact, I—"

"Has Hal called," Irene interrupted. "A Mr. Harold Hall?"

"I checked a quarter of an hour ago," Ernestine said, "there was no message for you."

"My best friend! When I need him, where is he? In a department store window. Would you please call Mr. Hall again and tell him to get his ass over here?"

Ernestine looked at her father. "Go ahead, darling, I'd like to be alone with Mrs. Connor for a moment."

Irene looked at him suspiciously. It nettled Mr. Bryant. He didn't like all those kids on his lawn, this woman, the notoriety, and the public fuss, it wasn't good for the image he'd created with years of effort and thousands of dollars in advertising.

"Now," he insisted softly, "there is one way our problem can be terminated with the kind of peace any dead person deserves."

"What's that?"

"Have you considered cremation?"

"What?"

Bryant persisted. "We have the finest facilities for that kind of service, right here in this building."

"You mean burn him?"

"The body is reduced to ashes and given to you in a beautiful urn, which can be kept indefinitely, wherever you—"

"What do you think I am?"

"Kindly consider, you do have a situation here. What those kids said—they threatened me, too, you know—was that they'd keep a group out there on my front lawn all day and all through the night and then tomorrow they propose to follow our little cortege to the grave, and who knows what kind of outlandish show they might put on there. In fact, I must tell you that I am on the verge of regretting that I— my institution—was ever involved in this affair."

"Are you threatening me, you son of a bitch?" Irene had a flask in her large handbag and fumbled for it now.

"Like son, like mother," Mr. Bryant said under his breath as he gave up, turning away from the woman just in time to see his daughter rush into the room.

"They're coming in, the whole bunch of them!"

Irene collared Mr. Bryant. "Stop them."

Mr. Bryant threw her hands off his jacket and left the room.

"Actually, they seemed very orderly," Ernestine said to her father.

"Phone the police!" Irene called after the pair leaving the room.

Downstairs, Mr. Bryant saw that he had nothing to worry about, at least for the moment. A group of about forty young people were filing past the body. A rather plump girl with a Mexican look was standing at the head of the coffin. Those going by, after they looked at the body, seemed to be stopping to say a word of comfort to her.

Irene Connor had found a dime and was asking Information for the number of the police. "This is an emergency!" she shouted into the phone.

Juana kept looking at Vinnie's face. She was surprised to see how handsome he looked freed of beard and the fall of hair. But when she turned to Michael, the last of the line to go by, she said, "Will you look what they did to him, Michael?"

Ernestine whispered to her father, "She's calling the police."

"That settles it," he said. "Either she allows this body to be cremated, or she will have to move him to another home. You call the police. Tell them you're speaking for me and there is absolutely nothing wrong with the conduct of these young people. Aside from the fact that they are filthy and smell of God knows what, they are behaving perfectly, which is more than I can say for the mother. Tell them, Jesus Christ, I don't want cops all over my place, it'll ruin my business!"

Cy Walker, the county prosecutor, left his office early that day. He had just been notified that it was his duty to prosecute Flores on behalf of the county, and he had a lot of thinking to do.

He had left a lucrative law practice in the East eight years ago to live in a drier, cleaner climate. He'd found his professional place in Southwest society very quickly, but his job as county prosecutor paid much less than what he had earned in his best years of private practice in Camden, New Jersey.

So a few weeks earlier Cy Walker had announced his resignation; this would be his last case. There was so much money to be made in real estate law, with the great boom in business and in the swelling insurance trade, that Cy couldn't afford to continue in the service of the public. The day after he resigned, in anticipation of an early renewal of lush earnings, he had bought himself a second car, a Camaro convertible, a pledge to himself that better days were coming.

"Sounds open and shut," his wife, Corky, said when he got home and told her about the case. "How can you not win? What's the matter?"

"Can I afford to win?"

"The man did it with premeditation and in cold blood, he—" She stopped. "Oh, I see what you mean."

"Yeah."

"You mean you might win, but it could be an unpopular victory?"

"I mean I can't help but win, and for sure it will be unpopular."

"Hmm."

"A lawyer in private practice doesn't need to know much law, baby, but popular he's got to be."

"You're popular, Cy."

"Will I be after my courtroom triumph? That sergeant in the U.S. Air Force, he's liable to be the town hero by the time the trial is over."

"Have a drink?"

"I will."

When Colonel Dowd got back to the base, he sent for the Judge Advocate. While he waited, he figured out the answer to Don Wheeler's question.

It wasn't what Wheeler had suggested; Francis Dowd would not have done what Flores did.

"Sometimes force is necessary," he'd said to the man, "our anger finally saves us," he'd said.

Flores had pulled the trigger, but hadn't he put the gun in the man's hand? Well, no, not that bad, but still, hadn't he encouraged, even pressured Flores into what he did? Wasn't he defending himself?

When he informed McCord that his son-in-law, Lieutenant Alan Kidd, was to be assigned to the defense of Master Sergeant Cesario Flores, McCord said, "May I ask your reasons?"

"No, you may not. Flores is going to be defended in fact by Mr. Don Wheeler, nominally by a young lawyer in his office named Gavin McAndrews. Our representation in court is to be negligible."

"Then, sir, you've got the right man."

Later that day, sitting next to Alan in the officer's club, Dowd was ashamed of feeding McCord that word "negligible." Person to person, Alan was anything but.

McCord had trouble finding Alan to notify him, finally tracked him down in the twilight of the Officers' Club where Alan was entertaining a group of young marrieds that included his wife. He was sitting at ease in an overstuffed chair, two martinis into his evening.

"Didn't you hear your name on the P.A.?" McCord scolded.

"I'm trying to discourage the use of public address in the lounge areas on the base. It tends to make social intercourse edgy."

When McCord told him the news, Alan didn't comment. He turned and looked at Marian.

McCord left. They all ordered a final round before dinner. Alan seemed to be studying his wife over the martini.

Finally she had to ask him, "What is it, Alan?"

At this he rose, nodded graciously to the others, and excused himself.

With dessert, the waiter brought Marian a note, one word, "Bowling."

"Remember," he said later in bed, "I told you my father died with a smile on his face?"

She nodded suspiciously.

"Some day I'll tell you what he was smiling about."

"Stop playing games with me, Alan."

"I'm not going to stay in law when I get through here, Marian."

"What are you going to do?"

"I don't know."

"What's that mean?"

"It's every man for himself now."

"Oh, Alan, stop it!"

"I revered that old man but never so much as on the day he died. What he said with his last breath was that the people who manipulated the law had turned it into an instrument to protect privilege."

"And that's why he was smiling?"

"No. He was smiling because it had taken him a lifetime to find out."

"Well, why hadn't he done something about it? He was in a position where he could have—he had the power, the prestige."

"He said he was leaving that to me."

"And your first step is to quit?"

"No, that was just to put you on notice in case that's how it turns out. You married a certain person. You are not obligated to persevere when that person changes identity."

"You have a very low estimate of me, Alan."

"Not of your realism, Marian."

He smiled at her, turned over, and was asleep long before she was.

Hal to the rescue! He had found another funeral home, at the far end of town. The Southside Home for the Dead, once the old city morgue, used the facilities left behind when that institution was sold off. Here came the poor who couldn't afford Bryant's prices.

The owner of the place was Isaac Bulgaros, a man of uncertain derivation, "Izzy" to the trade. His commodity was not the white-carnation respectability of Mr. and Miss Bryant, but a sort of friendly adaptability. Izzy, for instance, quickly got Hal's point. He sent to Bryant's for the body, and although the signs of the hippie siege had disappeared, he used caution. The car that drove through the white colonial gate and into a covered passage under Bryant's Funeral Home was a panel truck without windows or lettering on its sides.

Half an hour later, Hal drove to Bryant's, found Irene disconsolate in the lobby.

" 'Bout time," she said, getting up in pieces.

"Would you let me handle this, dear? I've done pretty well so far. The body is at Izzy's and from every indication got there unobserved. So don't snipe at me, I've got my period today and I'm a bit jumpy, so watch your shanty Irish lip!"

"Don't be mean to me, Hal. I'm—"

"A little drunk."

"Wish I were." In Hal's car, Irene was crying again. "I've never hurt anybody in my life. Why is everybody so mean to me? Hal, hold me for a minute, will you?"

"I'm gay, baby, very very gay, remember?"

"Just hold me, for chrissake, you're human, aren't you?"

Hal put his arm around her, and she slumped against his shoulder.

"Did you see Vinnie, Hal, isn't he beautiful? Like an executive!"

"Well, he was wearing my suit."

"I never had a chance to love him, Hal."

"Which brings me to—"

"Only now, when it's too late, maybe now I can do a little something for—"

"I'm going to tell you how."

"If only those little bastards will—"

"Irene, stop whining and listen! We did the job perfectly, Izzy and I. There hasn't been a sign of the insect army. And the same peerless duo will plan and carry out the funeral. I ask only one thing of you."

"Anything, Hal, only let me love up my boy a little."

"First! Lay off the sauce till he's in the ground."

"Don't talk to me that way, Hal."

"Second! Remember that they're going to find out pretty damn soon that the body's been cleared out of Bryant's and that it's lying in state, if you'll excuse the expression, somewhere else. They won't know, however, because I was so brilliant, where that somewhere else is, are you following? But they'll start looking, get on the phone, well, Izzy knows what to say. Their next step will be to follow you. Now I want you to stay away from Vinnie—is that your son's name?"

"Vincent. Yes."

"Till the morning of the funeral. I don't want anyone to

go out to Izzy's till then. They don't know where the body is now, and I don't want them to learn. Can you remember that, dearie?"

They not only knew the body had been moved, they knew it was at Izzy's. In a Country Squire station wagon borrowed by Sandy from her grandfather's stable, some pretty sharp eyes had taken note of the panel truck when it drove into Bryant's. The driver, dressed as moneyed innocence, had walked into Bryant's and inquired about rates and arrangements.

There, in the lobby, Sandy had been witness to Irene's big scene. A woman, Vinnie's mother Sandy assumed, had stormed up out of the basement and attacekd the manager of the establishment, a dyke in her mid-thirties, insisting she didn't want that other body, the black one, she only wanted her son.

"Well, who is the other young man? The Negro? We're billing you."

"How in the hell would I know? Do I look like a nigger? Just keep his black ass out of my son's car!"

"Shshsh," Ernestine begged, looking anxiously at Sandy. Then she rushed downstairs, leaving Sandy to herself.

Sandy hurried out with the news. When the panel truck drove out, it was tailed by the Country Squire all the way to Izzy's. Then Sandy drove to Queen Street to report. The house was full, over a hundred people there. Many of them knew Vinnie only casually, but they were all enlisted. Every movement seeks a martyr.

"I want at least twenty of us outside that place at all times, night and day," Michael was saying. "If we can get more, more—as many as possible, all the time. No letups! We ran them out of Bryant's, and we'll have our way at the Southside. I got his mother's phone number. Someone or other should call her every ten minutes and tell her in a nice polite way, no need to sound uptight, that Vinnie was our friend, he left instructions how he wanted to be buried and—listen, man, if any of you have friends out of town, tell them to call, too. Also call the funeral home and be real nice to the man, he carries poor people they tell me, so explain to him what the deal is and what we care about."

So fifty kids jammed in what cars they could find or traveled on their thumbs to the pavement outside Izzy's. They were so quiet that for half an hour after they arrived Izzy and his assistant did not notice their presence. When they did, it was not because of any disturbance.

Izzy went out and talked to them—and listened.

"His mother never gave a damn about him," a boy, thin, near desiccation, said. "She gave him away when he was seven years old."

"How would you bury him?" Izzy asked.

They all knew the answer to that, it seemed, but it was too simple to explain simply. Finally, the same boy said, "Our way."

They behaved like a herd, Izzy thought, with a herd's instinctive singleness of purpose and need, one that couldn't be articulated but that nevertheless determined all their actions. "And what is that, your way?" Izzy said, asking them all.

There was a general movement of heads in the direction of the very thin one, who said, "It's got nothing to do with where you put the body."

Izzy had never had a conversation with a herd before. When their leader spoke, they all spoke through him. Other times, others said what he might have.

Izzy liked them, the way they covered the ungiving pavement as if it was their true turf, the attitudes of their bodies like those softly rounded humps sheep and cattle make when they cluster at their ease. But above all, it was that they were there—all the time more arriving—because they cared for one of their number. When the old man had to go to answer a telephone call, he hated to leave them.

The caller was Hal, checking. Izzy told him that there was quite a crowd of kids in front of his place, what was it all about?

Hal couldn't explain or tell Izzy what to do, decided to sleep on it. He undressed Irene, put her to bed, then locked the door to her tract house from the outside with the key Irene had given him in case—she'd said—her boyfriend killed her some night.

This bravo, incidentally, had disappeared. Irene's bed was no longer a place where a man could get a decent night's sleep, so he'd gone home to his wife, a wise decision. Irene's phone rang continously that night, rang until she pulled it off the hook and threw a blanket over it. Among the calls she'd taken was one from New Orleans, another from Madison, Wisconsin. Irene told Hal the next morning that they were up against a nationwide conspiracy.

———————————————————

Judge Thurston Breen was the pride of the county's judiciary. People in the know put no ceiling on how far the judge could go in the service of the public.

In the first place, he looked like a member of the Supreme Court, if not the one that sits in Washington, certainly the one that wears the first robes of his state. He was of medium height and absolutely erect. He kept himself in superb physical condition by horseback riding and tennis—he and Lieutenant Alan Kidd were regulars on the same *en tout cas*— and by not eating lunch.

But that glow of his, everyone knew, came from inside. The judge enjoyed his life and who he was, enjoyed other people and who they were, had a happy home and a loyal wife, not too pretty, plenty smart. The judge was intelligent and not embarrassed by it, sported an air of culture without being a phony. In other words, he had every reason to feel the way he looked, confident and proud.

He wore dark suits of conservative cut. But instead of a white shirt and dark blue tie, which might have made him look like a gang lord dressed to look respectable, Judge Breen would wear a pink shirt and a tie which combined the colors in his suit and shirt. People remarked that he had an artist's eye for color.

His choice in shoes was unforgivable; brown shoes with a dark blue suit. But, by some treatment, a cream imported from England perhaps, or simply weathering under great care, they glowed darkly like the leather binding of a precious book.

His symmetrical face combined the elite virtues—firmness, clarity, strength—with simple human warmth. This was not altogether the endowment of a kind nature. Judge Breen's tan was uniform, summer and winter. On cloudy days, he spent five minutes under a lamp.

But the basic thing, the wonder, about Judge Breen was his courtroom deportment. He was the greatest show in the state. When a case was tried in front of him, people came to watch. Other judges dropped by to learn, stayed to envy.

Not that there were pyrotechnics. Breen's court had a chatty air. The way he conducted it demonstrated at every instant that ours was the best of all possible ways to deal with human error and determine socially imposed penalties. All present, the plaintiff and the defendant, the lawyers on both sides, the clerks, the secretaries, the court reporter, the bailiff and his charges, the members of the jury, all felt they were being included in the true process of democratic justice.

Juries listened to his instructions, spoken softly in a didactic but gentle tone, as if the words had never been used before. They hadn't, not the way Judge Breen put them together. He had rewritten the standard remarks of a judge to his jury into the common idiom, sprinkled the new text with personal observations and insights, wittily put, but without loss in cogency. He had a writer's ear for words.

He planned to write a book on the jury system one day and include these speeches, pointing out through the body of the text how human our system of justice is *au fond*. His hope was to make the law available to the understanding of the simplest person in this democracy.

His notes for the book, as well as the speeches, waited in large looseleaf notebooks locked in his office. The judge had decided not to publish anything until he had reached the pinnacle of his career, whatever that might turn out to be.

Governor was the goal in their sights—his wife, Sally, was an equal partner in this.

Although he had never given the least hint of this outside his bedroom, there were a lot of busy minds around the county courthouse who suspected what he was going for. That's how Judge Thurston Breen got his nickname, "Thurstie." It had quickly got back to the judge, and he didn't like it, not a damn bit. A nickname can hurt a man.

Judge Breen had himself to blame; he had chosen Thurston. Furthermore, Breen had been Green, and Green had been Greenbaum, and Thurston had been Theodore, and Theodore Teddy, and that was the story of his life. Judge Thurston Breen was—had been—a Jewish kid brought up on the streets of Chicago's South Side. He had gone to the Albert Leonard High School and to the University of Chicago, where he made acceptable grades, slipped through law school, passed the bar, and when he saw that he wasn't going to be rushed by one of the big firms, began in a small one which had a varied clientele.

Then it had happened. Sally warned him that he was in with people she did not trust. It turned out that the head of the firm had been facilitating certain kickback payments, had in fact carried forth the little black bag empty and returned with it full.

The Breen crisis came one day when Sally found Teddy in his bedroom crying and in that weakened condition he told her what his firm was into—more revelations were to be made soon—and that he feared his career, as well as the firm's, was ruined.

Sally threw her arms around him, reassured him with her love. Then she urged him to resign, immediately, to disassociate himself publicly from the sewer about to be uncovered. She gave him some further advice—suspecting that perhaps he might be in deeper than he'd admitted, even to himself. "Let's get out of here!" she urged. "Let's go somewhere far away and start all over."

That's how they'd come to the great Southwest.

And with Sally's help it had worked.

Sally had had a career, too, before she married. She'd been Sarah Rittman, a member of the staff of Adlai Stevenson. A diligent and able worker who organized well behind the scenes, her particular fields were the slums of Chicago's South Side, where she'd been born and raised. She was the patrician's bridge to people who might not otherwise have understood him, one of Adlai's foot soldiers, stubborn, resilient, outspoken, down-to-earth.

When her political god passed on to the greener fields of Washington and the U.N., Sarah decided it was time for her to marry and reproduce. She selected her man, the best-looking young lawyer in view, a prize for a plain girl, persisted till pregnant, then married. She made him happy, too.

Sarah Rittman had been further Left than she'd allowed to Stevenson or even to Teddy. Not that it would have mattered at the time in either case. On the contrary, she came equipped with a valuable street Marxism—and strong nails.

When Teddy had to start over again, she changed her name to Sally, went back to work—for him. She was there to open his law office, in fact she'd chosen it, his secretary, his letterheads, his first clients. Teddy's public image was largely her creation, Judge Breen-to-be. They chose certain friends, developed certain habits, cultivated certain tastes and hobbies—horseback riding, for instance. The idea of a collection of branding irons was hers, and it was soon known that the Breens had one of the best in the state. Sally chose their charity, too, the Indians who were the original inhabitants of that land. Thurston was on the committee concerned with the welfare of their young people.

As soon as the money started coming in, Sally began to entertain usefully. The coterie of friends who frequented their ranch-style home on the outskirts of the city was carefully chosen. Sally had a nose for power, for influence, for growth stocks in humans. It was the happiest period of their lives since their courtship.

What had happened in Chicago was long forgotten.

They even began to hint—this was one of her cleverest suggestions—to certain selected friends that they were Jewish. There followed a swelling belief in the judge's honesty and candor.

Having achieved his first peak, having enjoyed the exhilaration of working together successfully, they set their course for the governor's mansion. Again, the technique was to be proper exposure of the correct image.

Which is why Judge Breen wanted this case so badly, why he dropped hints in the right places, entertained certain people at lunch.

When he was informed that he had the assignment, the first thing he did was rush home to tell Sally the details, what had happened, how, who the people involved were, the lawyers, Cy Walker, Don Wheeler, Gavin McAndrews, his tennis buddy, Alan Kidd—

Then he got a shock.

"You're on the wrong side, Teddy," Sally said.

Judge Breen respected Sally's instinct, never went against it, not when it counted. But this time he debated her. This case was going to get more attention and more publicity, he told her, than any he had ever conducted.

"You're on the wrong side, Teddy," she sang.

"I'm not on anybody's side." He sounded more certain than he felt. "I represent the people of this state."

"Which people?"

"Oh, shit, Sare, don't give me that tired YCL crap. This is a long time later, kid, stop thinking ritualistically—"

"Okay, Thurstie."

"And fuck you, too," said Judge Thurston Breen. "I'm going for a ride."

"There you go again. Every time we disagree, you go for a horseback ride. You pay attention to me only after the ax. Then you say, why didn't you make me listen to you?"

"All right, make your point."

"Stay out of this one. I know it's tempting. I know you'll be center stage for the next three months, your name on the front page every day, and all the rest of it. But, darling, think ahead! Who're you going to be dealing with in a few years? The kids. There's an awful lot of them, and they're not the voters of tomorrow; most of them are already voting. Do you want them to refer to you, for the rest of your life, as the judge who got the Establishment's hit man off?"

"How the hell do you know which way this case is going?"

"You mean to tell me that this sun-burned, horse-ass, wife-swapping, whiskey-swilling bag of Wasps is actually going to sentence a member of their air force to death? You actually believe that? Because if you do, kid, you've lost touch with reality. Back to Chicago for you, Thurstie."

"Stop calling me that, Sare."

"Teddy, I'm trying to help you. No matter how many charming, educational speeches you make to the jury, you will be the whitewash judge—"

"And the lackey of the ruling class!"

"You said it! Because when this man gets off, the kids aren't going to blame Mr. Don Wheeler and his circus animals. They'll say he's true to form. But you, the man who's trying to bridge all classes and all age groups, who hopes to be elected governor of this state by offending as few people as possible, that man in the middle, the liberal conservative, he, you, are going to get the big black shiner, baby, and remember your ugly Jew-girl wife said it!"

"So what do you say I should do?"

"Let's go to the Greek Islands like we've been talking about."

"Sare, I've been assigned."

"Say you got the shingles—who's going to take your shirt off and look? Walk away. Let somebody else have the honor.

Or are you so thirsty that—I'm sorry, I didn't mean that."

"Jesus, Sare, I'm going to belt you one!"

"You are like hell. Sweetheart, think, really think this time. We've worked so hard! Now you want to take a chance that one lousy trial can—why take that chance? I know it's like telling an actor not to go on in a part for which he's been acclaimed, but—"

"Will you stop saying things like that! I'm not an actor!"

"Oh, *no?*" Then she stopped. "I'm sorry. I don't know why I say those awful things. Fix me an old-fashioned, will you, Teddy? I don't want to be mean to you any more!"

He fixed her a double old-fashioned, then one for himself. Later, when he tried to make love to her, he couldn't. "Serves you right," he said.

He woke in the middle of the night with his mind made up, woke Sally, told her he was going to go ahead with the case.

"Okay," she said.

It sounded only a little like a warning.

In the morning, he was able to do what he couldn't do the night before.

At breakfast she didn't mention the case.

———————————————————

As Gavin McAndrews had hoped, Cy Walker won the first skirmish. He got on the phone first thing in the morning and raised a self-righteous clamor about Flores, a murderer loose on his own recognizance, wandering around the base like a celebrity.

The press got all this immediately—Mr. Don Wheeler saw to that—and so the opening exchange was a complete and uncontested victory for the prosecution. Cy Walker felt pretty chesty about it. "Every once in a while those air force buckos have to be reminded they cannot behave like occupation troops in a conquered country," he told his blond secretary, Donna.

An hour later he had his court order, signed by another judge, not Thurston Breen, instructing the county sheriff to get off his indolent ass and out to the base, pick up Sergeant Flores, and immediately see to it that he was detained in a cell like a man about to go on trial for first-degree murder. Within another hour this transfer had been effected.

And that was how the prosecution got its first black eye in the community.

"Well," Cy Walker said to Donna, "that's only round one. The round that counts is the last."

Donna had a cunning developed over years of working for lawyers. "What worries you?" she asked.

"The fact that no one fought back. What's Wheeler up to?" Then he went into his office, closed the door, picked up the intercom, told Donna he was out, and lit his morning cigar.

What Cy was trying to figure out was just how unobtrusively he could win the case and still lose it, let Flores off easy—say manslaughter two, maybe five years—without looking inept and losing a case that even his wife had called open and shut. Of course, after it was over, he could wink, as the man was serving his three years—he had it down to that in his mind—and say privately in public that he simply could not believe that a man who had protected his daughter from a gang of potheads should be—but then— How could he be distinguished from the defense? It was a tough line Cy had to walk, and critical for his coming career in private practice.

Donna brought him his eleven o'clock coffee and one of her goodies. "When I used to work for Mr. Don Wheeler," she said, "I noticed that most cases, they'd just have a little talk, the lawyers on both sides, a little private talk and then the next morning I'd read in the paper that the case had been settled. I never knew how, but—" She liked to close the door in the middle of a sentence.

Why the hell did everybody refer to Wheeler as Mr. Don, not Mr. Wheeler, Mr. Don Wheeler? And there wasn't a secretary in town with any experience in a law office who didn't work for Mr. Don Wheeler.

"Didn't?" He meant "hadn't worked." A slip of the tongue. Cy wouldn't put it past that son of a bitch to have a spy in every big law office in town.

Then he picked up what she had dropped, her eleven o'clock brick. Maybe that was it! At some point in the trial when it looked like he was going good, when he had effectively displayed his moral indignation, he'd get hold of

Wheeler or that other fellow from his office, no, he'd do it through the lawyer the air force assigned, that's it, Cy had met him at a few parties, Alan Something, strictly country club, Cy had had to laugh when he heard who the air force had picked to defend, maybe they wanted to lose, too. Well, anyway, he'd drop manslaughter two in this Alan-what-the-hell-was-his-last-name's lap, just drop it and walk away, he couldn't be so dumb he wouldn't see the point right away and call everybody concerned together in Judge Thirsty's chambers, why not; and there he'd rattle his brass a bit and then suggest manslaughter two like it was his idea, it would get him a promotion for sure because would they ever grab at it. Wheeler's probably thinking along the same lines himself. Only one thing, the earlier in the trial, the better, right? Before the public gets all hot and bothered about the case, right?

And so County Prosecutor Cyrus Marshall Walker could conclude his service as public prosecutor with a case that would leave him admired on all sides—and ride home to his wife and kiddies in his new blue Camaro.

And when he opened his own offices, he'd take Donna along. Even if she did spy for Mr. Don Wheeler.

Gavin and Alan met for lunch, to get acquainted and to establish a working relationship. Gavin noticed Alan seemed to like him, looked at him intently, smiled from time to time as Gavin brought him up to date.

"I know they've told you I'm supposed to quarterback this," Gavin said, "but I like to work with people, not—"

"Oh, don't worry about me," Alan replied, "you'd be wise to think of me as someone you have to put up with."

Gavin treated that remark as humor and went on to describe what he thought their problems were.

Then he stopped. Alan seemed attentive but in a curious way, more watching Gavin than listening to the tactics he'd been laying down. "What do you think?" Gavin asked, though he was far from through.

"I was thinking," Alan said, "that you remind me of a road runner, you know that bird that always runs tipped forward?"

"A road runner?"

"I mean it as a compliment. I only wish I had some of that."

"Of what?" Gavin concealed his irritation perfectly.

"Of—you know, ambition, drive—"

"Oh! Okay," Gavin said. The guy was a weirdo, no question. "But did you hear what I've been saying?"

"Would you repeat just the last part? I have to admit my mind wandered there."

Gavin did.

When it came time to pay the check, Alan insisted. "Colonel McCord said I could charge it to the base. Don't deprive me of the pleasure of spending their money."

"I'll get it next time," Gavin said.

Alan thought, She should've married someone like him.

Gavin's immediate plan was for them to go out to the county jail and meet with Sergeant Flores for the first time. Each had his car, Gavin a Merc wagon he'd bought in the hope that his wife would soon provide extra passengers, and Alan his Karmann-Ghia, Marian's gift, which he described as a "real good-looking boat with a kinda disappointing power plant, representing, I suppose, what she's come to think of me."

Gavin laughed at this, but he was beginning to notice how many of Alan's quips were at himself.

The idea was for Gavin to lead the way—he knew a short cut—and for Alan to follow. But Alan, Gavin couldn't imagine how, lost contact, disappeared.

Later, when Gavin had come to know Alan better, he would have immediately realized this was not an accident.

In back of the jail, just outside the large double glass doors of the sheriff's office, there was a rose garden; and there Gavin found Cesario working, once again at a sort of liberty.

Roses, Cesario had informed Chief Burns that morning when they were sitting around his office, roses are an easy mark for aphids and other nearly invisible but extremely destructive pests, and if you don't look after them every minute, you might as well not have bothered to put them in. Cesario had volunteered to do something about them, and the chief accepted the offer.

So Cesario received Gavin in the rose garden, kneeling on the ground, troweling the soil around the plant stalks, his face turned away while Gavin was making his acquaintance. They had a good half-hour before Alan made it out there, and during that half-hour Gavin learned only that the man was contented with what he'd done.

"Did you meet my daughter?"

"Haven't had that pleasure."

"Well, when you meet her, you'll see she's worth it."

When Alan finally arrived, Cesario got up, excused himsef. The sight of the air force uniform seemed to turn him off.

When he returned, Cesario was carrying a can of Slug-a-Bug. "I don't think this is going to do it, the underside of these leaves are just covered with aphids." And that's all he said. He lay on his back and sprayed up at the leaves, pinching his nostrils tight as he did.

Gavin made a sign to Alan that they should go.

It occurred to Gavin that it might be embarrassing for Alan to be told, just after he arrived, that the interview was at an end.

But Alan didn't show—or feel—any embarrassment. Nor did he apologize for being late.

"Sorry you missed it," Gavin said. "We had a good talk."

"I know Flores," Alan countered, "never liked him."

This shocked Gavin. "Why the hell not? I've never seen anyone more honest. What don't you like about him?"

"I'm not compatible with the military end product."

"Then perhaps you shouldn't be on the case." This out before Gavin realized how far he was going.

"Wasn't my idea," Alan grinned at him. "What did you learn?"

"I've got to work on his daughters. Those two kids said a few things they may have to change their minds about."

"But you can't do that!"

Gavin didn't answer.

"Weren't you telling me at lunch that his daughter said right after the shooting that she wished it was him lying there instead of her boyfriend?"

"Mr. Don Wheeler says, 'Don't pay attention to what people say right after a murder.' Look, her boyfriend is dead, her father's alive. You don't think even the funkiest daughter is going to sit by and watch her father be executed, do you?"

"No," Alan admitted.

"I want to talk to that Juana. Can you find out where she is, right this minute?"

"I know where she is. She's sitting on the sidewalk in front of the Southside Home for the Dead. That's why I was late. I saw them all there. I never had a close look at a whole bunch of those kids before, so I got out and—" He stopped.

"What's the matter?"

"Did you mean what you said—about the girls changing their statements?"

"I'm going down there. You going home, Alan?"

"I'm going wherever you go, friend."

━━━━━━━━━━━━━━━━━━━━━━

When Alan arrived there was a small commotion in front of the entrance to the Southside Home for the Dead. Two cops had driven up in a squad car and were preparing to clear the pavement.

Alan saw over fifty kids sitting there, ignoring police orders. There was only one standing, a thin boy whose face reminded Alan of pictures he'd seen of his Vermont Yankee forefathers; hard-drawn, obdurate. Officers Palumbo and Koch were trying to be patient, Alan could see. The thought of pushing these kids off the sidewalk simply bored the perspiring police.

"Come on, will you, fella," Palumbo pleaded, "it's a hot day." He was speaking to Michael.

"Nobody's moving," Michael said. He turned and bumped into Alan, who was standing directly behind him, listening. Michael looked at Alan's uniform, saw an enemy, sat down.

"See that, lieutenant?" Officer Palumbo was appealing to Alan, "They're going to make me send for the riot car."

"Who're they harming?" Alan wondered out loud.

"What do they want? Hi, Bill." Gavin had just arrived, gone straight for the brass buttons.

"Hello, Mr. McAndrews," Palumbo said. "Don't ask me what they want. Hey, Twiggy, what you want?"

Michael, now sitting in a perfect lotus position, ignored the question.

"So far as the owner can make out," Officer Koch pointed to the old morgue building, "what they want is the body of one of their buddies, the one the air force guy shot."

"Naturally, the mother wants to bury her son." Officer Palumbo's voice, Alan thought, strained for dignity. "Hey, you, Twiggy," he nudged Michael between the buttocks with his foot, "don't you think a mother has a God-given right to bury her son? What are you, a Buddhist or something, sitting like that?"

Michael didn't respond.

Fat Freddie didn't move, nor did he look around.

There was not a stir anywhere.

Rosalie and Juana were lying on the pavement as if it was green grass, Rosalie on her back, Juana on her stomach, right-angled, her face over her friend's.

Juana was telling Rosalie how badly she felt about what had developed between her and Michael.

"Don't let it bug you," Rosalie said, "because I'm not tight about things like that."

"I love you, Rosalie."

"Actually, I'm relieved. I mean, look at me, I'm getting pretty big. You really helped me make up my mind. I'm going to disappear."

"What?"

"Split."

"To where?"

"Seattle, where my folks live. And I'm going to get married. Have the baby first, I couldn't get rid of it now if I wanted to, which I don't, because it's Vinnie's. Then I'm going to get me a nice nine-to-fiver and—"

"What will you say about whose it is?"

"I'll say its daddy died in the war."

At that instant, Officer Palumbo made his move, brushed by Alan, grabbed Michael under the armpits, and started to drag him toward the squad car.

Freddie went after Palumbo, pulling his arms off his friend. The second cop, Koch, went for Freddie, clubbing him over his head and shoulders and back.

Relieved of Freddie, Palumbo grabbed Michael again. Michael twisted at the waist, flailed with his legs, broke loose.

When he did, Palumbo also took to his stick.

And then Alan surprised himself. He pulled Palumbo around and heard his father's voice of command come out: "What are you doing, officer? Stop that! I said stop it!"

The words weren't out before Palumbo, who thought he

was being attacked from the rear by some of the other protestors, turned and clubbed Alan where neck meets shoulder, trying too late to stop the blow when he saw whom he was hitting.

But the blow landed.

For the first time in my life, Alan thought, I'm on the wrong side!

Well, there it was. A policeman had struck an officer of the air force with his club.

Everyone had seen it; everyone stopped.

There was an instant of irresolution on both sides.

It was at this moment that Irene and Hal appeared, walking through the crowd to the entrance of the old morgue. Irene was at her most ladylike, "Excuse me, excuse me, please, if you will?" not a bit frightened, she'd seen a few barroom brawls.

The police made the decision, hustled to their squad car to call for reinforcements.

"Which one is Juana Flores?" Gavin asked the nearest of the kids.

"You can't talk to her," Freddie said.

"Why not?"

"Because he won't let her." Freddie indicated Michael.

"Which one's Juana?" Gavin turned to ask Alan.

Alan was rushing to where the police were talking short wave. "Don't do that," he demanded, "I'll get them to move."

The police paid the fool no mind.

"See how they are!" Palumbo was saying to Koch. "They start a fight, then they holler police brutality."

Koch was jiggling a tooth he was going to lose to Fat Freddie's fist.

"You have your facts wrong, officer," Alan said. "You started it."

Palumbo pulled the car door closed.

Alan decided to enlist Gavin's help. When he got to where Gavin was, he saw a remarkable thing.

Gavin was scared.

"How can you defend that man?" Michael was saying.

Gavin couldn't answer his accuser's face.

"Where's your conscience?"

Then Michael walked away.

"You'd better stop them." Alan indicated the squad car.

"They're sending for the National Guard or something." Alan saw that Gavin resented being bossed. He didn't care. "Do it!" he ordered, and then caught up with Michael.

"Who're you?" Michael asked.

"I'm a lawyer, too," Alan said. "Air force."

"You defending her father?"

"Yes, I am."

"Who's ours?"

"You mean your lawyer?"

"Who's for us?" Michael demanded.

"The county prosecutor. Walker's his name."

"Where's he at?"

"County courthouse building. Downtown."

Michael nodded, stood there thinking a minute. Alan felt a surprising inhibition against interrupting his thought. Before he could turn the boy's attention his way again, Michael left him.

The others compacted around Michael, listening.

Gavin was talking to the police, his back turned to Alan, when he caught a sudden shift in Palumbo's eye and turned to look.

Gavin hunted birds. You are in the presence of wild turkeys, he recalled, and before you become aware it's happening, they've disappeared.

The whole gang was moving swiftly down the street.

"How the hell did he do that?" Palumbo asked Gavin. "How did you do that?" he asked Alan as he came toward them.

"I didn't," Alan said.

"Sorry I hit you," Palumbo said.

"Glad you did." Alan got into his little white Karmann-Ghia as a riot car roared up screaming.

━━━━━━━━━━━━━━━━━━━━━━━

Irene was cool walking through the fight, but inside she took one look at Vinnie's body and fell apart like a jigsaw puzzle turned over. She started for the ladies' room.

"Give me your flask before you go," Hal said.

"Go fuck yourself, you pederast."

Hal laughed and Irene disappeared.

Then Hal and Izzy had a talk.

"You got a good-looking girl friend," Izzy said.

"Her nerves are shot," Hal said.

"It'd be unnatural if she weren't, a fine sincere woman, I can see that."

"Sincere she is."

"What is the exact nature of her problem here?"

Hal told him and by the time Irene came out of the ladies' room, fortified, Izzy had made a suggestion, and Hal liked it.

They withdrew to Izzy's office.

"Mr. Hall has explained everything to me. Your problem is an unusual one but not so unusual as you might think. These children, they're very upset, apparently your son was a sort of hero to them and you have to respect—"

Irene was off. "But Mister—whatever the hell your name—"

Hal stopped her just in time. "Irene, be quiet! Now! Not a word. Mr. Bulgaros has been kind enough to make a suggestion which—"

"Yes, yes," Irene said, suddenly clinging, "forgive me, please, I want very much to hear what you have to say."

"I have here," Mr. Bulgaros began, "in fairly good working order, the complete equipment of the old city morgue. Now my suggestion, dear lady, is to delay the funeral. Let things cool down. The youngsters, very sincere, will come to the conclusion that the funeral has taken place, that we were able to bury the boy without their detecting it. Or they can easily be led to believe that a cremation took place. We have vaults which can be maintained at the proper temperature, so that you, in your good time, may choose when to bury your son. Meantime, he rests."

Irene looked at Hal uncertainly.

"In perfect condition," added Mr. Bulgaros.

"I think it's the solution," Hal said positively.

"For how long can he—?"

"Indefinitely," Izzy swore. "Months!"

"Let me think about it," Irene said.

"Meantime, let me offer you a drink," Izzy's smile inspired trust.

And that's how it was settled. For the time being.

Cy Walker told Donna to say Yes, he'd see them all right, in fact he'd been wanting to talk to them, but could they please limit their attendance at the conference to a small number of those most involved? More than thirty had already come into the county courthouse building, padded through the halls mostly on bare feet to Cy's office, and more were arriving all the time. Cy wasn't going to sit down with half a hundred hippies. "Tell 'em six, Donna, no more."

They were all gathering in a corner of his waiting room, in the open doorway, and out into the hall. The ones close in were trying to listen to Michael talking to Donna. Michael nodded, chose six, and told the rest to go out to the arcades where the fountains played and wait.

Freddie was still unsatisfied. The violence that his encounter with the police had stirred up had not been released, was still eating at him. He pulled Michael over to one side.

"I'm not going in there. I made up my mind," he whispered, "I ain't gonna wait on all this shit."

"I haven't made up mine," Michael said.

"Okay, I'm splitting."

"Okay."

"Because this is like—nothing."

"What would you do?"

"They're fixing to let him go, and they'll dress it up in all that legal shit, but that's what it's going to amount to and so I'm going to take care of it myself."

"I don't want you to do it."

"Fuck you."

"I said I don't want you to do it, Freddie."

"Because you're balling his daughter?"

"Split, Freddie."

"Well, what the hell else?" Freddie turned, but didn't go. "Michael," he said, "Jeezuz, I tried to go see Jeff's mother yesterday—in my imagination, you know—I walked up to the house, and I couldn't go in, because what the hell did I have to tell her?"

"Freddie, listen," Michael said, "I want to give it a couple of weeks. I don't like these legal types either. But I want to give them a go. If we see this trial is a phony, Vinnie was my best friend, so I do it to Flores, not at night, not in the dark when he's not looking. I'm going to walk up to him in the court, the place where they do justice, and I'm going to tell the judge what I'm going to do and why and then I'll shoot him, right there. That's my promise, all right, Freddie?"

Donna was heard announcing, "Mr. Walker will see you now."

"Okay, Freddie?"

"I ain't saying yes," Freddie said. And Michael had to take it that way, so he turned and led the way into Cy Walker's office.

The first thing Cy thought when he saw them walk in was, "Christ, what's a Southwest jury going to think of this gang of seed heads?"

And Donna must be thinking, "The place'll have to be fumigated!"

What Cy had not expected was the reticence and modest tone of their leader. His fellows sat around him, some in the available chairs, the rest on the floor. And then they were all silent, looking up at Cy, waiting for what he had to say.

"I'm awfully glad to see you all," Cy began. "My name is Cyrus Walker, Cy Walker, and I am the county prosecutor. I have the responsibility of prosecuting acts against the people of this county, and it is my responsibility to use my best efforts to see that justice is done."

There was a silence as Cy took them in and they waited for Michael to make their move.

"What are the chances?" Michael said abruptly.

"Chances?"

"For justice."

"Oh, I think, I really think," Cy said, "well, this is open and shut."

"Means what?"

"There's no way in the world that I can think of where we—I'm including you, you see—can lose this case."

"You really believe that?" Michael asked.

"I really believe everything I say, Mr.—"

"Call me Michael."

"Thanks. I hope we will all be on a first name basis soon, because we'll be working together a lot and any time—" Cy stopped himself. He'd been on the precipice of inviting them to come see him any time they had an idea they wanted to talk about. Jesus! So he picked up where he'd dropped it,

"Any time I need you I want to know where to get you quick."

"Suppose we want to get you?" Michael said.

"Call up Miss Lynn, and she'll get the message to me wherever I am; my work takes me out a lot, but you can talk to her. Let's get her in here now." He pressed a button, and Donna came in.

"Kids, this is Miss Donna Lynn, my secretary. I'm going to ask you a lot of questions now—have you time?"

"We don't have anywhere to go."

"That's the spirit. I want you to know, Michael and all of you, that I come from the East. I'm not one of those desert squares. They have some very old-fashioned attitudes out here. For instance—what?"

"Is it all right to smoke?" Freddie was asking.

"Yes, sure, have one of mine?"

"No thanks." Freddie took out his little sack and began to pack a little brass pipe. As the conversation progressed, he passed it around.

"What I was going to say was—I'm not, I mean I won't be surprised at anything you say or do—what's that? Marijuana?"

"Hash."

"Well, why not?" Cy looked at his watch. The afternoon was tailing off; this would be the last meeting of the day and the room could be thoroughly aired by morning. "Donna, I tell you what," Cy had an inspiration, "in the interests of concentration and privacy, let's turn off the phone, lock the door, and have one hell of a rap session, really nail down absolutely every detail of what happened. By the way, although several of you were eyewitnesses, no statements were ever taken from any of you, were there?"

No one answered. Cy felt that he had to hold up the conversation, why the hell did he feel compelled to do that?

"Why not?" Michael asked.

"I think that's outrageous, and I'll certainly bring that out in court—what was that? Oh, I see, why was your testimony not taken?"

"Right."

"You think this thing is rigged?" Freddie asked.

"No, sir. I don't. That's impossible in our system."

"You really believe that?" Michael asked.

"I do indeed. The very concept of a trial by a jury of the accused man's peers makes any manipulation, rigging, impossible."

"What peers?" Freddie asked.

"Peers. Equals."

"Same breed of cat," Michael translated.

"I look my juries over pretty carefully. Sit down, Donna. Door locked?"

"Yes, sir."

"Now, take everything down."

"Who picks the peers?" Michael asked.

"There's a regular system of doing it which works between the judge, the defense attorney, and myself. There's a list, and we all have a certain number of challenges."

"Where does that list come from?"

"It's taken from the voters list."

"And everybody is on that?"

"No, not everybody."

"What kind of people are on it?"

"All kinds, store owners, professionals, housewives—ah, I see, yes, you've got a point there, it's a problem. Those lists stick pretty much to the middle-income groups of people, and they are, at least in this community, people who have rather firm ideas of what's right and wrong. They have prejudices, this is not my taste, or anything to do with me, but the jury is what it is, and we have to convince and sway them, and I'm going to suggest, therefore, that you all wear shoes when you come to court. I think some of you girls could be pretty, I mean you are, but when I put you on the witness stand, especially if one of you—is one of you Miss Flores?"

Michael pointed to Juana.

"I'm awfully glad to meet you," Cy said.

Juana nodded.

Michael spoke next. "Can I come and sit with you when you pass on them?"

"Who?"

"The jury."

"Would you like to?"

"Yeah. I want to."

"Well—? I mean I think you'll find it pretty long-drawn-out and boring, but as far as my office is concerned—welcome."

So Cy Walker got himself a daily visitor in his office. And outside, around the courthouse fountains, Michael's Arabs camped each day; the lawn suffered.

When Cy was busy, Michael sat quietly in the outer office, his hands, surprisingly large, folded in his lap, his eyes alive but undirected. Occasionally he would read from the office's stock of magazines. *Forbes* was his favorite, Donna noted. His father, he explained to her, was in the market. He smiled, including her in the appreciation of that irony. "He's sort of rich," he added.

Donna, despite the fact that she failed to engage Michael in much conversation, liked him. His smile, she told her roommate, "makes you want to cry."

"He's probably on something," the roommate said, "now don't get involved with him, too."

There wasn't a day that Michael didn't come to Cy with a suggestion or a report. He told the lawyer that he'd found out Flores was not the perfectly controlled professional he appeared to be. Juana had described her father's fits of rage at home and shown him a long scar across her back where Flores had struck her with a switch when she was fifteen and first beginning to run around.

"Maybe," Michael said, "you can dream up some way of busting him loose in court, make him go wild, you know?"

"You've seen too many TV shows," Cy said.

It was Michael who informed Cy that Gavin McAndrews was seeing Juana, which did interest the lawyer.

It happened like this. After Rosalie had left, Juana stayed with Michael for several days. But she seemed jumpy, and Michael wasn't surprised when she announced she was moving back to the base. Her mother had cracked up, she said, and there was no one at home to take care of her sisters and little brother.

What Michael did not then know was that Gavin McAndrews had brought her the news of her mother's "collapse," a description which turned out to be highly exaggerated. It was Gavin who convinced Juana it was her duty to go back.

Gavin, the blue-ribbon bull of sorority row in his college days, knew the power of persistence for a woman, that and simple physical proximity. He'd made up his mind to visit Juana every day.

Juana several times left the base after she had made the family's supper, went to Queen Street, and spent the night. What drove her was less the itch than a growing need for drugs. With Vinnie dead, some control in Juana had died.

One night she dropped acid and had an extremely bad trip, got crying and hysterically argumentative. It was that night she told Michael that Gavin was coming onto the base every day to talk to her.

"What's he say to you?"

"You don't have to be jealous."

"I'm not jealous."

"Why not? He's sorta cute."

"I want you to tell me what he says to you, what he— Juana, pay attention. What's he—?"

"Don't you want to know if he's coming on with me?"

"No, I want to know—"

"Why not? Why don't you?" She began to cry again. "Oh, Vinnie," she said, "Vinnie was so good to me. You don't care about me. Why don't you like to ball me, Michael?"

"I like to ball you."

"No you don't. Vinnie wouldn't have cared. He would have wanted you to. He told me that once."

"Juana, stop it!"

"Ah, off you! This is a terrible trip. That goddamn acid you gave me is no good. Vinnie wouldn't have given me that kind of acid." She leaped out of bed and began to dress.

From the window he saw her striding down the street in steps uncharacteristically long, her head thrown back.

"I never got anything more out of her," Michael told Cy.

"Gavin goes right to it, doesn't he?"

"Right to what?"

"The weak spot," Cy said.

"Whose?"

"His. Which he hopes to make ours."

"I don't get you."

"On the night after the killing, both Juana and Elizabeth gave statements to the police. Those two signed statements are our case! That son of a bitch, McAndrews, he's—"

"Can he make her change what she said?"

"He just might!"

"Won't the jury know the girls are lying? Won't they know somebody's been talking to them?"

"I should think so, yes."

"But you're not positive?"

"It's all there, black on white, with their signatures and that of the examining officer. How could I be more positive? Sure I'm positive."

But he wasn't. He wasn't even positive he wanted to win this case.

The fact was that Michael had begun to make Cy feel ashamed of himself. Against his better judgment, he made the boy welcome in his office, talked to him a little more candidly, even allowed him to hear him grumbling over his troubles, a chance to see his weaknesses. He told Donna to give Michael coffee at the times she served him and when she sent out for a sandwich to buy one for the kid. "He looks like he's been living off locusts," he said to her. "Fatten him up with some of that petty cash."

Michael and Cy discussed the case at the end of each office day. This boy was curious, wanted to know everything, the contours of the case as seen from the inside, both insides, the procedures of the court, ritual and real, the theoretical basis of the legal system, its strengths and its abuses. Michael was particularly concerned with the jury system, and Cy gave him a book which the boy took home, read through the night, finishing it about noon the next day, then hitchhiked out to Cy's office, holding the book into which he had inserted litttle slips of paper to mark the questions he wanted Cy to answer. On one slip of paper, he had written in his small, firm hand, "The juror is the judge."

Michael asked, "Then the most important thing is who the jurors are?"

"Well, it is important, yes."

"A jury of his peers, that's what it says, that word again, it says they must be peers."

"Well, they will be," Cy lied. He knew damn well what the jury would be like.

The boy caught him. "Whose peers?"

"The defendant's, of course."

"You mean, mechanics, Mexicans, air force?"

"Well, we have had Mexicans." Cy couldn't remember the last time he'd seen a Chicano on a jury.

"Where do they get the names from?" Michael asked.

Cy described the enormous rotating metal drum, a hot-water boiler by manufacture, which was in a locked room in the courthouse building and contained the names of every voter in the city.

"Who picks?"

Cy explained, step by step, the procedures of choice, sometimes taking days before twelve jurors and two alternates were found who could meet the challenges to their impartiality that Judge Breen and the opposing lawyers would put. And he told how each side, Gavin and himself, had eight rejections they didn't have to explain.

Then Cy stopped. Michael was not listening.

He was looking at Cy. If Cy ever felt judged, it was at that instant.

Was he frightened of this one-hundred-twenty-pound kid and what he was thinking? "What's the matter?" he asked, his annoyance at himself directed at the boy.

"Nothing," Michael said. "I'd like to watch this jury-picking thing, okay?"

"Well, maybe—some of it anyway. I'll do my best."

He realized he had just lied to the boy again. Of course he could get him in to see the selection of the jury, lots of people with nothing to do sat around watching the show. "Some of it! I'll do my best!" Why should the boy trust him?

So it happened that Michael sat through the long sessions when jurors were being selected, occupying the end seat of the last row of the courtroom, aloof, separate, elegantly dressed in soft-worn, bleached-out Lee's, scuffed sandals, and someone's old white shirt, the long sleeves cuffed back.

He was a sight to see. He had lost weight; his hair seemed thicker and more fully curled. His soft faun's beard had grown from just under his eyes to under the frayed collar of his shirt. His eyes glowed—without focus, not directed at the events or personages around him.

Michael was the first one there in the morning. And at the end of the day when Judge Breen vanished through the sliding panel into his chambers, and the others, released at last, began to gather their papers and fill their packets and cases, Michael rose, and, with a languor that seemed insolently elaborated, walked slowly out of the courtroom, leaving behind him a buzz of resentment.

The fact was that all the personnel of the court had the feeling they were being judged, and they didn't like it. They covered their self-consciousness with more jollity than is customary at these functions.

But behind the jokes was hostility and suspicion. People became convinced not only that Michael was "on" something, but that he was in some way malignant, even dangerous; someone suggested he should be searched. Such thoughts were too absurd to be expressed directly, of course, but what the hell was he doing there every day anyway?

One morning Gavin walked up to him and asked him, "What do you think of all this?" He got a few eccentric nods of the head which could mean anything, but no answer. Gavin, left standing there, had to pretend someone was calling him and walk away, furious!

It was at this time that Alan Kidd began to show his interest in the outsider.

Alan was not involved in the mechanics of selecting the jury; Gavin took care of that. Alan's opinion was never sought by his associate or offered by Alan himself. So he had the leisure to pursue a purely personal investigation.

He sat near Michael. Every morning he greeted the boy and every afternoon smiled a goodbye, pretending not to be put off when Michael did not respond. Alan was making his acquaintance as one does that of a dog or a child, offering himself for conversation but not insisting on it.

He was rewarded.

"Why are they so friendly?" Michael asked.

"Who?"

Michael indicated the people within the courtroom.

"Well—they're all old friends," Alan answered.

He didn't understand right away what Michael meant, but he was glad to have those first few words, and after lunch he sat in the seat next to him. Although they still didn't talk much, they watched the proceedings together.

That night Alan dreamed he was frantic to get Michael on the phone. In the morning he couldn't remember what he wanted to say to him.

Alan had begun to see what the others could not, that while Michael's eyes were a little glazed, he was absorbing it all, experiencing it as one does events in retrospect, totally, not hung up on bits, turns, and trifles.

Others noticed that Alan habitually sat next to Michael and that Michael murmured something to him from time to time. At the end of one day, Gavin asked Alan, "What goes on with that freak?"

"I really don't know," Alan said.

"Well, try to find out, will you, and let me in on it?"

So Alan asked Michael, "How about a cup of coffee?" got back a nod which meant anything and nothing, persisted till Michael got up and followed him out and across the street into the coffee shop. Michael looked the place over as if he'd never been in anything like it before, then sat, unrelating. Alan did find out one thing about the courtroom's mystery guest very quickly; he was short of cash and hungry. Michael ordered buckwheat cakes and, waiting for them, ate the soda crackers on the table.

"What are you thinking?" Alan asked finally.

"You defending Flores?"

"I was assigned by the air force."

"You do everything the air force orders you?"

"I guess I do."

Michael nodded his head a few times, ate, silent again. Then, "Do lawyers have to believe in what they do?"

"Good question. There are all kinds."

"What kind are you?"

"Reluctant. I think I became a lawyer only because my father wanted me to."

"What kind of a lawyer was he? The believing kind?"

"And how! Well I am, too—to the extent that I'm a lawyer."

"Your father, though, he was a man of principle?"

"Though! Well, let it pass. He used to say that the world is best run by men who don't have too many principles. He didn't mean principles like it's best not to lie or steal and so on. He meant that life is so complicated—what the hell was that word he used? Dark! By which he meant inscrutable. So dark that a man who professes there is only one right way, and that he knows it, is a damn fool. The wise man, he used to say, is not ever completely sure he's right."

"What's a lawyer when he's not right?"

"Jesus, that was my father's joke! He used to say that. He didn't think much of lawyers."

Michael had finished his cakes, started on the crackers again.

"Have some more pancakes," Alan suggested.

"Okay."

"When was the last time you ate?"

"Well—not yesterday." He looked at Alan. "You're the only guy I ever met who liked his father."

"I did. Another thing he'd say, 'Most evil is done in the name of a good so absolute that it excuses anything and everything.'"

"Sounds cynical."

"He was a true believer."

"And you?"

"Me, too."

"What do you believe in?"

"That foolish show going on in there," Alan said.

"You're kidding."

"No. It's all we've got. Principles keep collapsing, so we have to rely on the good sense of common people."

"You believe that—what you're saying?"

"Yep. My father used to say that the jury system is based on an absurd premise which is that a fool is a fool, but twelve fools are wise."

"You really believe that?"

"I do."

Michael suddenly burst out laughing. "I just got it," he said. "Your father's crack."

"Why do you keep asking me if I believe what I say I believe?"

"Because a couple of days ago another fellow was laying that same shit on me, but I think you mean it."

"Yeah. You're looking at one of them."

"One of what?"

"Dupes of the system."

Michael nodded a few times.

The second order of pancakes had come, and Michael carefully spread margarine on each one.

"Why do you keep nodding your head that way?" Alan persisted.

"So people don't see I'm really shaking it the other way."

"I wish you'd have lunch with me every day," Alan said. "I enjoy your company."

"You really mean that?"

"Why would I say it if I didn't mean it?"

"That's what I'm trying to figure out," Michael said.

They did eat together the next day, too. By the third lunch, Michael was amazed to find he could talk to Alan more easily than he ever had to anyone. "I got to keep reminding myself," he told him, "that you're on the wrong side of this."

Alan surprised him. "I know."

A strange thing happened. Sitting next to Michael, Alan had begun to watch the spectacle not as one favored, which he was, not as a member of the winning team, which he was, but as Michael did, from the outside where Alan had never been before.

He suddenly realized, for instance, what Michael meant by "all that friendliness." Here were people trying murder, nothing less, in an atmosphere of twittering cordiality.

"You mean they're all on the same side?" he said to Michael one day, without prelude. Michael looked up at him, but didn't answer.

Both of them knew as they watched Cy Walker and Gavin McAndrews making their show of contesting each selection, that these two were going to have no difficulty selecting the twelve good men and true women, and that it would be the same jury it always was.

The court, Alan now saw, was like a reunion of classmates, newly returned from a perfect summer vacation, delighted to be seeing each other. As for the business of the case, they'd been through it before, they looked forward to going through it again, the occasion of their fraternity.

There were hours, minutes, seconds as Alan sat in that place when he had the oddest sensation, one he couldn't describe except that it was of falling down, down into some unknown state of feeling, of being. And even though it made him apprehensive now and then, this totally new sensation, even when he felt he might grip a familiar guardrail and decelerate the plunge, he didn't want to, knew nothing back up there he wanted to stay with. So he let himself fall—into what? Apartness? Isolation? Distrust of whom? Himself?

Michael was on another chute, falling even faster. Sometimes as bits of his skin chilled, he thought of Vinnie, as he heard the secretaries of the opposing lawyers greeting each other, swapping cigarettes and stories, bringing each other coffee in containers, sugaring it, stirring it, biting into each other's Danish, he thought of Vinnie, hearing their babble, "Darling! Sis! How are you? Did you hear? Who do you think? Not him? Yes, him! No! Really? Yes," Michael thought of his murdered friend.

He remembered their days together as he watched the play in that courtroom, the women showing off their wares, tits, ass, arms, legs as far up as they were passably good, their swift eyes checking out the attention they drew from the men, and the men, fresh from barber ministrations, watching each calculated display so they could themselves calculate their next move, the exchange of phone numbers and addresses, then of partners, that was coming for sure, whatever else would be accomplished in the days ahead.

Watching all this foreplay, Michael remembered the resolve he and Vinnie had made a half-hour before he was shot five times with the weapon that was now Exhibit One. Michael recalled—"Mexico!"

Michael knew where he was going, down, down into what? Mania? Maybe. Into undifferentiating hatred? Sure. But he, too, let it go. Because he didn't doubt the distortion he was risking was closer to the truth than the surface reality of the happenings around him.

He got up—it was a natural intermission after the acceptance of both sides of the fifth juror—and he walked slowly out of the room and down the hall, not looking up, remembering the day when he took the gun out of Vinnie's hand; and so, his eyes on the floor, he almost walked into Cy Walker and his mortal opponent, Gavin McAndrews, together, their backs to the corridor, in an embrace without touching, their tongues quivering in the act of laughter. So Michael saw it, that sick boy.

He knew this was a distortion. But they shouldn't have been laughing that way together. What were they doing? Reassuring each other of final friendship? Of their mutual good fortune? Hedging bets? Plotting? Conniving? Conspiracy?

And there it began, that terrible pressure in the center of his body where the blood collects and pumps and pounds.

Instinctively he ducked his head, passed them unnoticed.

Behind him, he heard Gavin and Cy's common laughter.

———————————————————————

Michael walked the mile and a half to Queen Street.

Some time earlier, someone official had decided it would be a good idea to put the Queen Street house under surveillance. When Michael left in the morning, he'd pass a car containing two men in business suits—these other uniforms deceived no one—using two-way radios that were never standard Detroit equipment. When he returned, the same car, or one just like it, was in the same place with two other men, dressed like their fellow protectors of the law, on the same mission, to watch and report who came and who went, carrying what, meeting whom?

Michael and Freddie had hidden Vinnie's gun under the same planks in the closet where he had stashed his life's savings, the large Hellmann's Mayonnaise jar full of H. Both boys knew it would be only a matter of time before the men in the parked car would find the legal excuse they needed to search the house.

Freddie's parking tickets gave them one. That afternoon Freddie had driven up in Jeff's car, and one of the men had walked up to the vehicle and around it and there inspected the stop light Flores had shot out. He advised Freddie to have it fixed.

"Your gun-for-hire shot it out," Freddie said. "I'm waiting on him to get out of jail and have it fixed for me."

"Spare me the lip, kid, will you?" The detective leaned in and picked a parking violation summons off the floor, one of several in that place of honor. As he was reading it Freddie made a mistake. He got out and walked into the house. The officer followed, didn't feel he needed an invitation or a warrant, knocked on the door, and, when the knock was ignored, entered.

In the hall facing the door was a table, and on the table a very large hub cap turned inside up, one of several family-size ashtrays. Scattered in the rubbish it contained were nineteen other parking tickets.

When Michael came home that night, Freddie was gone. Sandy, the only one left in the house, told him his friend was in a jail cell.

When Michael got in to see him, the prisoner greeted him casually from the dark corner of the tank. He talked with difficulty, his lips were bulbous. Someone—Michael remembered Officer Koch in front of the Southside Home for the Dead—had "straightened Freddie out."

Freddie laughed, sort of, indignation seemed absurd in this circumstance, he was way past anger. He owed, he said, three hundred and thirty-six dollars.

Freddie was content to be there for now, had "more friends in than out."

"How long you going to be there?" Michael asked.

"Ten days, but they'll find some way to keep me longer. When I come out, though, I'll be ready."

Michael knew what he meant, nodded a few times. Then Freddie went back to his corner, walking through the brawlers and the drunks, the purse-snatchers and the operator of the town's dirty-movie club.

That same evening, while Juana's sisters and brother finished the dinner she had prepared, Juana sat with Gavin on the porch and for the first time permitted him to speak about the case. In their earlier talks he had carefully kept the conversation to irrelevancies, such as his war experiences, told in great detail. This was his first venture to the point, carefully timed.

"Whether you like it or not," Gavin finally told her, "your father's life is in your hands."

"I don't care about him."

"You want him to die?"

Juana didn't answer. Her sisters and Diego, dinner finished, came out on the porch.

Gavin got up to go. "That's all it's really about, this trial, whether or not your father is put to death. It's up to you," he said so all the children could hear.

They looked at Juana.

"I'll be back tomorrow." Gavin waved goodbye to them all.

"Don't bother," Juana said.

At the bottom of the porch steps, Gavin turned. "By the

way," he said, "do you know where your friend Rosalie is? She seems to have disappeared."

"What do you want her for?"

"The police want her. There's a shoplifting charge out, pressed by Connally's against her and a couple of her girl friends."

"I don't know where Rosalie is," Juana said.

"They've got pictures from a hidden camera for proof. If you see her or hear from her, tell her I might be able to help her."

Gavin left.

The next day, Gavin, who had noticed Michael studying him, made it his business to stop by the last row.

"What have you two boys decided?" he said to Michael and Alan. Michael shrugged. "You been following what's happening here?" Gavin asked him.

"I think he's beginning to understand what's happening here," Alan said.

Despite Gavin's nice-guy cordiality, Michael felt in danger, just as Vinnie had been unprotected and in mortal danger when he drove onto the air force base. Michael was beginning to see the courtroom as an extension of the base. He looked at Alan. "Why aren't you wearing your uniform?" he asked.

"I don't like it," Alan said, part of the truth.

Back to silence. Michael had begun to suspect Alan, too. Perhaps Alan had been assigned to get in with him, to see what he was thinking. Of course. Nothing was accidental here.

Down, down.

He'd better get that gun out of Queen Street, bury it in the desert, near the dobe house, no, better, on reservation land. But how get it past the police guard? That gun would be all they needed.

And if they ever guessed what was on his mind, they would soon enough drop their cordiality, leave off dancing seductive capers on the grave of his friend, and devour him alive.

And so Michael, frightened, wore the *caro palo* of the ghetto person, that mask of imperturbability which says, "You can't hurt me. I do not hurt! In fact, I'm not really here." The mask covered the murder ready in Michael's heart.

That night Gavin didn't go to the base. A day's neglect might be just the thing to make Juana tumble.

Instead he and Alan took his boss out to the county jail to visit with Cesario Flores. "I'd very much appreciate knowing what you think, sir," he said to Mr. Don Wheeler.

Cesario seemed at peace, repeated his determination to allow his life to be ended without a struggle.

"I think, Sergeant Flores, you're forgetting something," Wheeler said in the harsh voice of a stockcaller.

"Yes, sir, I probably am, sir."

"Talk man to man to me, Flores, I'm not in the air force, though I know a lot about it. What you're forgetting is your duty."

"To the air force?"

"You're goddamn right. And to your family."

"I think I've taken care of those duties," Cesario said.

"Like hell you have," Wheeler said.

"I think the rest is up to you, sir. I've done my part."

"Don't tell me what's up to me. I know my duty, you don't know yours. I'm disgusted with you, sergeant."

"Yes, sir."

"I had a talk with your commanding officer, Colonel Dowd, last night. We're making arrangements for you to resign from the air force."

Alan saw the man's mask fall to the floor in pieces.

"Why is that, sir?" he finally asked.

"For your family's sake. It hasn't occurred to you, has it, that if you're convicted, which you are sure to be if you maintain the attitude you're showing me, your pension, twenty-two years' accumulation of service benefits will be invalidated?"

Cesario was thinking hard.

"Your family will be left without one cent. A man who is a confessed murderer and so convicted is dishonorably discharged. His accumulated benefits go down the drain. Is that what you want?"

Cesario thought some more, then he said, "Thank you for talking to me about it, sir. Yes, sir, I'll resign."

As they walked to their cars, Wheeler said, "An ordinary man, a very ordinary man."

"He doesn't seem quite right up here." Gavin tapped his head. "Does he to you?"

"No crazier than anybody else," Wheeler said. "But that may be your case."

"What's my case?" Gavin asked.

"That they drove him temporarily insane."

"I was thinking in the direction of defense of home and family, that sort of thing—"

"That's implicit in whatever you do." Wheeler stopped him. "You know, Gavin, nothing cracks like the well-organized, highly trained mind. You agree, Lieutenant Kidd? A man like this can be perfect under the kind of pressure he's been trained to meet, but put him up against a kind his training has not prepared him for, he'll puncture like a balloon. If you had a daughter and her boyfriend was introducing her to drugs, wouldn't you be pretty damned frantic? Didn't they drive this man off his rocker? Wasn't he, in that last moment, insane?"

"There's no history of any mental disturbance in Flores's family. I checked that out."

"So much better. It must have taken constant harassment, mental torture, which you can describe in the courtroom to wring every concerned parent's—you are getting people with kids on the jury?"

"Just about everyone."

"Good. Imagine the psychic laceration it took to drive this completely disciplined man—you're planning to put Dowd on?"

"Yes, sir."

"Don't take any suggestions from me if you don't agree with them. This is your case. And yours, lieutenant."

"Yes, sir," Gavin said.

"I want you to hire a couple of psychiatrists, pay them well, let them write a scholarly description of the nature of Flores's derangement. Medical stuff. Big words. Latin. That always impresses hell out of a jury."

"Yes, sir."

"Another thing. You're not going to put that Mexican son of a bitch on the stand looking the way he does."

"What's the matter with him?"

"Fat! Bloated! Looks like he's been on the bottom of a lake for a month."

"Chief Burns tells me he's been eating up a storm."

"You can't put a man weighing in at two hundred and whatever the hell pounds up against that little hairy ghost you pointed out to me in court yesterday."

"But how can I stop him from eating?"

"Don't give him any food. Starve the son of a bitch!"

"But Mr. Wheeler—"

"Last, and listen carefully to this, don't let Cy Walker try Flores. You try the hippies. Step by step, paint a picture of what those perverted, addicted young savages did to this decent, responsible, concerned man who's devoted his whole life to defending our country! The same thing these bastards are doing to every decent head of family. This community has had it with those kids, agree or not?"

"I surely do," Gavin said.

"You?" Wheeler turned to Alan.

"No, sir," Alan said blandly.

"What'd you say?"

"I haven't agreed with most of what you've said here today."

He looked at Alan without the least evidence that he was angry or annoyed. "I better be getting on home," he said. "You know, lieutenant, Mrs. Wheeler has been ill?"

"I was awfully sorry to hear that, sir," Alan replied.

Later Mr. Don Wheeler called Gavin from Hope's bedside.

"Did I hear that boy right, the lieutenant?"

"Yes, you did. I'm sorry."

"Well, I'll be damned!"

———————————————————

By the end of the week, the twelfth juror and the two alternates were agreed on by all. Friday morning's session was a short one, devoted to the swearing in of the jury and to Judge Breen's introductory remarks to the chosen.

"You and I are the judges in this case," he said. "I am the judge of the law, you the judges of the facts. But you alone are to determine the credibility to be given each wit-

ness. In judging this you have the right to consider their
manner and appearance, their means of knowledge, any
interest or motive they may have, the probability or im-
probability of the truth of their statements when considered
with all other evidence in the case."

Judge Breen concluded on an informal note. He told the
jurors how privileged they were to be on a case which was
to be tried by two such exceptional attorneys, introduced
Cyrus Walker and Gavin McAndrews, made a few flattering
remarks about each, and forgot to introduce Alan.

He noticed his wife in the courtroom, watching him as
she might a stranger.

Later he called home. "To what do I owe the honor?"

"I was watching the lay of the land."

"What's that mean?"

"Just what I said, Teddy."

He was still thinking about it when she said "See you,"
and clicked off.

Alan insisted on walking Michael home. "Curious to see
where you live," he said.

Michael was silent, and Alan, feeling how troubled the
boy was, made conversation. He showed Michael the black
and blue mark between his neck and shoulder. "That's the
first time anything like that has happened to me," he said.
"I was brought up to believe the cops are there to defend
me."

"They do," Michael said, "they do defend you."

Passers-by remarked on the strange pair, the handsome
young air force officer and the boy from another world,
walking as friends.

Alan tried again. "What are you doing this weekend?"

"Might go out to the desert," Michael said. "Tomorrow."

"Why don't you have lunch with me again tomorrow?"

"No thanks."

They turned a corner. "We live in the middle of this
block," Michael said, stopping.

Alan got the hint, turned to leave, hesitated. "Who's we?"
he asked. When Michael didn't answer, he added, "Whom
do you live with?"

"See that car, the black Galaxie? Those are police."

"What are they doing there?"

"They'll start following you, too, if you hang around with me."

"For chrissake," Alan was disgusted, "why don't you report it?"

"To whom?" Michael laughed. "I don't mind any more." Then he looked directly at Alan and said it plainly. "Goodbye."

Alan left.

In front of the house on Queen Street, Michael stopped and chatted with the police in the car.

"How're you cats getting along today?" he asked.

"Groovy!" said the cop at the wheel, pretty bored with this assignment. "How are you?"

"Very good. Anybody come looking for me?"

"Not a soul."

"Right on." Michael started toward the house.

"Oh, hey, you! Michael! There was somebody this morning. Said he had some bad news."

"Who said?"

"Don't know. You all look alike to me."

"How many times have I told you to ask for the name and write it down?"

"Sorry."

"Don't let it happen again."

Inside, under the hub-cap ashtray, Michael found a note. That morning, one of the kids Michael had posted outside the Southside Home for the Dead had had a casual conversation with a mortuary technician who told him they could all stop bothering. Vinnie had been cremated two days ago.

Don Wheeler had arranged a clubhouse luncheon to be followed by eighteen holes of golf. He planned to introduce Gavin to a pair of insurance company executives from one of his firm's most lucrative accounts. Waiting for the men to show up, they had an old-fashioned and dug into the potted cheddar while Gavin brought his boss up to the minute on the news.

Wheeler was satisfied with the jury.

"And Flores has lost ten pounds," Gavin boasted.

"Ten? That's nothing!"

"He's hardly getting anything to eat."

"Cut down on his water."

Their guests arrived, and they had a most convivial lunch of London broil.

There was no one in the house on Queen Street. The police surveillance and Fat Freddie's arrest had driven everyone away. Even Sandy had gone to visit her grandfather in his mountaintop home near the Mexican border.

Someone living in the house had always come up with money for food and rent. Now Michael was alone, he was hungry, and the rent hadn't been paid for months.

Michael's father sent his son an allowance of seventy-five dollars a month. It had not arrived.

The milk in the icebox had curdled. Michael began to cut away the green parts from the end of a loaf of bread, then threw it all away. At the back of the bottom shelf was a half bottle of lime extract. On the table were two old bottles of ketchup. Michael had what was left in them.

Aside from his hunger, Michael was contented to be alone, so when a little old man with clips on his trousers arrived on a bike to deliver a telegram informing Michael that his father was about to pay him a visit, he wasn't pleased.

Clifford Winter tried to keep up with his son, which wasn't always easy because the boy didn't write home except to inform his parents where they could send his allowance when he moved. But when Mr. Winter had to go to Los Angeles and San Diego to work out contracts between his firm and the aircraft companies, he would from time to time break his trips and spend a day or an evening with his son.

Michael didn't want to be distracted on this day. He had a lot to figure out.

In the kitchen a newspaper photograph of Cesario Flores was held to the wall by a paring knife through the left eye. Gently Michael pulled out the blade and took the picture in his hand. For a long time he studied the heavy, anxious face. He recalled their drive into the desert, how quickly they'd become friends, he and this authority freak.

He decided to see if he could borrow a couple of dollars from Donna—she'd been real friendly—and maybe eat some of the tollhouse cookies she kept on her desk. Then he'd go out into the desert and try to put the pieces of his feelings together.

On the rubbing table next to the one where Wheeler was getting his post-game massage was a prominent member of an international organization of Italians, who, after an extremely active career in a more populous area of the country, had decided to move to the great Southwest for reasons of health and safety. Wheeler had, at one critical juncture, helped this man with certain tax problems.

"I'm glad you're on this case, Don," the old Sicilian said, "where some of those hippies gang-banged that air force fellow's daughter and he had to shoot them."

"I don't think you've got the facts straight," Wheeler said.

"Oh, I got 'em straight, all right. Those kids are beginning to give this community a bad name. I'm glad you're in there."

Finally Cy had to pretend he was someone else, a friend writing the most prominent law firm in the state's capital city, calling their attention to the fact that Mr. Cyrus Walker was trying his last case as county prosecutor and might be interested in an association with a—and so on, all to be typed under a borrowed letterhead.

The letter drafted, Cy ripped off the top sheet of the legal pad and began to make notes for his opening remarks. But that was heavy going, too. He just couldn't go out there with notes and wing it. He had to impress; he was auditioning for a job, however disguised; he had to knock the ball out of the park.

Cy needed a drink.

In his outer office, he found Michael eating out of Donna's cookie jar while he studied some papers and made notes in the little book he carried.

Cy poured his drink. "What're you reading there?"

"The jury list," Michael said.

Judge Breen's bailiff had sent to Cy's office the list of the jurors chosen, name, sex, profession, marital status, and the ages of the children.

"Don't you think I should see what comes into my office first?" Cy asked Donna as he went back into his room and closed the door.

Donna took the papers out of Michael's hand and hurried to her boss's desk.

"What the hell's he doing here?" Cy asked her.

"I think he was just hungry."

"Donna, stop encouraging him, will you?"

"You told me to."

"Now, I'm telling you not to. I don't want him hanging around here. He's sort of nuts or something, don't you think?"

"No, sir, but I'll be less welcoming if you like."

"Get him in here, I'll tell him myself."

Michael came in munching a tollhouse cookie.

"Well, what do you think of our jury?" Cy asked.

"They're what I expected."

"You think they're his peers?"

"Do you?"

"You mean no Chicanos?"

"For one thing."

"They're all people who work for a living, Michael, same income level as Flores, aren't they?"

"Yeah, that's obvious."

"What's not obvious?"

"I've been thinking—maybe you have to be a murderer to understand a murderer."

"Jesus, Michael, we can't have a jury of murderers!"

"That's not what I meant. Those people you and that other lawyer picked, they look to me like they've been fixed not to feel anything."

"Are you ever patronizing!"

"What do they know about someone like Vinnie except that he was a threat to them?"

"Bullshit!"

"And that's why you picked them—because they've sold a piece of their asses."

"Like me and that other lawyer?"

"And the judge, too. I've begun to feel sorry for Flores. I'm not sure any more he's the one who killed—"

"Everybody saw it!"

"For twenty years they trained Flores to kill. What else would he do in a crisis?"

"So it's the system again, right?"

"I don't blame Flores any more."

"Who the fuck do you blame?"

Michael looked at Cy unblinking, then walked out of the office. He trotted two blocks to where the desert road went through the city and stuck up his thumb.

CHAPTER THREE

Clifford Winter, traveling west, set down on schedule at quarter to eleven Saturday morning. He had tennis clothes and a new steel racket in a carry-on bag, and, finding the chauffeured limo his secretary had engaged by long-distance telephone, he didn't bother with the rest of his luggage, went straight to the Tennis Club where the same resourceful girl had arranged for a lesson.

Clifford prized the hours of his life, left the chores to others. Accompanying him on this trip was Sam Underhill, a lawyer's lawyer, one of a small staff of these creatures maintained by Amalgamated Chemical, the giant corporation where Clifford was now fifth, perhaps fourth, man. Clifford, on his way to San Diego to oversee the legalities relating to certain large orders from aircraft companies, needed someone with him who could read small print without falling asleep. He had picked Sam because he knew from past trips that the man wasn't offended when called upon to perform small errands, even enjoyed these exercises in place, time, and means. Clifford would play tennis that morning in the confidence that he could leave it to Sam— all and whatever.

So Sam picked up the bags, Clifford's and his own, put them in a cab, checked in at the hotel, and cuddled with the phone. His main job was to find Mr. Winter's son, Michael. But he had other things to do before he got on to what he felt would be a difficult task. He called New York, checked that Mr. Winter's secretary had not failed to remember Mrs. Winter with flowers on her birthday and that they were mums. Then he called a local number, asked for Doris, found he was speaking to Doris, informed her that Mr. Winter was expecting her for lunch at the hotel and wasn't surprised that the young lady wasn't surprised. She too had been arranged for over the long-distance telephone.

Then to Michael.

The Winters hadn't had a letter from their only son since October, and Mrs. Winter, an unhappy woman who was for all purposes except support separated from her husband, had grown panicky about Michael's prolonged silence.

So Clifford had engaged a confidential service in the area to put them back in touch with the boy's whereabouts and doings. Through this agency, Clifford knew about the Cesario Flores case and something of Michael's involvement in it.

He was sympathetic with his son's feelings and what he knew of his doings. Clifford had had dealings with the military, held a candid view of the men who made the nation go, knew the magnetic fields of influence under the tissue of propriety that determined the actions of judges and lawyers. A young man at forty-four, outgoing and open-minded, Clifford was an extraordinary person.

But there was a tragedy in his life, and it wasn't his broken marriage. Being existentialist, he did not expect continuity in anything and had quickly accepted the inevitability of a new domestic arrangement when he observed his wife descending into an early menopause.

Clifford's pain, gentle but abiding, came from a deeper source. He had started life as a chemist, one who aspired to be an innovator in his field. But he found he did not have the imagination for this kind of speculation; what he did have was a gift for salesmanship. In a company with operations all over the world, a man who searched out and sold new markets was invaluable; no one in the field was more able or more successful than Clifford Winter.

This success was his disaster.

In work he made use of his knowledge of chemistry, of course, but his chief asset was charm, and the main source of his charm was that delicate sadness, the tenderness that unexpectedly lit his face, perhaps during the after-conference drink with a client, or even in a moment of relaxation during the business itself. When his sales energies relaxed—Clifford sold everything, even the morrow's weather—his self could be savored. The sadness was real; it had its roots in the man's sweet and sour disappointment at the turn of his life.

So while most of Michael's generation despised their fathers, Michael had to fight off an attraction to his. "The only thing I have against you, daddy," he once said, "is that you never gave me anything to fight against."

When Michael did not write for months at a time, when he changed his address without notifying his people, when he cut himself off from home in every way he could, it was out of a need to find out who he was as an independent person. Michael fought off his father to save himself.

When Clifford burst into the hotel room, perspiring in good health, the girl was there, waiting. He kissed her lightly, poured her a drink, himself a Gatorade, and began to strip for his shower.

"No luck with Michael," Sam said. "I tried all our usual—"

"He's in the desert."

"How did you find out?"

"The first person I asked, my doubles partner, not only told me where he was, but said the most perceptive thing. Your son, he said, is an extraordinary person."

"The desert is a big place," Sam complained. "Where in—?"

"The kids have a place on the edge of the reservation. All we got to do is go to the Indian trading store and ask."

"Where's the Indian—"

"Doris is a native, she can guide us."

He disappeared, and they heard the shower.

"I don't like the desert," Doris said.

Clifford came back, dripping.

"Say, wouldn't it be great fun," he said, "if we got us some books on the desert, the animal life and so on, the variety of cactuses, or is it cact-eye? I've always wanted to know more about what lives in the desert and how they manage without all that water we're used to. Sam, be a pal, go out to the university, they're sure to have books on all aspects of the subject. Get a load of them! Splurge! The car's downstairs. It should only take you fifteen minutes, but take an hour. And Sam, buy a couple of broadbrimmed hats, mine's seven and a half. I've got these tennis shoes, but you better buy yourself some footgear—"

"Jesus, Clifford, we're not going to walk into the desert. I'm not the type. You go without—"

"Wouldn't consider it, Sam. Now come on, don't be a creep. If Doris can do it, you certainly—"

"Who said I would?" Doris asked.

"It will be great fun!" Clifford ran into the bedroom and reappeared carrying a lot of paper money. "Here, buy Doris something beautiful for her feet. What size are you, dear?"

"Six." Doris looked as if she wished she'd never come into the company of this madman.

"Buy her three different sixes."

"Where? I don't know anything about ladies' shoes."

"I'll go with you," Doris offered.

"Like hell you will! Now go on, Sam, old buddy, I'm dying to see you in a pair of cowboy boots—"

"I can't wear anything like that. My joint's enlarged and—"

"Sam, there's a lady present!"

"I've got to have high box shoes."

"Well, whatever they are, get 'em. Now get out of here. Pour yourself another drink, Doris, and bring me a Scotch on the rocks."

When Sam got back an hour later, Doris was more relaxed and rather too talkative. But Clifford took care of that, too. He broke open one of the books and had her read the descriptions of the various flora of the Southwest desert as he dressed. "Charming, isn't it," he said to Sam, "all that biological writ in her flat western voice?"

The trip that followed was horrible for everyone but Clifford. He kept Doris reading all the way until he saw something that interested him, upon which he'd stop the car, stride out into the desert, and compare the plant to a photograph in the book. Doris and Sam followed him the first time, but gave up after that. It was well past four by then, the hottest part of the day. Both the local young lady and Sam began to dread what else might be ahead.

They finally came, by an uncertain road, to the town on

the reservation, to a general store, a post office, a garage
flanked by a flotilla of cannibalized cars, and a meeting hall
that looked unused. Clifford bought some rock crystals at
the store, three Dr. Peppers, and band-aids to put over the
places in Sam's feet where the new moccasins had pinched.

They inquired after Michael. No one knew a damned
thing about him, but they said the chief's house was out
that way, pointing where there was no path. The chief kept
white friends, and he'd be able to tell them where the boy
might be—if anyone could.

Clifford's caravan set out on foot. Doris by now was tired,
silent, and resentful, but she had no choice except to go
with Clifford. She certainly didn't want to stay in the limo
with those dirty Indian kids giggling through the windows
at her. So they all three set forth, Clifford carrying Doris's
three pairs of shoes, Sam the books.

Clifford's anticipation of pleasure seemed to swell at the
prospect of finally seeing his son, and though Sam remained
skeptical, Clifford's optimism turned out to be well-founded.
Michael was waiting for them at the chief's house.

He embraced his father and laughed with delight at the
sight and condition of his little platoon, then introduced
them all to Arthur, his Indian friend, who showed his good
sense by immediately taking a liking to Clifford. He invited
them all to dinner. Clifford accepted without hesitation, but
Sam looked at the hands and dress of Arthur's wife, who
was going to cook the meal, and asked could he return to
the hotel in the limo and send it back for Clifford.

Clifford hadn't heard Sam, was talking with Arthur and
walking in the opposite direction.

"Clifford," Sam called, "did you hear me?"

"Talking to the chief, Sam."

"The sun is setting, Clifford."

"I know, it's going to be beautiful. There's a full moon
tonight."

"Would you like to stay with us overnight?" the chief
asked.

"I was hoping you'd ask that," Clifford said.

That was when Doris began to cry. She did it modestly,
without the least effort to call attention to herself, sat on a
rock and let the tears roll.

"She's just tired," Clifford explained. "Doris, dear, what's the matter?"

"I hate the desert," she said. "I hate it, I hate it, I hate it, and I hate you!"

"That's all right," Clifford said. "Most people do once they get to know me."

Michael laughed.

"Tell you what," Clifford continued, "I'm going to give you Sam and vice versa. You can ride back to the hotel together, have some drinks and dinner, and enjoy each other. First, of course, you have to walk back to the car, it's thataway!" He pointed uncertainly.

"I know where it is." Sam glared at Clifford. "Remember, we're on the eight-ten tomorrow morning."

"Cancel it. Get us something in the afternoon. I had a tough time finding this bastard." He indicated Michael. "I'm not going to be rushed."

"They're waiting for us in San Diego."

"Tomorrow's Sunday, Sam, relax."

Sam walked over to him and whispered, "I'm perfectly capable of getting my own girls, you know."

"Glad to hear it. But now you have a choice." Then Clifford told Doris, "Call you next time I'm in town."

She shook her head and left, wobbling across the desert on her destroyed shoes.

It was a beautiful night.

After dinner, Arthur led them up onto the flat roof of his house. The furrowed metal retained some of the heat of the day as the air cooled. The moon hit the desert like it does the sea, leaving a broad path over it. They turned on to some choice grass, father and son, passing the joint back and forth, watching the splendid heavens.

After a while they heard Arthur snoring lightly. They were alone.

Clifford told Michael about his afternoon. "They thought I was doing it to torture them, poor things, but we've been making some experiments, the company has. You see, Michael, conventional industrial chemistry—well, everybody's manufacturing synthetic fertilizers now, there's no fun in that and very little profit. Follow? But my company— and I think I had a lot to do with this—is stepping out.

One of the things we've been working on is something you can spray from an airplane that will stop the stomata, that's a word from a Greek base, meaning—what do you think? Where's your education? 'Mouths.' Okay? Of these plants out here. Still with me? The idea being to cut down the loss of liquid so that growths will prosper with much less water than we've ever thought possible. Are you with me?"

Michael was stirred by his father's enthusiasm, he didn't know quite why. He'd seen it before, but now, in their gentle grass high, it exhilarated him.

"You see, with the population growth, we're going to have a protein problem. We're doing something with seaweed, harvesting it, but here, look at these enormous expanses of unused land, you see? I've got to tell you Michael, I got the idea from you."

"When?"

"Remember last fall when I was here, you told me all this arid expanse was once the bottom of an ocean, and I asked you if a movement can go one way why can't it be made to go the other? Of course, the water table here is down to what? A thousand feet? And that's dangerous, but it got me thinking. I want to thank you for that. I remember how interested you were in the earth that day, its history and its future, too. Are you still?"

"Not much."

"I thought you got such a boot out of all that?"

"I did."

"You know, Michael, nowadays the dream moves so quickly toward the practical. You're at a point I've long passed. I live like the world does, by compromise. But you can still go for something big. I've always believed in you, I always saw a light in you, from the time you were a kid—"

Here it comes, Michael thought.

"You see, you still have a choice where you go."

The joint passed back and forth.

Then Clifford stepped into it. "An associate of mine in town here sent me clippings on that case, the one where your friend got killed. I've been following it."

"What do you think?" Michael asked.

"Probably the same thing you do. It's obvious. This community—I mean the nation, not just the military—is not going to kill a man it has spent hundreds of thousands of dollars to train. Nor, of course, are they going to condone it. We're all Christians. So they'll compromise, send him to jail for a lot of years, like twenty, which will be cut down by good conduct to maybe—"

"It's amazing."

"What is?"

"Everybody thinks that, and it doesn't make anybody mad."

"It does you?"

"Well—Vinnie was my friend."

"May I ask you one question about that?" The joint went back and forth while Clifford figured out just how to phrase what he was determined to say. "That was an awful thing the air force guy did, right. But, truthfully, correct me if I'm wrong, didn't your friend threaten him with death too? Knowing how an air force sergeant would likely react? Didn't your friend take his daughter and—you know what that means to a Mexican raised in that Virgin Mary-oriented society. Your friend knew the chance he was taking, and he took it. Am I right?"

"Yes, I think so."

"So, he's dead, and that's a shame. But you're here. Let's think of yourself. Either you're going to live looking forward or die looking back. Most people have no choice because they have no gifts. But you do, Michael—"

"What gifts? Oh, dad, cut the shit."

"It's not. Do you want to live as a punisher? Is that the role you want to play, being angry at a twisted little man who's been corrupted by too much air force?"

"I don't blame Flores any more."

"Good."

"The murderer is—is—"

Clifford thought he'd stopped.

Then Michael said, "Who?"

"That's what I think, too. It's something bigger than this knee-jerk marionette. So ask yourself, who's responsible for the way of thinking that makes a man in difficulty wait with a gun to kill? Who condones it? Who encourages it? And then ask yourself, can you really fight that, change that? Here? In this case? In this place?"

"Where else?"

"Michael, things change because of ideas. Before there

is any real change, there is always someone who has said
something, some artist, philosopher, a thinker, even a poli-
tician. The idea, that's the strongest thing."

"I don't have that gift."

"You do."

"I'm not interested in saying anything. The opposite."

"You haven't given yourself a chance, Michael. For
chrissake, get out of this place. It's stagnant water. Get out
into the sea, where it moves, where there are currents and
storms, where the issues are being contested, where people
are fighting for what they believe. Go somewhere. Everywhere. Think of the parts of the world that are burning. Risk
your life, sure, but in a war worth winning."

"I have a feeling it's not out there, it's here, inside that
fence."

"What fence?"

"The one around the air force base."

The desert gets cold at night. Clifford felt it, gave up.

Then he tried again. "I've got to tell you something," he
said. "When I saw you this afternoon, I said to myself, he's
changed. I don't know how, but I wish I could do something about it."

"I don't think you can. I don't want to be like you, dad."

"I don't want you to be. But if you want to live a big
life, get a big cause. It doesn't matter to me that I don't
agree with your viewpoint. I think there's something fine in
this country, I know it will save itself. Don't you? Really?"

"No."

"Don't you see anything good here? Our tradition? Our
history?"

"Nothing. We say one thing, we do the opposite, so anything we say is hypocritical. As for our history, the parts
I know anything about are shameful. This has always been
a terrible country."

"That's too bad," Clifford said. "Too bad."

"That's what I think."

"No, you don't. What goes on in your head? What do
you really think when you're by yourself?"

"You want to hear?"

"That's why I came here!"

"I've thought—you sure? It doesn't make sense."

Clifford waited.

"I've thought of killing you."

"What?"

"That's right."

"Because this man killed your best friend, you—?"

"I told you, I don't make sense. And it's not because I don't love you."

Clifford tried. "I suppose," he said, "it's perfectly natural. It's classic, really, to dream of killing your father." He laughed.

"Not a dream. A thought."

"But why me?"

"I can't explain that. The thought did come to me."

"I think I understand."

"I don't think you do."

"Don't be so superior, kid, don't be so goddamn superior!" Clifford had trained himself not to get angry, ever. "I'm sorry," he said.

"That's okay. I don't blame you for getting mad."

They stopped talking, watched the heavens wheel.

"You mean that some way I'm responsible for my bit of it?"

A dusty owl passed close overhead, its wings spread and motionless.

"I'm sleepy, dad." Michael turned over on his stomach. "You know, Dad, you tried to kill me once."

"What do you mean—when?"

"Before I was born."

"That's silly, Michael."

"Didn't you try to talk mother into losing me?"

"Losing you?"

"An abortion, and she wouldn't?"

Clifford didn't know what to say.

"I wish I hadn't brought that up," Michael said.

"Oh, that's okay."

"Anyway, I heard you, what you said, and I wish I could please you. Anyway, thanks."

Michael turned his head and smiled at his father, then leaned over and kissed him on his cheek. "I'm glad you came out. And that we talked. Don't worry about what I said. I have these thoughts now, that's why I couldn't write."

"It was just your mother, she's been very hurt that you never answered her letters."

"Dad, you don't give a damn how she's hurt," Michael said very gently.

Clifford said nothing.

"There's one thing I do want from you," Michael said.

"Anything."

"I want you not to send me allowance money any more, okay?"

"If that's what you want." Clifford felt he was losing his last line of connection.

"I think one of my troubles," Michael said very quietly, "has been that there was always money. You had it, I took it."

"Seventy-five dollars a month? Michael!"

"Don't send it, okay?"

"Okay."

"I'll see you in the morning. I'm sleepy now. I really am." Michael rolled in on himself, head to knees, and was quiet.

Later, when Clifford was asleep, Michael turned on his back and looked at the stars where they were thickest. Then he looked at his father. The man's face, without the energy pushing it, had collapsed. It was forlorn.

Clifford left at dawn. "I think maybe I can make that early plane after all," he said. And then, for goodbye, "I wasn't hurt, you know, by what you said last night."

As Michael watched him go off in his best going-to-work bustle, his shoulders thrusting this way and that, the old super-optimo bounce in the arches of his feet, he knew his father was telling the truth. Clifford lived by each morning canceling out the previous day's experience.

"I wasn't hurt!"

His father had offered his son the final spectacle of parenthood, a man boxed in boxes he ridiculed, still gallant, still offering advice, asking simultaneously for pity and obedience.

"For that roof-top performance, many thanks, dad."

It was a windy day, the sky a sheet pulled taut not to flap. The wind hummed through the staves of the cactus, kicking up the sand.

At the first store, Michael called the base. To his surprise he was put right through to Alan.

"I want to see you," he said.

"Michael! Where are you?"

"Can you get me on the base?"

"Sure!"

"Hair and beard?"

"Sure, fuck 'em. I want you to meet my wife. And her, you! Where exactly are you?"

Michael told him.

"Don't move. I'm coming. I'm not on the case any more, did you know that?"

Riding back to town in the Karmann-Ghia, Alan set out to explain why he'd been taken off the case. But it seemed to Michael he was really trying to talk about something else, an intimate problem he was having with his wife, one that embarrassed him.

Michael finally decided to help him. "You mean you can't make it with her?"

"No—well, yes, yes, that's it. It never happened before, it's driving poor Marian nuts."

"You can't get it up?"

"No, that's not it. I get in fine, but then—" He made a sound like air escaping from a balloon.

Michael burst out laughing.

"Well, it's funny," Alan said. "And then it isn't."

"Is that why they took you off the case?"

"Yes. No!" Alan laughed. "I have to go through all this so you'll—"

"Maybe you just don't like her any more."

"No. The fact is she's very attractive. Anyway, Friday night she busted out with 'Okay, I don't excite you any more, okay, but what's so damn funny all the time?' Well, Christ I didn't know I'd been laughing about it. But you know when you're embarrassed— So I said, 'You excite me to begin with. Then something happens.' She got sweet again and said, 'Talk it out with me, darling, why don't you?' Well, I realized by then it had something to do with the case, I suppose the case is affecting everybody involved, one way or another. So I started to do what she asked, talk about it. She burst out, 'Will you stop talking about that goddamn case, that's all you've got on your mind!' "

"Is that true?"

"Yes, I'm obsessed with it. So then she starts a more direct approach, going after it—I once saw a terrier worrying a dead white mouse, you know—naturally, then, I couldn't even get it up to start with." Alan burst into laughter, stopped. "What the hell am I laughing at?" he said.

"Why does it bother you so much?"

"Wouldn't it you?"

"No."

"It bothers me. I could see she was getting very suspicious, and she comes out with, 'Who're you giving it to, anyway?' I said nobody, and that was true at the time. But then, I got more worried, so the next night, I'm wandering around the base like I do, and I come on the girl in the case, she's living at home now. She was walking around alone, nobody takes her out any more, they're afraid what her father might do. Anyway, I walked her out to where all those out-of-date planes are coming apart. There's never anybody out there. We walked right out to the fence, and she stood with her face against it, crying, and she told me why and I felt for her. On the way back she indicated some curiosity about what was in those planes in the way of equipment and I offered to show her, and it was rather confined in there, but I showed her the equipment she wanted to see. You know that's the first girl I ever made love to who wasn't a college graduate!" Alan laughed. "And the first time I've been untrue to my wife.

"So then we lay there, and she talked about the night of the murder and the way her father was and how Gavin's been working on her—she's got sort of a crush on him, his tactics are always very personal. Anyway, my mind got off my member, and there sure as hell is nothing the matter with me, because I did it to her again, which I've never done to Marian, not for a long time. Then you know what happened?"

"You did it to your wife."

"Right. I was like a sex fiend. And then—the same thing." He was laughing again, and Michael again felt a lot of pain there. "I looked at her, and I noticed she looks just like her father, Colonel Dowd. And *pfft!*"

"You just don't like your wife any more."

"I think she's a remarkable person. You'll see when you meet her. So I wanted to talk it out, and I started telling her about Miss Flores, not that I'd done it to her, but what she'd told me about her father's preparations for the murder. Marian blew her cork, said she didn't want to hear another word about that goddamn case! 'Ever since that case, you haven't fucked me'—she never used that word, not that way —and suddenly she's out of bed, bare-ass naked, and runs into the other room, locks the door, and that's where she spends the night. I could hear her crying in there."

Alan looked at Michael, but if he was expecting any sympathy for Marian on the boy's face, there wasn't any.

"Well, the next morning, when I got back from tennis, there's this slip from dear old dad, I'm off the case. Guess what they put me on?"

"Writing a sex book for soldiers' wives."

Alan laughed. "No, they got me studying Peruvian law."

"We invading Peru?"

"If we do, I'm ready. So then, that night, she comes back into our room and says, 'I don't want you to do it to me, I love you anyway, it's not dependent on that.' "

"And you did it to her."

"Perfect. And when it was over, I came out with it, 'Did you have me taken off this case?' Well, she looked at me, very sweet, very understanding, and she said, 'You're getting paranoid, darling.' Then she fell asleep looking beautiful and very pleased with herself. But I couldn't sleep. I was glad to be off the case, but it was the principle of the thing, don't you know?"

"You mean whether she had you fired?"

"Oh, that I know. Not that she would ask for it in so many words, she wouldn't have to—she and her father speak a language you can't hear."

"So I won't be seeing you around?"

"You mean because I'm off the case? Hell no! Now I'm really interested in it. Because she doesn't know you as people. She's never talked to someone like Juana Flores. Or met anyone like you. You're weirdos to her, freaks. She's lived in a garrison all her life. That's why I asked her to sit down quietly with you and listen to your side of it. More than that, to find out what you're like. I used to talk about you. I told her that I admired you and that she should open herself to the other side of this. Which is the way she's brought up. Fair-minded, if she gets a chance.

I mean she's a wonderful person. Okay with you? We'll just go over to my house and—"

They passed through the main gate.

"I didn't ask you," Alan said, "why did you want to come out here?"

"I want to see Colonel Dowd."

"You mean to talk to him?"

"I just want to look at him."

"Well, sure, why not? It'll help bring the wall down. I mean maybe he won't, but I'll ask him. Why not?"

Alan pulled up the car with a jerk. "This is his office; they'll know where he is."

A few minutes later, he came hurrying out. "What do you think," he said, "he's gone down to their house. And Marian's not home."

"Whose house?" Michael was standing in front of a large glassed-in map of the base, smoking a joint and marking a little spiral notebook with a pencil.

Vinson Village looked particularly bright and clean that Sunday morning; the sound of little rotating pinwheels watering the lawns and the hum of Sunday morning TV gentled the air. A couple of good-looking young airmen were sitting on the front steps of the Flores house, talking quietly. From inside came the sound of kids laughing.

Alan turned off the motor, and when he did, Michael could hear a man's voice telling a story. As he walked forward, he made out the words.

"Oh, yes, Chihuahua was a dangerous place before the Americans came. The army from the South had taken my father's village. In the middle of the night, the door to our house, it was kicked open, and in came this drunken general. He walked like this, almost fell forward, then like this, almost fell backward." The kids were laughing. "Anyway, this *jefe,* he had a *magnífico mostacho,* most of it in his mouth, like this, see? He had a voice, like *oom pa pa,* 'Which side you on, *hombre?*' he says." The kids laughed at the put-on voice. "My father didn't know what to say, he might guess wrong, you know, they were all killers those days."

Michael was approaching the house very slowly.

"Now my father, just to get time, he suggested the man sit down, which he did, *muy borracho,* you understand, colonel? Well, he said, 'Since you afraid to say, you must be from the army of Villa. Now my problem is this.' He had two pistols and put them on the table, and he looked from one to the other, like this, see? 'My problem is which pistol to kill you with, this one or that one. Which one you want, eh, *hombre?*' "

The kids were shrieking with laughter, and Michael, who was at the bottom of the steps by then, heard another voice, Colonel Dowd's he supposed, say, "I think it's a pretty good thing we came in and straightened you folks out."

"Oh, yes, sir, yes, sir."

"Well, one thing I've learned about Mexican stories, they don't necessarily have an ending. So if you'll excuse me, I'll get back to work. Remember, I promised Chief Burns you'd be back by noon."

"Twelve o'clock on the schnozz, sir."

Colonel Dowd came out the screen door and down the steps, Sergeant Jones following. The privates who'd been sitting on the steps got up, the driver running around Michael to get into the CO's car, the other standing to one side of the steps, waiting to fall in behind Sergeant Jones.

It was then that Alan noticed Marian sitting in the back of her father's car. She had not called his attention to her presence.

Michael was blocking the walk from the steps, and Colonel Dowd walked right up to him before he noticed who was there. Michael was looking at him intently, seemed to be making up his mind about something.

"Hey! Get out of the way!" Sergeant Jones barked. "Who the hell let you in?"

Alan stepped forward. "He's with me."

Michael was looking at the colonel and the colonel was looking at him.

"Can I talk to you?" Michael said.

At that instant Juana came into the doorway and, seeing Michael, made a frightened sound.

They must have thought that Juana had seen something they had not: Sergeant Jones grabbed Michael; the two privates held him while Jones went through his pockets and clapped him on the thighs and calves and under the arms.

"Sergeant Jones!" Alan shouted. "Release that man. That's an order!"

Alan had never spoken in that mode before, but it certainly sounded convincing. Jones jumped back, looked around; had they heard what he heard?

Colonel Dowd saw Jones's expression, had to laugh.

The others, permission granted, joined in.

Marian, sitting in the car, thought they were laughing at the spectacle of her husband giving orders.

Released, Michael again approached the colonel and asked, "Can I see you alone a minute please?"

"Well—what do you want?"

"Colonel Dowd!" It was Cesario's voice from inside the house. "He's one of them."

From Jones, Colonel Dowd got the news in a whisper: Michael was unarmed. "He's not doing any harm," he said, moving close to the boy and looking at him in the friendliest way. "Sure, you can talk to me. What about?"

Michael, flustered by his sudden cordiality, seemed to be trying to figure something out. Everybody waited for what he had to say. Finally he said, "I don't know."

"What did he say? What the hell did he say?" Sergeant Jones asked.

"He said he didn't know."

"I really would. Like to talk to you," Michael said.

"Fine. What about?"

There was another wait, and Alan, who was as puzzled as everyone else, saw Michael quit. His head dropped, he turned away, he didn't seem to know where he was.

Colonel Dowd waited. "Well," he finally said, patient, tolerant, "perhaps when you do know you can get Lieutenant Kidd to bring you out here again."

Michael shook his head and muttered something that sounded like "not necessary."

It was obvious; he was stoned. He didn't even look up when Dowd walked away. He'd apparently forgotten, or changed his mind, about why he'd come there.

The colonel, who had taken Alan by the arm, was talking to him at the side of his command car in a voice no one could hear, taking care not to humiliate his son-in-law. When he finished, he nodded at the airman standing with his hand on the car door and was driven away.

Marian had kept her face averted and expressionless during Alan's dressing down. It was the regulation thing to do.

Sergeant Jones was left behind to keep an eye on the distracted boy till he was safely off the base.

Michael stood where he'd been left. Alan had to pull at his arm to get his attention. "He wants you off the base," he whispered.

"Will you drive me somewhere?" said Michael.

When they drove through the base gate, Michael still had not said where he wanted to go. Alan had to ask him.

"Cy Walker's office." Having communicated this, Michael was silent again.

Alan assumed he was puzzling out what had just taken place. "Did you recognize who was in their house?" he asked. "By his voice?"

Michael nodded. "Were you surprised?" he asked.

"In a way," Alan said. Michael nodded again, simply acknowledging he had heard. Alan tried another subject. "What did you want to ask Colonel Dowd?"

Michael didn't answer.

"Colonel Dowd didn't like it that you learned Flores was there. He didn't like it one bit."

"It doesn't make any difference," Michael said. "It's all the same." Then he looked at Alan and said, "That your wife in the car?"

"Yes."

"Why do people get married? Do they really trust each other that much?" He smiled. "You knew he was there, didn't you? You pretended you were surprised, but you knew Flores was there."

"That's true," Alan said. "But I forgot. So when I heard his voice, I was surprised. Like I said."

"You're not telling the truth again."

"No, I'm not," Alan admitted.

"Did you want me to know Flores was there?"

"Yes."

"Do they think it's all right to do that? Legal?"

"I don't know. I'm telling you the truth now. When I first heard about it, I thought it was a natural thing to do. No, more than that, I thought it was humane. Let him visit his family, why not? And—I'm telling you the truth again—I still can't imagine why you're so mad about it. I almost can, but—"

"You weren't mad? When you heard his voice in there?"

"Should I have been?"

Michael shrugged. "No you're a nice guy, too." Then he said, "Nobody gets made at anything. I said something terrible to my father last night, and he said he wasn't mad at me. The colonel, you say he was pissed, but he spoke to me very politely, didn't he? Still, I have the feeling people wish me dead. They think I'm dangerous."

"Because of the rough way they searched you? I guess they thought you were there to shoot somebody."

"And that's illogical?"

"Of course."

"But it isn't."

"Oh, Michael, come on!"

"You know the only one I think is honest? Not you, that heavy-set sergeant, what's his name?"

"Jones. He's just what he looks like. A big shit."

Michael nodded.

"I don't think you're that kind of person," Alan said. "You're not a murderer."

"Neither is Flores."

"And I don't think anyone wants you dead." Alan was worried about Michael, the desperate way he looked. It was his responsibility, Alan felt, to do something about it. But what?

They were both silent for a few blocks, then Michael asked, "Do you believe Colonel Dowd encouraged him?"

"Encouraged whom? To do what?"

"Flores to kill Vinnie?"

"My God, how can you think that?"

"I can't tell about people any more. Maybe he ordered Flores to do it?"

"Michael, what's the matter with you?"

"You never had that suspicion?"

"No! When he puts me down I get mad at him, but mostly I think he's a pretty decent guy. At bottom, he's a *real* nice guy."

"Everybody is," Michael said. "Even Flores. I talked to him once all afternoon and night. We were together in the desert, and I liked him. This is a nice guy, I remember I said to myself. I could even see his side of it against Vinnie. And my father, he's a nice guy. I like him. And your wife, after you found out what she did to you, you made it with her, which proves you think at bottom she's a nice guy, too. And Mr. Gavin McAndrews—he's what?—like a great guy!"

"He's something, all right."

"And that other lawyer, ours? He's a real gentleman, gives me coffee, sandwiches, tells his secretary, a wonderful girl, to look after me like she was my mother, which she does, but better. And that Judge Breen, my God, everybody thinks he's like great! I mean the whole country is made up exclusively of nice guys. I look at the pictures in those magazines in Walker's office, *Life* and *Newsweek* and *Forbes,* everybody in them is tops. And I'm a freak. Right. I know it. But you want to know what I think?"

"I do, I really do."

Michael waited a moment, then suddenly veered. "Forget it," he said. "We're here? Thanks a lot for everything."

"Tell me what you were going to?"

"No. I'm not talking sense. I'm like suspicious of everybody. I see concealed motives, even with you. You better stay away from me. Don't think of me as a friend, I'm not safe as a friend any more. For instance, I've thought seriously of killing my father. I did it—in my mind. That's pretty sick, isn't it? And here's the thing—" Michael stopped, shook his head.

"What's the thing?"

Michael hesitated, then said, "It's okay. I don't care if you tell them what I've been saying to you."

"My God, Michael, I'm not going to tell anybody what we talk about."

"It's okay, you can. When they ask you, which they will. Here's the thing. There has to be some mark left behind. Doesn't there? Some evidence that somebody gave a shit? When Vinnie was shot to death that way? It can't just all soak into the ground like the blood of a dog someone ran over on the highway. Can it?"

"Michael, Flores is going to spend the rest of his life in jail, like maybe twenty years."

"Maybe."

"Everybody saw him do it."

"But he didn't do it."

"God's sake, I can't talk to you!"

"We've been electrocuting people for years and years. It's not the man who pulls the switch."

"That's no parallel."

"Who's guilty here? Will he get punished? Or will it go down this way and be forgotten? Well, say."

Suddenly Alan didn't feel sure enough to answer that question.

Michael started to get out of the car. "Thanks again."

"Where are you going to stay tonight? I drove by your house this morning—in case you were there. I guess your landlord has evicted you all. You didn't know that?"

"It doesn't matter."

"I wish I could invite you to stay with me, but—"

"That's okay."

"I'd like to talk to you. I'm worried."

"We've been talking." Then Michael smiled. "Last week, the week before, whenever it was, in the courtroom, you kept sitting next to me, making up to me, remember?"

Alan was caught, again.

"Did Mr. McAndrews tell you to sit next to me and find out what was on my mind?"

"No."

"But he did ask you what I said?"

"Yes."

"Every day?"

"Often. No, every day. Well, for chrissake, you sat there so quietly all the time with that punched-out look on your face, you can't blame him for being curious."

Michael got out of the car. "Thanks," he said, "and don't worry about it—I mean me. Punched-out look!" He laughed. "Right! Right!" He laughed again.

By the time Michael had walked halfway to the entrance of the county courthouse building, Alan had caught up with him.

"And you, you're not a nice guy?"

"I am. That's what I'm worried about."

Cy Walker wasn't in. "He's working on his opening presentation for tomorrow," Donna told Michael, "and I'm waiting to type it."

"Where is he?"

"Home." She saw his look and said, "No, I can't give you his address, Michael. He doesn't want to be interrupted."

"Will he be calling in?"

"He might."

"I'll wait."

"He told me not to let you hang around any more."

"Come on, Michael," Alan said.

"You better go," Michael said, suddenly cold.

Alan left.

"You want some coffee?" Donna asked. "Sit down. I brought some cookies from home. My roommate made them. Sit down!"

The strain of the trial was felt most the day before it started.

On this one day, Cy needed quiet. But something had broken down in the order of the Walker home. Their three boys, limited by domestic decree to one hour of TV a day, had this Sunday been watching since breakfast. Now he heard them squabbling over what to turn to next.

Cy burst into the room where they were, the den, originally his den, now the TV den, yanked one plug out of the wall, the other out of the set, stuffed the wire into his pocket, went looking for his wife.

Corky was on the floor in the darkest corner of the bedroom, directly under the air conditioner, studying a spread of solitaire, her face frozen over the stalled cards.

"You know what day this is! You know I have to work today!"

"You have to work every day," Corky said, "and I've got them on my back every day."

"Tell them to go outside and play."

"It's too hot outside."

"All the other kids play outside."

"Our kids are smarter. They won't breathe smog. They don't want to die."

"Then what do you suggest, goddamn it?"

"Gas masks!" She messed her game and got up. "I'm not going to live here any more. I hate this place. It's flat and it's hot and you can't breathe the air, that's the least you should expect from the place where you live—"

"I told you, as soon as I'm making real money, we'll get a place above the smog line."

"There's no such line. That's a myth to keep wives quiet."
The phone rang.

It was Donna, sounding impatient.

"Can you tell me when you actually need me. And if?"

"Go to a movie, Donna, and come back at maybe four—"

Then as Corky listened, Cy Walker had a tantrum.

"What the hell are you doing there?" he shouted. Corky thought he was talking to Donna. "I told you I don't want you hanging around my office. Put Donna back, get the hell off this line. Donna! Hello! Didn't I tell you to stop mothering that dirty little son of a bitch? Right, first I told you to mother him, then I told you to stop, so stop! I know you're not a cop, you don't have to be a cop to put him out. Well, fuck you, too. Go ahead, quit, who needs you, you can't even make a decent cup of coffee! You can both quit!" His look included Corky. "You can all quit!"

He hung up, fell on the bed.

Corky sat close to him. "How would you like a decent cup of coffee?" she said.

Just as she kissed him, there was a burst of sound from the den, a three-way quarrel, something falling. Corky marched on the enemy. He could hear her, the boys griping, then leaving the house.

The front door slammed. The air conditioner vibrated in its phases.

Sunday was the day of Judge Bo Barton's annual barbecue. Judge Bo was the thorny old man of the bench of that state. People had been waiting twenty-five years for him to die, but like some scraggly desert plant, he'd found a way to live without sustenance. He got thinner, he got meaner, but he wouldn't retire and he wouldn't die. And he kept giving his annual barbecue.

It was the one best chance every year for meeting new arrivals on the political scene and weighing their heft, for forming new alliances and strengthening old ones, for measuring the progress up or down of friend or foe. Many an appointee was chewed out over a sparerib, many a patron buttered with the sour-dough rolls.

The guest everyone was eager to meet this year was the brilliant young lawyer about to be given sudden prominence by the Flores case.

Sally Breen refused to go.

At first she wouldn't give Teddy a reason, not a real one. "I don't like baked pinto beans and chuck-wagon dowdy, I don't enjoy chicken barbecued till stiff, and the sparerib sauce is too greasy, and—"

"I thought you liked Judge Bo."

"I like him okay. At least he's mean. But I don't want to kiss his cactus-covered ass this year. I'm not in that line of work any more."

"What line of work?"

"Sucking."

"What the hell will I tell him?"

"I'll tell you what you'll tell him. Sally is indisposed, Bo your honor"—this said in the mincing voice of the poke-bonnet prissy of the Old West—"but she'll be bright as a pup in the mornin'."

"Boy, are you two-faced. When you want something from somebody, you're all over him! I remember how you buttered that old man's fly."

"Not this year!"

"Sare, the governor's flying down! Come on! You know what this means to me."

"Sure," she said, "enjoy yourself."

That was the day Don Wheeler sent for the ambulance.

Hope was hallucinating. Even in the speeding ambulance she was convinced they were going to their home on the side of a mountain in the north of the state.

Don sat on a little white stool and held her hand as Hope rambled, back at a large house party they'd thrown two years ago. Their guests on that occasion, the executives responsible for Wheeler's most lucrative accounts, had been asked up for a weekend of deer hunting. All well through middle age, they had been positioned, seated, at "stands" and the dogs sent out to drive the deer by. The men were dressed ruggedly, but no more exertion was required of them than lifting a gun and pressing a trigger. They had all brought down at least one head.

Just to the side of their house, a strong frame had been erected, and as the trophies were brought in by jeep, gutted for the dogs, hung by their heels, there developed a triumphant display.

The ambulance siren sounded as they rounded a corner.

"I don't know what to do with all that meat, Don," she said.

"Well, now, honey, the fellows will take most of it back home with them and we'll freeze the rest. Close your eyes."

"But there's so much, so—"

She lost consciousness, slept for a minute. Wheeler found himself making plans, what he'd do when she was gone, where he'd go. Only lately had he realized he hadn't done the things he most wanted, safari in East Africa, hunt bear in Kodiak Island, fish for marlin off the shores of Peru.

"Forty? Did you say forty—?"

"Forty-four, darling."

"Promise me you won't kill any more, Don. I just love to see them come down to the meadow in the morning."

Hope had placed great cubes of salt in the field below their bedroom window.

"That's the only thing I don't like about you, Don, you've been so good to me. Promise me that."

"I promise, darling, now be quiet."

All the way from Cy's office Alan chewed himself out. "It's your home, invite anybody you want."

By the time he got home he was furious. He stacked his old Perez Prado 78s, the ones Marian hated, fell out on the sofa, and let the Havana sound in.

She came down after a couple of sides and turned the player off. "The McCords will be here any minute," she said.

Alan had forgotten.

He loaded McCord's cocktails, baited him over the beef. "Justice is the order the armed impose on the unarmed," he said, holding the wine bottle over the judge advocate's glass.

McCord ignored the philosophy, accepted the burgundy.

Marian had planned the dinner to mend fences; McCord and Alan didn't talk from the last of the roast through the second brandy.

Marian saw the guests to their car, locked the front door, pulled off her girdle.

Alan stacked the player again, Sibelius.

"What the hell's eating you?" she asked in her mistress-of-the-castle voice.

"I wanted to bring somebody home to spend the night, and I didn't because I thought you wouldn't like it."

Marian laughed, relieved. "One of those hippie girls with plenty toe-cheese?"

"I'm not kidding."

"Alan, darling, really! You can have anybody here you want. Now let's talk about why you were so rude to the McCords and what we're going to do about it."

"I hesitate to bring someone I like to my own home."

"But, darling, you can't blame me for that. Who was it?"

"Michael Winter."

"You can have him if you want, Alan, of course."

"I will."

She turned and started up the stairs. "But if you decide to, let me know because I won't be here for the event."

"What does that mean?" Marian kept mounting the stairs. "Hey, boss lady, what the hell does that mean?"

She stopped. "You know how I feel about that case, everyone in it, everything about it. That case has come close to wrecking my marriage."

"What's the matter with him?"

"He's dirty."

"That's all?"

"And I had a good look at him today. He smells. At a distance. He also smells of drugs. What's *not* the matter with him?"

"I think he's—I mean he's just a kid, but there's something about him—"

"Christlike?"

"Don't make fun of him."

"Put a beard on a drug habit, take away his will power and energy, dirty him up good all over, and even if he slits throats, he's still some sort of Messiah. Look, let's leave it like I left it. He's dirty."

"He's the only one here bothering about the right and wrong—"

"If you mean to bring him here, go ahead. It would embarrass me, and it would certainly embarrass my father, who has already forbidden you to bring him on the base. But it's your home, do what you want. Okay? Satisfied?"

"No."

"Then I'd like to make a suggestion, a sincere one, really

Alan—if you're so crazy about him and what he is, why don't you go live with him in one of those hippie pods or whatever they're called for a while?"

Alan got up. "He has no place to stay tonight."

"I doubt if this is the first time he's had that problem."

"Don't give me that *Ladies' Home Journal* piss!" said Alan.

Marian continued up the stairs.

Alan decided to go on.

"The reason I can't fuck you now, Marian," he said, "is that I can't talk to you."

"Are you sure that's the reason?"

"I made sure."

"Oh, that's good news!"

She was at the top of the stairs.

"If you don't mind," she said, in a different voice, "I'm going to sleep. You can stay here or sleep in the guest room, alone or with your boyfriend, or go sleep with him in the park. Just don't disturb me. And I'd rather, if you care, I'd rather you didn't take any more of whatever he's been giving you to make you talk to me that way."

"You know that's not true, Marian."

Walking to the foot of the stairs, he saw that she was crying. "Maybe you're right, maybe I'm blaming you for what's my fault. But I think a lot of Michael, and I only wish you knew him."

"No, thanks."

"He's the only one in this whole thing who sees what they're getting ready here."

"Oh, Alan, baby, he's just a drug addict."

Alan shook his head.

"I guess you'll see it someday, Alan, but now—"

"I really do love him. I have that kind of feeling for him."

"Well, in the morning, when I come down for my Cheeri-oats, if Jesus is here, I go."

From the bedroom door she called down. "Alan, if you don't mind, turn the player down. I like Beethoven or who-ever that is better than your Cuban music-to-hump-by, but not when I'm trying to sleep."

He heard the bedroom door lock, thought about going downtown to see if he could find Michael, decided not to. Inch by inch, he knew it now, he'd given himself up to Marian. It wasn't her fault, it was his.

Hours later he'd made up his mind. His wife, his home on the base, which was not his anyway, his profession, which was also not his, his uniform, which belonged to the air force —what the hell was he doing in the air force?—he'd quit them all.

He went over and put Beethoven's middle quartets, the optimistic ones, on the spindle, turned the sound down for the sake of the lady upstairs, poured himself what he used to drink before his marriage, Early Times, straight. Then he stretched out on the sofa and enjoyed the heat running through him.

Vinnie lay on a battered metal tray slid into a bank of cubicles, his body preserved at forty degrees. As the skin of his face had tightened, his hair and beard appeared to be growing back. He looked better than the day he died.

———————————————————————

At eight Monday morning, Bailiff Lansing was in Judge Breen's courtroom, the first one there. Quietly, gracefully, he moved about, making sure everything was in place and ready for the start of the trial for murder.

When Cy Walker got to his office in the county courthouse building, Michael was waiting for him. Both of them behaved as if the unpleasantness over the phone the day before had not occurred. There was no time for anything but the work at hand.

Cy listened to Michael tell about Cesario's visit to the base. "Somewhere along the line it may be useful," Cy said. He noticed the disarray in his office. "Did you sleep here last night?"

"On the sofa."

"I wish you wouldn't hang around my office any more," he said. "I'll call you before your testimony to help you with what you're going to say. Where will you be?"

"I don't know," Michael said.

"Well, if and when you know, leave your telephone number and address with whoever is here."

Then Cy noticed his desk top. Two large folders were out. Michael explained, "I would have put them back, but

I lost the place in the files and didn't want to put them in the wrong place."

"You've got some goddamn nerve! Don't you recognize any privacies?"

"Sure. I only read those on the case."

"You have no right to do that!"

In one of the folders, Cy knew, was his private record, the one he kept on every case he handled, put down in his own hand in a bound diary with a clasp lock. Cy quickly found it. The clasp had been broken.

"Did you read this?"

"Yes."

"It was locked."

"I opened it."

"Get out of here. Right now!"

"I noticed you wish you didn't have to try this case," Michael said calmly, "that you think it may have, what did you say, counterproductive results on your career?"

Cy walked to the door and called for the guard. "Ernie!"

Through the open door, Donna walked in. Cy was too enraged to say anything to her.

She took in the desk top, the open files, the diary, and hurried to put them all together again into the metal file cases. "I'm sorry, Mr. Walker," she called to him in the hall, "I left in such a hurry yesterday I didn't lock the files."

"Ernie!" Cy roared. The guard on the floor was hurrying toward him at last.

"I read only what you had on this case," Michael said. "Actually, one thing you wrote is very interesting—that no one involved in this case will ever be the same—"

"Throw him out of here," Cy ordered. The uniformed guard started toward Michael. Michael lifted a thin hand; the guard stopped.

"I think you should take yourself off this case, Mr. Walker," Michael said. "We need a lawyer on this case who wants to win it."

"Goddamn it, Ernie, what the hell are you standing there for?"

The guard, an old man lucky in his sinecure, was not in good shape; he had concealed a hernia from his employers. Fortunately for him there was no need to provide force.

"You don't have to do that," Michael said, as Ernie

trudged up, looking as formidable as he possibly could, "I'm going."

Michael sauntered down the stairs and out of the building, strolled through the people on the walk, his neck erect, his head thrown back. At that instant he understood his friend Vinnie, what it was that had made Vinnie walk the way he walked, not arrogance, but the knowledge that those against him were frightened and uncertain and, by that, inferior.

These people were afraid of him; that was the fact. Cy calling for muscle was not demonstrating power but fear. That was the force Vinnie had had, the confidence that in a confrontation those opposing him would not dare go as far as he would. "They might beat me," Vinnie used to say, "but they'll have to kill me to do it."

Facing the square, Michael stopped and asked the kids sitting on the edge of the lawn for a joint, waited while it was turned, accepted it without acknowledgment or thanks, walked off.

Out from under the shade trees, the morning sun hit him. Michael had spent most of the night transcribing bits from Cy Walker's files into the notebook he carried. He had been so agitated by what he found out that when he tried to sleep on the leather sofa, he'd soon be up again, walking around and around the dark office, talking to himself. "But Jesus! But Jesus!" Now, he was exhausted.

Across the blazing square, massed against the elevated side of the Interstate, was an enormous motor hotel, the Western Star. Michael had read somewhere that it was owned by insurance companies. Facing the courthouse, this three-storied mass, arms and wings of simulated dobe, crouched over its prize of old land. Above the entrance was a flaring metal frame supporting a design worked in neon tubing of gold and green, the Indian tribal symbol for "Welcome." Michael knew the symbol well, he had studied the Indians driven off this piece of the West. Welcome! The symbol for the Western Star should have been an Indian chief with a bleeding hole in his forehead.

He stood for an instant facing the structure, Orestes before the palace at Mycenae, a figure of revenge and right, inade-quate perhaps, as Orestes had been inadequate, a prince as Vinnie had been a prince.

He passed through the parking lot, along the rows of gleaming cars. Then off the far edge he dropped, looking for a place to rest. There was a ragged glen below one wing of the Western Star. Here, at the base of the fortress wall, the prince fell to earth.

Lying on his back, ankles crossed, he put another match to the stick of weed, pulled in the smoke, held it, pulled in again.

Above him were hundreds of feet of bedroom windows, all in a row, all closed, under each was an air conditioner, sucking air through a screened mouth, providing the cool, shaded rooms where the privileged breathed. Michael could hear the chorus of pumping motors.

There was a particular odor in the air. At the end of the wall where he lay, behind a huge square screen, was the exhaust from the pumps that fed the public rooms. Three befouled colored ribbons, tied to the grating, rode the torrent of dead air.

The trial was starting before another hour passed; he might miss it if he let himself sleep. Whatever he was going to do, he would have to do soon. The rituals of justice would be observed and concluded. In the fewest possible days, Vinnie's murder would be dropped into the bin of silence, there to disappear forever from human account. Actually such trial as they intended was already over; the issue at law had been decided. Justice, if there was to be justice, was up to him.

He had to sleep, even for a few minutes. He pulled off his shirt, put the joint back behind his lips, sucked in, flipped off his sandals, and did his shoulder-stand *asanas*. He relaxed in the posture, his lungs full of the sweet smoke; he breathed, filling and emptying his lungs. Finally he tensed each extremity, then relaxed.

He pillowed his shirt under one cheek, closed his eyes, and little by little let himself down into a sort of sleep. He stopped hearing the cars driving in and out of the Western Star's parking area and the cries of the gang of kids in the gulch of the dry stream beneath him, picking over the rubbish the housekeepers had dumped there.

Neither asleep nor awake, call it dreaming, he saw himself.

He walked through the corridors of that palace, through a series of antechambers that led to the seat of power. At their positions of responsibility were the stewards and attendants and guards, surrogates of the throne. They were, he could recognize, the personages of this trial for murder: Cy Walker, Gavin McAndrews, Bailliff Lansing, Judge Breen, Colonel Dowd, even Sergeant Jones and his wife, flanked by the guards at the main gate of the base, he thought he'd forgotten them. They were all dressed in the same uniform, stiffened by the braid of authority not their own, their attitudes enigmatic but watchful, each jealously protecting what eminence he had, however minor. Michael walked through a series of rooms lit by the Indian chief with the red light in his forehead. He knew he was coming to the throne room, because the chorus of little electric motors had swelled to a roar and the smell of death in the air smarted his nostrils.

Threading his way along the guarded paths, receiving from each station of authority the indifferent nod which passed him through—what harm could he do, a person so inconsequential? Michael finally reached a vast chamber, alive with the echoes of past violence, vibrating to the sound of motors. There he found the throne itself.

It was unoccupied.

Michael had wondered about that. Was there anyone to take that responsibility? Was there a final authority? An establishment of power? Or were they all surrogates for someone not known, not there?

Who then must he try? On whose body mark retaliation?

One thing he settled immediately. He himself was the only one strong enough, unafraid enough, the only one with nothing to lose. He would sit on the throne.

From there he called out, "Bring the defendants before me!" In his sleep he laughed at the tone of his voice. It was from some old movie that voice, Bogart, Cagney, Robinson? Pretty corny!

The doors at the back of the room opened, and in rows of eight abreast the army of defendants marched into the room to face him. As they entered, the room got bigger, like one of Disney's effects, the viewpoint higher, until Michael saw that they were a multitude, everyone he'd been watching not only around the courthouse, but all his life through, their frightened bodies pressed together for insect safety, complaining and grumbling, protesting. "We were only following orders! Don't blame us!"

When they spoke, he knew who they were, not only the
people of the trial, but the people of his life, of the nation's
streets and buildings, his father among them, his teachers,
too, yes, as well as the public figures who during his life had
played out history on television. They were all awaiting his
judgment.

They knew what he was thinking, they fell on their knees
and begged for mercy, buzzing and scraping.

He was honest with them. "I admit I cannot give you a
fair trial," he said. "I have made up my mind you are all
guilty. But I don't intend to punish you. You don't merit
punishment. You are inferior creatures, I can see that, you
are nothing, you only do what you are told. Even you with
the gun, you, Sergeant Flores, you had no choice but to—"

Flores was firing his pistol, but it seemed of no importance.

Michael stood. "There's only one among you," he continued, "who—"

At that instant in his dream, he stopped.

He didn't want to go on, knowing what was ahead.

The joint had died in his mouth; carefully he relit it.

Yes, he thought, that was exactly what he had to do, try
the people who were trying the case.

What was he ducking? Why was he avoiding what it was
all about?

He decided to take the chance, let himself go again, down
into his vision.

Accusations of duplicity filled the air, confessions of guilt!
The multitude pointed at each other.

Then Michael spoke again, gently and sadly. "There is
only one among you worthy of trial, only one of you who
is not trapped in his past, his allegiances and obligations.
He is the best of you."

He made an imperious gesture with his right hand, signal-
ing that this man be brought before him.

Among the others there was great relief. Released by
Michael's decision, some ran, making their escape off the
sides of the parking lot into the gulch where the rubbish of
the palace had been dumped. Others simply disappeared into
the ground where they stood. Michael never saw them go.

He only saw Alan standing suppliant before him, with his
open, old-time face that had always been friendly and was
now.

"When was the last time you ate?" Alan said.

Michael woke, perspiring, horrified.

"That was a lot of shit, that dream," he said out loud.

The big heat was moving in, the sun striking through the scrubby trees under the motel wall.

How much time had passed? He looked at the sun. It had moved up; the trial must have started.

He got to his feet, swaying a little. His mouth tasted stale, he rubbed his gums with the side of a forefinger. Then he pulled his shirt over his head and looked around for his sandals.

They were gone. He was not surprised.

He entered the courtroom barefoot.

"You're a mess," Donna said to Michael, hurrying past him into the courtroom with some papers for her boss. As she went through the door, Michael heard Cy Walker making his opening presentation. He hadn't missed much.

He followed Donna in. "Lieutenant Kidd talked to me," she whispered as the door swung closed behind them. "It's okay for tonight." What was she talking about?

The three rows of seats at the end of the courtroom were packed. Michael tried to squeeze into the back row, but when the spectators took a look at him they wouldn't move over.

He saw Alan in the front row. Michael sidled in past newspapermen who tilted their steno pads and uncrossed their legs to let him by, slumped into the space Alan made for him, and pretended to be intent on what Cy Walker was saying. Michael couldn't look at Alan yet, he hadn't shaken off the dream.

"No one has and no one can controvert the very simple facts"—Cy noticed Michael—"of this sad case. There are witnesses—"

Bailliff Lansing became aware of two bare feet on the barrier rail.

"—to every instant of what took place. The actual deed of murder was witnessed—"

A nimble little lawyer's clerk slipped into the courtroom and up to Gavin McAndrews with a whispered message. Gavin rushed out.

"—by Elizabeth Flores, Sergeant Flores's daughter. We have her sworn and signed statement describing—"

Alan was aware that Michael was studying him with cold eyes. "What's the matter?" he said. When Michael didn't

answer, he added, "A lot's happened since I saw you, a lot!"

"—that awful moment in detail. Regretfully we will be putting this young girl on the stand."

Bailliff Lansing tapped Michael's knee with a long middle finger. His eyes indicated Michael's bare feet, then swiveled to the door.

"We also have," Cy rattled the papers Donna had just brought him, "the sworn and signed statement of Juana Flores—" Cy stopped talking, watched the confrontation.

"Put your feet under your seat," Alan whispered.

Along each wall a deputy moved in slowly.

Michael turned to Alan. "What? What's happened?"

Out in the corridor, the Flores family led by Mother Elsa had finally shown, an hour late. Gavin had carefully instructed them to be there for the opening of the trial. It was obvious what had caused the delay. Mrs. Flores had dressed her darlings as if they were to be guests at a tea dance.

Bailiff Lansing stood over Michael, waiting.

"Well, what happened?" Michael asked again.

"We had a showdown," Alan said.

Lansing leaned over and whispered something to Michael, who nodded absentmindedly but didn't move his feet. The jury was enjoying the first moment of drama. At the back, spectators raised up to watch the dirty little hippie get his.

"What's the matter with the way we're dressed?" Elsa demanded of Gavin.

"I haven't got time to explain. Here's five dollars, get them into a cab and home and—haven't they got—? Especially you, Juana. Haven't you got a plain blue dress?"

"If that's what you wanted, why didn't you say so?" Elsa protested from under her polka-dot veil.

"And without the uplift, Juana."

"I'm not going in there dressed like some old nun!" Juana said, quite ready to do anything he asked.

Gavin grabbed Juana's elbow, pulled her away from the others, talked to her in language she understood. "Now you go home and cover your tits before I rap you right across your fat little ass. Move it!"

He looked ferocious, Juana thought, and most attractive. She turned to Elsa. "Mom, come on, let's hurry. I know what he wants."

The guards moved in discreetly except for the squeak in one's shoes. Michael had to be lifted out of his chair, a dead weight. The jury enjoyed the show.

Judge Breen used his gavel, tried to conceal a smile.

Michael struggled, was overcome.

Judge Breen played up to his audience. "A victory for the culture of shoes!" His aside was enjoyed; laughter was permitted in the court.

"Put me down, please," Michael said as the deputies carried him through the door. "Will you please put me down?"

On his feet, he said, "May I have your names, please?" He pulled the spiral pad out of his back pocket.

"You trying to get wise or something?" the smaller and more aggressive of the deputies asked.

Alan rushed up. "He's got a right to know your name, officer, it's his legal right. I'm Lieutenant Kidd from the air force base. What is your name?"

The deputies gave their names to the uniform.

"Thank you very much," Michael said.

"That will be all," Alan added.

"Judge Breen's very strict," the larger deputy explained.

"I know he is," Michael said, accepting the apology.

The deputies gone, Alan sat next to Michael, who didn't look up. "I've got a lot to tell you," he said.

"Not now," Michael said. He had stopped writing but was bent over the little pad.

"What the hell are you mad at me about? Because I used to talk to Gavin about you?"

"No."

"Well, whatever your reason, stop it, I'm on your side now."

"I had a dream about you."

"Oh, Michael, come on. A dream!"

"A dream is the truest—"

"Look, now, I'm your lawyer, all right? Free. No pay."

Michael shook his head. "Give me ten dollars," he said. "I'll have plenty tomorrow. I'll pay you back."

Alan reached into his pocket quickly. "What happened to your shoes?"

"It's not for shoes."

"Then what?"

"None of your business."

"You know," he separated out two fives, "I shouldn't give you a goddamn cent."

"Then don't."

Alan gave him the money.

Michael reached into his pocket for the little tin of aspirin he carried, took two. Then he looked at Alan, his own face suddenly haggard. "I'm getting a headache again," he said. "I have one all the time now."

"You just need sleep, friend. I forgot to tell you, I spoke to Donna and she said you can stay at her place. And listen—"

"I haven't got time now. I got to go somewhere."

"Where?"

Michael tensed. "Don't ask me questions like that," he said.

"You still don't trust me?"

"Why should I?" Michael looked at him, then said, "You studied this case. You know the fellow on trial here, you know he's just the finger that pulled the trigger. You know who's really guilty here and how to bring it out in court—"

"But I don't know. I'm with you, but—"

"You're not with me because you don't think like me. I'm going to get a lawyer. I'll have nearly a thousand dollars tomorrow."

"How will you—? I'm sorry, I don't want to know."

"You see, you keep asking me questions like that. What I need is a lawyer who's one of us, a freak or a black, somebody who's got no stake in this scene, who's got nothing to lose."

"That's me."

Michael looked at him a long time. "Bullshit!" he said.

Alan swallowed it. "Go buy yourself whatever it is," he said.

Standing where Michael had left him, Alan remembered he'd made a tennis date for what could be excellent doubles.

There's another way to live through this life, he reminded himself. He could walk out of that courthouse building, keep the date at the club, go home, shower, half make up with Marian, then all the way; it had happened before, quarrels in the living room, reconciliations in bed.

What the hell was he doing here, enduring the scorn of this twisted kid?

Why the hell did he feel responsible for the outcome of this bloody trial? Let his old man's puritanism lie where it was buried, in a Massachusetts graveyard. Read about the trial in the papers! Feel concern, at no personal cost.

He moved to the courtroom, opened the door a little, glanced in.

Cy was making his opening statement, nailing up the calendar of events as any competent lawyer would. His choice of facts was okay. Alan thought, but everybody knew them, no one would contest them.

And there was no illumination, Alan felt, no insight. He kept wanting to correct almost everything Cy was saying in some particular, put it so it would cut through and jolt the jury to attention. Alan remembered a professor who used to quote Robert Frost: "Squeeze out the water!" Cy was verbose. He wandered.

There was an empty seat in the front row, and Alan took it. He was there for the duration.

He had to prove to a boy who didn't want to hear about it, and wouldn't believe it when it was shown him, that this old ritual in a courtroom still worked.

He'd be Michael's lawyer whether the boy wanted it or not, Cy's associate whether Cy accepted him or not. And he'd do it openly, for all to see.

"What the hell is Kidd doing?" Gavin asked Earl McCord, who had taken Alan's place at the defense table. "He was out there before, whispering to that insane kid."

"Why sit here wondering?" McCord said. "Let's put a tail on him."

In the back of the army-navy store were the footlockers and suitcases standing on their ends. Michael selected a case of thin, stiff metal, long enough to hold a carbine.

If Gavin's opening presentation was disappointing, it was because he kept being distracted by Lieutenant Kidd in the front row, writing all through Gavin's talk, obviously nothing related to what he was saying.

Actually there was one moment in Gavin's presentation that did catch Alan's attention completely; a gesture, casual and probably unconscious.

"I will ask you to do one very simple thing through the course of this trial," Gavin said to the jury. "Put yourself inside this man." As he said this, Gavin moved behind Cesario Flores and put both his hands on the man's shoulders, a son protecting his father.

Alan knew, at exactly that moment, how this case was going to be decided.

Thurston Breen had heard the morning's news over his car radio, but he wanted to read the paper carefully, had stolen looks at his copy all through Cy's talk and Gavin's.

The journal of that sun-drenched community was informing its readers, particularly the thousands of senior citizens who'd come to the Southwest to live out their years on coupons, that some sort of bottom had dropped out of the market. The pressmen had enjoyed this solemn duty as they enjoyed recording all the East Coast's troubles; there was a perverse delight between the lines of the lead story.

The one stock Judge Breen had been sure of, that of the greatest utility in the country, was particularly sick. And that "can't-miss" growth stock of his!

"Your broker isn't in," his secretary told him, "but Mrs. Breen is on the line."

"Tell them I'll be calling back at precisely three o'clock New York time," he told the girl. "And I want him to be there! Then put my wife on."

"Read the paper this morning, Teddy?" Sally asked.

"The market'll come back," Breen answered. "This is a healthy country."

That morning Hope had her last moment when she thought recovery possible. No one else did, and it's possible Hope was pretending. But she did have a four-minute egg, her cup of Constant Comment tea, and a buttered English muffin.

Don Wheeler, watching bedside, returned her smiles as she told him about the naughty dream she'd had the night before.

"Actually, it wasn't naughty," she said, "because it was all about you, only you. Will you make love to me when I get better, Don?"

"You just wait."

She was laughing now. "Who did you go out to call just before? You haven't got another girl warming up in the bull pen, have you?"

"Darling, why do you say that?"

"Puh! Wouldn't put it past you!"

"I was calling Gavin. It's his first day."

"I like Gavin. They don't make them like Gavin any more."

"I'll tell him what you said someday," Don Wheeler said.

"Tell him myself," Hope said.

Then she looked at her husband's face and saw the truth.

It had taken Cy Walker almost the entire recess to get the man on the phone, but he finally did, just before court was to reconvene.

In the folder of mail Donna had handed her boss that morning was an offer from the largest law firm in the state's capital, a concrete offer with a starting date. He was being offered a bare five hundred dollars a year more than he got as county prosecutor.

"It just wouldn't pay me to move," he said to the firm's senior partner.

The man was cordial. "I really wish we could do better," he said. "But I'm sure you can appreciate our problem. Read the morning papers, ho, ho, here we go again, life on a precipice?"

"Maybe we could meet halfway," Cy suggested. "If the firm would help me buy a house up there—"

"Then what could we possibly tell the other fellows in the office?"

"Could you pay for our transportation?"

"Suppose I do that personally, out of my own pocket."

"I couldn't accept it."

"Look Cy—may I call you Cy right from the start—you've got a week. That's really the best we can do. Think it over. Whatever you decide you have our cordial esteem."

"*You* think it over," Cy said. "Goodbye."

His anger lasted the three seconds it took him to remember that his resignation as county prosecutor had gone through.

When Cy put the ruddy-faced pathologist on the stand he gave the foreman a photograph of Vin Connor, naked on the stone slab of the morgue, asked him to pass it around.

Alan suspected that when the jurors looked at the photograph they saw only the savagery in the boy's face. The five little black holes in the body, once seen, said nothing more. The face, on the other hand, was a terrifying sculpture which revealed to the jury everything about the drug culture that threatened the decent society of their Southwest land.

Alan decided he had to convince Cy to put the issue of the trial on the broadest-possible base, justice was being defended here, the tradition itself, did it or did it not work? Alan began to write. "What trust can our children ever again have if—"

Bailiff Lansing handed him a folded note. Earl McCord was asking him to lunch.

"I've just talked to the base commander." McCord touched his mouth with a corner of his napkin to remove a dab of lime jello.

"Why don't you reconsider and have some of this blueberry pie?" Alan said. "It's delicious."

"You are to go back to the base immediately after lunch, and you are to be restricted to the base until you receive other instructions." He lifted more jello to his mouth. "That's an order," he added.

Alan carefully mixed coffee ice cream and blueberry filling on his spoon. "I think I'll hang around here a while," he said.

"That's a decision I'd give a great deal of thought to if I were you." McCord signaled for the check.

"I have." Alan nodded a few times, then gave McCord Michael Winter's best faraway look.

The afternoon session opened with the entrance of the family of Master Sergeant Flores. They had gone to the other extreme, broken out every black or navy dress in their closets. There was a faint aroma of moth repellent.

Gavin's immediate impression was that they were rushing Flores's funeral.

The jury, however, saw that the man on trial was proud of his family, heartened by their presence. For them, the family in black was a flash-forward of what must not be allowed to happen.

Cy was finishing with the pathologist, identifying each bullet, where it had entered the body, what internal damage it had done. He made particular reference to the two bullet holes below the line of pubic hair.

But Alan saw again that Cy's tactics weren't working as he had hoped. The boy's groin was covered by a card bearing his name and morgue record number. But the presence of that penis under the card was felt by the members of the jury, male and female, all middle-aged, as another kind of threat, one they all knew well but couldn't have talked about.

He's playing into Gavin's hands, Alan thought.

Alan noticed that although Cy showed the jury a photograph of the black boy Flores had killed and pointed out the two bullet holes at the base of the skull, he did not pass that photograph around. Apparently he had decided to play down the second killing. Alan thought this a mistake, too.

He got up and left the court. He would write a brief for Cy, urge another attack, list the points that must be made, perhaps even sketch out what his closing remarks should be, that, too.

He had to find a quiet place to think.

While Cy was putting on record the testimony of the white A.P. that Vin Connor did not have a weapon, that of the black A.P. that Cesario Flores did have, evidence from the police that there was no sign of drugs, Earl McCord was looking for Kidd.

He found him on a white stool in a corner of the men's room.

"What are you doing in here?" he asked.

"Writing. Kindly don't disturb me."

"Walker's putting you on the stand."

"When? You just told me to go back to the base."

"Next. Any minute now."

"Send somebody for me when the time comes."

The man trailing Michael had an uneventful afternoon. He saw Michael put the metal case he was carrying in a white Karmann-Ghia, whose license number the man jotted down. As Michael walked away, the man took a peek inside the case. It was empty. Then he followed Michael to Queen Street; the boy was either exhausted or under the influence, it must be the latter, he looked like he was walking through a foot of water. From the middle of the next block he watched what Michael was watching, the movers carrying the new tenants' appliances into the house on Queen Street. When they were done, the man followed Michael back to the Karmann-Ghia, saw him enter it, put up the windows, and drop back out of sight. Twenty minutes later he took a peek. Michael was fast asleep over two bucket seats. He walked to a phone booth and called headquarters.

"Nothing," he said.

Gavin watched Alan on the stand. The man was up to something.

"Sergeant Flores was sitting in a wicker chair," Alan said, "fussing with his leg, not paying the least—"

"Fussing with his leg?" Cy prompted.

"Yes, sir. He was picking at a place with a knife's point. That was when we realized he had a bullet in it."

"Where?"

"Just above the knee."

"Did he seem deranged or—what has been suggested— insane, temporarily or any other way?"

"Quite the opposite." Alan looked at Gavin. "That's the truth, Gavin, I was there."

Judge Breen came down with his gavel. "The witness will confine himself to answering questions put to him," he said. "As a lawyer, he knows trial procedure."

"Your honor, Mr. McAndrews keeps glaring at me as if I was doing something wrong by telling the truth here."

"Your honor!" Gavin jumped to his feet.

"Witness, I am asking you again," Judge Breen said, "to confine yourself strictly to Mr. Walker's questions and not to address the lawyer for the defense or the jury."

Alan nodded. "I know trial procedure, your honor."

"Was that when Colonel Dowd ordered Sergeant Flores taken to the base hospital?" Cy asked.

"Yes, sir."

"Did you follow him there?"

"I did."

"What was his behavior there? Calm? Perfectly at—?"

"Your honor," Gavin interrupted, "I wonder if you could find a way to influence the county prosecutor to refrain from putting words in the witness's—"

"Well, here are my own words," Alan said, "Flores was enjoying the calm that follows victory."

"Then you wouldn't characterize his behavior as that of a person who was temporarily insane."

Gavin had had enough. "Your honor," he pleaded. "This is a judgment to which I will produce the expert testimony of two qualified psychiatrists. It is not an easy judgment to make. Perhaps the very fact that he behaved so calmly in these circumstances—"

"You should have seen him," Alan said.

Judge Breen came down with his gavel. "Mr. Walker," he said. "I will hold you responsible the next time your witness breaks trial procedure."

"Go on," Cy said, "and please address no one but me."

"He was sitting on the operating table," Alan continued, "and he said, 'Can somebody get me some strawberry ice cream?' The medics were probing his wound, so I went for it."

"And then?"

"He ate it, all of it, and fell asleep like a baby. So I got talking to the medics. They were amazed at what the sergeant had told them while—"

"Objection, your honor," Gavin said. "We can't have what this witness says the medics said Sergeant Flores said. If those doctors have anything of value to contribute, let them be——"

"But, Gavin, they've been shipped overseas," Alan said. "You told me so yourself."

Gavin had forgotten he'd told that to Alan in their first good days, rather boastfully, as he now remembered.

"I have no further questions for this witness at this time," Cy said. It was a good moment for the jury to gather impressions.

"I have one." Gavin advanced on Alan stiff-legged. "Lieutenant, you didn't tell us how Sergeant Flores got the wound."

"That's because, by the rules of court procedure, I must confine myself strictly to what I've seen or heard. Flores *said* he shot himself."

"Would you maintain that is the conduct of a man in perfect possession of his good sense?"

"I'm sure you'll have expert testimony to that," Alan said.

Gavin controlled himself. "That is all I have for this witness, your honor," and walked away.

Cy was up again and, with the judge's permission, asked, "When in the series of events that night did Sergeant Flores shoot himself?"

"He didn't say."

"Did he mention anything about a struggle?"

"No, sir."

"Did the medics who were rushed overseas—?"

"I object to that!" Gavin was on his feet, furious. "That's a scurrilous allegation!"

"He's absolutely right, Mr. Walker," Judge Breen said.

"Absolutely right, again, is he?"

Judge Breen boiled over. "You should remember, Mr. County Prosecutor, that when you are impudent and disrespectful to me, you are being impudent and disrespectful to the Bench, and the Bench, Mr. Walker, has means provided by law, means with which you are familiar." Thurston Breen looked at the jury, noticed how impressed they were, and his tone of warning became even more majestic. "The Bench does not want to use the weapon of contempt, but you can believe me that any further—"

At this moment the sliding door behind the judge's chair opened, and the court saw the arm of a woman reach in to hand Judge Breen a slip of paper. His secretary had typed out some closing prices.

He had lost, while presiding over the case that day, close to three thousand dollars.

————————————————

"Sergeant Flores," Cy said in a gentle tone, "I have only three questions to ask you. You can answer them with one word, yes or no, then I'll let you step down."

Cy's voice suggested concern and mercy.

"Sergeant Flores, did you shoot five bullets into the body of Vin Connor?"

Cesario did not raise his head. "Yes, sir," he said.

"Did you mean to kill him?"

"Yes, sir."

"Did you plan it beforehand?"

"Yes, sir."

"I have no further questions, your honor," Cy said. Then he looked at Gavin.

"Sergeant Flores," Gavin began, "I wonder if you could, slowly and in your own time, tell us the full story leading up to and—I'm really sorry to have to put you through this."

"Sure I will, if you want me to, sure."

Cesario sighed, didn't seem to have the strength to do what Gavin was asking. He looked around at the faces waiting for him to speak, then closed his eyes.

When he opened them again, he apologized to the jury. "I'm awfully tired, you know. I don't seem to be able to rest up." Then he turned to his defender. "It's just what everybody said. The papers had it right. But if you—" He looked back at the jury. "I don't want to take up any more of your time," he said.

"Your honor," Cy started, "I must object—"

"Maybe if I could just say this, your honor, judge." The man was continuing, and Thurston Breen knew the feeling for Cesario in that courtroom was so strong no one who wanted the approval of that community would dare stop him.

Cy decided to let him go, too. After all, the man was about to make a confession of guilt.

"You men all have work to do and you women children of your own to take care of. So maybe I can just say it, and you can go home, and I can go to where they're keeping me. Because what that air force officer was trying to get on the record before, that was true, what I said to the doctors in the hospital, I would do what I did right over again."

Both lawyers were silent, each for his own reason.

"I love her more than anything, my daughter. I couldn't let her go on that way, could I?"

Thurston Breen was wishing he was that close to his child.

"Perhaps if I was a better man I could have figured out, with the help of the *madrecita,* some way I didn't have to do what I did. I'm not what they call an educated man, I know something about the XF-4A jet engine, but not much else."

At that instant, Juana got up and walked out of the courtroom.

Her father watched her go, every step to the door and out. Then he said, "She can't stand the sight of me," and he smiled ruefully at the jury and looked at the empty chair. "God is punishing me," he said, then continued. "The truth is, I didn't have anything against those kids. I liked them. Isn't that strange? Still, they were hurting my daughter. I became convinced of that. So—"

Then he switched. "Another thing. I see now that I brought disgrace to the air force, which is the service I admire most on earth. Everything I am I owe to the—what was I saying? Before?"

He looked at Gavin for help, but Gavin didn't offer. Cy began to feel that this stumbling confession of guilt was the thing most likely to get the man off, didn't know how to stop it.

Cesario had dropped the points of his elbows on his knees and hunched over, once a massive man, now wasted and drawn. He lifted his head. "Sorry," he said.

"Take your time," Gavin reached out.

"Thank you," Cesario said. "I want to take any load of worry off you people. I knew it was going to cost me my life when I did it. It was worth it to me not to have her with that fellow."

The jurors remembered the photograph of Vinnie they'd studied; not the bullet holes in the body but the hatred in the face.

"Convict me," Cesario continued, speaking to the members of the jury as individuals now. "That would be a great thing for me. My daughter would know—if I gave my life for her—she'd remember that all her life."

He dropped his eyes again, and the jury heard him ask, "Wouldn't she?"

Then he gave the most delicate, the most Latin shrug and said, "Mr. McAndrews, if you like I can tell the story now."

"You don't have to," Gavin said. "You can step down now."

"I'm sorry if I took too much time," Cesario said. He walked slowly to his chair, straightened his blouse as he sat. The jury could hear his heavy breathing.

Cy knew that at the end of a day which should have been all his, something had gone wrong.

Judge Breen knew it, too. "Call your next witness," he said briskly.

The bailiff told Judge Breen: Juana wasn't in the anteroom. She had left the building, he thought.

"Will counsel approach the bench?" Judge Breen asked.

There was a whispered consultation. "She's my next witness," Cy protested, loudly enough for the jury to hear. A look from Judge Breen moderated his tone. The discussion at the bench continued in whispers.

The jury could see that the prosecutor was put out by the disappearance of his next witness, but they were not impressed. Whatever the trial had been for them originally, it was a drama now: how to reunite a family, a father and daughter, the most traditional American love unit.

From now on it was only a matter of how to legally effect what the tide of the jury's feelings already demanded.

As they filed into the jury room, Bailiff Lansing checked them off, making sure he had them all. Then he closed the door and locked it. Some of his charges were past fifty and didn't hold their water the way they used to; Lansing admitted elders to the facilities first.

Again he cautioned them against discussing the case. Not that it wasn't a good idea to get them at ease with each other as early as possible; it would save time later on.

The foreman was a quiet, sober man who worked for a corporation that manufactured airplanes. One thing puzzled this man; after asking others on the jury what *"madrecita"* meant, he asked Lansing.

"It's an affectionate term for the Mother of God, Mex for little mother," Lansing told him. "Sergeant Flores, as you have seen, is a religious man."

The men and women of the jury nodded; they were themselves religious.

"We might take our first vote on where we eat," Lansing said. "We can eat at Jack's, you know Jack's, steaks, or that little Mexican place on Boyle Street, Las Palmas, it's very clean. I recommend it."

Las Palmas won.

Cesario Flores was mistaken. Juana had not left the court-room because she "couldn't stand the sight of her father." The fact was that she admired his forthrightness, was par-ticularly affected when he said he loved her better than anything in the world. Gavin had taken her to a Chinese restaurant the night before and, over sweet and sour pork, had made it clear that her father's life was in her hands. She felt herself about to be untrue to Vinnie; he was already growing dim in her memory.

A few minutes before she got up and left the courtroom, her left eyelid had begun to twitch. She rubbed hard, closed the eye, waited; the twitch wouldn't stop. This scared her; she had to break the short circuit in the reflex that controlled that eyelid, had to have something to quiet her nerves.

A person who knew drugs might have guessed by the bug-eyed urgency with which she left the court what she was out to find.

On the lawn she saw all Queen Street, along with many faces she didn't recognize. Or was it that they were looking at her differently, she wondered, as if at an outsider?

Juana didn't trust herself any more. Was she imagining it bad? She had begun doing that lately, imagining it bad. Then she saw the familiar face. "Oh, Sandy," Juana said, "can you—?" She plumped down next to her. "It's like I start shaking and can't—"

Sandy, by temperament an aristocrat, was unconcerned about anyone's favor or good opinion. The others had turned their faces away from Juana when she passed them; not Sandy. Sandy looked at her and said, "It's all that Chinese food your new boyfriend's been feeding you. Get away from me."

Juana sat where she was, her eyes lowered. After a minute she got up. "Fuck you all!" she said to Sandy. "I knew you hated me from the beginning, didn't you?"

"I did," Sandy said, "I sure as hell did."

"Because I got Vinnie?"

"Because you got two faces," Sandy said. "Now split. I've got nothing for you."

Juana stood there affronting them all. Her eyelid had stopped twitching. The admission of hatred had acted like a drug, stimulating the pumping of blood, bringing fresh color to her cheeks.

"Juanie!" Elizabeth was calling from the courthouse door. "We're going to his office, Mr. McAndrews. He wants to talk to us. Juana!"

The police were busy that afternoon, closing down a free store some of the university students had set up and refused to vacate when the owner of the building got a court order. By the time a squad car got to the courthouse parking lot to check on the Karmann-Ghia, it was gone.

The chief alerted every squad car in the city. Three cars closed in on the convertible as it was pulling into the parking area at the side of an apartment house. The police were in time to see Lieutenant Kidd and his bedraggled companion go into the condominium. The air force lieutenant was talking energetically; the boy with the shoulder-length curls didn't seem to be listening.

One of their number walked into the hallway of the place and made a list of the tenants, fifty-six in all. The names were transmitted by short wave to police headquarters, processed; the only person in the condominium who had any connection with the case was Donna Lynn, secretary to the county prosecutor.

A search into Miss Lynn's connections and past turned up nothing special. But headquarters further analyzed the situation and decided that Lieutenant Kidd and the "hippie leader" were probably guests in Miss Lynn's apartment.

At the instant this conclusion was being reached Michael was in Donna's shower; Donna was picking his clothes up off the floor. What she saw aroused her mother feeling. Not only was the T-shirt filthy, the socks rags, but the boy did not wear underwear and the inside seam of his trousers' seat was soiled beyond redemption. There was nothing to do but throw the whole mess away.

Alan, meanwhile, was watching the evening news.

When Michael came out of the bathroom Donna had a towel ready, one of her best, part of the trousseau she had prepared for her marriage, a seven-week catastrophe. Michael, not observing the usual modesties, did a poor job drying himself; she had to finish it. She felt how thin he had become, his chest caved in, his ribs stretching the skin. When she was through he seemed exhausted again, sat on the edge of her sofa, and didn't say anything.

"Are you hungry?" Donna asked.

He nodded, but when she put food in front of him, he didn't eat. He seemed to be sleepy.

"Wake me up at one o'clock," he said.

"In the morning?" She took him by the hand, led him into the bedroom, threw her bed open, and told him to get in. He did.

"Tell Alan we're going at one-thirty," he said as he fell asleep.

A few minutes later Donna's roommate came home, a motherly soul who clerked at a large department store. When Donna showed her Michael's clothes, they decided to go to the store and get a complete outfit, a light suit, shirt, tie, socks, underwear, shoes, everything.

"He won't wear a suit," Alan said. "Get him a new pair of Lee's."

"He'll wear it," Donna said.

The door swung open and Mr. Don Wheeler entered, Gavin following at a respectful distance.

"They all here?" he asked Gavin, looking at the Flores family.

"Yes, sir."

"The girl, too?"

Gavin indicated Juana, who was standing against the wall next to the door they had just entered.

Wheeler turned. "Are you the one who had the temerity to walk out of the courtroom this afternoon while your father was testifying?"

Juana nodded. Her eyelid was twitching again.

Wheeler looked at the others, wondering how his office ever got mixed up with such a crummy crew. He sighed.

But when he spoke his voice was measured, controlled.

"Thank you for coming," he said, a way of opening a meeting he always used. "I asked Mr. McAndrews to bring you together so I could tell you that our firm is dropping the defense of Sergeant Flores. You will have to look for other counsel."

Twenty minutes later, everything was straightened out. "Let me say it again so there will be no misunderstanding whatsoever," Wheeler said. "You have agreed, all of you, to do everything that Mr. McAndrews asks you to do, no matter what it is? Is that correct?"

There was a murmur of assent.

"Speak up, please," Wheeler said. He looked at Juana.

"Yes, sir," Juana said.

"Very well," Wheeler said, and walked over to Juana, sat next to her, and spoke to her softly.

"Miss Juana, your father feels defeated now. He has resigned himself to death. But I know the man a little, and I'm here to tell you that if you pay him the smallest gesture of concern, not love, not even approval of what he did, but simple concern for a man whose thoughts have been only of you and who, for your sake, Miss Juana, unless we act quickly, very quickly, is going to be locked in a room, a room from which—"

"Stop it," Juana cried suddenly, "please—"

"Do you want that, Miss Juana?"

Juana made a sound.

"Speak up!"

"No, sir, I don't."

"Then why have you been making it inevitable? Reach out your hand, girl, touch him! That man will be reborn. He will fight for his life, I know it! I believe now that this man shouldn't—and will not—serve a single day. Gavin! Do you hear me, Gavin? Not one single day!"

"I hear you, sir," Gavin said.

Later, when the family had left and Wheeler was preparing to return to the hospital where the chill in his wife's feet had mounted to her ankles, Gavin walked him to his car. Wheeler said, "Imagine having to talk a girl into defending her father! I despise those people, Gavin."

Gavin nodded solemnly. "I'll be over to the hospital later," he said.

"I don't know if Mrs. Wheeler will recognize you, but if she does, she'll be glad to see you."

He put his hand on Gavin's hair and roughed it up. "I think a lot of you, Gavin," he said. Then he made one of his jokes. "What did I tell you yesterday that you swore you'd never forget that you have already forgotten?"

"Temp insanity, let the jury see it first."

"Wrong. Think, boy, think!"

"Try the hippies. Right?"

"Try the shit out of them! Pile it on. They're dirty! They're ignorant! They're liars! They're diseased! They're drugged! They're pregnant! And there's one under the bed of every member of that jury of geldings and maiden aunts."

He stopped, his energy suddenly collapsed. "Poor Hope," he said, "the good ones go." He sighed. "Look what's left! Offal!" Then he got in his car and drove away.

———————————————————

Donna was shaking Michael gently. "It's one-thirty, but don't get up, baby. Sleep, you need it."

"Wake him up, wake Alan." Michael sat up with a jerk of his body. He seemed to shiver.

"Michael, baby," she felt his chest under her hands, a bird cage covered with cloth, his heart fluttering, "where the hell are you going this time of night?"

Michael stood. His cock was erect. Donna wanted to kiss it. It seemed to be the biggest thing on the boy.

Michael looked around for his pants. "You know a good lawyer?"

"I know a lot of lawyers, all I've ever done my whole lousy life is work for lawyers."

"A labor lawyer? Civil rights? Some new kid? Someone honest?"

"I've always worked for lawyers who paid salaries, that's been my trouble. You have to pay a fee before they'll say good morning."

"I'll have money."

"You going out this time of night looking for an honest lawyer? Baby, go back to bed, I'll get in with you if you go back to bed."

He put on the pants of the suit she'd bought him.

Donna went into the other room and woke Alan.

Outside, the two police in business suits were fast asleep in their unmarked car. Alan and Michael drove off without a tail.

"Throw a right here. Turn off your lights."

They moved slowly down Queen Street, and Michael told him where to stop, across the street from the house.

"What are you going to do?" Alan asked.

"I'm trusting you now, so don't ask questions."

Michael opened the door, swinging it out as far as it would go so he could take out the long metal case. "Get down in your seat and sit still, don't turn on the radio or anything dumb like that," he said. "I'll be right back."

Michael crossed the street and disappeared alongside one of the houses.

Alan hesitated, then did as he was told, got down in his seat as far as he could. Just as he settled, he heard the sound of breaking glass.

All Michael had wanted to do was clear a hole around the window clasp, but the putty was old and loose and a corner of heavy glass had come down on his hand, cutting it. Michael wiped it on his new pants, then climbed into the house. The drops of blood falling on the floor didn't matter, he figured; there was no way to conceal that the house had been broken into.

He walked through the silent rooms, smelling the new paint. On the floor his tread was gummy. The only sound was the hum of the refrigerator turned on to be ready for the new tenants in the morning. When he got to the room where Vinnie used to sleep, Michael pulled a screwdriver out of his pocket and felt around till he found the crack between the strips of flooring. Then he pried up a plank.

The space under the floor was empty. The gun was gone. So was the mayonnaise jar.

A squad car driving down Queen Street came on the Karmann-Ghia by accident, drove past it, turned the corner, stopped, and called H.Q. for instructions. They were told to wait till the license number was checked. They waited. "That's the one!" the answer came.

The police in business suits, sleeping in their unmarked car outside Donna's, were rudely awakened. "What the hell is he doing out this time of night?" they protested.

"That's what you're supposed to tell us."

"What should we do?" the squad car asked from Queen Street.

"Keep your eye on them till we get back to you."

"He's coming out of the house again," the squad car reported three minutes later, "carrying some kind of suitcase. What do you want us to do?"

"Do what comes natural, nothing. Tail him when he moves, but don't lose him again."

"Let's go," Michael said, getting into the car.

"Where?" Alan asked.

"Donna's."

Alan could see Michael was upset. "What happened?" he asked.

"Nothing," Michael said. "Anyway, that's settled—" He put his hand between his legs and pressed on it to stop the flow of blood.

"What's settled?"

"That is," Michael said, nodding his head a few times. "That's the end of that."

The police outside Donna's condominium waited for the white convertible to reappear, eager to make an arrest to justify themselves.

The squad car following the Karmann-Ghia stayed close, its lights off. "Maybe we ought to see what's in that suitcase?" they asked headquarters.

The captain in charge, not wanting the responsibility for a false arrest, called the chief of police. The chief said he'd get right back, to keep the line open.

Alan drove into the parking lot outside Donna's, the squad car following. The occupants of the unmarked car waited.

The chief woke Colonel Dowd. "I don't know the ins and outs of this," he said. "Why don't you call Don Wheeler?"

Michael was pulling the case out of the back of the white car.

The door of the unmarked car was ajar.

The chief got Mr. Wheeler at the hospital. "There seems to be a conspiracy here," Wheeler reasoned. "Why don't you wait, he'll lead you to the others, and you'll get all of them. What the hell is that air force lieutenant doing in this anyway? Christ!"

At that instant the police in business suits piled out of their unmarked car and rushed Alan and Michael, jerking the suitcase out of Michael's hands.

There was a shout from the squad car, which had pulled up alongside. Something was said, Michael and Alan couldn't hear it, but it caused the men in the business suits to apologize. Shamefaced, they gave the case back, got into their unmarked car, and made a show of driving off.

It all happened so quickly that Michael and Alan didn't react.

Donna was waiting for them. Alan started to tell her what had happened, but Michael walked into the bedroom. He took off his clothes, got into bed, face down. "Wake me when you get up," he said. "I want to sleep."

Donna closed the door.

"He's getting in some kind of bad trouble," Alan said to her. "Find out what he's doing."

Then he described the incident with the police.

"Are they still out there?"

"Sure they are," Alan said. "I tell you he's up to something that—well, he won't tell me, he doesn't trust me."

Donna wasn't sure she did either. "He didn't tell you what he was doing in that house?"

"Not a word. You've got to find out and tell me, okay?"

"Okay." Now Donna was sure she didn't like Alan.

"Because they'll take him apart. All he's got to do is give them an excuse. Did you see his hand? Don't let him get out of here without me. If he wakes, wake me. Okay?"

"Okay. What about his hand?"

"It's bleeding."

Donna had to wake Michael to clean the cut, which was small but deep. "This needs a stitch," she said. Michael shook his head. "Well then hold still and I'll see what I can do."

"Alan tell you what happened?" he asked her.

Donna came close. "You trust him?"

"Why?"

"He asked me to find out what you were up to and tell him. Says he's worried about you."

Michael nodded.

"Have to bandage this real tight, pull it together, so—" She stripped another band-aid. "What did you want a lawyer for?"

"I don't any more. About Alan, sometimes I think he's okay. But I always have to remember he used to work with Mr. McAndrews, used to tell him what I said and what I was thinking. You know Mr. McAndrews?"

"I used to work for him."

"Would he get the police to follow me and—?"

"Yes."

"What else would he do?"

"To win a case? Name it."

"What makes you so sure?"

"I know him. I used to be his girl."

"For real?"

"Well, no, not that, not real, but—you better go to sleep now." She'd finished the bandaging. "This will hold all right." She looked at him. "Feel okay?"

"Pretty good."

"Mind if I—?"

Every other man Donna had gotten into bed with had immediately tried to put it into her, ready or not. Michael accepted her against him as if they'd been lovers for years, friends. Donna, finding herself not taken, had mixed feelings.

"Do you mind that I was his girl?" she asked.

"Why should I?" Michael said.

"Well," Donna said, "anything you want to know about Gavin the Mac, I'm the authority."

Michael nodded. They were silent for quite a while; then Donna took off the T-shirt she was wearing. "This is Gavin's," she said, and threw it on the floor.

"How long were you his—?"

"That turned you off, didn't it? Off me?"

"No, why?"

"You mean you do like me?"

"Why do you keep worrying about that? Sure I like you, I think you're a good person."

"That's all I ever wanted to be."

"You got a boyfriend?"

"Hasn't everybody? But I go to *his* place. So I can leave any time. After Gavin I don't trust anybody, to give myself to, I mean. Look, you want to hear about Gavin?"

"Yeah."

"He's going to be president of the United States."

"He's that smart?"

"Did I say smart? What he is is, throw him into a cage of tigers, he walks out and they send an ambulance for the tigers."

"You mean that, president of the United States?"

"That's a secret. Hasn't even told his wife. Well, he doesn't tell anybody anything. That man was fucking me for nearly two years and nobody ever found out."

"How'd he work that?"

"He had the right kind of linthead. Me. Mount Olive Junior College, for girls only, specializing in Catholic virgin squab from good homes. I graduated with honors and when I get out I've got nothing to get a job with but my legs. They're good legs, you noticed?"

"Yeah, they're O.K."

"Fuck you! So before you know it, I'm a leg model and they're photographing nothing on me from the crotch up. I had to go to college for that! Of course, that should have wised me up to the way men wanted me to be. But no, not me, I'm too pure, which means too dumb. So Gavin, he's making these business trips to Southern Cal, it turned out later, it's to see some other girl. He meets me in the intermissions, you might say. Well, anyway, you know the first time you see Gavin—you know—like that little limp, it gets to you. And he's so damned sure of himself, and I'm sure of nothing except the virgin birth. So before I know it I'm a member of the sorority, his. I'm crying at confession and half an hour later, I'm in the hay with him. He used to wait outside the church in his car and drive me right to the motel!"

"You mean that was his idea of—"

"Kicks. So then it happens to him, success, at twenty-five, the youngest member ever of Don Wheeler and Associates-at-Law. And he can't make those long California weekends any more. Respectability, that starts. So he decides to bring

me here, give me a job—I'd been going to secretarial school
—he picks me out of the whole harem. I feel honored, too.
He sets me up in a place. I was crazy, I mean crazy and
crazy about him, both. I was part of his baggage, he checked
me when he wanted to and picked me up when he wanted to.
When he said come, I came. I thought he had the only key
to the lock—"

Michael interrupted. "You got something against men?"

"No!" Donna said. "I got something against—maybe I do."

"You got something against me?"

"Well, you're not exactly a man, are you? You're more
of what you said I was—a person."

"I've never been able to hold a girl," Michael said without
regret. "I don't know why, but it doesn't last. Like my friend,
Vinnie, he used to treat them terrible, but they stayed with
him. Do women want to be scared, or dominated? I don't
do that."

She was silent, then she said, "I'm going to tell you the
truth, I still think of him, even though I hate him. Maybe
it's because of his arrogance, like you say, maybe I miss that.
He used to lay back and watch me camp on it, watch me
with that funny smile on his face. I can still see it. Like he
was doing me a favor, which I suppose he was. He'd lie
back and let me do the work, for openers. And it stayed up,
like forever, there was nothing I could do to make him come.
After a while I took it for what it was, a put-down, right?
Don't worry, he used to say to me—no pills for a good R.C.
girl—don't worry, I'm not like other men, I come when I
want to. And he did. When he wanted to. He used to keep
it up so long I got frantic, tired and frantic. I'd come and
come and he'd just look at me with that tight little smile.
Finally he'd decide, like now. Nothing to do with anything
that was happening between us, you understand. He had his
own best way of doing that, too. He'd lay me out on the
bed, face down, and he'd do me like a dog. He used to tell
me, you got nothing much up front, kid—his wife, Betty,
he was just courting her then, she's big-breasted—but what
an ass! Then he'd do me that way. That was the first thing
I remember resenting and having the nerve to say so. After
I left him I figured it out. I didn't like it because I couldn't
look at his face when he came, and he liked it because I

couldn't look at his face. Because when he finally did, he was weak, was like unarmed without his goddamn club. He'd fall over my back, helpless, and stay like that. He didn't want me to see him when he was weak."

"Why'd you stay with him?"

"I got pregnant—like everybody else. Now he can't get his wife pregnant, but he sure as hell did me. I could see from the day I told him how he resented it. Well, then I began to resent him back, better late than never. The one thing I wanted was the kid I had in me. I thought that might make some sense of my fucked-up life. So I told him I was going to have it, that I knew he'd never marry me and so on, but I was going to have it anyway."

"Why didn't you?"

"Well, brother Michael, that man got frantic! He told me people had begun to suspect I was his girl, what a disaster this would be if they knew about it. And you know the truth? I was enjoying it. I'd finally turned the tables on the son of a bitch. But I was too good, you know, too Catholic brought-up to think it right I should enjoy it. I was so sincere, I told him nobody would ever know, don't worry, and after the kid was born I'd move to another town. Of course you say that now, he said, but suppose later you think it over and get sore at me or if you get broke, it could be blackmail, you'd have something on me. And he got more and more frantic, then more and more abusive. He'd fuck me and hit me, then fuck me and hit me. Then what he did you wouldn't believe."

"I'll believe it."

"He went to my priest. I don't know if he gave him money or what or helped him in some way, those priests are awful political, but this one talked to me about being engaged now, Gavin was, and that we had both done wrong and all the rest of it. So I told him I wanted to keep the kid, what do you advise, Father, and he said he couldn't advise me.

"The day after the abortion instead of doing what he said he'd do, which was see me and be nice to me, which was all I wanted, Gavin dropped me. Six weeks later I was fired, and he was married. And I never saw him except around the courthouse. He's never spoken to me since, not a damned word. Not a look. I'm dead for him!"

"You should have had the kid."

"That's why I hate him. I know he wanted me to leave town. But I stayed, I did the circuit, every lawyer in this town and his close friends twice."

"Including Mr. Wheeler?"

"Him, too, they're all the same. I despise lawyers. All that big front shit about justice and right, that game they play that they know all the answers. When the fact is they're thieves, with their discreet bills, they're so damned crooked and so arrogant and so spoiled. You know a lawyer can have his pick, any woman in town? People are terrified of lawyers. They're the power in this country. If a boy wants to be a wheel, what does he do? Go to law school! Nixon and Mitchell. Every one of those Kennedys. Three-quarters of the Congress—they boast about that! Why isn't a philosopher president? Or a doctor? That would be more like it. Or a poet, a writer, a biologist, a guy that draws comic strips, anybody! No, it's always a lawyer. Bastards!"

"Why do you work for one, then?"

"Because I do everything I can, where it counts, to ruin them. That's why I gave you Cy Walker's diary and file. Because I could see when you kids came into his office that first day, you were so sincere and straight, and all that bastard had on his mind was how not to win the case and still make it look like he'd tried. If he got Flores executed, he'd be finished in this state. Half an hour before you kids came in he was on the telephone with a big law firm up north trying to get another job, feeling around, how they'd go if he won it and how they'd go if he lost it. He even asked my advice. I tell you, this is the age of the lawyers, kid, you haven't got a chance. They're the country!"

"We are."

"Bullshit! I know what's going on, and you're not going to beat them. Look at you! You're nothing but a soft-hearted bag of bones! Gavin McAndrews pushed me into that abortionist's office and told the man to pull the kid out of me. I should have taken a pistol and killed the son of a bitch, because that other stuff, please be nice, see my side of it, have pity and all that, it doesn't move them, they're the law. Like this trial—you want justice? Take a gun and shoot him dead, Flores. But don't wait for justice from the lawyers, because that's not what they're dealing. Hell, that Flores did just what they wanted him to do. When I heard you tell that to Walter, I knew you had the score. But I thought, he knows what the score is, but he can't do anything, he's too weak. It takes an assassin to kill an assassin. You've got to do something so terrible that they finally realize they can't get away with it any more."

"Donna," Michael whispered, "that's it! What I've been thinking."

"Then what you think is right. Only don't underestimate them. They know everything about everybody, and they know about you. They know you're in this house. I can't promise you they don't know you're in my bed. Like that fellow out there, your buddy, are you sure he's not at that door listening? They followed you down to the house where you went, did you know that? Who told them where you were all day?"

"I don't know."

"They followed you back here, and you saw what happened! And they have a reason for not taking you tonight. Did that occur to you?"

"No. It didn't."

"You're such a child to be playing this game. When I used to see you in that courtroom, sitting there studying the method of jury selection and all that shit, making your notes in your little book, figuring out how to fight these guys, all alone—I mean it was pitiful. Nothing but a child, so naive, so sweet, you know, you are sweet, let me kiss you, I got to kiss your mouth—"

Then she said, "I don't know why any girl would leave you. I wouldn't leave you for anybody on earth, if you would stay with me. But I know you wouldn't. I'm so scared for you, baby. I'm so frightened what's going to happen to you, you little skinny thing, you don't know what you're up against."

"I know the score. I found out."

"The more you know, the more you're in danger. And you don't seem to care what happens to you. You'll die. The moment I saw your sweet face, I said to myself, that boy is going to get killed. And I think you may want it, too."

"Donna, no one is going to kill me. And I don't want it,

but thank you, thank you for saying all that, and—I like you, Donna."

"Now you want me? Now?"

He laughed. "Sure I want you."

They made love and fell asleep.

All through that night, he writhed and turned. Finally, as the first light was coming in, Donna couldn't take it any more, woke him.

Rescued, he lay on his back, catching at the flying ends of what he'd been dreaming as it slipped away.

"You were going on like that all night," she said.

Suddenly he put his arms around her, his head in the space between her chin and her chest, eyes closed, breathing hard.

Donna held the child she'd lost.

Outside they could hear the garbage pickup in the alley below. Michael was recalling all she'd said to him the night before; the words he remembered again; the images, he saw.

He got out of bed. "Be right back."

In the other room the shades were drawn. Michael felt his way past Alan, asleep on the sofa, and into the kitchen, closing the door carefully before he turned on the light.

In the trash he found his old trousers, and in the back pocket wrapped in a piece of cigarette foil, a tiny square of blotting paper, and in the middle of that, a medallion of congealed white powder.

He decided not to drop the acid till Donna had gone to work. Slipping the tiny packet between the mattress and the spring, he got back into bed.

Donna opened her arms for him, put her leg between his and pressed. She wanted to comfort him, but he did not respond.

After a while he turned his back to her, curled knee to chin.

"What are you going to do today?" she asked.

"I got a lot to figure out," he said, without turning. "Is it all right if I stay here all day?"

"Stay here the rest of your life."

She got up and went into the bathroom. When she came back out, half an hour later, he was in the same position.

She dressed, then sat on the side of the bed. His eyes

were open, and she leaned forward to kiss them closed. "Sleep a while," she said, "you didn't rest all night." Then she got up to leave. "But you better be here when I get back tonight, hear?"

When Donna had gone, Michael closed the bedroom door —Alan was still fast asleep—got back into bed and took the first step on his trip. It was, as he saw it, a voyage into light.

CHAPTER FOUR

_____

The youngest of Cy Walker's three sons, the only one who still entered his parents' bedroom without knocking, brought his father the morning paper. "Your picture's in there," he said.

"How's he look?" Corky Walker asked.

"Terrible," the boy said. "Who's that other guy?"

Marian Kidd gave up trying to sleep, put on the coffee, then opened the front door and picked up the morning paper. On the front page was Alan's picture and the story of his about-face.

Some fifty of the kids passed the night on the courthouse lawn. They were still burned up over the way the police had closed—and trashed—their free store. This pig action made a two-inch item on an inside page of the paper. A story on the front page made them feel better. "What's coming," a black revolutionary had declared in an eastern city, "is a period of sabotage of capitalist institutions and symbolic murder."

This quote also made Don Wheeler feel better. He read it to Gavin over the phone just down the hall from Hope's hospital room. "That'll help us," he said.

"With the case? Sure it will," Gavin agreed.

230

"Stuff the case!" Wheeler said. "I mean it will wake people up to what's going on inside those bastards' heads."

Judge Thurston Breen, at his French toast, was reading an adjoining column which, as if to immediately confirm the black leader's prediction, reported an explosion in a New York police station. The judge showed the story to his wife. Their only son was at college in that city, and he wore his hair long.

When Mrs. Muriel Dowd showed her husband the newspaper, the colonel's reaction was to pick up the phone and give orders that Lieutenant Alan Kidd be brought back to the base, by force if necessary, and be there confined.

Juana couldn't remember, looking at Alan's picture, whether she'd been with him or not. Such is fame.

On his way in, Cy thought things over. He knew his own case had gone reasonably well; he knew he might not do that well again. The story of the bomb explosion would hurt his cause. Today'd be the best time to go for a settlement. Later, as he walked through the herd of kids on the courthouse lawn, Cy was applauded, a public demonstration of favor he would rather have done without. Yes, he decided, push hard till noon, then, during the lunch break, settle.

Four young executives—so they appeared to be—drove into town. Each arrived in his own rented car, each stayed at a different motel. Later they met at the office of the Grand Mesa Copper Company.

There was no Grand Mesa Copper Company.

As they sat around discussing the news in the morning paper, there was a knock on the door. Two college undergraduates were ushered in.

The four men put their informants through a rigorous questioning.

"About symbolic murder, what do you kids mean by that?" they asked.

"Like the buddhist monks burning themselves," one of

the students explained. "It's a way of making death mean something."

Marian had pleaded with her father to give her that one day, one last chance. Reluctantly he'd agreed. After giving her the address of Donna's apartment, where Alan was staying, he warned her, "But if he's not here for supper, I'll bring him in like a pig in a sling."

She couldn't make up her mind what to wear, realized she didn't know, after five years of marriage, what there was about her that turned her husband on. If anything! Now, in this crisis, she certainly should know what tack to take: plead, flirt, insist, reason, play helpless?

A pants suit, she decided, with a ruffled blouse. This costume would conceal her weak points, slightly meaty legs, and put a mystery around her breasts which were fine but placed low. The coat of the rust-colored suit worried her a little; it was severe and might give her a boss-lady look. But open, loose? She decided it was okay.

Anyway, her husband had never shown much interest in her; he wasn't, she'd always told herself, very highly sexed. As she dressed, she began, for the first time, to consider other possibilities. Perhaps this crisis was a good thing; perhaps now they might really sort things out.

———————————————————

Cy had a good morning. His decision to offer an out-of-court settlement that day had taken pressure off him.

And Elsa Flores, that morning, was a perfect foil. She'd obviously been coached to answer "I don't remember" whenever she was in trouble, and Cy had her in trouble most of the time. "You do remember there were shots, your husband shot and killed Mr. Vincent Connor, you do remember that? That's what this trial is all about, does that refresh your memory? Now, did these shots take place after the young man came into the house?"

"I don't remember."

"Well, there were shots, right?"

"I didn't hear them. The television was on."

Cy made a show of collapsing. "You mean to tell us you

couldn't hear shots fired in your own house because a television program drowned them out?"

"Why not? Yes." Despite herself she looked at Gavin.

"What was the program, do you remember that?"

"Some kind of gangster film, cheap stuff."

"And, of course, the shots were synchronized precisely to drown out the shots that were fired in the very next room, the ones that killed Vincent—?"

"It's possible!"

"Mrs. Flores!"

"Well! It's possible—why not?"

"That must have been one loud TV show!"

People in the room laughed. Breen silenced them with his gavel, but they kept on whispering. Mrs. Flores succeeded where the judge had failed; she glared at the spectators. "Manners don't exist in this country," she said.

"Tell me, Mrs. Flores," Cy said, "are you a truthful person?"

"I have told the truth always."

"What were you doing at the time the shots were fired?"

"I was talking to my daughter, Juana."

"What about, may I ask?"

"A private matter."

"And since it was a private matter, you certainly weren't shouting, were you, you certainly wouldn't want the younger girls in the room to hear, is that correct?"

"That is correct."

"You mean you were able," Cy pressed on, "to talk in an intimate, private tone to your daughter despite the gangster film on the TV screen right next to you where they were shooting it up so continuously that you couldn't hear the five pistol shots your husband fired into the body of Vincent Connor?"

Mrs. Flores looked at Gavin, openly.

"Did you forget what you were supposed to say, Mrs. Flores? Was it, perhaps, 'I don't remember'?"

Elsa searched in her bag for a kleenex. Cy brought her one from a box at his table. "Here we are," he said with a flourish of courtesy. She glared at him, and Cy turned to Gavin. "I think she wants some help from you," he said, "she doesn't know what you want her to say."

Gavin didn't object. He instinctively knew what Cy did

not, that when Cy was winning, the jury liked him least.

"My truth has never been doubted—by anyone," she said. "My word—by anyone! Ever!" Then she was in tears again.

Through it all ex-Master Sergeant Flores did not once stir, not a muscle, not a turn of the head.

"Your witness," Cy said.

Gavin let Cy Walker's victim sit there sobbing.

"Mr. Andrews," Judge Breen finally had to ask, "are you going to question the witness?"

"Not in the condition to which she has been reduced," Gavin said. He looked at the jury, saw that even if Elsa had lost them he had not. "Will it be all right, your honor, if we give her a rest? You can step down, Mrs. Flores," he continued without waiting for the judge's answer, went to the witness chair, extended his hand, and escorted her out of the courtroom.

"I suppose," Judge Breen said, "we should proceed with the next witness."

Knowing that the Flores girls had been coached, Cy put them on the stand in turn, asking them to confirm that the signatures on the statements they made the night of the murders were theirs. He then had the transcripts marked as exhibits.

What the court reporter then read in a voice without expression established incontrovertibly that the girls' father had invited—"ordered," Elizabeth had said—Vin Connor to the base; had insisted that he come out to his house; had been seen by Elizabeth loading a pistol an hour before the killing, which meant premeditation; had fired the shots immediately after the boy entered the house, which meant there had been no time for discussion, argument, or struggle. Both girls' statements gave the impression, furthermore, that during the minutes before the killing, their father had been composed and quietly determined.

Cy commented only that since memories had been failing that morning, he was fortunate to have these transcripts taken within an hour of the murder, before the witnesses' memories had had a chance to fade.

The most damaging thing in the girls' statements was Juana's assertion that she had warned Vinnie not to come out to the house, that she knew her father had a gun and intended to use it.

Which destroyed the defense's defense: that Sergeant Flores had gone temporarily insane at the sight of a boy who forced his way into his house to abduct his daughter.

Juana agreed, sentence by sentence, that what Cy was reading the jury was precisely what she had said that night. Cy's voice had gotten softer and gentler, his manner less and less aggressive.

The facts spoke for themselves.

Cy and Gavin stood in front of adjoining urinals.

"You're missing out on a lot of good golf today," Cy said. It was the opening day of the Desert Cup.

"I know it," Gavin said. Gavin, one of the officers of the club where the tournament was taking place, had been photographed last year handing an enormous cup of baroque silver-work to the winner.

"I'm not eager to hurt that family, Gavin," Cy said. "Christ knows they've had enough pain for a lifetime. We'll take murder two. With good behavior, the man will be out in five years."

"Uh-huh," Gavin said.

"With a little push here and there, he could be out in three. Where you going for lunch?"

"Cross the street, I guess."

"Suggestion. Why don't you see if you can get hold of Mr. Wheeler. We can meet tonight and wrap this up in five quick minutes."

"He's at the hospital. You know his wife's dying?"

"Sorry to hear that—"

"But I'll be talking to him sometime this afternoon."

"Do that."

As he walked down the stairs, Cy was pleased. Gavin seemed in favor of his offer. When he got to the front door he hesitated, then turned back, walked through a long series of corridors and out the back door. He didn't want to chance being publicly applauded again by the wrong people.

Michael could hear his parents quarreling in the next room. This time he didn't put his fingers in his ears, wasn't terrified; he listened.

It was difficult because there were other sounds in his head, too.

He heard his father say something he couldn't make out, calming his mother down as he always had when Michael was a kid, probably lying to her, as he always had—

Then he heard his mother, "I don't care what he is to you." His father said, "Shshsh," then murmured something, and he heard his mother again, "I can't feel sorry for him. I'm thinking of my own life, do you mind? And I want him out of it!"

Then Michael heard footsteps, and Donna's bedroom door was thrown open and someone said, "I want you the hell out of our life! Do you hear me?"

What Marian saw stopped her as if she'd run into a brick wall. Naked, on a disordered bed, was Michael, bones and skin, his eyes red and swollen. The muscles of his stomach clenching, his attention insecure, shifting from one thing to another, never fixed.

Marian stood in shock.

For Michael time was scrambled, seconds were hours, hours instants. There was distance without directions. The colors he saw were neither what they had been in his bedroom long ago nor what they were at Donna's now. He felt the heat, blinding amber, shot through a doorway against a rust silhouette of—his mother? No, a split silhouette, a man's? He couldn't make out the face, except the outline, didn't recognize the figure, but it was out of the comics, for sure, a conglomerate of threatening distortions he did not fear at all now.

Nevertheless it stood, whoever it was, he or she, prepared to strike, the possessor of magic powers, rays that bent around corners to kill even as the deep amber light bent around—whom? Neither one parent nor the other. "Get out of my life!" she said, homing on him, on target, a woman, he could see that now.

"Are you Alan's wife?"

"Alan!" Marian called for help.

Alan hurried to Michael's side. "What's the matter?" Alan had never seen anything like this before, knew it had to be drugs, what else? But which and how long it might last he didn't know. "What's the matter, Michael?"

Michael didn't answer immediately, kept staring at him.

"Are you his wife?" Michael asked.

"Yes," she said. Michael tried to get up, didn't make it, sat down on the bed again.

"Alan," she asked, "should we call somebody? Put something on him, Alan."

Michael's eyes turned up, then seemed to be looking inward. "I'm fine." He nodded a few times.

Alan got him Donna's terry-cloth robe.

"Don't worry about how I look," Michael said.

"Alan," Marian whispered, "you think some strong coffee? How long does it take to wear off?"

Alan didn't know.

Michael's habitual gentleness was not in evidence. "I'm glad you're here," he said to Marian. "I want to talk to you." Then he turned to Alan. "Tell her to sit down, I'm not going to hurt her, I want to talk to her. Why does she look at me that way?"

"I don't know," Alan said.

Marian couldn't stand it any more. "Because you're a pretty strange sight, that's why. What have you been taking?"

"Acid," Michael said.

"Well, I can't talk to anyone in this condition. Do you talk to him when he's like this, Alan?"

"You can talk to me better this way than the other!"

"Alan," Marian said, "let's go."

"Let's not go," Michael said. "What did you mean when you came in here and said, 'Get out of our lives!' What did you mean? The truth! I'm sick and tired of lying."

"Do you lie?"

"All the time. Don't you?"

"No."

"Every word I usually say is a lie. When I drop acid I get back to what I really am. Can you understand that?"

"No," Marian said, "I know who I am."

"You're lucky. I want to talk to you even more now. You don't have to stay, Alan."

"Alan, don't you dare move." Then she looked at Michael, making another effort to get up, clutching Donna's robe around him. But his legs gave out again, he wobbled and almost fell. "It's only my legs," Michael said, "my mind is stronger than ever." Then he stood up. "I want to go into the other room," he proclaimed, smiling at himself, "where we can sit and I can talk to her. Alan, help me."

Alan started to, but Michael tipped forward and made a forward-falling dash for the other room, struck the wall at the side of the door, then got through the door okay and onto the sofa, turned around with a sly, triumphant smile on his face, and asked, "Where are you? Alan, bring her here!"

Marian came into the room, cautiously, found her bag. "I've got a few things to pick up at the cleaners—"

"You don't have to pick up a few things anywhere," Michael said. "Now, you see, you said you didn't lie, but you lie so naturally you don't even know—"

"Don't you dare talk to me that way! Not in that condition."

"My condition is very good," Michael said. "I wish I was always in this condition." His tongue was suddenly thick, but he went on. "I'm the way I want to be, sit down!"

Marian sat.

"I want to talk to you about the trial," Michael said.

"Alan!"

"Alan can't do anything unless I tell him to. Now sit down and stay put. Remember, no matter how I look I'm friendly. How do I look? Friendly?"

"You look simply terrible."

Michael laughed. "I asked for that, didn't I?" His face seemed to fall apart; for an instant he looked drunk. Then, just as quickly, he pulled himself together and said, "What do you intend to do about the trial?"

"I have no responsibility for that goddamn trial."

"Well, you know we all have, you, I, all of us, but that's so obvious it's not worth saying, right? What I meant was—"

Again he fell silent, seemed to be searching in his mind for something he couldn't find.

"I think you should get a good night's sleep," Marian said, getting up. "It'll clear your mind."

"Then I'll be back where I was, you know, friendly and phony. Alan knows what I mean." Then he noticed. "Are you up again? Alan, tell her to stay put."

"Do sit a minute, Marian," Alan said, watching the scene from a judge's seat, measuring them.

"If I could only reach you," Michael continued. "Do you have any children? You see if this is just passed over"— he was making a great effort now—"like it's *being* passed over, they won't trust what they call justice again, I mean your children won't, I'm talking about them now, do you have any?"

"Not yet."

"You shouldn't unless this is straightened out. No one should have any children for a while. Not until we see what happens here. I mean my generation's messed up, imagine the next!"

"May I be candid with you?" Marian took hold. "What you do is transfer your own neurotic problems into dubious social generalizations. I mean, because you're sick, it really doesn't follow that society is sick."

"I'm so glad you finally said something. That was wonderful, now we can talk. Listen, this is serious. There's going to be a lot of killing. You know that, don't you?"

"Where?"

"Everywhere! All over. Every state and city."

"Nonsense."

"It's the only thing that's going to make people realize—"

"Realize *what?*"

"Well, you can see this, can't you, that a price has to be paid in someone's blood for what happened? Forgetting he was my best friend."

"That's sheer nonsense, I mean, really you are sick—"

"You know, crime can't just be absolved," Michael said gently.

"No one's planning to absolve—"

"They've already done it. When they picked the jury. But you see we, no, not we, I have to—" he stopped and dropped his head. Then he raised it and looked at Alan a long time.

"I don't understand." Marian turned to her husband. "Alan—did you hear—?"

"You better listen," Michael said, "I'm trying to tell you something. Or part of me is."

Looking at him, she got it. "I think," she said, "you're threatening something."

He was rubbing his eyes.

"I'll tell you one thing," Marian said, "between you and authority, between the police, however crude and ignorant they may sometimes be, and a person like yourself who can't control his saliva no less his mind—I'll take the police any time. Any day!"

Marian turned to Alan, and this time there was no denying her. "I'm going, Alan," she said, walked to the door and waited.

"No, you're not. Not yet." Now in much better control of himself, Michael rushed to where she stood in the doorway. When he put his hands on her, Donna's robe fell to the floor. "You're going to stay," he ordered. "You're going to talk to me!"

She struggled against him, but he held on, jerking her, pulling her back into the room.

And then she did it, turned in his grip and thrust her knee straight up, hitting the mark her father had taught her to hit when she was a girl of twelve.

Michael collapsed like a folding chair.

Marian, in her terror, struck him and was about to strike him again when Alan seized her from the rear and held her arms.

"Let me go, you bastard!" she said, she the irrational one now.

Alan held her with all his strength, binding her arms. Her head turned from side to side as she tried frantically to bite her husband's arms and hands where they held her.

Michael was up off the floor where he had knelt, bending a little backward, as if to ease the pain that way, then forward over his knees again, then back, holding his genitals. "It's all right, it will be all right in a minute, don't leave, Alan, tell her—" Then he hobbled over to where Alan was holding Marian and said, "Let her go."

Marian escaped from the room.

Alan examined his wrists where Marian had bitten them.

"She was pretty frightened," Michael offered.

"She had no business doing what she did. I'll see you tomorrow."

"Don't," Michael said. "I'm stoned so here's the truth. You're like my brother, okay? You're the only one of them who—well, Donna doesn't trust you for shit, and man you're a fool, but—go on home. Don't mess around with me any more."

"I'll see you tomorrow."

"I'm ashamed of you," Alan said. "He's just a kid in bad trouble, the kind you've never known. You've lived in a compound all your life, under guard! When someone crosses you, you order him the hell out of your life."

"All right, Alan, all right." Marian was soaking in her bath, Alan in the doorway. "I'm tired," she said.

He started away.

"Alan, don't go." Untrained for apology, she couldn't look at him. "I'm sort of embarrassed, I don't know why I got so—violent. I've never known anyone like that, you're right about what you said, okay?"

Alan put the seat down, sat.

"Only why are you so hard on me and yourself and so easy on him? Isn't that a kind of snobbery? Isn't he pretty sick?"

"He has good reason."

"Did you hear what that—pardon me—maniac was saying?"

"When he's turned on, he talks that way."

"Which way?"

"In metaphors. You take him literally."

"Read the morning paper. He wants your life. I heard him, *I* wasn't stoned."

She got out of the tub and covered herself quickly with a towel. "How does more killing undo a killing?"

Alan didn't answer.

"Good night," she said, indicating the door.

Alan didn't move.

"I think it's best if you don't come near me—until we get past this."

She waited for him to leave.

"Daddy told me to remind you you're not to leave the base. He'll have to put you in detention if you do. Okay? And, till this mess is over, darling, I really wish you'd go live in the Officers' Dorm or—"

"You go live in the Officers' Dorm."

Alan went downstairs, poured himself a drink. The morning paper was on the coffee table. He read the black intellectual's prediction. Symbolic murders, he'd said, white martyrs, he'd said.

He looked at the photograph of the black staring right back at him. Alan closed the paper over the man's face.

His father would not have ducked a picture in a newspaper. He opened the page again.

――――――――――――――――――――――

Hope's eyes opened, and she looked at the ceiling as if she was having difficulty recalling something. Her lips would move; no sound. Once she reached out her hand, and Wheeler gave her his to hold. She made sure he was still there, then she said her last words.

"What am I going to do with all that meat?"

When the nurse called him to the phone, he was relieved.

"Walker just suggested we settle for murder two," Gavin told him.

"He can go and fuck himself," Wheeler said. Then, "Well, maybe that's too hasty. What do you think?"

"I'm for it," Gavin said, the first time he ever bucked his boss.

There was a long silence. Wheeler was disappointed in his protégé. "Of course, we'll have to leave it up to Flores, won't we?"

"Yes, sir."

"Let's meet with him after court's out."

"Yes, sir." Then Gavin asked, "How's Mrs. Wheeler?"

Wheeler didn't answer for a moment; when he did, he sounded furious. "The same," he said, "and I'm the same! I'm against it. I say no compromises. Didn't you hear what that bastard said in the paper this morning?"

"Yes, sir, but this is—"

"Was that man threatening us?"

"Well, maybe he was—"

"Maybe, my ass! I value the people of this country, Gavin, and I won't stand for this. I want that Mexican son of a bitch vindicated."

Gavin, cross-examining Juana the next morning, went far back into her relationship with Vinnie, where they met, how they came together, her father's early objections.

"But nevertheless you continued seeing Vin Connor?"

"Yes, sir."

"Was Vin Connor supplying you with drugs, Juana?"

"Yes, sir."

"He introduced you to their use?"

"Yes, sir."

"What were these drugs?"

"You know—"

"No, I don't and neither do the ladies and gentlemen of the jury. They are not in common use among decent people, at least not yet. Describe the drugs he supplied you with, if you will."

"Marijuana."

"What is that?"

"You know, grass."

"No, I don't, not really. Describe it, please."

"You smoke it, it turns you on."

"And what else?"

"Speed."

"Which is—?"

"I don't know exactly, but it's stronger."

"Anything else?"

"LSD. He always had some tabs of LSD on him."

"Tabs?"

"Like pills. Tablets, I guess."

"This was frequent? The marijuana, for instance?"

"Oh, that? Every day."

"The others?"

"I guess I must have dropped acid a couple of times a week."

"Your father knew about this?"

"He did."

"What was his attitude?"

"Against it."

"But you kept on anyway?"

Juana nodded.

"Now, did your father know where you were all through this?"

"Not for a long time."

"Did you know he was searching for you?"

"Yes, sir."

"But you didn't contact him?"

"Once I did, I wrote him."

"Did you tell him where you were?"

"No, sir."

"You knew your father was looking frantically all over town, that he was driving around all night looking?"

"Bennie told me that, yes."

"Not sleeping? Not able to do his normal fine job at the base?"

"Yes."

"How do you feel about that now?"

"I'm ashamed of myself."

For the first time in the trial Cesario Flores raised his head and looked at his daughter. His face opened.

"How did you feel then?"

"I felt ashamed of myself then. But I couldn't do anything about it."

"Why not?"

"Well, when I was with Vinnie, it was like I didn't have a mind of my own."

"Would you say he had hypnotic power over—"

"Objection, your honor," Cy said.

"I suggest you rephrase the question," Judge Breen said.

"Thank you, your honor, but it's not necessary. Now, I understand Vin Connor took a trip to San Francisco. Do you know why he went there?"

"To get some more acid."

"And during that interval, what did you do?"

"I went home."

"Were your parents glad to see you?"

"They were very relieved."

"And you?"

"Like I was free of something."

"Now, Juana, tell us, in your own words, exactly what happened."

"He came back, sent me a letter, and told me to meet him."

"Did you decide to meet him?"

"No. I decided not to. But then I did."

"Where?"

"At the fence where they put the old planes."

"And what happened?"

"He told me to come out through the gate."

"What did you say?"

"I said I didn't want to."

"And then?"

"He said if I didn't he'd come in there—on the base with a gun and take me away."

"With a gun and take you?"

"Yes. So I came out through the gate."

"And he was waiting for you?"

"In a car."

"And then?"

"He drove me home."

"You mean where he lived?"

"Yes."

"And what happened there?"

"He beat me up."

"Struck you?"

"Yes."

"Many times?"

"Yes."

"And then?"

"You know."

"No. How would I know?"

"He made it with me."

"He made love to you?"

"That's what they call it."

"And then?"

"He hit me a few more times. Just in case I forgot from before."

"Did it hurt?"

"No. Not really. He had a way which—I remember when he did it, I felt I had it coming to me. So it didn't really hurt. He could do that, make you feel that whatever he wanted was right."

"And then?"

"Everything was like before."

"And you were contented?"

Juana hesitated. Then she said, "I was more than contented. I was—I belonged to him, that's all there is to it. I didn't care what happened. It was like I didn't have a mind of my own."

"During this time, did Mr. Connor consort with other girls?"

"Oh, yes."

"How did you feel about that?"

"I didn't mind."

"Did he warn you not to ever run away again?"

"When he was hitting me, yes."

"What did he say?"

"He said that if my father ever took me away again, he'd kill him."

"He'd kill him?"

"Yes."

"He didn't mean that literally, did he?"

"He did."

"Well, did he have a gun?"

It was then that Juana heard a growling sound.

Michael was sitting in the back of the courtroom, she could see he was just coming off a trip. She knew him like that.

Bailiff Lansing and a guard moved toward the boy, but when Judge Breen used his gavel, Michael was quiet.

"Go on, Juana, please," Gavin said. He'd noticed Michael too, and, behind him, his tail.

"Vinnie had a gun in the house," Juana said.

"So when you heard Vin Connor say that if your father ever took you away again, he'd kill him, you believed he would?"

"I did, yes."

"One last question, Juana. What would you say the nature of the hold Vin Connor had on you was?"

"I couldn't really understand it."

"Were you—forgive my asking—a virgin before you met Vin Connor?"

"Yes, sir."

"Do you think Vin Connor's hold on you was sexual in nature?"

"Part of it."

"What do you mean by that?"

"He was the first and—I would have done anything he asked me to do."

"Thank you, Juana, thank you for being so honest."

"That's all?"

Cy rose. "May I refer," he said, "to your statement, the one you made on the night of the murder? You said, on this occasion when your memory was fresh, that your father insisted that Vinnie come out to your home?"

"He did, yes."

"And that you felt your father might kill him if the boy came out?"

"I also felt that Vinnie might kill *him*."

"Just answer my question, yes or no."

"Okay. I mean, yes."

"And because you felt your father might kill him, you grabbed the phone and begged Vinnie not to come out?"

"That's right. I did that."

"Why?"

"Because my father was not himself."

"Not himself? But you said on the night this testimony was taken that your father seemed quiet and—"

"My father gets very quiet when he's upset or mad—"

"Why didn't you want Vinnie to come out to your house that night?"

"For one thing, I was ashamed of him."

"Ashamed of him! You'd been living with him for four months; now suddenly you're ashamed of him?"

"I was. Every time I got away from him, I was ashamed of him and ashamed he had me that way, the way he did."

"Miss Flores, that is not quite what you said! You said that night, did you not, that you felt your father had laid a trap and intended to kill him in cold blood."

"I didn't say cold blood. My father was not himself that night, I could tell—"

Michael was standing up. "You're a liar," he shouted. "Tell the truth," he shouted. "It was cold blood. He knew everyone here would be with him. He knew he could get away with it. Like he *is* getting away with it! Because you're all liars here!"

The deputy sheriffs had him out of the courtroom.

When he was gone, Juana spoke into the silence. "That's not true, what he said. I—I drove my father crazy. He was only trying to, I couldn't save myself, so he was trying to save me, best way he could, that's all he was doing. I was proud of him then, that I meant that much to him, that he is that kind of man, that he would do that for me, even kill for me. I'm still proud of him."

Judge Breen called a recess. Before he left the courtroom, he asked both lawyers to meet with him in his chambers.

After he was gone, no one, not the two lawyers, not the reporters, left. They were watching father and daughter.

Cesario was looking at her intently, directly, for the first time in the trial, nakedly. It was a love scene.

Juana stepped down from the witness stand, walked slowly to where her father sat, touched his shoulder. Then she went on by.

What Don Wheeler had hoped would happen, happened. From that instant, Cesario Flores was fighting for his life.

――――――――――――――――――――

"Strictly between us," Judge Breen said, "don't you think this trial has made its point? It seems to me it's clearly something you can settle here between yourselves, say manslaughter two. I'll leave you alone and—what the hell is it, Geraldine?"

His secretary leaned over and whispered something to him.

"Well, let's see it!"

Geraldine handed him an open telegram. Cy and Gavin waited, but it didn't look like there was going to be more conversation. Breen was staring at the wire.

"I made a similar suggestion this noon," Cy said.

"He did, your honor," Gavin said.

"Well," Judge Breen said, forcing his attention back to them, "I'm glad we all agree, because we're on the verge of some very ugly revelations here, concerning drugs and sex and the privileges of the air force. I mean once you start opening Pandora's box in this"—he looked at the telegram—"hell, it's not going to do any of us any good. What do you say, Gavin?"

"It's strictly up to my client," Gavin said.

After they'd left, Breen called his wife and told her he had to fly to New York.

"When?"

"Yesterday! First chance I get, tomorrow, tonight. As soon as this goddamn trial is over."

In Cesario Flores's cell, Gavin explained the issue and the possibilities carefully and by the book, and then Mr. Don Wheeler explained it all over again.

But Flores had been touched, his daughter had touched him on the shoulder, and his smile was triumphant.

"You want me to say what should be?" he asked.

"It's your life," Wheeler said.

"So what do you say," Gavin said.

"I say, roll de dice!"

"What does that mean?" Gavin asked; he knew.

"Deal!"

"Which means?"

"Let it ride! All or nothing! Roll de dice!"

Mr. Don Wheeler burst into laughter. For the first time he liked that Mex son of a bitch. He even extended his hand and chortled as he repeated, "Roll de dice!"

———————————————————

Cy got a most irregular call at home that night from Thurston Breen. "Who the hell was the bearded hippie who made all that fuss at the end of court today?"

"A friend of the dead boy's. Why?" Cy asked.

"I've had some inquiries about him."

"From whom?"

"I can't say."

It crossed Cy's mind that the judge was making this up. But a few minutes after he hung up, a tall, rather handsome man, well dressed in the model of a young business executive, ruggedness carefully concealed, came to Cy Walker's door and introduced himself by flipping open one side of a small flat wallet.

Cy told him everything he knew about Michael.

That night Juana had a call.

"Michael?" she said.

"No," the voice said. "This is Vinnie talking. You don't remember me any more, do you?"

It was a voice she'd heard before, but couldn't place.

"I heard everything you said about me today, and I won't forget it, so be careful where you go, because, what's going to happen to you, you two-face tramp, I'm going to cut you open from your snatch to your mouth."

Juana hung up, dialed Gavin, and told him what had happened.

"That's him," Gavin said, "Michael."

"Michael isn't like that," Juana said.

"When he's tripping? I'll bet you'll be getting calls like that all night. Leave your phone off the hook."

Fat Freddie Povich, released from jail a few days before, had gotten under the floor of the house on Queen Street before Michael and had dealt the contents of the mayonnaise jar. Now, waiting his turn on the witness stand, he was holed up in the Western Star Motel with over five hundred dollars in his pocket.

Under the mattress of the bed was the carbine.

Freddie's pilot fish, Che Weill, came to see him at the end of court each day—it was just across the square—to tell Freddie what had happened. That afternoon it had been Juana's testimony, word for word.

Donna brought Michael a message to telephone Alan right away and use a booth.

Alan sounded excited. "I'm really on to something big, so don't give up, Michael."

"You think I'm giving up?" Michael asked.

"I did, yes, and I know it looks bad." It was at this point that Alan's line was tapped, on the base side. "I've got something that may be crucial for you, and when I make sure, which should be tomorrow, I'll get in touch with you."

"Don't come here," Michael said.

"Stop that, Michael," Alan said. "I'm confined to the base now, but—"

"Like I told you, stay away from me." He hung up.

There was a short conference in the office of the Grand Mesa Copper Company, then a phone call to Colonel Dowd. Certain identifications were made, then the base commander was asked to allow Lieutenant Alan Kidd to leave the base and go anywhere he wished, there'd be a safety tail on him.

Sally Breen slid open the glass door of the shower and shouted to her husband, "Gavin McAndrews just called. He said to tell you the answer is no. They're going with what they have." She closed the door quickly, anticipating a reaction that might splatter her dress.

Then she dialed the office and canceled her husband's reservation to New York that evening.

Judge Breen was in much deeper than he'd told his wife,

the victim of a really brilliant idea his brother had promised would set him for life. He had borrowed half a million from a New York bank. With that sum he had bought AAA bonds which, at maturity would yield a profit taxable on a capital-gains basis. The interest on the loan was deductible. It seemed a completely safe finagle; it was even legal.

It was this New York bank which had urgently wired him asking for six thousand dollars additional collateral. He had nothing in hand he could use—the bank already had all his paper except his life insurance.

At a quarter to seven the next morning, a store on the main street of that city was getting a new window display. This establishment had always featured fine hunting rifles and shotguns. These were being taken out of the window by a man who wore cowboy boots, and replaced by a display of side arms, some of a size suitable for bedside tables, some that would fit into a lady's purse.

Among the collection of pistols, prominently placed, were a number of small metal cylinders, marked to sell at $3.95, labeled "Paralyzers." The owner of the store evidently anticipated a demand. With them were to be sold small metal clasps that could be fastened with screws to the inside frame of a front door, holding the paralyzers ready for instant use. Behind this display of metal cylinders was the sign that explained it: EVERY HOME SHOULD HAVE ONE.

———————————————————

The next morning, Cy rested. It became Gavin's case.

Gavin's brains were in his gut; he was a natural trial lawyer. Never superior to his jury as Cy was, especially when he was trying not to be, Gavin was made of the same stuff. All he did was provide them with a stand-up spectacle of the license to be what they were, sanctify what they secretly felt but what Christian society had told them from their earliest days they must not feel: prejudice, jealousy, fear of strangers, distrust of intellect, their most secret therefore most profound hatreds. Gavin dealt in humanity as it was, not in the logic of laws, in natural panic, not the structure of testimony.

So where Cy had built his whole case on a framework of

facts, Gavin's case had one purpose triggered by one impression: the ecstasy on Flores's face when his daughter touched him. Wheeler had told him, "Try the hippies!" But when Gavin saw the lightning flash of feeling on the father's face, he changed his tactic. He wanted the jury to experience, again and again, the look which had so moved him.

This tack wasn't merely calculated; it came from what was deepest in Gavin. An orphan, he responded to intense love between father and child with pure longing. His secretary told the other girls that Gavin often came back from long conversations in Flores's cell with the evidence of tears in his eyes.

So when Bennie told the court his memories of Flores driving around town all night looking for his daughter and ended with, "I don't understand how a daughter could treat her father that way," and Flores murmured, "You're wrong on that, Bennie, she's still a good girl, Bennie," Gavin saw what the jury saw, the look on Flores's face, and that it was getting to them.

What Gavin had planned happened so naturally, so quietly, that it didn't occur to Judge Breen to silence Flores.

Then, instead of going on to another argument, another effect, Gavin did the same thing with Jones, the beefy sergeant, who ended his testimony with, "She was just no good. They say love is blind but he treated her like she was the Virgin Mary."

"You just didn't know her, Jack," Flores said.

"I lived next door to her."

"But I lived in the same house with her," and again Flores shrugged that delicate Latin way.

This time Judge Breen did silence him, and Flores apologized to the judge and said he wouldn't speak out of turn again; but the jury had seen the look again, which was all Gavin wanted.

It was inconceivable that anyone watching the man at this moment could believe he was on trial for murder.

At the end of the day Gavin, for his climax, rolled in the big brass. Colonel Dowd told a story about a crisis in Asia. A lot of very expensive hardware had been shot down, and there was a frantic call from Washington for more combat-quick planes. Dowd had decided to share the problem with his most trusted heads of department. It was Flores's suggestion that his men be put on a twelve-hour shift till the crisis was over.

"And that's what happened," Dowd said. "He made his men feel like Americans, even though he was from Mexico and the rest of the men from here. I tried to get some of those other heads of department to go along on the twelve-twelve day on a voluntary basis, but they refused. When I told this to Sergeant Flores, he said—I can remember his words like they'd been written and I'd read them over and over—'I was born outside,' he said, 'and I've traveled many countries, so I know what it's like other places. Maybe that's why I appreciate here more than the other fellows do. Because to work twelve hours a day for a few weeks, *Madre de Dios'* "—Colonel Dowd was imitating the man's Tex-Mex accent—" 'what is that? The least I can do, *verdad?* When I remember what it is I have here?' "

Through all this, Cesario de las Flores sat with his head up. Some of the jurors had tears in their eyes.

The real measure of how well Gavin did on his first day was that Cy passed up cross-examining witness after witness. What was there to ask them?

Irene had taken to attending the trial for a few hours every day, enjoying the notoriety.

There had quickly become attached to her a guard of newsmen, one in particular, a bright girl with close-cropped red hair. She was writing a series called "Our Permissive Parents," the first article made up largely of material she'd milked from Irene by encouraging her to carry on about her son, her memories of his vanished father, her problems being both mother and father to the boy, her opinions on life and love and sin. She needed a few juicy quotes before it went to press, and she was getting them.

"What's a woman supposed to do when the man she's married to just doesn't come from work one night, disappears, leaves her to raise a son, not to mention a daughter, who's also disappeared, damn if I know where?"

The sharp girl-reporter, hungry for everything she could get before Mrs. Connor saw the next day's paper, followed her out to the yard of the courthouse building, sat with her there on a bench around the "eternal fountain," gave her what encouragement was necessary, very little indeed.

Some of the kids who were camping on the courthouse lawn night and day, not about to pass up any entertainment, crowded round.

Within half an hour, Irene, riding the vodka, was saying, "It's the fault of the men, I could have helped that boy, but I never had a chance, I had to spend all my spare time looking around for another man to take up with so I could maybe make a home for Vinnie. But it just didn't work out, it's my Irish fate they tell me, and the way men are these days, so suspicious, faggots, like secret ones, they can't take a woman with a mind of her own, can't handle her. So who's to blame, tell me? Not me!" Irene was in a rage now. "Who's to blame that my boy's lying in that filthy funeral home, run by that dirty old Bulgarian with the yellow finger-nails, you think I like that, my son locked up in an icebox there—"

Hal, who was standing at a little distance with some potential trade, waiting while the woman had her public fling, saw some of the kids—he thought he recognized one from the night at the morgue—walk away, consult, then run off.

He hurried to where he could hear Irene. "He should have shot that whore daughter of his, not my son. It's those filthy little hippies who aren't letting me give my Vinnie a Christian burial!"

Hal grabbed her hand and pulled her out of the circle of listeners. "What the hell have you been saying?"

All that day through, Michael had sat at the window of Donna's bedroom. Outside, the parking lot was nearly empty; everybody was at work. Michael was looking at a pepper tree which had come through the black-top at one corner. Apparently the tree's roots weren't finding all they needed under the macadam, because its leaf growth was thin. The tree was up against a bank of fill held back by concrete blocks arranged in a pattern of crosses. This low bank supported the ground at the rear of a small concrete building, a dry-cleaning establishment. From a pipe at the bottom of the building, a scalding vapor was pressured in spurts, souring the air. The steam rose through the sun's rays. When there was a breeze, the tree seemed to be quivering in lemon mist. Michael had sat there all the previous day watching the tree endure its destiny. The phone rang at regular intervals. How frantic a phone sounds when it's denied! Michael thought. He watched the tree as he might a human tragedy he couldn't do anything about.

He'd made up his mind. He wasn't going to court again; his outburst at Juana yesterday was all he had to say.

At six Donna came home. She found him in the dark room looking into the floodlight at the corner of the parking lot, unblinking. Donna stirred some honey into a coffee yogurt. While Michael was eating it, the phone rang again. Donna told Alan that Michael didn't want to talk to him.

She knelt next to Michael and put her head in his lap. "He says he's got something good for you," she said. "And he says did you know Vinnie's still in the vault?"

By nine that night, the watch on the pavement outside the funeral home had been resumed, and Izzy Bulgaros heard how Irene had characterized him in the most public place of all, the morning's newspaper. To be referred to as a dirty old man was bad for business. Who'd want someone with yellow fingernails to handle the body of their loved one? Bulgaros decided to get rid of the body.

"That reporter made a fucking fool of you!"

It was noon, and Hal and Irene were sitting in her kitchen.

"Icebox, you had to give her! Yellow fingernails!"

Irene bit her lip, finished her drink, found the bottle, poured her lunch.

"I mean, couldn't you keep in mind the one simple thing I told you?"

"What did you tell me, for chrissake, you tell me so many things and they're all so brilliant!"

"I told you that little red-headed dyke was going to cut you up! And all you did was help her, going on and on about what a flake your son was, which he was, but what were you—?"

"I only told the truth."

"Who gives a shit about the truth? What do you think people are going to say when they read this paper, that Vinnie's mother told the truth? They're going to say he was no good because she's no good."

"Well—well—"

"You're the town joke!"

"Stop it! Stop biting at me!"

She made a move, but he beat her to it, throwing the rest

of his drink into her face. When she went for him with her nails, he walloped her. She fell on the bed and cried like a child who's given up on absolutely everything.

He began to stroke her hair.

"I'm a mess," she said. "I'm a failure, Hal, in every way, no good."

"That's right," he said affectionately, "you're nothing, a nothing mother, a nothing woman, you're a—"

"Well stop putting me down, and tell me what to do, Hal, tell me how to be!"

"Recognize friends."

"What friends?" She rubbed her jaw. "You hurt me."

"I'm talking about Vinnie's friends."

"You mean that little Mex whore?"

"No, I mean the people sitting out front of the Southside Home for the Dead this minute, the only people in the world who loved your son."

"Those creeps?"

"Yes. Tell me who cared enough for your no-good kid to stick up for him in court? Did you hear what that boy said, the skinny one? He told them, didn't he, Irene? Didn't he?"

"Yes he did," she admitted, her eyes like a child's.

"He told them they are liars, which is what they are. He told them the whole trial was rigged, which it sure as hell is. You put your son down for the whole town to read, but that kid had the guts to—"

"Yes, yes," Irene said, "he did—"

"You owe that boy an apology, Irene baby, you ought to get down on your knees in front of that boy! And all of them! Forgetting how dirty they are. You fart in bed, too, baby, what the hell are you so high class about?"

"I don't know, Hal, don't be mean to me, Hal."

"Did you read what that Bulgaros said, did you get his message? He's a businessman, baby, and if you don't get your son's dead ass out of his icebox quick, he's going to throw his body on the town dump for the dogs."

"He said that?"

"He doesn't have to say it. He's sick of the mess out there, and he knows you don't have the bills to pay for your hair set yet—you had to borrow from me yesterday, how the hell you gonna pay for a funeral?"

"Don't say those things to me, Hal, don't be mean to me. Tell me what you want me to do."

"If I were a mother, I'd give my son his wish. I'd let the people who loved him bury him like he wanted."

Irene rushed to where Hal was and kissed him. "I'd do anything for you, Hal."

"Don't do it for me, do it for the good of your black soul. Do it for them, his friends, because they're the only ones who care enough to camp on their asses in front of that place and let this goddamn town know that someone once cared for somebody, that somebody will stick up for someone, just out of feeling, you understand, just out of what they laughingly refer to as love, you understand?"

"I do, Hal, I love you, even though you're a faggot, I really love you."

"You got no choice, baby, because there isn't anybody else in this whole world who'd put up with you."

Irene kissed Hal. "So tell me what to wear?" she said.

——————————————————————

Cy yearned to get laid, he'd have liked to play golf, he would have settled for a movie, or even to sit in the shade and very slowly eat an apple, anything except what he was doing, going back to that courtroom.

He'd had lunch alone, broken his diet just to get some satisfaction out of something. With the key-lime pie he'd written out a telegram accepting their lousy offer. He knew by the time he'd paid the movers and the redecorating and settling-in expenses, he'd be behind for at least two years. But the telegram was in his pocket, and he was going to send it at the end of that court session.

He heard running footsteps, felt a hand on his arm. Alan.

"Hello there." Cy showed his public-service smile. "Can't talk right now, I've got to—"

Alan read his wristwatch. "You've got five minutes." He took Cy by the elbow, steered him through the courthouse door. "We'll use the stairs," he said, "I'd prefer not to bump into Gavin."

Cy didn't want to climb the stairs, but he did.

"Gavin's keeping the base psychiatrist off the stand,"

Alan said in a voice louder than necessary. "Do you know why?"

"No," Cy said. The guy had him taking the stairs by twos.

"Because Dr. Stevens saw Flores an hour after the murder and found him—what's the opposite of temporarily insane? Like us? That's it. Gavin is taking you apart in there, and they're going to get this guy off—stop looking around and listen!"

"I'm listening," Cy said.

"The two psychiatrists he's putting on the stand didn't even see Flores till last week and after, repeat, after Gavin had talked to him."

"Well, isn't that normal?" Cy had stopped the rush at the courtroom door.

"And he paid them."

"That's normal."

"Listen, you haven't much time—are you paying attention? Stevens has got a problem. Booze. I'll call him and tell him we're coming out to the base to see him tonight and to stay dry. We'll have dinner together, we can't let this happen, what's—"

Gavin, coming out of the elevator, said hello to Cy, looked at Alan, didn't speak, passed by.

"Gavin," Alan called out, "come back here a minute."

Gavin wouldn't be caught dead refusing a challenge.

"Tell me, Gavin," Alan said, "what is the time lapse between the moment you first stop telling the truth and the moment you no longer know what it is?"

Gavin offered Alan his Cagney smile, then turned and walked away. As he sat down behind the defense table, he decided to put Alan on the stand. He'd publicly waste that two-faced son of a bitch.

Subpoenaed in Seattle, air-fare prepaid, motel expense vouched for, Rosalie had been brought to town by the defense. She was outside the Southside Home for the Dead now, with the others. Rosalie, who had been with Vinnie, who had been with Michael, had brought with her, in a rapture of good fortune, the young man she'd found in Seattle, not her boyfriend, her fiancé. This Lonnie was not what she had determined to look for, a nine-to-fiver, nor was he a hippie or a head; he was an anachronism, a flower person. She had told him the truth about the father of who was in her belly; they were going to be married, "like any minute."

The word went around; Rosalie had found the right guy. Tipping back a little to balance her five-month's bundle, she walked here and there, greeting old friends, bringing them one by one to meet Lonnie. He was a tall boy, affably stooped, and blessed with a soft, perfectly oval face and heavy plum eyes. The first thing they all noticed was how proud he was of Rosalie, as proud as she was of him. This square miracle, clearly deserved by both, cast an air of cheer and good fellowship and hope over the group gathered outside the old morgue.

There were many strangers among the two hundred-odd sitting or lying in easy postures, summoned no one really knew how, from far off and often surprising places, Butte, Montana, for instance, one from Hawaii, L.A., of course. And, of course, everyone from the house on Queen Street was there, except one, Fat Freddie Povich. The story that moved around with the joints was that he'd been released from jail, some people had seen him afterward and said he looked all right, but, for him, very subdued, very quiet. He had disappeared then; no one knew where he was, but everyone expected him there any minute.

Although Lonnie and Rosalie were the nucleus of this happy assembly, there were other clusters, swarming here and there over the sidewalk and in the parking lot at the side of the building. The general air of affection and celebration gave the dour old institution an incongruous atmosphere: a promise of some sort of fulfillment coming.

Here and there people picked on guitars and sang, but in voices which permitted groups close by to have another song going. Others were rapping, exchanging accounts of adventures, of people encountered, loving and hateful, of travel and the general persecution under which they were living out their lives. Occasionally someone stood to act out something that had happened to him in Alien Amerika, an instant of primitive theater. Laughter broke out here, then there. It was a congress of old friends; even those who'd never seen each other before thought of the event as a reunion.

A few bikers who had roared up out of nowhere, among the first to show, even they were gentled, some asleep, others fussing quietly with their Harley-Davidsons and Yamahas.

Then, as if summoned by a general unspoken wish, the person they all wanted most to see appeared: Michael.

Without discussing it among themselves, they all knew that whatever was going to happen there, in that city, on that case, would happen through Michael.

Michael's outburst in court had reached everyone in every corner of this society; it had become part of the culture. The fact that his eyes were glazed, that he walked through them now without really seeing any of them, seemed natural to them. It was the way a leader should behave.

The only one he embraced was Rosalie, but this as if he'd seen her the day before. He nodded a few times at Lonnie and smiled vaguely, but it was obvious that the next time he saw him they would have to be introduced. Lonnie told Rosalie in a whisper, "He's on a big head trip."

"He always is," Rosalie replied.

After that moment's stop Michael progressed swiftly into the funeral home; the time had come for him to speak to Mr. Bulgaros.

"Dr. Deming, I have had the opportunity to read your psychiatric report on Cesario Flores, Court Order 14322. May I ask you a few questions?"

"Yes, yes, of course, that's what we're here for."

The psychiatrist was a heavy, lax man. A smile frequented his lips, he didn't seem to be taking either Cy or the occasion seriously.

"Dr. Deming, you say here that when the defendant was brought to your office to be examined he was cooperative, candid, and forthright. Does that mean you believed he was telling you the truth?"

"Yes, yes, as he knew it to be, yes."

"As he knew it to be?"

"That's all any of us can do, Mr.—?"

"Walker. You also say here that your examination showed his memory to be excellent."

"Yes, yes, generally excellent, yes."

"Now may I call your attention to certain discrepancies between what your patient and his wife told you last week and what his daughters told the police on the night of the murder seven weeks before?"

"Of course, why not?"

"For instance, according to your report Flores said it was the dead boy who insisted he must see Flores, while both girls said on the night of the murder that it was Flores who insisted that the boy come out to the base."

"That's correct!"

"Which is correct?"

"You are correct. There is a discrepancy there."

"Well, then, which is true?"

"That is for the jury to determine, is it not?"

"What is your judgment?"

"Does that matter? After all, my value here, if any, is simply to make a personality evaluation."

"Of course. May I ask, were you paid for this 'personality evaluation,' Dr. Deming?"

"Yes, I was."

"I see. Another thing that puzzles me. Your report quotes Flores as saying that the boy insisted he come to the house—rather than meet at the main gate—while the girls told the police that on the night of the murder their father insisted Connor come out to the house."

"Yes, yes." Dr. Deming purred and smiled.

"Yes, yes, what?"

"They were all pretty distraught that night."

"But, of course, seven weeks later in your office, Mr. Flores seemed in good shape."

"Yes, he did, yes."

"It didn't occur to you that in the intervening time he might have been carefully coached—"

"Objection, your honor," Gavin said. "That's an improper allegation."

"Sustained."

"What does amnesic mean, Dr. Deming?"

"You know what it means. Well, if you like. It means that after the pistol went off the first time—"

"You say in your report accidentally, after the pistol accidentally went off the first time."

"That is not my statement, Mr. Walker, I am only reporting what my patient told me."

"I know. Go on."

"He told me after the pistol went off accidentally the first time and struck him in the leg, he became amnesic."

"Your word."

"Yes, of course. He had only a very fragmentary grasp of the sequence of events that transpired after—"

"But you said his memory was excellent. Your word."

"In ordinary circumstances, yes. The night of the murder was not an ordinary circumstance." Dr. Deming laughed.

"May I read from your report?"

"Of course, why not?"

"Quote. 'I don't remember any more shots or hearing the gun go off, but I do remember kids yelling something like "help" and that the front door was open. I was immediately overwhelmed with fear that they had taken Juana away, kidnapped her, and I ran out and the car was coming right at me and I fired several shots at the car. I don't remember what happened then, but I was told later that—'" Cy stopped. "Dr. Deming," he said, "did you ask your patient why, if he thought his daughter was in the car, he wasn't afraid he might hit her when he fired?"

"Of course, I asked that, of course."

"What did he say?"

"He wasn't able to respond reasonably to that question."

"And that is amnesic?"

"Yes, right, now you have it. He didn't recall the precise sequence of events after the shooting."

"And you believed him?"

"I didn't say that. I was there only to make a personality judgment—to the best of my ability."

"But it did seem quite possible to you that a man could forget certain things that were important to forget and remember certain other things that were important to—"

"Objection, your honor," Gavin said wearily, "there's no need to make allegations of that kind."

"Sustained."

"May I just point out one other bit that worries me?"

"I'm waiting," Dr. Deming said cheerily.

"If the first shot, the accidental one, entered his leg, how could Flores run out of the house and nimbly avoiding the efforts of the driver of the car to run him down, pump four shots into the—" Cy stopped.

Dr. Deming was laughing. "That is the mystery of the human organism," he said.

"May I suggest a less mysterious interpretation? That he shot himself intentionally, not accidentally? After he murdered the driver, not before?"

"Yes, that's possible, it's possible, Mr. Walter."

"Walker."

"Walker. Sorry. Many apologies."

"You seem to be a little amnesic, too."

"I may have a resistance to remembering your name because you're sort of getting on me, aren't you?"

Everybody in the courtroom, including the judge, laughed.

"What I was going to say," Dr. Deming proceeded, "was that under the stress of a psychic disorder as severe as this one, people do extraordinary things."

"So I've heard. Now, Dr. Deming, what does dissociative mean? You use that word repeatedly in your conclusion."

"It means that he, Sergeant Flores, had lost—temporarily —the ability to put bits of experience together, that is, to reason in the usual logical way, so he acted, that night, primarily from emotion. It appeared to me that at that time he was not capable of forming a reasoned intent and that he was not able to consider the difference between right and wrong and that, therefore, he did not have control over his actions at that time."

"That is your best professional judgment?"

"Absolutely."

"Does that mean he was not responsible for his actions that night?"

"I didn't say *quite* that."

"I thought you did. But you would say, would you not, that he should not be held legally responsible for his behavior that night?"

"Well, let me be precise, let me choose my own words, may I?"

"Of course, of course, why not, that's what we're here for."

"There's no need to mock me, Mr. Walter, really it doesn't serve any purpose. We all do the best we can. All I wanted to say is that at the time of the shooting, in my best professional judgment, the combination of chronic pressures plus the acute aggravation resulting from the deceased's insistence on taking the defendant's daughter away resulted in the defendant's personality being overwhelmed by primitive emotions of fear and rage. During this period of what I called dissociation, I feel that Sergeant Flores's ability to control his behavior was temporarily nil. It is extremely difficult to say if he knew right from wrong at the time the shooting occurred."

"But don't we all live under pressure, and don't we all have to be responsible for our behavior despite the pressures?"

"Yes, yes, of course," Dr. Deming said. Then he looked at the jury and said, "But I don't think many of us have had a drug-crazed boy come into our homes to take our daughter away." He asked the jury directly, "Have we?" Then he turned to the flabbergasted Cy Walker and said, "I even wonder how you might have behaved under those circumstances."

"But you don't think Mr. Flores should be confined to a mental hospital?" Cy asked.

"Of course not. We've all seen that he is able to understand the nature of the proceedings against him, is able to assist in his own defense, doesn't have a chronic psychopathic personality disorder, that's clear. He is able to reason and control his conduct and is not likely to engage in violent or dangerous behavior. Therefore he does not need to be institutionalized."

"But he did kill two men. Isn't he a threat to—?"

"I seriously doubt that he would be a danger to society unless a situation closely approximating the one which occurred should recur at some future time—which you will admit is a highly unlikely possibility."

Cy sat down, shook his head.

"Is there anything else you want to ask Dr. Deming?" Judge Breen asked him.

Cy made a sound with his lips.

"Why do you make that peculiar clucking sound, Mr.—?"

"Walker. I do that in admiration."

"Of what?"

"Of the remarkable flexibility of your profession." He sat down before the judge could reprimand him.

"Yes, yes, I see, thank you," said Dr. Deming.

Hal helped Irene choose what to wear, a blue jersey. Then, though her hands were shaking, she made herself up decent, which was a trick considering that she and Hal had killed a fifth since noon.

They drove out together, sharing the responsibility of spotting the cars coming at them, shrieking with laughter and cursing the other drivers and each other as they swung to avoid the malignant efforts of everyone else on the road to run them down.

They turned off the throughway at the wrong exit. Then, to help them find their way, they picked up a little Mexican boy whom they found so adorable that by the time they arrived at the Southside Home for the Dead he ran off without taking the money they'd promised.

The fact that their bearing was uncertain rather pleased the assembly there. Someone rushed to get Irene a box to sit on.

The word reached Michael just as he came out of the building after his talk with Mr. Bulgaros. Escorted to Irene, he sat on his heels at her feet. She was so touched by this attitude of devotion that she suddenly clutched his hand to her mouth and kissed it.

When he told her what they planned to do with Vinnie, it wasn't clear that she understood or even heard what he said, only that she could see Michael loved her son and so loved him for that.

There were more than fifty young people close around her, more coming all the time, brought there by the memory and meaning of her son. Her eyes glistened as she looked around at the young worshippers, warmed by the light in their faces.

"We want you very much to come," Michael said.

"How could I miss it, for chrissake!"

"If you like, we'll come and get you in a car."

"We got a car."

"But you may not be able to find the place—so if we drove by in the morning you could follow us out."

"I'd like that."

Impulsively, she took his hand again. Irene had become, for the first and only time in her life, Vinnie's mother.

"Dr. O'Rear, were you in the armed services?"

"Yes," the psychiatrist answered, "but I really don't see what that has to do with what I've been saying."

"I thought you showed an especially sympathetic understanding of the nature of a lifer, you do know what a lifer is, don't you?"

"Mr. Walker, neither my report nor my testimony show any special understanding and sympathy for the lifer, and I resent whatever innuendo lies in that choice of word. My report came to almost exactly the same conclusion Dr. Deming's did."

"So I noticed. To the choice of words! 'Dissociative,' for instance. I still don't really know what that word means."

"Oh, come on, Mr. Walker, you understand very well what the word means. If you don't, you certainly aren't going to after I've explained it because I couldn't do it nearly as well as Dr. Deming did."

"May I ask you about a few points you made that Dr. Deming did not?"

"Yes, yes, of course, that's what we're here for, isn't it?"

The courtroom adored Dr. O'Rear. He wasn't taking any crap from Cy.

"Now, doctor, you say in your report that Mr. Flores's, formerly Sergeant Flores's, record has been impeccable, regular promotions, no reprimands. You further say that he seems to you to perhaps overconform. You end your—praise—by saying that you found he strongly adheres to the military dictum that a good officer should be able to control his family problems and that he saw family disruptions as potential threats to his military station and career."

"I meant that as praise."

"Would you then call him the perfect soldier, psychologically speaking?"

"I didn't say that. Don't put words in my mouth."

"Would you say that those qualities are a part of every good soldier—to comply with orders? Yes or no."

"Yes."

"You go on to say that you found him overly polite and

formal and that—well, let me read from your report, that he 'relates in an approval-seeking manner.' Right?"

"Yes."

"Would you then say that Sergeant Flores would have to be sure of the approval of his superiors before he would do something?"

"Do you mean in his line of duty in the air force?"

"To begin with?"

"There. Yes."

"Would you say that he would have to have or believe he had, however mistakenly, the approval of his superiors before he murdered Vincent Connor?"

"No."

"But he would be concerned about it?"

"Yes."

"Might even believe, mistakenly, that he had it?"

"Yes."

"Would he in his dissociative reactive phase believe that his deed would find general approval?"

"He might mistakenly believe that."

"Then you would say that he was trying to win the approval of his superiors by what he did?"

"No."

"Then what does it mean, your statement that he relates in an approval-seeking manner, it sounds scholarly, but what does it mean?"

"I told you that doesn't apply here."

"Does it mean, possibly, that he was certain, in his deranged mind, of course, of the approval of others before he acted?"

"No."

"Then does it mean anything at all?"

"Not the way you're trying to twist it."

"Do you think that Sergeant Flores was encouraged in what he did?"

"By whom?"

"His superiors?"

"Of course not."

"By the general moral and intellectual atmosphere of the base?"

"No."

"By the general moral and intellectual atmosphere of the country?"

"No."

"Don't you really think that?"

"What do you think I am!"

"I think you are finding it difficult to tell the truth."

"I don't have to take that. I was hired to do a job, and—"

"And you did it. Let me ask you one more question. Did Sergeant Flores at any time in your examination of him show the least remorse for killing another human being? Two! Two other human beings? Tell the truth!"

"No."

"Isn't that a quality a good soldier should have, too?"

"Show remorse?"

"No, *not* show remorse, not *feel* remorse. To do his duty as he understands it to be and not allow ordinary human inhibitions especially those of a moral nature to interfere with his efficiency?"

"I resent that."

"Then show me that he showed remorse, just once, once, anywhere, of any kind, in anything he said or did."

"He was defending his home and—" He stopped.

"Were you going to say—country, defending his home and country?"

"Yes, I was. I think that boy was a menace."

"And that he should have been killed?"

"No. But I'm not ashamed to say it, I think he should have been restrained, confined until—"

"In a concentration camp?"

"I wouldn't call it that."

"What would you call it?"

Dr. O'Rear decided he'd gone too far, decided not to answer that question.

Cy Walker decided he'd gone far enough, decided not to question Dr. O'Rear further.

Judge Breen recessed court early that Friday, at ten minutes before four, saying that everyone needed a good rest and particularly advising the jury to get lots of sleep over the weekend.

His plane left at five. Sarah had insisted on taking him

to the airport; on the way she read him a letter they'd had that morning from their son Arthur. It was even shorter than his usual.

"I've left school," he wrote. "Don't worry. Love."

Teddy didn't comment. It was one more load than he could carry that day.

"I think it's a good idea," Sarah said.

"Okay." Teddy seemed beat.

"What's college? He'll turn out another authority addict like the others. But you might see him in New York, see if he needs—"

"Okay, I will." Teddy sighed.

They parked at the airport, and she did something she hadn't done in many weeks, slid over against him and pulled his head down and kissed him on the lips.

"I love you, Teddy," she said.

"Since when all of a sudden?"

"I know I haven't sounded like it lately. But I do. You can count on it."

"You're just worried about your boy."

"*You're* my boy, and I'm sorry I said those mean things to you."

"Oh, that's okay, I don't mind."

"It's not okay! And you do mind! Why do you say that? Anyway, I didn't want you flying off without knowing it. I love you, Teddy."

"Not like you used to."

"Nobody loves anybody like they used to. But I've thought a lot about it, and you're no worse than anyone else—"

He laughed. "I've received more flattering compliments."

"Well, that's maturity, isn't it? I mean, I don't see stars any more. What I mean is you're better than the others, you've got a good heart, not many of those around! I want you to know I'll be yours anywhere, anytime, anything you decide to do."

He felt the beginning of tears. He was tired and didn't have much hope ahead.

He began to tell her about the trial—she seemed interested for a change—particularly about Dr. O'Rear.

"That son of a bitch is a fascist, Sare, he wants to put these kids in concentration camps. He actually said it, detain them somewhere till they've straightened out, that's what he said. And that goddamn jury ate it up! What the hell am I defending here, Sare? I've worked like a nigger all my life, and now some anonymous goniffs in New York are shooting craps with my life's savings."

Sarah was very tender with him. "Your problem, baby, is that you still believe if you're a good boy, you'll be rewarded. When you're a good boy, they eat you."

She kissed him where his eyes had closed for an instant, and suddenly Teddy Breen told her everything, the whole story, about the loan he was carrying and that he had indeed shared in the take of his old office in Chicago; that was the money invested, now disappearing.

She was not surprised.

"Anyway," Teddy said, "it's dirty money that's going."

"Clean money goes the same way. Fast."

At the gate he kissed her goodbye. He felt much better.

"If you decide not to come back," she said, "just call me. I'm packed."

That thought had crossed his mind—often. In court, that very afternoon! To just pull up stakes again and—

"Think of it," she said, "you could be Teddy Greenbaum again, and I'd love you like I used to love him."

───────────────────────

Alan and Cy had trouble finding the base psychiatrist. Ed Stevens wasn't home, and his wife had no idea where he was. "Sometimes he just takes off Friday night, and I don't see him till Monday morning. His 'liberty drunks,' he calls them. He's not reliable over the weekends."

"You must worry about him," Alan said.

"I worry, sure, but I'm not going to tell the man how to live his life, not at this late date. He's been through a lot, you know. Here, look."

She pointed to some photographs on the wall, and Alan and Cy looked at one taken by a navy cameraman of the flattop *Lexington* as it went down. Next to it was a very unofficial-looking snapshot of some sailors grouped under the muzzles of three eight-inchers.

"That's him there with his buddies," she said, "can you believe it? They all went down with the *Lexington*, all except him. He never got over it. One drink and he's on them again."

"That's too bad," Alan said. "You got any idea where he might be drinking?"

"Not the foggiest. I just hope I can get him through another two years. Then we'll be set, twenty years' pension, benefits, buy a trailer, go down to Florida, and live near the warm water. About the only thing he likes besides drinking is swimming and maybe an occasional girl, he still likes that."

"Don't you mind?" Cy asked.

"You mean you'd expect me to deny the man that at the end of his life? He can do anything that makes him happy, fellow. Look, I'll tell you where he is. I even know the girl—by the way, I didn't offer you a beer. I'm going to have another, can I get you one?"

"No, thank you," Alan said.

"No, thanks," Cy said.

"Well, aren't you admirable," she laughed. "Anyway, I'm a cheap drunk, right? Just a cheap drunk from Podunk!" she sang from the kitchen. She came back to the table, laughing, tore off a corner of *Life* magazine, and began to write an address on it, laboriously. "My mother had arthritis and it's coming on me, too. Well, hell, so? I told the doctor, I'm not going to be writing my memoirs. Long as I can open a beer and turn on the television. Here, take it. And tell him everything's okay here."

Ed Stevens was alone and reading a book, *The Crock of Gold*, taking his liquor slowly, as if he had all night, which he had.

He offered them a jolt, apologized he had no mixer but water. His guests quickly murmured that was all they ever used. Then they invited them to dinner, him and his girl, was she home?

"Oh, I don't think she'll be in for a while, she's being courted, you know, figures it's time she had children and maybe get married, too. So she's giving the field a once-over. Can't blame her. I'm not much use to her any more, but it's nice here and—well, I'm comfortable, it's nice, isn't it?"

They agreed it was, and they were sincere, even envious. Then they gave him his wife's message.

"She's a good old girl, isn't she! I don't come here, you understand, to get away from my wife. It's the base, I can't stand those creeps out there, you know."

"Why don't we have dinner," Alan said. "I'm hungry."

"Well, to tell you the truth, I stopped eating a couple of years ago. And I'm too lazy to move, enjoying this too much. You're hungry, though. Let's see, she's got some cheese—it's here—and some franks, days old but they're cooked, well, you can have anything she's got, look around. Hell, relax! It's cool and nice. I can keep the windows open here. At the base, every time I have a snort I have to pull the shades down. The women there—I actually caught one of them lifting a corner of my shade to peek into my house. I happened to be in the backyard at the time, it was after dark and hot as hell. So I said to her, 'What the hell you doing there, Mabel?' She scooted like a cat. And I'm supposed to dispense sanity and good sense out there!" He laughed till he was tired. Then he asked abruptly, "What did you fellows want to have dinner with me for?"

Cy told him about the testimony of the two psychiatrists, and Alan reminded him that he had brought Gavin out to see him, weeks ago, just after Gavin was put on the case.

"I never heard from him again," Stevens said, laughing again, "soon as he understood I thought Flores was sane, he didn't come visiting any more. Hell, I don't want Flores killed anyway. He's no worse than the rest of the damned air force. You're not going to try to put me on the stand, are you?"

"Well, we were, yes," Alan said.

"Not on your life! I don't want to go near that place. I'll tell you something, they'll never let me on the stand. Never! Hell, I know the truth. That man was boasting to me about what he'd done. All that shit about love for his daughter, hell, he used to beat that little girl's brains out, she used to come home late and he'd whale the piss out of her. They don't want to hear all that."

"That's why we want to put you on the stand," Alan said.

"They won't let you do it. No one wants to believe Flores was sane. It's one of those lies that makes life possible. Flores was temporarily insane, that's why he did it, otherwise he was a model man and model air force and he didn't know what he was doing, just a passing aberration."

"Well, let me tell you what's got me," Alan said. "Can I?"

"Sure, go 'head!" He poured them another drink, and they waited while he got some water. "Glad you guys came out," he said, "go ahead. I'm listening."

"What's being proved in that court," Alan said, "is that if a man doesn't like his daughter's boyfriend, he can shoot him dead, and if he's air force he can get away with it, especially if the ideas of the guy he killed are unpopular and if he lives different from——"

"Oh, come on, there's nothing new there. 'Rank has its privileges,' ever hear that?"

"But they're going to get away with it."

"Sure they are! Was it ever different?"

"Not only is he going to get away with it, he's going to be a hero."

"Ah! That's the charm of it."

"But we can't let them——"

"Why the hell not? They get away with everything else."

"Dr. Stevens," Alan said, "I saw that photograph in your house, you and those fellows on the deck of the *Lexington,* and the picture next to it—the flattop going down, and your wife told me that all your buddies, all of them in that picture, went down and only you were left. Well, those fellows were lost for something, weren't they?"

"Then? Yes. We believed in that war! We wanted to go to that war! But after it was over and all those fellows were gone, it was no different. It was the same, the pistols ran it for the moneyman. They don't even pretend around here. You don't mean to tell me you still believe in that garbage, do you?"

"Not still. Again."

"I'm sorry for you."

"I want you to go on the stand. I want you to say what you told me, that he boasted about killing the boy, that he was sane and smart and prepared and——"

"You believe it'll make any damned difference?"

"Dr. Stevens, I'll tell you how corny I am. I even believe that you may have been spared when the *Lexington* went down so you could stand in that court and for five minutes tell the truth."

"You know that's bullshit."

Alan watched Ed fill the glasses again, this time not bothering with ice or water.

"Well, then," Alan said, "do it to spite them. Go in there and say a true word—just because they don't want you to. You know he was sane."

"Sane as hell."

"And that if he didn't do it, his name would have been cat-shit around here."

"True."

"Say it so you'll remember when you die that you once had five minutes when your buddies who went down would have been—"

"Will you cut that shit out!" Stevens yelled. "Lay off them! You don't know anything about them."

"Well, I'll tell you the truth," Alan said. "I have a friend, he's one of those kids with dirty feet and long hair, blows grass and drops acid and all the rest of it. I was like you till I met him, I had given up. Well, this kid, he's been sitting watching the preparations for the trial, the whole show, and he's gotten more and more disgusted, and now he's beginning to give up. I'm beginning to believe, and he's giving up. I gave him a lot of rhetoric about the judicial process and the jury system and the final strength of democratic institutions and all that stuff including the common decency of everybody, even those in the army, and day by day, minute by minute, the way that trial went, everything that happened in court made me a liar. Now, Dr. Stevens, he's turned against me. In fact, he sees that people like me are the ones who tell everybody that everything is basically okay, that everything will finally work out okay. We're the dupes, but we're also the perverters, we're the ones who keep this thing going. So I feel I have to show him, can you understand that? Prove there's something good, something honest? I mean just so it won't be a total fake! He's about at the end of disgust now, like the ones who are bombing the buildings, only I think he's gone a step further in his mind. He thinks it's necessary to start killing people now or else no one will pay attention. I need your testimony, Dr. Stevens."

"They'll say it's privileged."

"They already did. But that applies to consultations, not to what you heard and saw and. . . ."

"They'll never let me."

"But if we find a way to make them, will you testify?"

"If you want me to."

They stayed there, drinking, until the girl came home and then excused themselves.

Alan had drunk more than Cy, so Cy drove to where his car was parked. "Can you make it back to the base?" he asked as Alan got out.

"Oh, sure, don't worry about me."

"You didn't mean that, did you, what you said about Michael? That he might kill somebody, as a sort of demonstration? That's insanity—or kid talk, I don't know which."

"I believe he's thinking along those lines."

"Then he ought to be put away."

"That's just what he figures you'd say."

"Why does he hold you responsible?"

"He doesn't. I do. You know, Cy, I originally became a lawyer because I thought our way of justice was worth devoting a life to, excuse the corn. But gradually I forgot about it, I married and settled into the air force, I played a hell of a game of tennis and made with the jokes, I didn't let myself look around and think about anything. Well, Michael started me up again. Anyway, it's come down to this, either I'm full of it or I'm not, either I've spent my whole life lying to myself, or—you see what I mean, it's not him? It's me."

CHAPTER FIVE
_____

Don Wheeler sat at the foot of one of the eight beds in the Special Care Ward, his hand on Hope's ankle, the tips of his first and second fingers on the pulse there. The Special Care Ward was empty that night except for one other person dying under an oxygen tent and a child into whom glucose was being fed from a suspended bottle. They were unattended. The only sounds were those of the muffled counters in the automatic devices, falling and engaging, the dripping of forced fluids.

Alan drove to Donna's. He buzzed from downstairs, but there was no answer. A couple came home and he passed in with them, hammered on the door of Donna's apartment until her roommate opened it to the length of the safety chain. Alan insisted she tell him where Michael was. "How the hell do I know?" she said. "He's not here." So Alan went down to the Karmann-Ghia and, putting half of himself on each seat, fell asleep. He had no other place to go.

It wasn't until Cy got home that he remembered the telegram form still in his pocket. He undressed by the light from the bathroom, looking at Corky. She woke a little and looked at the white electric clock on the bedside table. "It's awful late," she said, "where you been?" She fell asleep before he could answer. Cy took the telegram out of his pocket and read it. They were getting the better of him, he felt it again; he didn't want to send that fucking knuckle-under-gram. Possibly, he thought, as he sat down to evacuate, it was just a matter of principle with them, to get a short-hair hold on all their employees from the beginning. Well, it was a matter of principle with him not to let them. He tore up the telegram and stuffed the bits down between his legs.

Suddenly he wanted very much to win the Flores case.

It was an off-news night at the local TV station, and somebody there had the idea of taping what was happening at the Southside Home for the Dead.

The word got around. By eleven, the night people, outcasts, criminals, dropouts, freaks, radicals, freight yard workers, late shifts out of the bean wagons, the heads and the drunks, the bikers and dealers, the homeless, the rootless, wanderers all, were beginning to make the scene.

The news first reached the taxi drivers who had to go through that part of town to bring their fares back from the ball game.

The news went through the dormitories of the university, out to the students spread on the lawns and under the trees. Most of them didn't need an excuse not to study, but this one served, and they had the wheels to make it out to the Southside.

The news reached the massage parlor near the hotel where the visiting ball team stayed. The swinging second baseman and the flakey right fielder got into a free-for-all with three visiting appliance salesmen. The girls broke it up—to their regret because the men made up, decided to go out together and see the show.

The news scattered an engagement party on the other side of town. A lot of the nice kids who knew no other way out of the prevailing boredom except to get bombed out of their minds piled into their Cutlasses and Cougars and zapped down the quiet streets to the south side of town.

The news reached Mextown. A bunch of the bloods, including a rivet catcher who claimed to be a distant relative of Cesario Flores, piled into a panel truck and headed for the fun.

The news reached a tavern on the El Paso Road where

a newly formed musical group was trying out on a pass-the-bucket basis. They had a slim showing that night, decided to quit and go.

The news broke up a stud game of seven bush-mafia who'd moved to the Southwest in an act of loyalty to their capo. Their verdict on the social life of that community? No action! They were grateful for any diversion.

The news reached the air force base, where the only entertainment for a squadron of fighter pilots just in from Con Minh was Walt Disney's *The Love Bug*. Juana was there, and when she heard what was happening she asked her escort to drive her to the scene. When she got there she stayed in the car so none of her old friends could see her. But air force personnel, two days out of the sky over Asia, mingled and marveled.

Among the hippies, joints and makings were passed for free. But a couple of dealers with the hard stuff took the opportunity to move it. A lot of the kids knew they were in for a long party, decided to hoard what they could afford.

The police sat in their squad cars, coats unbuttoned, dragging on cigarettes as they watched drugs being dealt, the passing of paper, the pressing of hands. They saw men with records, some of whom they'd faced in court on less-festive occasions. They nodded and their lips said hello, and they got the same back. There was a general moratorium on the exercise of every kind of authority that night.

From a decent distance two aging priests watched. They lived across the street from the old morgue; the music had awakened them. They seemed unperturbed, chattered at each other like two old white monkeys.

A breeze, coming down from the mountains to the north-east, stirred the air, kept it fresh and cool.

People walked here and there, looking at each other, like the crowds in the small plaza of a Mexican mountain town, or along the courting walk of a near-eastern city back in the days when people were entertained by encountering each other, still liked and didn't fear each other, back in the long-gone beginnings of this century.

Through it all, Irene sat on her box in quiet euphoria, empress acknowledged. Hal stood close up behind her, ready to steady her if necessary.

"Who are all these people?" The TV newsman was interviewing Irene. She looked at Michael, sitting at her feet.

"There's some who know who he is and some who just heard about him," he said. "But they're all friends of Vinnie's, he was murdered and they don't know what to do about it."

In the black middle of the night, Don Wheeler woke with a start. There was no pulse in Hope's ankle. The foot was cold—well, it had been cold for over a day, but now there was no pulse. He looked up. An intern, a young man he'd never seen before, was standing at the head of the bed, holding Hope's wrist. He put it down on her chickenbone chest, then covered her face with the top of the sheet. Then he moved to where the widower sat and covered Hope's feet with the bottom of the sheet. He whispered to Wheeler; there was no point in staying now. Wheeler shook his head. The intern walked away.

The T.V. truck had gone. The visitors began to disappear. The grounds around the old morgue were quiet.

About three o'clock, Irene fell asleep where she was sitting. Hal, with help from Michael, got her into his car, and they drove off.

Some of the kids slept in dark corners, others in cars parked up and down the street.

But those most involved with Vinnie and what he meant walked to the highway leading into the desert where tomorrow's events would take place.

After a hearty breakfast of pancakes and eggs that he made for himself, Gavin read the sports page carefully, then folded the paper, went to the bedroom, and put on his best sport coat.

"I'm going to the hospital," he said to Betty who was still in bed. "You don't want to come, do you?"

Gavin didn't like Betty around when he was with Mr. Wheeler.

"No," Betty said, "I'm going to stay in bed, it's too delicious to leave. See if Pup got home all right, will you?"

"Don't worry about him," Gavin said, "he was somewhere doing the same thing we were last night." He smiled and closed the door.

Pup was a large, overfed boxer. When Gavin opened the front door, he found him at his feet. His belly had been ripped open with long knife slashes; his guts were all over the steps.

The caravan was a short one. Michael, in Donna's car, came first. Sitting up front with him was Irene. She had insisted on it, but once she'd got her way, she slept the whole trip out. So did Rosalie and Lonnie in the back seat. Sandy was there too, awake, not talking, not stoned.

Behind Donna's car was Mr. Bulgaros, driving his hearse. He had intended to have the regular driver on the job, uniform and all. But the man, not entering into the spirit of the event, had asked double time for Sunday.

Finally there was Hal's car. From the side it looked empty, but actually Hal had picked up six people who were all over the back seat and the floor, fast asleep.

By the time Gavin got to the hospital, his boss had left and Hope Wheeler was on her way to Bryant's Funeral Home.

Just on the chance, Gavin went to the office. His guess was shrewd; Don Wheeler was at his desk. Wheeler always kept it tidy, none of the usual calendars, pictures, letter trays. Just a clean surface—and on it, now, a single letter written in a woman's hand, and a single envelope with a name on it.

Wheeler nodded at Gavin as if he'd been expecting him.

"I'm awfully sorry, sir," Gavin said.

Wheeler picked up the envelope he'd found under Hope's pillow at the hospital. It was dated a month ago. He read it to Gavin, first the envelope, "Open after I'm gone," then the letter:

"Darling Dee-dee: I'm sorry this has been so long and boring for you. But now I'm gone and you're free. Just do one last thing for me. Don't have a funeral. I detest them. I don't really have any friends, and no relatives who'd be interested to hear I'm dead. I couldn't stand for a lot of people I don't really know sitting there, doing their best to look doleful just because you're a big shot. Take what's left of me to a crematorium as soon as I'm gone, the same

day if you can. When they burn me up, I don't want anyone
else in the place. Just you and me, alone, the way it was
in the beginning, the way I liked it best when I was alive.
There isn't much of me left, it won't take long. While it's
happening, remember, really do, that I loved you all my
life and I couldn't have asked for anything more than you
gave me and that I have no regrets except maybe that you
didn't make love to me one more time. And know that I
trusted you and believed every word you ever said to me
and was always proud to have been your wife. I don't
believe in an afterlife or any of that, so just tell them to
throw my ashes where they throw everyone else's. Yours
still, Hope."

——————————————————————

While Vinnie's body lay in Mr. Bulgaros's hearse, the boys
took turns with a pair of shovels he'd provided to dig a
grave in the hollow on the other side of the little rise where
the dobe house stood.

Sandy and Rosalie wrapped the body in some sheets they
had washed in a laundromat on the way out. The sheets,
Sandy's, had hem-stitched edges and the embroidered initials
of her grandmother.

At the bottom of the shallow grave two Indian blankets
were put down. The body was lowered and placed on top
of them. Then the face and chest were bared, down to the
top of the trousers.

Two of the bikers had ripped off some flowers somewhere,
and these were arranged around the body. Mr. Bulgaros
had brought out flowers left over from another funeral.
They didn't look bad, considering.

Everyone was turned on, and everyone was turned on
to what was happening. When they began to come down,
there was the wherewithal to pick them up. The whole
place smelled of grass.

No one had arranged procedure, but people began to
come up and throw things into the open grave. The idea
seemed to be to provide for Vinnie in the future. Some
who believed in reincarnation left amulets to protect the
dead man. A biker left a charm of bear teeth on a leather
thong; it had seen him safely through ninety thousand miles.

Another biker, after reading excerpts, mostly sections having to do with the correct way to break in a motor, threw his Harley-Davidson handbook into the grave.

To make sure that Vinnie would never lack what he might need to turn on, or possibly because it was the only valuable thing many of them had, lids of grass were thrown into the grave and those who were not so well provided threw in what they thought they could spare, some only a couple of joints.

A girl took a tiny white solid state radio off the belt of her jeans and placed it carefully by Vinnie's ear.

A sixteen-year-old boy with bloodshot eyes, no one knew who he was or where he'd come from, threw in a fix kit.

Sandy took off her elephant hair ring, fell on her knees, reached down, put it on one of Vinnie's closed eyes.

Mr. Bulgaros had nothing to give; they assured him it wasn't necessary, he had already done enough. But he finally, after considerable hesitation, threw in his Chinese good-luck coin, the one he always carried. Then he got back into his hearse and drove off.

A young girl with a snub nose and many freckles, who'd never seen Vinnie alive, took her panties off and threw them in.

Rosalie had a little photograph of Lonnie in her wallet. She asked him if it would be okay, then leaned down and put it on Vinnie's chest.

A man of thirty who'd just done six months in jail for taking part in a "train" involving two fifteen-year-old girls tore a swastika patch off the side of his sleeve and threw it in. Another pulled off a 2nd Armored patch and threw it in.

A boy hitchhiking west with a young black woman went into his knapsack and pulled out a spiked kaiser helmet, the only thing his father had ever given him. He placed it near Vinnie's head.

As the music and the drugs heated their spirits, the gifts began to have a sacrificial air.

A boy who'd lived at Queen Street for a time cut off the hair from one side of his head and threw it in; he was stoned.

A black boy, Vinnie had dealt him and he remembered a time when he was balls-of-his-ass-broke and Vinnie gave him what he needed, cut his hand and let the blood drip in.

A musician who'd been singing the same melodic phrase over and over, drawing twenty people around him into the monotonous, maddening chant, smashed his guitar against the side of the grave.

A boy from the neighborhood who had joined the assembly by accident, but immediately dug it, put his knife and leather sheath at Vinnie's groin. A girl saw him do it, left the boy she'd come with, kissed the stranger, and stayed with him. The boy who had brought her out didn't mind, not that day.

A girl with long black hair and a large hooked nose supporting small granny glasses stood at the side of the grave and said a message. "Sex," she announced, "is politically important. People who are inhibited sexually are also oppressed."

None of this happened in quick sequence. The demonstrations of sorrow and devotion, loss, love and inspiration came at irregular and erratically spaced intervals.

By mid-afternoon many of the assembly were into heavier drugs.

There was an argument on the sidelines. A girl was debating quite seriously whether it was good politics at this moment in history to kill white babies, considering the way the world was going. Weathermen, she said, were advocating this.

A boy next to her said she was lying, that was pig talk.

Some people close by who hadn't heard the argument did hear the word "pig" and began to murmur, "Off the pig, hit the pig," and so on that way.

A tall boy who looked like Jon Voight was shouting, "Right, right! That's what I said! The Weathermen are into guilt politics because they're all from affluent families!"

A very small boy stood at the grave, took a brass peace amulet that hung from a leather thong around his neck, threw it in. He seemed unsteady, his eyes were full of hate. "There are four power groups in this state," he announced. "They are one, real estate. Two, the military, there are now almost twenty thousand men at the base, including two hundred and fifty South Korean pilots in training. Three, the university, nationally known as a brainwashing, playboy school. And four, the copper mining industry. Those are the realities of our lives." People shshshed him.

For a while there was silence.

Michael decided it was time to close the grave.

The sun was very low, very red, very hot. Some of the kids were scattering, looking for shade or privacy.

But they all stopped where they were when they heard the size and sound of Irene's grief. The woman, drunk for two days, was inspired by the demonstrations all around her and spiritually elevated by her position as mother of the martyr. In another era she might have thrown herself into the grave to be buried alive with her loved one. Hal had to restrain her from climbing down into the pit. She struck at him, but he held on until others came up to help. Irene was out of a west Ireland woman by a Donegal stone farmer and surprisingly strong. Finally her screams and the cries of people trying to subdue her brought Michael. He spoke to her; she seized his hand, kissed it, and was quiet.

She told Hal to go get her a drink. He said the bottle was empty and she said, for chrissake, that's what she meant, go get her a drink. The nearest package store was six miles; Hal didn't dare leave her alone that long, so he decided to pretend, walk to the car but not drive off.

The moment his back was turned Irene put the clutch on Michael, whom she outweighed by thirty pounds, whispering hoarsely in his ear, "I don't sleep with that goddamn faggot, I want you to know that."

It was time to cover the body. What with the grave's being used by strangers for a political platform and Irene's threat to throw herself in, which she seemed in condition to carry out, Vinnie was no longer the focus of the occasion.

Michael dropped into the shallow pit, crouched there out of sight. An instant's curiosity, then the assembly picked up on whatever they'd been doing.

Michael got out and looked around, went over to a group of people he'd never seen before, asked for their blanket. He covered the face with the cotton sheet, the body with the coarse wool.

He told Irene to throw in the first handful of dirt.

Then, chasing away everyone who tried to help, Michael shoveled the body over with heavy sand. He alone stamped the ground covering Vinnie until it was level.

Remembering what he'd read the Indians did, he threw bits of dead cactus and dried roots, rocks and old bones over the place, everywhere scuffing the surface to disguise where the dead had been put down. Still he fussed, adding bits of dried rubbish as he found them, stopping, sitting on the ground, seeing something more, pulling it to where Vinnie was, working the place over again, then again.

Finally it was done. Michael sat without moving, giving no sign of what he was thinking or feeling, exhausted. The cause that had kept him going for so long was no longer there.

The sun in the desert is hottest at the end of the day. People found shade at the side of a car, under a pickup, or by rigging a blanket for an awning.

There was music and smoking; nearly a hundred people turned on that afternoon and evening. There was the buzz of laughter and the hum of general talk, storytelling, and the exchange of views. And even before the sun disappeared, there was balling in the open.

All was harmony, no one competed, no one put anyone down. For a few minutes, they were a nation.

Then it happened.

Sandy started it. In the spirit of the day, she had an irresistible desire to ride. The bike she picked was not an ordinary one; Sandy knew the best when she saw it. The Suzuki TM400R is a racer and nothing else, no trim, no rack, no frills, just forty horse under the seat, thirty-three pounds of torque to propel two hundred and thirty-six pounds of bike. This beast will do wheelies in all five gears. On any kind of paved surface, the rider must lean down hard on the handle bars just to keep the front wheels on the ground. And in sand? Loose dirt! Very few riders know what to do with that much horsepower, how to get it on the ground without getting themselves on the ground.

This was the first TM400R in the area; the owner had never let anyone else touch it, so when he heard the rasp of the unmuffled explosion chamber, he moved like a cat. Sandy was used to getting what she wanted; she would not get down. The biker pulled her off and flung her five feet.

Sandy came up holding a rock, which she threw at the biker. The rock didn't hit him, it hit the bike, chipping off a piece of the paint.

Whether the people who moved in when Sandy was smacked across the face were her friends or crazy with

the heat or just stoned, they were spoiling. Everyone saw
the knife come out, no one could really blame the biker
for pulling out his belt with a buckle the size and weight
of a large Yale lock.

The fight, observed from above, would have suggested a
struggle between two snakes, heads locked, tails lashing this
way and that. Almost everyone in the place followed the
running battle for the two hundred yards it covered.

Except Michael. The last of it happened near to where
he sat, in fact the fighters passed just over him as they cut
and lashed at each other. Michael made no effort to stop
it; his role as a leader had been played out. He did not
raise his face, didn't even appear to be waiting for it to be
over.

The biker's face was cut, but not deeply.

The scalp of one of Sandy's friends was ripped open by
the belt buckle. A flap of skin, hair attached, hung loose,
the size of a baby's hand. The boy fell over, staggered up,
then dropped. He was stunned—or worse. The fight stopped
for the moment.

The biker turned his back, walked away, began to fuss
with his bike, inspecting the place where the rock had
dented the side. Bleeding from the cut on his face, he
wiped the drops of blood as they fell on his bike.

On the other side, someone was urging that they take
the boy to the hospital—he appeared to be in shock. Much
loud discussion: Where was the nearest hospital? Others
had the heat up to go on with the fight. The biker's friends
were moving in around him.

Michael knew this scene: a riot, full scale, was about to
blow. He made no move to stop it.

What settled the day was the boy with the cracked skull;
he began to vomit. No one could figure out why—vomit
from a cracked skull? Much anxious whispering. The decision: Get him to a hospital. The tail gate of a wagon was
lowered, the body gently lifted in. The boy wasn't dead,
but very white, at least a concussion, serious. One final
crisis: Was he "clean"? His girl friend went through his
pockets, removed a sack of grass and some other stuff they
didn't want found at the hospital. Another car filled with
his friends followed the wagon off.

As they pulled out, the biker was showboating his indifference to the injured man. Michael despised him. After maybe ten minutes more of fussing with his bike, he looked up at the setting sun and frowned, as if making a judgment about something. Why the act? He's a fake, Michael thought, a pig. Then the man mounted. So did his friends. They left, but only after cutting circles through the crowd again and again, raising the dust, their expression of scorn for the terrorized, daring them to respond.

They didn't. No one spoke a word in anger, or even reproach. In the middle of the cloud the bikers raised, they sat and ate dust. Michael despised them, too, they were no more human than the rest of humanity, no more civilized than the civilization they scorned.

For Michael this was the end of that part of the story. Whatever cause had once held these people together, given them some kind of unity and meaning, no longer existed. Vinnie was in the ground.

Michael got up and walked across the desert, now darkening, down the dirt road trace to the dobe hut he and Vinnie had once planned to occupy, now black as death. He stood in front of it and remembered. Then he turned and walked into the desert until everything behind him had disappeared.

Somewhere he lay down like an animal and fell asleep.

CHAPTER SIX

The men who fly the F-4s out of Collins, the Fighting Fifty-fifth, are an elite. The purpose of the base is to put them in the air perfectly trained, perfectly equipped. They are highly motivated, mission-oriented, combat-ready.

Uniformly young, dressed in one-piece zip-ups, it is not easy to tell the instructors fresh out of the air over Asia from the young men they train. Only when they wear their dress uniforms can the majors and baby colonels be detected. There is about them all an air of innocence marvelously wedded to a highly trained technological intelligence. Their specialized education has saved them, their faces reveal, from the unpleasant and demoralizing questions that more abstruse preoccupations would have raised. Physically there is about them all a confident lift of body and head that only the very young and the very favored enjoy.

For them all, pain has been eliminated from the art of war: Killing has become an abstract of scope smudges and calculus curves, of cross hairs and coordinates, of following orders phrased in the vocabulary of high arithmetic. Their innocence, it is plain to see, is not spoiled by the killing they've been trained to perform. Easygoing, they do their jobs with minds clean of complicating factors. They are nice guys, relieved of the burden of conscience.

They are perfect mates for their F-4s.

They are also automated, also programmed, the highest expression of a technological society.

They know not what they do.

Because the air force lives by technology, no one can become part of it except by enlisting for four years. Whenever one of its number decides not to re-enlist, there is the tremendous waste of the time and money invested in each man. And so the air force does everything possible to keep its members in the service.

These men are pampered to the limits of the Christian tradition and military necessity. The part of the base where they stay resembles nothing so much as the campus of a country-club college devoted to postgraduate studies. The men don't live in barracks; they live in dorms. They have maid service. They are allowed beer in their rooms. Even the question of sexual release has been given official attention. Discreet but energetic efforts are made to bring girls within range.

The Balinese room of the Officers' Club, its thatched roof and walls, its easy chairs of highly polished woods and plantation slump seats, stirs that traditional erotic vision of the middle-aged American male, the bare-breasted South Seas, simultaneously making a subtle promise to the young men in training: Something like this is waiting for them in Southeast Asia.

Here are to be found the women in waiting, many of them wives of the pilots, dead, captured, missing. These wives are not there because they are waiting, but because they are not. It is odd, perhaps, that they should be looking for this kind of help from the very men who were or could have been their husband's best buddies.

What is immediately obvious is that it is the women who pursue. Outnumbered ten to one, they move with the directness which comes only with experience and the first realization that time moves faster for a woman. The men enjoy this state of affairs, do not press, move when and if they choose. The women, after all, aren't going anywhere.

The fact is that the boy-pilots are a perfect fraternity, moving outside their circle of male comradeship only for something biological they cannot control. This gives them that particular air of indifference so attractive to the anxious woman.

When Marian Kidd, née Dowd, had been in her last year of college, her daddy was doing the first of his two tours on the base. His lovely daughter, home for the holidays, would make it her custom to sit on his terrace and be lusted for in a genteel way.

When she married Alan Kidd that closed the chapter.

But not the book. Recently she had resumed her visits to the Officers' Club. At least once a week now, she walked again onto the terrace of the Balinese room, accompanied by that congenial if ineffectual man she'd married. Now, however, there was something anxious about the movements of her body. Perhaps she came there to be reassured that she was still admired, still alluring. Even if the cold light of her bathroom mirror revealed a slight down-stiffening of her mouth and a crinkle or two extra around her eyes, the light reflected off these soft-thatched walls gave away no such trifling defects. The boys still rallied round. The fact she was married was not a deterrent; most of the women there were.

Now, on this Saturday night, she was the nucleus of a cluster of perhaps a dozen lounge chairs, designed with a middle so low that both avenues to the treasures they held, head and knees, were tilted up, the flower and stems of desire. Marian's was surrounded by admirers who were—she couldn't help letting them believe—making time with her. Her smile, flashing this way and that, was a delighted display. And why not? What could be more exhilarating? To be a pretty woman, to be crowded, leaned over, rubbed against accidentally, then on purpose, to be sought, measured, to be—this promised—devoured.

She had missed it. Who could blame her for wanting it back?

At a huge metal barbecue trough, broiling two filets, was her husband. Next to him at the coals stood that fine professional, Lieutenant Colonel Earl McCord. And with him a man in civilian clothes who could have been a young advertising executive from one of the less-flamboyant agencies, could have been an engineer or a top-level electronics salesman, was none of these. As confident in his bearing as any of the pilots, he was a member of another elite.

"I'm worried about him," this man said to Alan, turning over his steak. "You're his close friend, aren't you?"

"I like Michael," Alan said cautiously, "but I don't think we're close friends." He moved to a large frosted bowl of fine fresh greens.

"Well, I think we should do something about helping him, don't you?" The man followed Alan and helped himself to salad. "I saw him in court the day I got into town, and he looked pretty shook up."

"He has been." Alan ladled green goddess dressing on Marian's salad, Russian on his own. "What do you plan to do?"

"I don't know. I was going to ask you—"

"I think you know," Alan said. "What's your plan?"

The man seemed a little hurt by Alan's distrust. "I think," he said, opening a potato baked in foil, "that we should influence him to leave town—for a while. He's in danger here, not because of anything he's done, but—" The man put three patties of sweet butter into the heart of his spud. "I mean, he's a nice kid, from everything I can gather, and not political at all, is he?"

"Try some of these chives," Alan said.

"But he's in with a bad bunch, don't you think so?"

"I do," Alan admitted.

"Incidentally," the man said, "do you know where he is now? I'm not asking for information, I'm about to tell you if you don't know."

"I don't," Alan said. He lifted the linen skirt off the basket of hot rolls and pulled out two for himself and two for his wife.

"We've just been informed—they've all been out in the desert, you know, burying the young man, and after they performed the ceremony there was an extremely ugly scrap. One kid has been brought into the hospital here, he's in Emergency now, with part of his scalp off."

"Not Michael, it wasn't Michael, was it?"

"No, but he was right into the middle of it."

"How do you know all this—so soon after it's happened?"

"It's our business to know."

Alan went back to the barbecue, picked up the long fork, and turned the filet.

The man followed. "We need to know everything that affects his thinking."

"Shall I turn yours?"

"Thanks," the man said.

"And to what end is it affecting his thinking?"

"Hasn't he threatened your life?"

"No," Alan said.

The man looked down at his steak, seemed sad about Alan's answer. "We were led to believe he had."

"By my wife?"

"If it were, you realize I couldn't say so. But it wasn't Mrs.—"

"Kidd."

"Thank you." The man hesitated, looked at Lieutenant McCord, then back at Alan. "Well, you ought to know," he said.

"Yes, I ought to." He wished he hadn't had to lie, but the man had lied, too. He pronged Marian's steak, dropped it on her plate. He was furious with her.

"Your wife sure likes her steak rare," the man observed.

"She's a base brat." Alan started away.

"Wait a minute," the man said.

"Wait a minute," McCord said. "We'd like your help in—"

"I can't help you."

"Why not?" snapped McCord.

Alan resented having to explain, but he tried. "Because I don't have the slightest influence on him any more. Because he won't even talk to me now—"

"You better take your wife her steak," the man suggested.

Alan nodded and walked over to where Marian was entertaining her suitors.

"I'm afraid that he was lying to us," the man said to McCord, with genuine regret.

Lieutenant Colonel McCord was embarrassed for the air force.

Alan was worried. He had, despite every predisposition and prejudice, liked the man. He, too, felt Michael was in trouble. He resented Marian's informing, but the information she'd conveyed was—accurate. And Alan was afraid as the man said he was of what Michael might be moved to do next.

There was an announcement from inside the Balinese room. Happy Hour, all drinks half price, was coming to an end. Alan saw McCord say something to his guest, then pick up their empties and hurry into the bar.

As McCord left, Alan returned to where the man sat. "I didn't want to talk to you in front of Colonel McCord," Alan lied, "but I am worried about Michael Winter."

"I realize that," the man said, "sit down."

"You know," Alan said, "there's something very good about him."

"And we must never forget," the man agreed, "that what's got him so shook up is the murder of his best friend. That's a big load for a kid to carry. But we can't forget, either, he's just a kid, but some of these kids now have deadly weapons—and convictions to go with them. Many of these crimes around the country come out of some kind of idealism, don't they?"

"Yes," Alan admitted. "True!"

"A gun or a pistol in the hands of a kid like this, even the most naïve, the most pure, is just as deadly. Isn't it?"

Alan nodded. "You see, he doesn't believe people pay any attention to words any more, only deeds. And he's on the verge—I think you're right about that—of doing something that may ruin his life."

"Or yours?"

"Well, I suppose—"

"What we're worried about is what might happen here if Master Sergeant Flores is exonerated."

"You mean when."

"It's very likely, I know. We want to be ready—"

"Here comes McCord," Alan said, getting up. Then he leaned over, said, "Anything I can do to help Michael, not you, Michael, understand? I don't know where the justice in this thing is, but it's certainly not in exonerating Flores."

"I don't think so either." The man spoke quickly, aware of McCord approaching.

"So anything you ask me to do that I believe will help him, I'll be glad to perform."

"I may take you up on that," the man said. "You're doing the right thing."

"I haven't done anything yet," Alan said. He surprised the man—and himself—by shaking his hand, nodded stiffly to Earl McCord, and walked away.

——————————————————————

Don Wheeler, observing his wife's last wish, disposed of her body immediately. She had also asked that he sit alone in the memorial chapel, and he did that too, in the front row, by himself.

Gavin had sent flowers; he was the only one of Wheeler's associates who knew Hope had died.

The ceremony was as brief as possible. There was an organ interlude, reflection music during which Wheeler looked at the small white casket. Then a panel opened at the back of the little stage and the coffin, on a concealed treadmill, rode back to music of a more religious character. As it moved the music got louder, to cover the sound of the wheels and gears, Wheeler supposed. When the casket had disappeared, the panel dropped back into place. The music swelled into an inspirational andante, then got very quiet, and a voiceover on tape began "The Lord Is My Shepherd."

Wheeler sat there for another ten minutes. The chapel was very still.

A man in black jacket and striped trousers opened the door at the back and approached. He sat in the row behind Wheeler for a moment, then leaned forward respectfully.

"Are you sure about the ashes?" he asked. "Mix them in, confuse them with those of—others?"

"That's what she wanted."

"What others?"

"Whoever they are. Today. Tomorrow."

"Well, let's see, there will be a Mr.—"

"I don't want to know," he said, turning around and facing Ernest Bryant. Don Wheeler's face was frightening. "Is it over?" he asked.

"Yes," Bryant said gently, "the earthly remains have been consumed."

"If you'd like your bill paid promptly, better give it to me now," Wheeler said. "I'm leaving town Tuesday for a long time."

Bryant hurried off.

The foyer was filled with the next funeral.

Wheeler walked to the offices of Don Wheeler and Associates. The streets were empty except for two old Indian women sitting on the two main corners. They held up beads and amulets for sale, and religious trinkets, crosses of pitted cactus wood hung on beaded strings.

His building was empty. So were the company offices.

He suddenly decided to do what he'd said, leave town Tuesday. He didn't want to go through the business of accepting condolences.

In the stationery closet he found the stack of folded corrugated cartons he'd had the foresight to order. He took his coat off and began to pack.

There was only one important thing he had to do before he left town. He called Gavin's number. "Wake him," he told Betty. Betty, he realized, didn't know Hope was dead. Don had told Gavin not to say anything to anybody; he was glad to see he could trust Gavin that way, too. "Get down here, will you?" he said. "I want you to help me pack."

After a long and demoralizing meeting with his broker, Judge Breen called his son. Arthur had a meeting that night —despite his dropout he still worked on a small dissident campus paper called *TH$ DOP$*—so the judge met him uptown.

The first question Arthur asked was, "What did you come here for?"

"Aren't you glad to see me?"

"I mean East, why did you come East? Sure I'm glad to—"

"I know, I was just kidding," Breen said, looking up at the waiter. "Don't you even want a beer?"

"I don't drink." Then, after his father had ordered, "It's you drunks who're putting us potheads in jail."

Breen was afraid to ask him how far into drugs he was. The boy looked fine, his eyes clear and bright, and there was a sassy, confident good humor about him that his father had never noticed before.

Then Thurston Breen found out Arthur knew all about the case. "You're going to be famous, dad," he promised, "if that guy gets off. Oh, you're going to be right in there with Hoffman."

"How do you know about that trial?" Breen asked. "There wasn't anything about it in the press, was there?"

"What's the press here, the *New York Times*? It was in our paper, the one I work on, all about it."

"I suppose you had the privilege of writing me up?"

"Who knows you better? I'll send you the back issues."

"Send them to the house, not the office, will you?" Breen laughed. "What do you mean famous?"

"That's what they called you in the *East Village Other*, the infamous Lynch Law Judge Breen. They ran a cartoon where you were a puppet and a couple of corny figures, Mr. Big Copper and Colonel Big Wings, were pulling the strings."

"Now you know that's a lot of shit."

The boy didn't comment, smiled that sassy smile.

"Am I an embarrassment to you, Arthur?"

"Not a bit. I don't consider myself responsible for what you've done or what you're going to do."

"That's right!" Breen suddenly felt belligerent as hell.

"Only one thing. I was going to write you, but I'd rather say it. I'm changing my name back to what it was, I'm Art Greenbaum now, okay?"

"No!" Breen shouted before he knew it.

"I've already done it," the boy said. "After all, I couldn't sign that piece about Judge Breen, 'Breen,' could I?" Then he smiled again and said, more gently, "There's nothing you can do about it." He looked up. "Here's my date."

She wore tattered dungarees and was barefoot, but she was a pretty girl. Breen wished she was with him.

Arthur introduced them, and the first thing she said was, "You mean you're going to let that murderer off?"

Breen tried his best to explain to them both that he only presided at the trial, that under the jury system, the jury was the judge and so on. But as he said it he knew what they knew, Flores was going to get off, no chance of any other verdict.

On his way downtown in a cab, he realized they had not discussed Art's dropping out. It hadn't seemed relevant.

The sheets in his hotel smelled of disinfectant. He couldn't sleep. He dressed and walked up Broadway. A hot pastrami sandwich! He remembered how much he'd liked them. But Lindy's had disappeared and the new places looked dirty and full of people he didn't like.

He walked down Broadway, across Forty-second Street,

up Eighth Avenue, had drinks at three different bars on Eighth, old haunts with new names and new clientele—threatening, he thought.

A black prostitute in a huge ash-blonde wig put it to him. He quickly turned away, realized he was afraid of her. Things were so open here now. Sex on the street! Nothing was discreet. He went to an all-night sex movie.

What struck him—it was the first one he'd ever seen, couldn't at home, of course—was how young, how well-endowed, how handsome the participants were. "What they won't do for a few bucks nowadays," he sighed. He was also surprised how long they were able to keep it up.

At two in the morning he was walking again down Broadway. The streets seemed to be populated at this hour entirely with criminal types; he hated to think what was ahead for the cities of this nation. He was glad there was a state of New Mexico, of Arizona, of Southern California.

That night, lying in his bed, Judge Thurston Breen faced facts. He was never coming back to New York or any other big city. For better for worse, but forever, he was in the great Southwest. And Teddy Greenbaum? Forget it!

―――――――――――――――――――

As Marian went upstairs to bed that night, Alan was coming down for his night walk.

They passed each other without a look.

"What did you think of that fellow?" Marian said from the top of the stairs. "The one at dinner."

Alan paused at the bottom. "I thought he made considerable sense."

"Well, that's big of you. And what else?"

"I detest informers."

"Meaning me?"

"Name yourself."

"Anything else?"

"You can go ahead—with my blessings."

"Which means?"

"Which means that you were announcing to all at dinner that you were giving me a choice. Fly right or you'll leave me for—to judge from tonight—most of the Fighting Fifty-fifth. Am I correct?"

"What you are, Alan, is paranoid." Marian clicked off the light in the upper hall.

As Alan walked out the front door he heard her from what had been their bedroom.

"I hate you," she was shouting after him. "I don't want to ever see you again."

All climaxes, Alan decided, are anticlimactic. They happen after they've happened. What Alan felt as he walked away was disemburdened and, for no reasonable reason, full of hope.

At quarter to one, Wheeler and Gavin finished. There was a stack of seven cartons in the middle of the floor, corner on corner, all properly tied with prickly brown twine. On top of these was the horned Mexican saddle Wheeler had kept on a saddletree in front of the north windows to "remind me of my cows."

In a dark corner away from the windows, there was an enormous pile of legal paper, letters and briefs, threats and promises, agreements, secret and open, transcripts of forgotten testimony, contracts long dead, and a couple of hundred jury lists and verdicts; most of what Wheeler had carefully collected for over twenty-five years he considered not worth keeping.

He washed his hands, put his coat back on. Then he sat down and told Gavin to sit down, he had something to tell him.

"I won't be here after Tuesday," he said. "Grace will send these up north," he indicated the seven cartons and the saddle, "and all that," he pointed to the pile of legal rubbish, "she'll throw away. I doubt I'll ever come back here. I don't expect to. This particular office is yours. It is my hope that in time—don't make the move till you feel ready for it—you will take my place at the head of this firm. That is my wish. I've decided to give you my shares and my vote. The timing will be up to you."

"Thank you, sir," Gavin said. He saw that Mr. Wheeler was looking at him intently, wondered what he was thinking. "Where will you be?" he asked.

"I'm leaving the country," Wheeler said. "I have built up substantial holdings—this is in confidence—in Switzerland

and also in Johannesburg, gold shares. I've never told anyone that."

"You know you can trust me, sir."

"Gavin, I have not, not for a long time, believed in the
future of this country. I know now that I can't do anything
about what's happening here, and I can't bear to watch it
happen any more."

"Yes, sir."

"In fact, I can't read the morning newspapers. They turn
my stomach."

Gavin decided not to tell him about his dog.

"I have something else to tell you." He seemed to be on
a precipice.

"Yes, sir."

"One reason—the other being that I truly like you, always
have, truly trust and admire you, always did—but one reason
I've always shown a strong interest in you is that you're my
son."

"Yes, sir."

They sat staring at each other.

"The details," Don Wheeler finally said, "do not matter.
Although if you like, I'll write them to you when I have
time."

"I'd like that, sir."

If it occurred to either of them to embrace, to express
physically any newfound feeling, there was no indication.

Finally, Gavin said, "May I ask one question?"

Wheeler expected Gavin would want to know about his
mother.

But what Gavin asked was, "Did Mrs. Wheeler know?"

"Mrs. Wheeler," his father said carefully, "always trusted
me completely. She had no cause to lose that trust, right
to the end."

━━━━━━━━━━━━━━━━━━━━━━━━

Michael woke, clenched like a foetus on the bottom of that
dead sea, shivering.

In the middle distance were the people who'd attended
the funeral and among them the car he was looking for,
Donna's. He got to his feet, tipped forward, walked to it,
seeing nothing on either side of his path.

Sleeping bodies were all over the bottom of the hollow, scattered up the hill and around behind it.

They were all strangers now.

He stood over Lonnie and Rosalie. Was this innocence or stupidity? Were they naïve or just living life come-what-may? Tomorrow or the next day or the next they'd have drifted off, somewhere, those feeble friendly smiles still on their faces, loving, gentle, ineffectual, with the memory span of animals, outcasts because of no principle but a shrinking passivity. Here they were perfectly expressing themselves, in each other's arms, asleep.

In the distance a hawk stooped from the top of a giant cactus, picked up a small animal which struggled for an instant, then was still. Michael marveled at how briefly the animal had struggled for its life.

Some of these humans at his feet talked revolution. They'll revolution shit, Michael thought.

Donna's car was full of people, front and back. Michael turned them out roughly with a few sharp words. He was glad to see they didn't like him when he was himself.

Then he drove out of their number.

He left the car outside Donna's house, dropping the keys in her mailbox. He noticed there were no police watching the house.

Michael wanted to stay indoors now, in the dark. He didn't want to answer questions, and he didn't want to see any friends, or any person who thought he was.

The place he chose was fathered by a boy from New York, Ben Rose, not a boy, a man, a Jew, spare, angular, intelligent, activist, his clothes hip but clean, his hair tied at the back of the neck. He was a neat man and ran an ordered house. Waiting in town for his trial, he had not jumped bail like some others, even though everyone knew he'd get one to five for possession.

Michael told him the truth, that he was followed. Could he stay? Ben hesitated, measuring him.

He's a rabbi, Michael thought.

The rabbi nodded.

Ben Rose thought in terms of future political good. All fugitives from pig justice were to be helped.

He led Michael through a room where a very heavy girl slept, an activist known for her fearlessness, also up for one to five. Then into another room, where Ben opened the door to a closet and showed Michael a framed hole in the ceiling, the way to the attic.

"Up there," he said.

In one corner of the attic was a young man. His name was Wally; he'd been a missileman, working out of the base in one of the many silos the air force had put down in the area. Wally, dishonorably discharged for being under the influence while on duty, boasted over a thousand acid trips. No one believed the number, but something sure as hell had juggled his marbles. He gave Michael half a tab "for later," waved off his thanks.

Michael went to the opposite corner, lay down on some discarded roofing, was asleep instantly.

He was never sure later whether what he next remembered happened or was dreamed. Che Weill was kneeling next to him, looking exactly like the famous poster, even to the beret. Michael remembered asking, "Where did you get the money?" He wasn't sure if Che answered, but when he woke much later he found a twenty-dollar bill in his fist. It must have happened.

Then he figured it out.

Michael had always assumed it was the police who'd gone under the boards of the closet in the house on Queen Street and taken the gun and the mayonnaise jar full of H. Now he knew who had.

Che was Fat Freddie's pilot fish. Fat Freddie had money—where else would Che get it? And where else would Freddie have gotten money?

Which meant: Fat Freddie was somewhere in the city, had bread and a gun—and knew where Michael was.

Betty McAndrews took two steelheads out of the freezer, fish they'd been saving for months. The dinner, delicious, was not a success. For the first time Gavin and Wheeler seemed tense with each other.

There were simply too many questions unanswered in Gavin's mind. Furthermore, everything seemed, at least superficially, exactly the same and this disturbed him.

Wheeler, he could see, had a problem. "I've packed all my clothes," he finally said, "but I don't know what to do with hers."

This was the first Betty knew of Hope's death.

Wheeler could not bear her condolences, her efforts to display concern and be, through it all, cheerful. "Shit," he said to himself, as Betty went on and on, "They hardly knew each other, Hope and this one."

"I'd be glad to go through her clothes for you," Betty was suggesting.

Wheeler didn't want her going through Hope's goddamn clothes.

"Perhaps we can give some of them to the Southside Community Center," she suggested in a mournful yet practical tone of voice.

Don turned her off. "No one could wear her size."

"Kids, perhaps, kids," Betty persisted. Then she caught Gavin's look. Wheeler had stood up.

"I'd prefer to do it myself. I think that's the right way. I hope you'll forgive me if I go—those were wonderful fish. But I don't seem to have an appetite."

He walked away from the table, Gavin and Betty following.

"You may not see me again for a long time," he said to Gavin, "but I'll write you soon, like I said, along those lines." He shook Betty's hand, then Gavin's. "You're doing great in court," he said. "Give them holy hell tomorrow."

"I will, sir," Gavin said, noticing that he was no less formal with his boss than he had been before.

"Did I do something wrong?" Betty whispered as soon as the door closed.

Don Wheeler drove downtown. The two old Indian women sitting on the corner were still trying to peddle their beads and amulets to the crowd coming out of the movie. He gave them each ten dollars and drove them up to his house on the mountain.

At the edge of his property, behind the house, there was a small outdoor furnace equipped with the shields and screens approved for disposal of garbage by burning. Wheeler built a fire.

Then he told the two women to clean everything, absolutely everything, out of Hope's closets, dresses, blouses, underwear, stockings, gloves, coats, hats, shoes, furs, pocketbooks, everything for every season, summer and winter, and to carry everything to the blazing furnace.

He handled nothing himself.

One of the Indians finally got up courage to ask if she could keep certain items. They would fit her young ones.

Wheeler gave them another pair of tens and told them he wanted everything destroyed.

They worked until three in the morning, until Wheeler was satisfied there was no remaining evidence of Hope's life on earth.

They had finished when the storm came; sudden, ferocious. Wheeler, not wanting to drive down the mountain through the rain, told the women to bed down where they were, in Hope's room; he would drive them down in the morning.

In July there are cloudbursts in the great southwest desert. The wind shifts, and the rain which has been stored up in the pockets of the mountains to the north suddenly moves in and comes down. People said this one was the heaviest in many years, but they always say that.

The holocaust of falling water woke the newly married couple and their friends. Lonnie and Rosalie had found a desert preacher the day before who would not let a loaded belly prevent him from welding a union less than perfect. His wife had provided the music, singing, "Ah, Sweet Mystery of Life!" after the "I do's." The preacher, in conclusion, had given them his card—and taken the last ten dollars Lonnie had.

The wedding night had been a community affair, so in the five minutes between three-five and three-ten, they were all equally soaked. There was no shelter.

At first many of them had enjoyed it, stretching up their arms and hands and turning on to it. But as the final effect of the drugs wore off, they felt the chill. At daybreak they could be seen straggling along the highway in the direction of the city. No one would pick up these soaking, sodden animals.

Except Rosalie, who stuck out her belly instead of her thumb. She and Lonnie soon had a ride, which was fortunate because Monday was Rosalie's day in court, the occasion for which Gavin had brought her back to the city.

Others walked the distance, eleven miles. When they got

back to whatever cover they had in the city, most of them had no change of clothing, so went to bed.

This storm, like others before it, was so heavy that the gulches were flooded and the creatures who lived in holes in the ground were driven up to dry land. That morning, the local radio stations broadcast rattlesnake warnings.

The airport was boxed in by the storm, and Judge Thurston Breen was put down in the middle of the night at an airport one hundred and twenty miles to the north. He had to wait till six, when the hungriest of the car-rental places opened. At breakfast, the headline read: Millions Adrift Across Pakistan.

Across the plateau, through the rain, the judge kept his car pushed to seventy, through Father Felipe Pass and down into the desert, reaching home at a quarter to eight.

He found police and his wife, hysterical, on his terrace. Their Great Dane had been killed with a knife, gutted; the entrails were all over the white porch furniture.

Bailiff Lansing recognized Monday as the day Gavin McAndrews would put the hippies on the stand by getting up a little earlier than usual, taking his service revolver out of his footlocker, cleaning it, loading it, and putting it into the attaché case he carried to court each morning. He placed the case, its clasp freed, on his desk.

No sooner had Judge Breen taken his seat than Cy rose and asked if he could approach the bench. Gavin followed to see what he was up to.

Cy underplayed it, asked permission rather casually to put the base psychiatrist on the stand, hinting it had originally been Gavin's plan to do so. Perhaps the defense now felt it had enough expert testimony, but the prosecution would value another opinion.

Gavin said that there were two reasons for his change of plan, the first being that he'd found out Dr. Stevens was a habitual drunk and—

"The second being that he'd testify Flores was as sane as any of us!" Alan, moving down the aisle, speaking in an unrestrained voice.

Judge Breen's gavel cut him down.

"The court reporter will strike that from the record," he

instructed. Then he turned to Alan: "Lieutenant Kidd!" beckoned him to the bench.

Judge Breen knew Alan from the tennis courts, moderated his rebuke. "Lieutenant Kidd, you have no standing here. Step back behind the rail and preserve your silence, or I'll have you escorted from the courtroom."

Alan sat in the front row, leaning forward to follow the long whispered hassle that followed. From there he heard Cy break out.

"Judge Breen, this man's testimony is critical to the prosecution. If you disallow it, I can't be responsible for the consequences." Cy's voice was pitched to a level where it would reach everyone in court, including the reporters.

Here Judge Breen, noted for his patience and for the smooth way he generally conducted the business of his court, did an uncharacteristic thing, slapped his hand down on the bench. "Are you threatening me?" he whispered. He started to go on, then invited the contending lawyers to adjourn to his chambers.

Cy thought he got an approving nod from Alan as he left the room.

"I'll say it again," Cy said in the judge's room. "You are arbitrarily choking off the evidence I consider the most crucial—"

"That testimony is privileged, you know the law. A man has the right to consult a psychiatrist about a delicate personal problem without having what passed between them broadcast. I'm not going to allow it."

"Then you're going to take the consequences."

"Don't threaten me, Cy!" The judge stood up, on the verge, then turned away and said, "Well, what are you going to do about it?"

"I have recourse. I can appeal your decision."

"Go ahead. The court of appeals is meeting right—"

"I know that and I know where. Thank you." He turned his back on the judge and left the room.

For the next hour, Gavin put on the stand a fashion show of freaks. Exhibited were seven alumni of the house on Queen Street, all of whom had spent the weekend in the desert, been soaked by the cloudburst, slept in their clothes.

For this show, Gavin had asked for and obtained the judge's permission to suspend temporarily Bailiff Lansing's prohibition against bare feet.

Of course, Gavin asked them all if they knew Vinnie, and they all did. Yes, they said, he was violent, yes, he could be dangerous, yes, he had an uncontrollable temper, he sure did, was given to sudden eruptions of rage, everyone was frightened of him, yes, yes. And he, like everyone else there, used drugs, but no, they didn't know how he made a living, how did any of them make a living, that wasn't important.

But on Sandy, Gavin tripped up. In the first place she had graduated from a prestigious eastern college, Swarthmore, and with honors in philosophy. "In what?" Gavin asked.

"My dear man," Sandy said, as if she were talking to a servant, "you heard perfectly well what I said, why do you require me to repeat it? May I answer that? Because you are trying to exhibit us as freaks, psychos, maniacs, and degenerates. It happens I did graduate and with honors, not that it's been worth a damn to me since. Now may I anticipate your other points, because this question and answer bit is just too boring."

Gavin looked at Judge Breen, who nodded. "Vinnie did have a lively temper. A short one. Can you blame him when you look around at this world? Look at the faces in this courtroom! I had to take three red ones before I dared come in here. Next question. Yes, Vinnie did make his living dealing drugs, and that is at least as honorable as ambulance chasing. Next question. Yes, Vinnie could be maddening, but then I find everyone quite intolerable. I wouldn't be able to stay in a room with any of you if I wasn't turned on to my hair roots."

Gavin felt he had to interrupt, *pro forma.* "Your honor, I'm afraid I'll have to—"

"Let her go on."

Sandy had talked right through this exchange. "Yes, I knew Vinnie well, which does mean, yes, I had sexual relations with him, as who didn't. How often? Every time I got lucky. About Private Jeff Wilson, whom that man murdered," she flipped her hand at Flores, "the black soldier no one of you has ever mentioned here? Yes, I did it with him, too, every time I got lucky. He was a very good human being, and he got into a fist fight with Flores about his feeling about war, said he wouldn't shoot at people of the same color, and Flores began to abuse him, tried to hit him, and—"

Gavin finally stopped her. Cy had no questions.

As she came down from the stand, everyone could see she was in another country. Bailiff Lansing had to give her a gentle push to guide her through the door.

The jury was horrified.

Which was why Gavin had let her go on as long as he had.

The thing about Rosalie that made the jury love her was that she was obviously so happy. She looked terrible, her hair in ropes, all the perk out of her maternity mini, her blouse crumpled except where her filling breasts pushed it out, watermarks from the rain on her black Mary Janes.

Before she started, Gavin, sensing the jury might get to like Rosalie, told her just what line of questioning he was going to follow. He said, tiptoeing, that he might have to ask her some personal questions, but after all they were dealing in a matter of life and death, so perhaps she'd forgive them.

Rosalie smiled and told him to go ahead.

Gavin noticed she kept looking at a boy among the spectators who was looking at her with equal interest.

"Forgive me for asking, Rosalie," Gavin said in his good-uncle voice, "but who is the father of your child?"

"Objection, your honor," Cy said, "are you really going to permit this line of questioning?"

"I don't mind answering," Rosalie said, smiling.

"That's not the point," Cy said.

"Your honor, trust me not only to handle this delicate matter delicately but also to make a point that even the prosecution will think important," Gavin pleaded.

"Go ahead," said Judge Breen.

"Go ahead, then, Rosalie," Gavin nodded at her.

"Vinnie," Rosalie said. "I believe Vinnie was the father."

"You believe?"

"I'm pretty sure."

"Did he know you were pregnant by him?"

"Oh, I told him."

"What was his reaction?"

"He took it okay."

"What do you mean?"

"He wasn't sore or anything. I told him I was going to go ahead and have it, and he said that was my business."

"And then?"

"Well, then, Juana—his daughter—began to hang around Vinnie, and pretty soon he was with her."

"Did that upset you?"

"That was his business."

"And you met somebody else?"

"Yeah!"

"Were you on the outs with Juana during this period?"

"No, we were best friends." She smiled at the boy in the back of the courtroom, and he at her. "And it all worked out for the best."

"Let me get this exactly right, Rosalie. While Juana was going with Vinnie, you were carrying Vinnie's baby and going out with someone else?"

"That's right, right."

"Is that the fellow in the back, the one you keep smiling at?"

"No, it was Michael, you know Michael, the thin one? I don't see him here, but you know who I mean?"

"Yes, he'll be here this afternoon," Gavin said. "May I ask who the fellow in the back is?"

"He's my husband," Rosalie said, and smiled at the jury.

"Since when?"

"We got married yesterday."

Gavin congratulated her and then said, "One more question, Rosalie. Suppose you had a daughter, and she was running around with a boy who was having a child by another girl, wouldn't you be upset, maybe even frantic?"

"I don't have those sex hang-ups," Rosalie said.

The jury got the point.

Judge Breen looked at his watch and called a recess. He was anxious to get on the phone.

Cy rushed to his office in the courtroom building, where Alan was waiting. He said that the request for an immediate hearing before the court of appeals had been denied. Cy could have one next Tuesday, eight days off.

"I told them the trial would be over by then," Alan said.

"What did they say?"

"You know Judge Barton?" Alan asked.

Judge Breen had a message to call Judge Bo Barton.

"Look, Breen," the old man said, "we just did a damn fool thing up here, refusing that young prosecutor's request for a hearing. I mean we told him he could have it Tuesday week. Who does that fool? Your court will be out then, correct?"

"I certainly hope so," Judge Breen said.

"Now if I were you I'd insist the man be heard. You know damned well we're not going to let him interrupt your procedure. If we did, every chicken-shit lawyer in town would be running up here with these extraordinary writs and stopping trials. But if you're going to refuse a man anyway, hear him first, that's the democratic way, correct? Are you listening to me?"

"Of course."

"So, my suggestion is, be the hero! Take the morning off tomorrow, send that man down here with his plea. We'll send him back to you very correct, you can believe me, sir, very correct."

———————————————————

Bailiff Lansing was the first to recognize Michael. "You look much better," he said, going up to him, "why, you're really a nice-looking young man! What happened? Fall in love?"

Michael's beard was off, his hair trimmed, and he wore the full regalia Donna had bought him, shirt, tie, coat, loafers. The idea to go to court "in disguise" had wakened him that morning. Donna's clothes bespoke the middle ground he now occupied. And, as clothes will, Michael's accentuated a natural elegance in his posture.

"I think the judge wants to speak to you," Michael said to the Bailiff, getting his attention off him.

Judge Breen wanted to talk to Cy Walker. When Bailiff Lansing had escorted the disgruntled lawyer to the bench, the judge informed him that he was going to arrange Cy's hearing in front of the court of appeals and insist that it take place tomorrow morning and that, further, he'd recess his own court till after lunch the next day so Cy would be taking no chances of being declared in contempt.

"What got into you?" Cy asked.

"When I thought it over," the judge said, "it seemed the right thing to do."

Some men waste in jail; Fat Freddie had gotten fatter. Where Michael had gone straight in his dress, Mr. Povich, as Bailiff Lansing called him when he invited him to the stand, had gone flamboyant. His new threads made him look like a star linebacker for a professional football team, who'd decided to live big, but live hip.

As he marched to the chair, Freddie looked at no one. Once there, he raised his head and glared at everybody. His tone, when he answered the first few questions—Present place of domicile? None. Education? None. Means of livelihood? Shrug, shrug—was even more truculent than Michael remembered it.

Gavin showed him certain objects taken from his car, a ten-inch piece of broom handle sharpened to an ice-pick's point, a bone-handle strip knife, a pair of brass knuckles.

"You wouldn't claim, as does the prosecution, that you went out to the base that night unarmed, would you?"

"Boy scouts," Freddie said, "that was us. Be prepared!"

"Be prepared for what?" Gavin asked.

"Anything, man."

"Would you say this motto applied to Vin Connor, too?"

"That boy didn't need any weapons."

"Which means?"

"He was able!"

"By the way, how did he make his living?"

"You don't ask people that, man."

"Someone here said he dealt drugs."

"That would be one way."

"You knew that for a fact?"

"I used to buy from him."

"Was he himself a user?"

"Never saw him when he wasn't on something."

"That include the evening you all went out to the base?"

"Never saw him when he wasn't on something."

Michael couldn't believe it. *What the hell was Freddie doing?*

"Would you say he was dangerous then?"

"I wouldn't turn my back on him, and I was his friend."

"Now, do you remember Sergeant Flores coming out of the house that night?"

"Can you forget a man running wild?"

"Did you feel threatened?"

"Wouldn't you? He was holding a hot pistol. That's why I told Jeff to run the son of a bitch down."

"Run him down?"

"With the car. That man was insane!"

Gavin paused, let the testimony sink in.

"Mr. Povich," he picked up, "you mentioned Jeff Wilson, the driver of the car. Do you know, was he acquainted with Sergeant Flores?"

"Acquainted? They had a fist fight, man!"

Gavin went on to get the details: that Sergeant Flores had had the better of it, Jeff being stoned, that Jeff had sworn he'd pay Flores back.

"Then," Gavin concluded, "might it be possible that when Sergeant Flores saw Private Wilson sitting in the car that night, he had cause for concern?"

"That knife you showed me, that belonged to Jeff, Flores knew sooner or later he'd cut him. So when he saw us coming down on him in the car, he must have figured, this is it."

Gavin consulted his notes again while the jury stared at Freddie and Freddie stared at them.

"Mr. Povich, do you have feelings of animosity toward Sergeant Flores?"

"Why should I?"

"He killed two of your close friends."

"I don't blame him. I mean if you tell a man you're going to come out and take his daughter away over his dead body, you got to take your chances, right?"

"Did Vin Connor say he was going to kill Sergeant Flores, did you hear him say that?"

"I heard him tell this man on the phone that's why he was coming out there that night."

He didn't hear that, Michael thought. *He's making it up.*

"So if you had been Sergeant Flores, what would you have done?"

"I'd have a piece in my belt. Loaded."

"Your honor," Gavin said, studying his notes, "I have no further questions to ask this witness."

"I'd like to say something," Freddie said.

Judge Breen nodded.

"I want permission to leave town tomorrow morning, Your Honor, I want to go back home. I talked to my uncle, he runs a garage, and he said he'd give me a job if I straightened out and became a decent human being again."

"Objection, Your Honor!" Cy approached the stand.

"Surely the Prosecutor doesn't object to someone trying to be a decent human being?"

"Before his release is taken under advisement, Your Honor, the People want to cross-examine."

"Proceed."

"Isn't it a fact," said Cy to Freddie, "that when Vin Connor drove out to the base the night of the murder, he was unarmed?"

"I don't know."

"Well, all his other friends say he was unarmed." Cy was furious.

"Are they sure?"

"The dead man was searched the minute the police got there. They found nothing on the body."

Freddie pointed to Michael. "Did they search him?"

"Why should anyone search him?"

"Because he was the first one to get to the body. I saw him run up into the house, like Flash whatshisname."

"You're a goddamn liar." Michael spoke quietly from his seat.

When Cy released Freddie Povich, the two-hundred-pounder swaggered slowly down the aisle, started past the seat where Michael was sitting, and once again the whole court heard Michael say, "You're a fink, Freddie."

Freddie grabbed Michael by the jacket, there was a flurry, like a dog fight, then Michael was on the floor.

The deputy sheriffs were on Freddie by then, as was an unidentified man in plain clothes, who followed Freddie when he was released a few minutes later.

Michael was stunned. A blow had glanced off his jaw. Putting his hands to the breast pocket of his suit coat, he felt something Freddie had left behind there when he first clasped him, something hard.

Later, in the men's room, Michael locked the cabinet door and took out of his pocket the key to room 347 in the Western Star Motel.

When Gavin put Michael on the stand, he congratulated him on his appearance. "I'll admit it's a shock," he said, "but a very pleasant one."

Michael smiled at the jury.

Alan, sitting in the front row, had never seen Michael this way, remote and receding, the last view of a person disappearing over a horizon.

"May I ask what accounts for this very attractive change?" Gavin asked.

"I've often wondered," Michael answered, with his breeze-cool smile, "what would have happened at this trial if the jury had been blindfolded."

"In other words, you think this jury is prejudiced?"

Michael smiled at them in what seemed a friendly if unfocused manner and said, "They know they are."

The members of the jury, seduced by Michael's smile, smiled back. Then they after-heard what Michael had said, and sobered.

Alan was the only one in the courtroom who laughed out loud.

Gavin took it up. "Michael, on the night of the murder, is it true that you and your friend had a bitter difference?"

"Not bitter."

"And it concerned?"

"Sergeant Flores."

"What was the issue?"

"I had nothing against Sergeant Flores, in fact"—he turned and smiled toward Cesario—"I told Vinnie I liked him."

"And you still do?"

"He's a victim, too. I'm sorry for him."

"Even though he killed your best friend?" Gavin asked.

"You can't blame him. He was trained to kill."

"Of course," Gavin said. "He was in the service."

"Right," said Michael," and that's necessary."

"What's necessary?"

"To be able to kill without your conscience bothering you."

"Michael, do you really believe Sergeant Flores has no conscience?"

"Not a twitch!" Michael said, smiling at Cesario. "Besides, he wouldn't have done it unless he believed, beforehand, that he had approval."

"Whose?"

"Yours. The community's."

"Unexpressed, you mean?"

"Are you sure of that?"

Cy could see that the jury was more horrified by this soft-spoken spook's testimony than by anyone else's; he had to stop it. "Irrelevant and immaterial," he said. "Your honor, I demand that defense stop this line of questioning and get to the point."

"He's right," Judge Breen said.

"Of course, he's right," Gavin said quickly. "It's simply that I'm fascinated, honestly I am, by this young man's view of us. Now tell me, Michael, did Vincent want to take a gun out to the base with him that night?"

"Yes, he did."

"Looking back now, you think he was right to take a gun out to the base?"

"Wait a minute, wait a minute. He didn't do that. That's what I talked him out of." Michael was laughing. "You're pretty tricky, aren't you?"

Alan burst out laughing, too, and this time the courtroom joined in.

Even Gavin. "But if you had it to do over you would not have dissuaded him?"

"I would have suggested he meet Sergeant Flores elsewhere."

"With a weapon?"

"Flores had one."

"But if we're going to kill when we disagree, isn't that savagery?"

"Then why are you defending Flores?"

Gavin changed faces. "Because he was driven out of his mind by someone just as twisted as you," he shouted. "Because he had to face a savage, degenerate man philosophically prepared just as you are to scuttle every moral value of this society, and to murder! A man who believed, as you do, that a gun is the only way men can settle their differences."

Michael didn't seem the least disturbed by Gavin's display of anger. "Do you hear any other sounds?" he asked gently. "Guns being manufactured, sold, bought, borrowed, loaded, fired! Those are the only sounds you can hear, anywhere. In the world!"

"That's all, thank you," Gavin said.

Cy was on his feet. "Michael," he began, "please answer yes or no, nothing more. Did Vin Connor have a gun on his person when he went into Sergeant Flores's home?"

"No."

"Was there a delay after he entered the home?"

"No."

"The sound of shooting was almost immediate?"

"Yes."

"Did you take a weapon off the dead boy's body when you rushed into the house?"

"No."

"That's all, thank you, Michael."

Gavin, approaching Michael for redirect, had that fourth-quarter look on his face.

"Michael, you said you knew Sergeant Flores before the night of the shooting?"

"I did."

"And that you liked him?"

"I did."

"You realize he's on trial here for his life?"

"No, I realize you're trying us here, for our lives."

"Michael, that is nonsense."

"You are trying us in Vinnie."

"Michael, I'm sorry for you, really I am. You're so wrong."

"I know it," Michael said, and his voice milder than ever. "I am wrong. The fact is—the real truth—that you are on trial here. You and the other lawyer, he's supposed to be against you, but you're both the same, and the jury, you're the same—"

"Your honor," Gavin appealed to the judge.

"Yes, you, too, your honor, you're on trial here, too. You're all being judged, and you will all be punished. And since the only sound you can hear is the sound of a gun, that's the sound you'll hear."

He stopped, looked at them, smiled faintly, and was silent.

CHAPTER SEVEN

Clifford's investigator met him at the airport. He wouldn't tell Clifford why he'd summoned him. He told him only that it concerned his son, Michael, and that he was to check in at the Western Star and expect a visitor later that night. He accompanied Clifford to the motel, watched him sign in, made a note of the room number, shook his hand, and left. Clifford bought the local paper and two cigars in metal tubes, then went to his room.

"Wait here," he told her. Donna had driven him to the Western Star, stopped at one of the small side entrances. "I won't be long," Michael said as he took the long metal suitcase out of the back of the car. He'd come for the gun.

As he approached room 347, he began to hear yowls of laughter. When he put the key in the lock, he heard the one-liners bouncing—*Laugh-In*—and Fat Freddie mimicking one of the clowns, the German accent very thick on his lips. When Michael opened the door, he saw what he'd guessed, Fat Freddie was high, way up there, all flags flying.

Michael closed the door, double-locked it, put the long metal suitcase across the arms of a chair, then turned the TV down so he could talk to the man.

"Don't do that," Freddie said quickly, and Michael could see that Freddie was on a sharp edge. "Turn it up where I had it, loud," he said.

322

Michael did, then talking above it, he said, "I came here for what you took of Vinnie's."

"Sure, sure," Freddie said, apparently agreeable again. He reached into his pocket, eyes never off the party on the tube, pulled out a rat's nest of bills, and threw them on the bed. "Leave me a couple of twenties, that's all I'm going to need," he said.

As Michael gathered and counted the maybe three hundred dollars, he figured it out, not only what Freddie had been doing in court that day—trying to throw the bastards off his ass—but what he was planning to do now. As he arranged the bills by denominations, Michael walked to the window of the room and looked out.

Across the square was the courthouse and the side door to which Michael knew Flores was brought every morning. It was partly concealed by a single story garage. When Michael raised the window and leaned out, he saw that directly over room 347 was the great "Bienvenidos" sign. From up there nothing would block the sight line to the side entrance.

"This all you got for it?" Michael came back into the room and threw two twenties onto Freddie's belly.

"Had to deal in a hurry," Freddie said. "Not the best way. Also I kept some of the scagg for myself. It was like Vinnie said, really fine."

"Now give me my gun."

There was a break for a commercial announcement.

"I ain't got your gun," Freddie said, getting up. Michael watched him strut his beef over to the long glass on the closet door and admire his image. "Also I bought me these threads," Fat Freddie said, "I'm gonna make my move in style." He was wearing flaring bells, broad peppermint stripes on white duck and a Cubano shirt with two rows of ruffles down the front. "You dig me?" he asked.

"What happened to your face?" Michael had noticed in court how it had been beaten lopsided.

"This was just for goodbye and hurry-back-you-all." He grinned, best he could, then turned back his upper lip where it had been split and inspected the swelling in the mirror. "Well," he said, "they say everything evens up, and this time they'll be right. In spades!"

Then he turned and looked at Michael, the high coming

down fast. Michael could even see the fear under the swagger.

"Gimme the gun, will you Freddie?" he said.

"I ain't got no gun for you, Michael."

Michael flipped the blanket off the outline he'd noticed on the bed. But he didn't get a good look. Freddie shoved him back in a corner, covering the carbine in an instant. But in that instant, Michael had seen the weapon was well-rubbed with oil, that the bullet clip was in place, and that there was a scope attached now. Vinnie hadn't had a scope on it.

The clowns were back and Freddie, the viewer, was on the bed, breathing hard now, not going with the wit.

"That ain't your gun," he said, slowly and plainly. "Like they say, the land belongs to them that works it, and you wouldn't do anything with that gun if you had it, so it's mine now."

"I know what you're going to do, Freddie, don't do it."

"I think you better get your ass out of here. Do what you were supposed to do, go to Saint Louis and tell Jeff's mother, did you do that?"

"No."

"Why not? That woman's sitting, wondering why she hasn't heard from her kid. Forget about me and the gun, I'll take care of that part of it. You got the bread now, make the trip, go, get out of town, because if you stay here they'll be picking you up tomorrow."

"It won't mean a damn thing, what you're going to do, Freddie, don't do it."

"How do you know what I'm going to do?"

"I saw through that act you put on in court even before you hit me, and when I looked out this window and saw where the courtroom door lay—Freddie, Christ, listen! If you take out Flores, it's the wrong man, it won't change anything, it will give them an excuse to bust anybody and everybody—"

"Excuse! What's the matter with you, man?" He was off the bed, ripping off his shirt, unzipping his bells. They fell to the floor, and Freddie stood naked, barrel-bellied and very white. His back and sides were covered with blue welts.

"You still say they need some kinda excuse, you son of a bitch?"

Michael had no answer.

"You say it can get worse? Look at me!"

Michael looked away.

Then Freddie spoke gently, "I don't dig you, man," he said, pulling on his clothes, slowly and sadly like a team-kid who'd just lost the big game. "But I decided not to hold it against you. You're just a talker, that's your nature. Maybe you're waiting for a sign from heaven or something. Are you, Michael baby?" he said with something like affection. "Well, those signs aren't coming down like they used to."

It was then Michael made his move for the carbine.

"Michael!" Freddie stopped him cold just with his voice. "Stay away from that! Back up! Now! More! Now turn around! And walk!"

Michael was up against the wall, failed, ashamed, proven in that instant to be what Freddie had said.

"I'll tell you something like a friend," he said, "the way I am, I'd just as soon kill you as not, so be real careful what you—"

He hesitated, then threw open the closet door and there, lying on his face, bound and gagged was—Michael recognized him by the hair and beret—Che.

"I think I found out who's been talking, it wasn't you like I thought for a while. I'm still checking it out, but if it's him, he's made his last squeak. You want to be in there with him?"

Michael couldn't move because of fear.

"I'm going to do a fool thing," Freddie said, "which I'll probably regret. Get out of here, Michael, go to Saint Louis like I told you. You know you ain't never gonna do anything. Leave the work to me."

Michael didn't take the long case with him.

━━━━━━━━━━━━━━━━━━━━━━━

Clifford's visitor knew Michael was in the Western Star, but he didn't so inform Clifford. It was important to find out where Michael would go when he left Freddie's room, important to establish whether he left with or without the long metal suitcase and its contents.

Clifford was warned that he should, as soon as possible,

take charge of his son and get him out of that scene. The boy was involved with a dangerous movement, and he should, in effect, be kidnapped.

"Will you be able to help me with that?" Clifford had to ask.

"We're an investigating body," his tall, well-dressed visitor said, "nothing more. I might make one very personal suggestion—from me to you. Be his father. Put your foot down. He's not twenty-one yet, is he?"

"Twenty. No—nineteen."

"Get him away from here—whether he wants to leave or not."

"But I don't even know where he is."

"Someone will call you first thing in the morning and tell you."

"Is there anywhere I can get you—in case I need help?"

"What kind of help?"

"Well, you know he's a slight kid and extremely mild-mannered, but he's become rather strong-willed."

"I'm sure you'll be able to handle him. I mean," the man smiled, "you look athletic and, as you say, he's—"

"I don't know if I want to do it that way," Clifford said.

"I'm not sure you have any choice," his visitor said.

In the beginning the cars following him had been police cars, marked or unmarked, souped-up Ford Galaxies, the faces in them look-alikes. To be tailed was a circumstance of his life; Michael accepted it.

But after he'd come back from his weekend in the desert, the familiar police cars and faces had disappeared. He still believed he was being watched, but had no idea when or how often or by whom.

Now, as he drove away from the Western Star, Donna at the wheel, he was aware again of a car following them. Nothing they did shook it off.

"Where'll I go?" Donna asked.

"Just keep driving, ride around."

They did.

"What's the matter with you?" Donna asked. "What happened?"

"I'm a coward."

"They live longer, cowards."

Michael looked back. The car was still on them. "Go out to the golf course," Michael said. "We'll neck."

"Michael, for sweet Jesus' sake, let's go home to bed."

The edge of the golf course was a lovers' lane, some fifteen cars under low-hanging trees.

'How's this?" Donna asked.

"Perfect. You must have plenty experience."

The car following them had turned in, three cars down the line.

"Where you going?" Donna asked.

"I'm going to do something bad," Michael said.

"He's coming," the man in the car with Alan said. "I suggest we leave. It'll be embarrassing for you." He put the car into reverse. It chugged, rocked a little.

"Turn the motor off," Alan said.

The man didn't.

Alan reached for the door handle. "I wouldn't consider leaving here now."

The man turned the motor off. "You know your usefulness will be destroyed," he said.

"I am not part of your organization," Alan said. "I want to talk to him. Alone. I'll nudge you when."

"You saw him walk into the motel with the gun case?"

"That it contained a gun is an assumption."

"He left without the case. You saw that, too."

"I'll take his word for what it contained."

"You won't have to. We'll have the transcript of their conversation in Povich's motel room."

"I despise your work," Alan said.

"But you can see it's necessary."

Alan didn't answer.

"When I called you this morning to witness this, I thought —well, obviously, your mind is closed."

Alan didn't answer.

"Here he comes," the man said, turning off his short-wave receiver.

If Michael was surprised to see Alan, he didn't show it. "I want to make a deal with you," he said, taking Alan's new—or revealed—identity for granted. "I imagine," he started, "that you people know—"

"Don't give me that 'you people' crap, Michael! This is

the first time I've done this, and I only did it because you—"

"Okay, okay," Michael said, indifferent to what concerned Alan. "I was going to ask," he proceeded evenly, "you and your friend there, whoever he is, you know where Freddie Povich is?"

Alan turned to the man behind the wheel, instantly regretted it. The man nodded, and Alan said, "He knows."

"So do you," Michael said, "right?"

Alan nodded.

"Do you know what he's planning to do?"

Alan looked at the man behind the wheel again. He felt trapped in behavior that made him seem part of the man's organization.

"We've got a pretty good idea," the man said.

"Well, I want to make a deal with you," Michael said. "I want to tell you exactly what he's planning, flat out, and I want you—Alan, I'm talking to you, I don't know this man."

Alan raised his head.

"He's only living for one thing," Michael went on, "and he's going to do it tomorrow in the morning."

"We had a notion," the man said.

"I want you to promise me, Alan," Michael said, "you, too, mister, I want you to get the police into Freddie's room sometime tonight, now, soon, and take him in. For possession. Grass. Or—there was a carbine on his bed when I left twenty minutes ago. I don't want him to do what he's set on doing tomorrow."

"Which is?" the man behind the wheel said.

"You just told me you knew."

"I want to hear you say it so we don't have a misunderstanding later."

Michael hesitated. "Are we making a deal on this?" he asked. "All he'll be held for is possession, right?"

"That's the idea," the man said.

"Give me your word, Alan."

"I give you my word."

"Tell me how it's going to be, Alan."

"We're going to go from here—to the police," Alan said. "We'll see that they take Freddie in tonight. For possession."

"So let's have the story," the man behind the wheel said.

Michael plunged. "He's on the top floor of the Western

Star, room 347. Near his room, there's a stairs to the roof. From there it's clear to the side door of the courthouse where they bring Flores in every morning. Freddie will be waiting for Flores tomorrow. His carbine's got a scope."

"Why are you telling us this?" the man behind the wheel asked.

"For his sake."

"You're doing the right thing," the man said.

"I don't want him to get into the other kind of trouble," Michael said.

"The other kind would be bad—and short."

The man felt Alan prod the side of his leg. The man got out of the car.

"Where you going?" Michael asked.

"Take a piss," the man said.

"So we got a deal, mister? Okay, mister?"

"I told you," the man said as he walked away, "your buddy's not going to spend the night in the Western Star."

They were alone.

"I got your word too, Alan?"

"Where do you get off being so goddamn superior, Michael? You're doing the same thing I am!"

"It doesn't matter what you think of me or what I think of you," he said. "We got a deal." He turned and walked away.

Alan was out of the car and after him. "Listen, Michael, was there a gun in that case? The one we saw you carry into the Western Star about an hour ago."

"You saw that, too?"

Alan nodded.

"No, there wasn't," Michael said.

"Well, I believe you. But they don't. These people have the idea you're running the show and Freddie is just—"

"There's no *show*," Michael said.

"They think there is. I'll tell you something else. Whatever you said to Freddie, just now, they know. There's a bug in his room. They know how deep in you are."

Michael's expression didn't change.

"Tell me—tell me and I'll believe you. Have you been planning this thing, what's supposed to happen tomorrow?"

"I don't know who I'm talking to," Michael said. Again he started back to Donna's car.

"Michael!" Alan held him, whispered, "I believe you. What are you afraid of if you're innocent?" Alan demanded. "If you run away now, you'll be a fugitive. What value is that? Nobody can touch you for what you have in your mind. Your intentions! Whatever they were—or are! Get out of that goddamn paranoid—Face them down! Tell them the truth!"

"You talking about turning myself in? Doing what you're doing?"

"No. I'm saying don't run scared, fight for your rights. Believe in the fairness of someone besides yourself. These people are not—"

Michael turned and walked back to Donna's car. This time Alan did not follow him.

When Alan got back to the car, the man was listening to the short wave.

"Did you tell him we have what he and Povich talked about in the room?" the man asked.

"Yes."

"Well, I just heard, what we have is one hell of a recording of 'Laugh-In.' And a sound of whispering." He laughed, then noticed Alan's face. "You're worried."

Alan nodded.

"You know, I'll tell you again, I like him. He's got something the rest of those kids don't. I'm going to make a suggestion, then leave it to you."

Alan nodded.

"Really think about this. The idea—well, it's what he's doing in behalf of his friend. I suggest we pick him up."

"For what?"

"Twenty different reasons. What we need in this country is a law for just such a situation. Protective detention. This kid's on the verge of doing something from which there is no—"

He noticed Alan wasn't going with him.

"You don't have to be there. I'll do it. We'll hold him for a week or two, then let him go on certain conditions. We could save his life that way. What do you say?"

"Absolutely not."

"All right, but I won't be responsible for what happens to your boy."

"I'm not asking you to. I'm responsible."

━━━━━━━━━━━━━━━━━━━━━━━━━━

When Michael told Donna who had been in the car, she wasn't surprised. "It figured," she said.

Michael asked her to drive him to the airport. After he saw Jeff's mother, he'd write Freddie in jail, tell him everything, not only what Jeff's mother had said, but why he'd done what he'd done.

They had a long wait for the plane. Michael thought of telling Donna where he was going and why, but she said, "Just tell me when you're coming back." Then she stopped. "I know you're not coming back," she said.

So there was no talk of destination or the future. She had him once more in the back seat, people all around. Then they sat propped against each other, slept, woke, time passing.

"I realize," Donna said just before he left, "that I'm too old for you. I mean it's ridiculous! But so are you. Even among freaks you're a freak. So I think you've found her, me, the girl for you. Think about that, will you? Wherever you're going, say a word and I'll come."

Michael kissed her on the cheek.

He felt sick on the plane, a claw hammer was working in his belly trying to pull something out, failing. He wondered if it was because he dreaded facing Jeff's mother.

In the lint at the bottom of one pocket, he found the half tab of acid that silo soldier Wally had given him, put it in his mouth, dropped it.

He was sitting next to a priest who was reading *Playboy*. He offered it to Michael when he got through. "They got some good articles in there," he said.

Michael couldn't take the magazine or the talk.

Later, he saw the priest's lips moving. "Who do you pray for?" he asked the black cloth.

"When I'm in my church, I pray for my parish or for our country or our president, worthy causes like that. But on a plane or a bus—"

"Then who?"

"For those I've left behind. I always feel I'm abandoning

someone when I travel." He started to explain, but Michael had turned him off.

Later the priest saw that Michael was crying, and offered himself. "Perhaps you'd like to talk to me," he said. "You look like you need help."

"Not from you."

The priest hummed a little tune.

"Do you pray for murderers?" Michael asked him later.

"Are you one?"

"That may be my calling."

"Oh, now, now."

"I haven't been called yet, but I'm waiting."

"For what?"

"For a sign." He kept looking at the priest. "You think there may be something for me in *Playboy?*" He laughed, picked up the magazine.

The priest laughed, too, but it crossed his mind that he ought to report this conversation to the police. Then he saw Michael laughing at a cartoon, noticed how gentle the boy's face was.

"You're going to be all right," he said.

"Yeah, this is just a bum trip."

Michael didn't remember anything that happened the rest of the way. He'd zonked out. The plane came down into Saint Louis through smog made mustard by the morning sun.

The cab put him down at 32 Edgemere Avenue, not in the ghetto. Why had he thought it would be? The building had a doorman.

Mrs. Wilson was no rocker-mammy; she was in her late thirties and wearing a small, strict dress. Later he couldn't remember anything about her face except the clear plum lipstick she wore. Or about the apartment except it was all white and there were mirrors glazed silver. There was a man—her lover?—deep purple.

She must have immediately complained to Michael that her son hadn't written her. Mr. Jeffrey, she called him sarcastically. Maybe that's what got Michael mad because he said, "One reason he hasn't written you is that he's dead."

That's how he told the woman.

After that, everything turned perverse. Instead of offering

sympathy, which was what he'd come to do, he couldn't stop needling.

She asked Michael who'd shot her son.

"A man in the air force, a real nice guy." Then Michael scolded. "You mustn't blame that man," he said.

"What? I mustn't what?"

"No, ma'am."

"You use drugs, too?"

"Yes, ma'am," Michael answered, "I sure do."

The deep purple male standing in the bedroom door was putting on heavy cuff links of unmatched bits of tortoise shell. Michael was to remember them, but not the man's face. He also remembered how the man filled the doorway to the white bedroom and how he looked at him.

"It's insane to cling to a body," Michael plunged on. "That's eye-for-an-eye-shit, it doesn't bring the boy back. Anyway, what would he do in this place? No wonder he left!"

"Get this little white bastard out of here before I kill him," Mrs. Wilson said to her purple lover.

Somewhere along here Michael recognized that he wasn't needling her, he was needling himself. "I advise you to forget all about it," he said, to himself, out loud, "just forget it. Everybody else has."

He faced the man coming at him.

"There isn't a damn thing you or anybody else can do about it."

The man hit him then. Again and again.

Later, at the airport, standing hopeless in front of a mirror, he saw with satisfaction that his face was lumped, his lips puffed and caked. He deserved it, he thought.

Where next? The alcove at the very end of the row of sales booths was Aeronaves de Mexico. He bought a ticket to Mexico City. He and Vinnie had planned to go there someday. This was someday.

The salesman asked the obligatory question, "First class?"

"Absolutely," Michael answered.

At Houston he had four hours to wait.

The man had just swabbed the floor of the men's room; it was still wet. A path of newspaper led to the stalls.

Michael's bowels were loose. It was a sign he must be doing something very wrong. Still it was a comfort to sit quietly with his head down in his own warm stink and just let go.

There were a few sheets of the local paper spread out in front of him under the bottom of the door, wet through but legible. Now that's an exceptionally considerate service, he thought.

Then he saw the name, "Fred Povich."

He opened the door and crouched in the opening, reading from the top the account of the attempt on the life of Sergeant Cesario Flores, the quick action of the police that had saved his life, and so on and on, skipping down, down to "the death of the would-be assassin, Fred Povich, a hippie type."

"Put that paper down."

Michael had lifted the wet sheet to read it better.

"Someone wanted that," he said. "Someone wanted it that way."

"Put it down, I said." The attendant was advancing on him. But Michael stood, his pants and jockey shorts on the floor, holding the wet front page. "Someone wanted it that way!"

The attendant snatched the paper out of his hand. "Buy your own, kid," he said, then reached in and closed the door.

There was a plane to L.A. that put down once at El Paso. Loading. Last call. Michael bought on.

Well, he thought, there it is!

CHAPTER EIGHT

In El Paso, he decided to start saving money. Now he might need it.

In the Greyhound Bus Terminal, Michael found refugees. They were camping on the floor between two benches, among old suitcases, army-surplus knapsacks, bundles in Indian blankets or newspapers, brown paper bags, water flasks of leather, guitars. They were heading for Santa Fe and Taos. These places were safe, they reported, at least for the time being.

Recognizing Michael, they told him what they knew. Following the attempt on Flores's life, there had been wholesale pickups and arrests. Police cars with cage-backs drove out of headquarters empty, drove back full. Every hippie who tried to leave town had been picked up. Major highways were patrolled; no one hitchhiked out that day. The bus terminal in town had been raided; as the bus carrying their group drove out, they'd seen the pigs moving in.

By noon the jails were glutted; there was nowhere to put more people. The kid who reported this had it straight from a pig, his father, who'd advised him on the phone to stay away a while.

They all advised Michael not to go back. He caught the next bus, but got off ten miles outside the city limits. He would wait for night and go in on a freight. No one watched trains any more.

Michael went to the one place for him in the city. The front door of the house was double-locked, the back wide open. Nobody was awake. When Ben Rose went for his morning piss an hour later, he found Michael sitting in the front room, looking out the window.

Ben quickly pulled him back from the view of the street, told him the news. The police had designated Michael mastermind of the plot to kill Flores. "Mastermind" cracked Michael up; Ben had a tough time making Michael feel danger. Michael played with the house kitten, asked about the pile of battered suitcases, bedrolls, and guitar cases near the door.

Ben told him the family, all seven, were splitting the next morning, going to Santa Fe in an old Estate Wagon and a VW rented from Dollar-a-Day.

Wally woke when Michael climbed into the attic. He had tripped the night before, was still loose, ready for anything.

Michael lay down in the corner opposite and petted the kitten while Ben told him more. The body of Che Weill had been found in Freddie's room at the Western Star. Apparently, Ben said, Freddie'd thought Che was an informer. He could well have been, Ben said.

As for Freddie's death, Ben had the answers. "They wanted it that way, man," he said to Michael, who had the kitten purring.

"Who wanted it, who's they?" Wally busted in, all this new to him, just two weeks out of the missile silos, stoned ever since.

Ben shrugged his rabbi shrug. "The power structure, man."

"What's that?" Wally demanded.

"You ought to know," Ben said, turning to Michael. "It was too good an opportunity for them to miss."

"Opportunity for what, man?" Wally persisted. "Talk to me, Ben, goddamnit, talk to me!"

"To get the public's head on straight." Ben gave him that much, then, to Michael, "they could have taken Freddie in the night before, they knew what he was going to do!"

Michael was amazed. "How do you know that?"

"They clocked him when he took a crap, man! When they saw their chance, they decided—"

"Who decided?" Wally shouted, "Who met with who?

Who called who on the phone?" Wally sounded what he was, flying. "What's this big 'they,' all the time?"

"They don't have to meet, man," Ben said. "They don't have to talk on the phone."

Wally burst out laughing. "You're so goddamn heavy, Ben, you know that, you're so downright puzzling? When did you learn it all?"

"Shut up, Wally, and show him the afternoon paper." Ben took the kitten away from Michael.

Michael looked at the photograph on the front page.

"Look at that! Analyze!" Ben slapped the picture with the back of his hand. "Just what they needed. See? The assassin falling through space, gun in hand. Analyze! After that picture, who can still believe hippies are just colorful members of a counterculture? Like innocent, like kids? Your dead buddy on that sidewalk, there's the proof. We're criminals!"

Wally was looking over Michael's shoulder. "It's safer in the air force," he said, "a whole lot safer!"

Ben was going on. "He even cut a throat! One of his own kind, yet! And he's got a pocketful not of dreams, but smack! Perfect! The life of someone as downright disgusting as Fat Freddie Povich is cheap to pay for that kind of demonstration. Okay? Want more? What happened after? A roundup of two-legged varmints by the pork! No warrants necessary, no evidence! They were grabbing hair by the handful, pulling it out. Search and seizure? You should have seen the way they busted in here yesterday! *Oink, oink!*"

"I do believe it's safer in the air," Wally said.

"The same all over the city. And do you hear any complaints?"

"*Oink, oink!*" Wally, rocking, laughing.

"Listen to Wally's radio, see if you hear any protests. Who heard from the liberals? The clergy? Congratulations you'll hear! Read the papers. Michael—Michael!"

Michael was falling asleep.

Ben was a little hurt that Michael hadn't followed his analysis. "You better get some rest," he said. "You're just not thinking. Wally, keep your eye on him, don't let him go out!"

After Ben had gone, Wally came over to pass a joint.

"Ben's real heavy." He touched his head. "Still he don't know nothing. Figure that one out."

"I was too tired to listen to him," Michael said, "hope I didn't hurt his feelings." He drew on the stick. "So what do you say?" he asked Wally.

"I say—turn him loose!"

"Who?"

"Turn the madman loose! Break the code box! Press every button! Throw the big switch! Let 'er blast! *Oink! oink!!*"

Michael drew on the joint once more, passed it back, turned over, and was asleep.

————————————————————

Gavin had more precise information, gave it to Wheeler as he drove him to the airport that morning.

"The man Povich put on the cross hairs of his scope was not Cesario Flores. He was about the same size, wore the same clothes over a bullet-proof vest, and—"

"A policeman?"

"A trainee who'd volunteered for the job. When he heard a whistle, he knew Povich had raised his rifle. As he threw himself on the ground and rolled behind the police van, he heard two shots from above, then three from where he was, then three more. He looked up in time to see this fat pig—he really was a pig—falling from the top of the sign, bouncing like a bale of cotton off the ledge at the bottom, and smashing down on the pavement—you know where the fountain is? The one with the Disney dwarfs that light up at night?"

"Then they knew all the time he had the gun?"

"He didn't. Guess who brought it to him. That boy you call the hairy ghost."

"Wouldn't have thought he had the gumption," Wheeler said.

"The opinion is he quarterbacked the whole show."

"They get a confession?"

"They haven't got the boy yet."

"They'll get him. The police here are finally learning their trade." They were silent for a while, riding the rim of the airport. Wheeler was very tense. "Gavin," he said suddenly, "something's bothering you. Why don't you tell me?"

"Well, it's that they knew all the time what Povich was going to do, and they let him go through with it—almost—then killed him."

Wheeler thought it over. "Those kids," he said, "they holler arson, revolution, sabotage of public buildings, disruption of the government, you name it! Okay. Dealer's choice. They call the game, we play it. Why should we take them less seriously than they take themselves?"

Gavin was silent.

Wheeler boiled over. "Take 'em at their goddamn word! They gave that son of a bitch on the welcome sign every chance to change his mind. But he didn't! He was part of a plan. There were others involved, am I right? Gavin?"

"I don't think we should behave as badly as they do."

"That's a lot of horse manure! You'd better protect your way of life, son," he said. "I mean your privileges. Or you won't have them long."

Wheeler checked in, looked at the clock, then at his son, bewildered by what had gone wrong between them. There wasn't much time.

"You understand I can't stay here right now," he said. It was as near to an apology as he had ever come. "Last night I found myself talking out loud to her. I'd say—this is insane—but I'd say, 'Where are you, Hope?' damn fool thing out loud, 'Why did you leave me, Hope?' " The recollection and the confession seemed to embarrass Wheeler and he choked himself down again. "You can see why I can't stay here, can't you?"

"Sure," Gavin said. "Sure."

What Wheeler had not told his son was that he had heard himself saying to his dead wife, "Why did you do it?," talking to Hope as to a person who'd committed suicide.

At the gate, Wheeler and Gavin shook hands, just as they always had, and parted.

Her questioners had never met anyone like Donna. When they told her they didn't believe she didn't know where Michael was, she showered them with apostate blue needles, defied them—a fine pair of clean-living R.C.s—her legs far apart like a man's, challenging them with her immodesty, too.

"Why don't you leave him alone?" she said. "He didn't kill anybody. You bastards did!"

They persisted, using their trained calm, a poor weapon in this circumstance. "So let's go back to where you said— so let's go back to the beginning one more time—" They were really trying to help the boy, get to him before he did something beyond the point of no return.

When they informed her that at the time she'd admitted driving to the airport there was only one flight, the milk-and-mail to Saint Louis, Memphis, Wheeling, Washington, Philadelphia, and New York, she said, "so that's where he is, St. Louis, Memphis, Wheeling, Washington, Philadelphia and New York, so now you know."

Donna was glad Michael hadn't told her where he was going.

"We still don't believe you," they said an hour later.

"Well, then how about this. He's right here in town?"

"All right," came back their practiced patience, "whereabouts?" Then they began to laugh, gave up, admiring in her what they wouldn't have tolerated in a man. There was nothing to do but let her go and send out a detective to hunt the refugee in the East Village; that's where they all went.

As Donna walked through the anteroom, she saw Alan Kidd waiting. She didn't acknowledge his greeting. The son of a bitch was wearing tennis clothes.

———————————————————————

Alan had left the arrest of Povich to the others, followed Michael and Donna to the airport in a taxi, stayed unobserved and at a distance. The fact that Michael had decided to run was a disaster for Alan.

With Michael gone, some kind of bottom dropped out of Alan's life. He went back to Donna's, where he'd left his car, drove around town till almost five, then went out to the base, entering his wife's house through a window— Marian had latched the front door with a chain—and again slept in the den.

He'd made up his mind to resign from the air force

immediately, and, until that could be effected, live off the base.

In the morning he stayed behind a closed door until he heard Marian leave the house. He dressed for tennis and drove off the base.

He heard the news about Freddie over the car radio. He pulled over to the side of the road the way someone does after a blowout, sat a full ten minutes staring straight ahead, then he went looking for the man.

He found the Grand Mesa Company's offices being abandoned, its personnel leaving town.

"We tried to call you last night," the man said. "You hadn't told your wife where you were. We even sent a car out to the base—"

"What did you have to say?"

"That we had reconsidered our tactics and—"

"How do you expect anyone to ever believe—"

"We don't exist to win people's favor. We exist to protect the security of this country. We looked everywhere we could for that kid you and I were talking to last night. How do you find someone like that? Since you followed him—where did he go?"

"I don't know."

"I think you do. The woman who walked out of here just before you was with him at the airport. She wouldn't tell us anything either. Why people don't help us, I'll never know."

"It should be obvious."

"There was only one place at that time of night. Michael is somewhere east of here. We are still anxious to talk to him, to tell him our reasons—"

"Which are?"

"Suppose we'd done what we said. Povich would have been sent down for maybe three months. Then he'd have been free to do what we—temporarily—prevented him from doing. Please, listen carefully if you possibly can."

"I am."

"We gave Povich every chance. The other fellows here convinced me we had to deal with what he was really up to, not a pretense. The guys with me thought I'd made a bad mistake agreeing to what I agreed to, that it would, in the end, do everyone more harm than good. If you read the

accounts in the papers this morning—they were accurate—
you'll see that all he had to do was follow our instructions,
drop his gun, and walk down. The penalty would have been
more severe than what he would have had for possession,
yes, he would have had time possibly to come to his senses.
It turned out we were dealing with a crazed person. He
knew the odds against him. He opened fire anyway. We
were lucky to have just one man fall, a member of the
force here, wounded. It could have been much worse. You
get my point?"

"I get it. I don't buy it."

"You will, when you're able to think about it. Forgive
me, I only have a few minutes, and I have something to
tell you. When we find him, we're putting Michael Winter
under protective surveillance. I advise you to stay away
from him. He is liable to do anything."

"Especially after he reads the morning paper."

He went right on. "From what I've observed about him,
I'd say that boy is far more intelligent than the man who
died this morning. He's got a good heart, not a natural
killer, not at all. He's worth saving. And while he has
committed a crime, it can be overlooked. Did you hear
that?"

"Yes."

"I'd like to at least have the chance to explain to him
why we did what we did last night. I see I have partially
convinced you. There is no reason why Michael can't live
happily and usefully from now on. I believe he will be
drawn to get in touch with you. I want you to put him in
touch with us. With me."

He gave Alan a card with two Chicago phone numbers
on it.

"Call collect. At night here, during the day there. I want
your help. Not for me, for him! It was obvious to me last
night that he had an ambivalent relationship with you, part
resentment, but another part some kind of genuine esteem.
I am convinced that if you arrange it so I can talk to him
as I am to you, there's a fighting chance he will listen. As
you have."

"Why should he call you? He didn't do anything."

"If we waited for him to do something, you might be

dead. Besides, lieutenant, he did. He was an accessory to attempted murder. He brought Povich the gun—"

"I don't believe that."

"As an accessory—the law says he is just as responsible as the man who died, and if he could become an accessory to one man, he can to another. There are all sorts of driven and desperate characters in that underworld of drugs and politics, eager to perform what the man this morning failed to."

"I don't agree."

"I wouldn't expect you to, not yet. You're still hung up on the least important aspect of this, the unfortunate agreement I made last night, one I should not have made, one I tried by every means I could think of to correct. This morning it was I who insisted that we give Povich two shots before we replied. I was on the bullhorn. I pleaded with that man. In the eyes of my mates—and my own—I am responsible for that cop in the hospital with a slug in his kidney. He'll probably lose that kidney, he might have lost his life. I'm lucky he didn't. That's why I can't be sentimental about this."

"And I am? Sentimental?"

"Worse. Forgive me. You betray yourself. That's your way of life."

"How?"

"You might have straightened that boy out with a few no-nonsense words. Instead you coddled him, spoiled him, bought everything he said. Did you ever once stick up for what *you* believe? Isn't that the duty of a friend? If not that, what?"

"Yes, but—"

"And isn't it about time all of us said this is how we want it to be here, and this is the way it's going to be here? You want to do him a favor? Get tough with him."

"Yes, but—"

"But! That says it all."

He stood, looked at his watch. "Sorry, I've got to rush off," he said.

They shook hands formally, and Alan was left with it.

———————————————————

Judge Bo Barton refused Cy's appeal. Any other decision, he said, would encourage every crackpot, every bomb-throwing anarchist in that part of the world, give them a way of disrupting and delaying trials and so impeding the process of justice. In the light of the morning's events, anyone could see how important quick justice was. "Back to the barrelhead!" he said.

As Gavin and Cy left Judge Barton's court, in the twilight of one of the long upstairs corridors, Gavin put his arm around the beaten man. This gesture, though momentary, drained Cy of the last of his resolve to contest the decision he now knew to be inevitable.

The sale of pistols and paralyzers boomed; there was a rush on American flags and patriotic decals. In a supermarket, guns were put on sale.

Judge Barton decided to adjourn court for the entire day.

The cops were especially rough with student leaders, using this opportunity to teach the future rulers of this territory a lesson they wouldn't forget.

In an office of the state capitol that same evening, there was an extraordinary meeting of the regents, worthies entrusted with the well-being of the state university and its students. It had become apparent that comfort, support, and shelter was being provided activists of the so-called youth revolution by students under the jurisdiction of these regents.

It was suggested that there be drawn up a code of conduct for students at the state universities.

There was no discussion.

"Distribution or wearing of armbands and buttons, the carrying of signs, banners, or posters having an obscene or controversial significance in a manner which substantially interferes with the normal activities of the university, etc., etc.

"Participation in any assembly, demonstration, sit-in, or similar event which substantially disrupts the normal activities of the university, etc., etc.

"Publishing or threatening to publish malicious writing, printing, or pictures which impeach the honesty, integrity, or reputation of any member of the university community or which bring such person into disrepute, contempt, or ridicule, etc., etc."

Ben Rose woke Michael just before dawn to insist that he go to the mountains with them. "They'll lay one on you, accessory to attempted murder."

"Don't talk to me about that," Michael ordered. "I understand what has to happen. Go your way."

Michael went back to sleep holding the cat.

Ben decided to leave the VW behind. The Estate Wagon could hold all seven, sleeping and driving in shifts.

An hour after they'd gone, the landlord came in to look his house over. To his surprise, Ben's family had left it clean and neat. The landlord was so pleased, he didn't think to look in the attic.

At nine the next morning, Bailiff Lansing called "All rise!", the door behind the judge's place was pulled open, and Judge Thurston Breen slid into his seat.

Everyone knew the trial was over. But Gavin was determined to put Alan Kidd on the stand.

Gavin had had an extraordinary phone call that morning from the base commander. Colonel Dowd, hinting that Kidd wasn't in condition to be put through an ordeal, asked Gavin if he could "get along without."

Gavin had said No. But if he'd expected from Dowd's request to be questioning a humbled man, he was mistaken. There are men like Alan, who, thrown down from a moral stand they've taken, climb back to the very same position, reoccupy it defiantly, more not less determined, more not less convinced that they were right, all along.

"You drove Michael Winter out to the house on Queen Street?"

"I did," Alan replied.

"How long was he in the house?"

"About twenty minutes, maybe half an hour."

"Did he take this long metal suitcase with him?" Gavin held up the exhibit which had been found in Freddie Povich's room.

"Yes, he did."

"May I ask what you did while he was in the house?"

"May I ask what relevance that question has to this trial?"

"I must say," Judge Breen interceded, "I was wondering the same thing."

"Your honor," Gavin replied, "trust me to show, not only the relevance of my line of questions to the outcome of this trial, but to the issues which this trial raises."

The mood of the community on this day was such that Judge Breen decided to let Gavin's answer, which was as irrelevant as his question, pass.

Gavin turned to Alan. "Answer my question, please," he said. "What did you do while he was in the house?"

"I waited."

"I need to know in what position you waited."

"I crouched," Alan said.

"Can you be more explicit?"

"Yes. I crouched like this," Alan illustrated, "in a cowardly and ridiculous position. Is that what you—"

"Crouched out of sight?"

"Yes. Like a criminal."

"So then it's true you cooperated with Michael Winter in every respect?"

"I was glad to."

"Deceiving and eluding the police of this city?"

"That wasn't hard."

"How was Michael Winter able to make you do this? Try to answer without sarcasm."

"Without sarcasm. Because I had the greatest respect for him."

"And you still hold that respect?"

"Yes."

"Despite the fact that Michael Winter has on two occasions here, derided the court, made fun of it, reviled it?"

"Not despite. Because of."

"And you say that now, despite the fact that Winter provided Povich with the weapon Povich used to make his assassination attempt?"

"If that's true, despite that."

"And despite that after he did this, Michael Winter

left town, by night, leaving his fellow conspirators to hold the bag?"

"There was nothing else for him to do."

"I think there was. Face the music."

"I believe he will, in time."

"Will what?"

"Claim his innocence."

"Here?"

"Not in this court. But here in these United States."

Judge Breen interrupted. "I think, counsel," he said, "that we may have pursued this line of questioning long enough. Will you show us its relevance, please?"

"Your honor, it must be obvious now that the same young person who planned the assassination attempt two mornings ago, using Freddie Povich to hit, also may have planned the killing which was to have taken place on the base, using Vin Connor to hit. What Sergeant Flores was up against then, was not a psychotic boy named Vin Connor, but a criminal conspiracy whose leader, Michael Winter, is a person with hypnotic powers of persuasion so great that he was able to involve someone else as dedicated and intelligent as the man on the stand, this misguided lieutenant in our air force. Thank you, witness, you may——"

"And you think you've shown that?" Alan asked coolly.

"I know it."

"Then you're a fool."

Alan got up and walked through the enclosure gate. Bailiff Lansing moved after him as Judge Breen asked Cy if he wanted to question the departing man.

Cy shook his head.

Alan was already out of the courtroom.

"Hey! You got your picture in here!" Wally had sneaked out for the papers. "Here's an air force dude says he intends to make you face the music."

"I know," Michael said.

The attic was very hot, and Michael very sleepy.

"Alan Kidd. You know him?"

"He's a friend of mine."

"Here!" Wally offered the paper.

"I don't want to read it," Michael said.

Wally turned to the funnies.

"Wally."

"Yeah?"

"Can you still get on the base?"

At the end of that afternoon, Alan reported to the office of the base commander.

"I can arrange, if you wish, to have you assigned to another base," Colonel Dowd told Alan. "It would be temporary, but you could leave Monday morning—or even Sunday night."

"That will be fine, sir, thank you, Sunday."

They both hesitated. Colonel Dowd, a kind man, had more feeling for Alan than Marian did at that moment.

"I'm sorry about you and Marian, Alan," he said.

"Thank you, sir, is that all?"

"Guess so. I really am sorry. I'll miss you."

Alan got up. They shook hands.

The final day of the trial was a time for generosity. Even Cy Walker was in a mood of harmony and healing.

"No one can deny," he said in his brief summary, "that Cesario Flores is a good man. But sometimes good men commit crimes. I have not told you that Vin Connor was a good person. But all men in our country live under the protection of the law. All you have to judge here," he told the jury, "is whether this good man killed Vin Connor in an act of premeditated murder."

Gavin's own summation put three simple questions to the members of the jury. "Place yourselves—each of you—in Master Sergeant Flores's shoes. What would you have done? Would you have done different? If you had, would you have liked yourself?"

The greater part of that morning was devoted to Judge Breen's charge to the jury. After telling them the choice of decisions they had, he made a philosophic observation.

"The law," he said, "is a living thing, which is to say it is always changing. Physiologists tell us our body is completely replaced every—what? Seven years? But the law changes in subtle ways even more frequently. It has to. I have never seen—have you?—so many profound, so many bewildering changes in our customs and values as over these last years.

"At the same time the law has the necessary quality of permanence. It must always be there, above and beyond us, our strength and our safeguard. The miracle is this, that the law achieves this permanence only by and because of its changing.

"It is your privilege to render a decision in this case. What you hand down here will be read not only for its finality but for its inferences, perhaps more importantly the latter. From the result of your deliberations we will know what of our law you consider needs bending to our changing ways and what you consider inviolable.

"So we look to you—I as well as your community—for guidance. Every decision changes the law if only by confirming it for a new circumstance."

▬▬▬▬▬▬▬▬▬▬▬▬▬▬▬▬▬▬▬▬

For their last lunch together the members of the jury selected the dining room of the Western Star. Over the nine days of meals together they had decided that when you get all through with the spices and sauces, the chilis and the curry powders, good, straight, western American food is best.

With their dessert they were chattering about staying in touch, exchanging addresses and phone numbers as they might have after a vacation cruise, when there was a sudden silence and a lady juror, a motherly soul in her forties, was heard to exclaim, "Well, I want that man home for his supper tonight!"

"You have breached my instructions, Mrs. Wycoff," Bailiff Lansing said. "I'm sorry you did that."

Mrs. Wycoff took the reprimand to heart. But the dessert, pecan pie a la mode, restored her good spirits. Like most of the jury she had gained weight during the trial.

Judge Breen had lunch at his desk and at the telephone. His broker had looked into the concerns Breen had brought up a couple of days ago in New York. The bank had accepted his life insurance as collateral, which stabilized the situation temporarily. There were two reasons, the broker said, why the judge might want to reconsider his instructions to replace his present growth stocks with tax-free municipals. The first, of course, was that the stocks were now so low that to sell would be really foolish and would show a lack of courage and belief in the system. Those stocks were going up again, sooner or later; they always had. As for the New York City bonds, the broker called his attention to an article in the preceding day's *New York Times* (he was sending it air special) which quoted the Mayor's assurance that New York City paid its creditors on time and always would. Statements of that kind, the broker observed, usually precede a collapse.

"Okay," Breen burst out, "then leave it alone, leave it alone!"

When he hung up he was in exactly the same condition he was in a week ago when he'd decided he was on the verge of disaster. Worse, his life insurance was on the line, too!

Still, for some reason, he didn't feel in danger any more.

The jury reached its verdict in a matter of minutes: Not guilty by reason of temporary insanity. But Bailiff Lansing thought it might be advisable for them to sit around for a while. If they came back in ten minutes, some people might believe they hadn't given the case proper consideration.

So they chatted. Out of that came a problem. Some of the people on the jury were concerned that the "insane" verdict, even qualified by the word "temporary," might damage Flores later in his professional life.

Others argued that the temporary-insanity verdict really was better because later on, if the sergeant had any qualms of conscience, he could always tell himself he didn't know what he was doing when he did it.

So when Judge Breen asked their foreman, "Have you reached a verdict?" the man stood up and said they had and that it was not guilty by reason of temporary insanity, "not guilty" said in good space and the other words very fast.

When he delivered the verdict, everyone's eyes went to the defendant, and they saw an odd thing. Flores's attention seemed not to be on the jury which was freeing him; he was looking around for someone.

It was Gavin who noticed Juana wasn't in the courtroom.

Elsa was there with Elizabeth and Diego and Linda, but Juana had not come.

Then Flores understood the verdict. He nodded, leaned over to Gavin and asked, "Can I go home now?"

Gavin laughed out loud. "Yes, sir," he said, "you can go home now."

But it was almost an hour before Cesario Flores got out of the courtroom. The newspapermen were all over him, writing down everything he said, including "This restores my faith in American justice." And "I prayed like I never prayed before." And "I knew God was watching over me."

Flores believed it all. He was the only one-hundred-percent believer in that room.

Colonel Dowd sent a car for him—Elsa and the kids had gone ahead—and Flores enjoyed that, too, being chauffeured in a car marked Base Commanding Officer. At the main gate the soldiers on duty saluted the car, and he accepted their respect as for himself.

He was driven straight to Dowd's office, where, on the porch, Sergeant Jones was waiting for him. He hit him on the biceps with his fist, which was as affectionate as he knew how to be. "You did it, you son of a bitch!" he hissed. "You really did it!"

"Had to be," Flores said. Then he made his little crap-shooter gesture and whispered to Jones, "Roll de dice!," laughed out loud and said, "What's right is right! Roll de dice!"

When Jones took him down the long hall, secretaries stood for him.

Colonel Dowd cleared his office, had the doors closed, and, still standing, said, "We're grateful to you, Sergeant Flores, all of us."

"That's all right, sir," Flores said.

They chatted about this and that; then there was a silence, and Flores got up and said he hadn't seen his family yet, not really, maybe he better go home.

"Sit down a minute, Sergeant," the colonel said, "because we've got a problem."

Cesario sat.

"It's about your resignation. We rushed it through, had to, for your sake. Who could have anticipated this? Total exoneration? I'll bet not even you figured on that!"

"Right is right," Flores said.

"I'll do my very best to have it rescinded. But the air force is starchy about—"

"I want to stay here, sir."

"God knows I want you to. In the meantime, you can live in your house."

"I want to stay in the air force, Colonel Dowd. That's all I am. Air force!"

"Incidentally, remember the foreman of the jury? Well, he's a foreman somewhere else, at Fairbank Aircraft. Of course, he knows you've retired here, and he called me yesterday and asked if you might—"

"I want to stay in the air force."

"It may be impossible. The job at Fairbank would pay nearly two hundred dollars a month more, and the man said he could easily find you a house near the plant—"

Colonel Dowd stopped.

Cesario Flores was weeping.

The house was full of his neighbors. Mrs. Jones had brought over a washtub full of Bud, and when he walked in there was one waiting for him and he put it down in two swallows, as thousands cheered, what a man, what a man, pull him another! They were all over him, popping open the cans and chewing the cud of the trial and asking for his autograph, even old friends who knew him too well to like him, shouting, "Sign this, will you, Sarge, it's for my kid to keep!" and "You sure showed them, boy, you really showed them something!"

After his second Flores began to go with it, believing it all, laughing it up. After his third he bellowed like a bull Mex style and everyone laughed, but no one louder than *el toro* himself.

Just then his whole maintenance outfit rolled up in the unit's trucks and emptied into the house, twenty, thirty guys laughing and admiring him and asking him questions he couldn't really hear, but answered anyway.

"Oh, oh, I wish Juanie was here," he kept saying; then he'd shout, "Juana, Goddammit, where the hell are you!"

Everybody laughed. Nobody knew where she was and nobody gave a shit.

The beer roused his appetite, and he walked into the kitchen.

"Now when would I have time to cook a dinner, *Liebchen?*" Elsa said for all to hear. "For goodness' sake!"

"I'm cooking tonight!" he shouted.

He took Diego by the hand, and they walked to the supermarket. Along the way the porches were decked out with people offering their congratulations. Kids came down with the newspaper that had his picture on the front page and pointed to where they wanted him to sign.

Along the heavy-stacked rows of food in the supermarket, shoppers came up, saying, "I just want to shake your hand," offered him anything they had for him to sign, the man who'd done it for them. Even the butcher, after he'd quartered the fresh-killed fowl, smoothed out a dollar bill and said, "Write something special, will you, Sarge?"

Flores wrote, "Right is right! Roll de dice!"

━━━━━━━━━━━━━━━━━━━━━━━━

The liberal community was outraged by the verdict.

They were all gathered at a semisecret cocktail party thrown by a lit prof to raise money for the Bolivian underground The drinking went on after the canapés and the tortilla chips were gone. Someone went out for more liquor. It was too important an occasion to cut short.

By eleven-thirty they were all in one hot huddle, in chairs, on the floor, on each other, around Stanley Hough, Whitehead Professor of Ancient History, author of a classic study of the Peloponnesian War and its contemporary relevance.

Old Man Hough was the campus firebrand, a heavy man with a mottled red face and very pale eyes, a man who was, in his own words, too old not to say what he thought. Which he was now doing, in roars.

Behind him his wife, a young woman with a long neck, a former pupil, watched anxiously. The professor had had one stroke and was not supposed to get riled. She had a way of humming to remind him, and she did this now.

He shook her off angrily. "You know damn well," he growled to the people at his feet, "if he had killed two cops, they'd have convicted him like a shot!"

Then he stood up, empty glass in hand, wobbling and

shaking, glaring at those sitting around him as if they were his enemies instead of his coreligionists.

His wife hummed again.

"Stop looking around and smiling at everyone, Olive!" he shouted. "Stop all that undercover humming and those damn apologetic laughs. I'm not going home till I'm ready!"

Olive hummed and laughed apologetically.

The professor got through the circle of bright heads and found what was left of the liquor. But before he poured, he wheeled and let go again.

"What's the matter with us all?" he shouted. "They're legalizing murder in this state!"

If the rage at that party seemed futile, it was to prove not to be, not entirely. Among those present had been an editor for the morning paper. His editorial, written at midnight, when every responsible person in the paper's offices had gone to bed, was headed A SHAMEFUL DECISION and concluded: "The verdict invites any father to become judge, jury, and executioner."

But that editorial, mightily applauded in liberal circles, had no effect. The reaction of the general public was simply: "Of course!"

Gavin also threw a party. It was a classy idea, but it didn't work out the way he hoped.

Never doubting the verdict, he had, during the lunch break, invited the judge and Sally and Cy and Corky to come over and help Betty and him get rid of three fat mallards Wheeler had turned over to them, along with the contents of his deep freeze.

The judge and Sally got there all right, but Corky called at the last minute and said Cy was not feeling well, could they have a rain check?

So it turned out to be a party for the victors, and a very jolly one. For a moment, during cocktails, Gavin even thought of inviting Cesario to come on over. "But what would we talk about?" he quipped to Thurston and Sally. "The restoration of his daughter's virginity by trial for murder?"

They were quickly flying on martinis, then wine and a Curaçao liqueur from Wheeler's reserve. Betty was particularly happy. Finally she said it, "I haven't even told him yet," pointing to Gavin. "The doctor told me today that we finally did it. I'm going to produce, I mean reproduce."

The judge and Sally were very flattered to be in on such a private occasion, and Gavin kept kissing Betty and looking at her, and they got so happy and so in harmony with all mankind that they began to worry about Cy, wishing he was there and saying what a really nice guy he was after all and finally, in a frenzy of good fellowship, they decided to get him on the phone.

This time Corky told the truth. Cy had not come home.

When Cy came back to his office after the verdict, he'd found Donna looking disgruntled again, so he called her in and fired her.

That was all Donna needed. She told Cy exactly how he'd sold out to the community of shit-heads and how Michael was worth ten of him any day. All these savage attacks at his worth struck him simply as true.

He asked her to get him a drink, then told her to sit down and drink with him, then go to dinner with him, to which she said she would like hell, she didn't go sneaking around with other women's husbands, she wouldn't go unless he promised to tell Mrs. Walker and take her openly to the most public restaurant in town.

It was on a hill for the affluent, overlooking the valley; they sat at a window table lit by candles set in hurricane lamps, and she told him after a couple more that she loved Michael, not so much sexually but as a person, and that the papers and the filthy TV and the muscle-head police and those plain-clothes prigs who quizzed her had Michael all wrong. he was anything but a criminal, pure and good and completely honest—

"Why don't you go to him?" he asked.

"In the first place I don't know where he is, and in the second place I'm too old for him, and in the last place he doesn't want me."

So Cy took her home. Before they got into bed, she made him promise that he'd tell his wife everything, she was not a double-dealing sneak. Cy had drunk enough to promise he would and mean it.

She found Cy nicer than she thought he'd be, if only because there was so much need in him.

He found her unresponsive.

Afterward he thanked her for everything she'd said, she'd convinced him, he was quitting the practice of law.

Donna didn't believe him, but she kissed him goodbye and pretended she did.

Five minutes later, there was a knock on the door. It was Michael. He had seen them come in, waited outside for Cy to go.

With him was a spacey freak he introduced as Wally.

Michael had come for help. His time had run out, new tenants were moving into Ben's old house the next morning, so he and Wally couldn't stay in the attic any longer. Could they stay there?

There was something else Michael wanted.

The editorial shocked some of the readers of Saturday's paper. But it was pulled out of the second edition and replaced by another editorial—a more "balanced" plea for quiet and forgetting and for a return to normal. The heading of the second editorial was "Let's Cool It." And the last line, written all in caps, said, REMEMBER WHAT A WONDERFUL PLACE THIS WAS TO LIVE IN ONCE? WELL, BELIEVE US, IT WILL BE AGAIN!

In the paper there was only one piece of news related to the trial. Judge Barton, despite his years, could, on occasion, act expeditiously. He had granted Gavin's request. The murder weapon could be returned to its owner, Sergeant Cesario Flores, Rtd.

Was Judge Barton aware of the symbolic meaning of his act? No one ever found out because no one dared ask him.

The odd thing was that when Gavin called Cesario to tell him he could come to the office Monday and get his pistol, Flores seemed bitter, said he didn't want it.

Then he told Gavin; it was definite, there was no way, Colonel Dowd had told him, that the air force could rescind his resignation. Oh, he'd been promised a job all right, with Fairbank, but—well, thank God for little favors, he had asked Colonel Dowd if he could continue to shop at the base commissary and the colonel had said it was against the rules, but the hell with the damn rules, Dowd gave him permission.

Gavin changed the subject. "Well, anyway," he said, "it must be nice to be back with your family. By the way, how's Juana?"

Juana had heard from Elizabeth that since her father was taking a job at the other end of town, the family would have to move off the base. She'd come for her clothes.

It was the first time her father had seen her since the trial, and she was wearing a new pair of bells. She told him straight out that she'd found someone, moved in with him and some other kids. She pointed and there he was, waiting for her to come out, a tall boy with very long hair and a scruff of beard, leaning against the side of the car and with an air of consummate indifference. When she'd packed her things and kissed them all goodbye, he drove her off.

"Take care of yourself," her father said. He had no fight left in him.

Riding off the base, Juana made her new boyfriend stop the car, opened the door, ran across the street, and hugged somebody.

It was Wally. "I thought they threw you out of here," she said. Juana liked Wally better than anyone she'd been with after Vinnie. He was wilder, meaner, funnier, and more everlastingly turned on.

"I came to borrow something," he said.

"Well, call me, will you?" She scribbled a number on the back of the odd-shaped parcel he was carrying. It was awful heavy. "Who are you going to use this on?" she asked, laughing.

The door to Lieutenant and Mrs. Kidd's home was open, and through the screen Wally could see the dining room where the couple were enjoying a lunch of tunafish salad and quartered tomatoes. They seemed to be in excellent spirits, sharing a joke with the maid, who went to the door when Wally knocked.

Alan had spent the night at Marian's. An "outrageous"

—Marian's word—thing had happened. They'd slept together. Marian was not nearly as surprised as Alan.

What had happened didn't in the least affect their decision to divorce. It was simply the "nicest"—Marian's word—way to break off, no hard feelings, nobody mad.

They'd enjoyed it, too. With the strain of commitment eased, they were, once again, able to appreciate each other's good points.

In fact they'd slept right through breakfast and were concluding a very pleasant lunch when Wally interrupted.

"What is it, Mary?" Marian Kidd asked the maid at the door.

"He says he's got a message for Lieutenant Kidd."

Alan Kidd knew Wally through his dishonorable discharge, processed in the judge advocate's office.

"Hello there," he said. "What's up?"

"I got a message for you, sir, from Donna. She said call her."

"Excuse me a minute, Marian." Alan took the steps in threes, closed the door, threw himself across the bed, and picked up Marian's trimline phone.

"Is it what I think?" he asked Donna.

Donna told him she wasn't sure the person he was referring to was coming to town, but if he did, the same boy who'd brought Alan her message would call for him early the next morning, really early, like maybe seven, could he be at the main gate, just outside, waiting?

There it was! Alan had his chance!

Michael must know he needed help now, must realize he had to have what only a true friend could give him, the truth spoken without qualification.

Alan remembered several times when his father, Judge Nicholas Kidd, had spoken to him with words that came down like boulders, remembered how they'd hurt at first and how much better he'd felt afterward.

Oh yes, he'd speak very straight to Mr. Michael in the morning! It was time for some hard New England talk, he'd sure as hell straighten that boy out this time.

Alan's heart beat as it might have before a tryst.

CHAPTER NINE

The hours after dawn on Sunday are the quiet ones. No one of account is on the streets. An occasional Indian, lost in his own land, a family of Mexicans, north for a weekend of shopping, the last of the night people, wanting sleep, the first of the old people who can no longer sleep, these separate humans pad aimlessly here and there or stand on corners waiting for the city to start moving again.

Even the bells of San Felipe are mellow; they lull, they don't summon. First mass is thin.

There is being built in the heart of that place a new civic center, a complex of buildings rising out of the pink sand, out of the old powdered stone. The architects have chosen for their designs reinforced concrete with the same cast of pinkish-brown. The half-finished structures already harmonize with the land, already seem to have been there a long time. Especially on Sunday, when nothing moves, they suggest landmarks left by some civilization long gone, the masses ponderous, the scale monumental, keyed to the ancient jagged mountains which stand behind and above in their own silence.

The people of the region are justly proud of what's going up in their mid-city. Excellent architects, artists who respect the traditions of the region are putting up a new county seat with its administrative offices and courtrooms and a new city hall housing an up-to-date police department adequate to the community's growing needs. There will also be two vast amphitheaters, suitable for all sports from ice hockey to tournament tennis and equally suited for political conventions.

The new county courthouse building is the most imposing of these structures, perhaps because its designers were aware of the inevitable symbolism of its façade. This one successfully suggests majesty and justice.

At about half past seven on this Sunday, two visitors entered these grounds through a piece of the wire link fence that the trucks had trampled. They walked through the outer ring of mobile air-conditioned offices, along the assembly of great earthmovers, the huge Empires and Internationals, the cats and the loaders; they walked past the mobile air compressors, now silent, and the Blue Brute monorotors. They skirted the tar wagons, still acrid though cool, past the plumbers' tables, standing uncovered just as the men had left them when they left for the weekend.

As the visitors strolled in the rhythm of that soft Sunday morning, they were in conversation. The older man, a lieutenant of the United States Air Force, was fair, classically handsome, perfectly proportioned. The other, a boy, walked as if he were by himself.

The lieutenant's manner was forceful. He seemed to be giving the young man instructions, at other times correcting him. It was impossible to tell from the behavior of the younger person whether he was agreeing or disagreeing, whether he was even listening. The lieutenant was answering what was unspoken.

"Yes, at this point, I do know what's the best for you. And I am making it my business! I haven't the least intention of standing by and watch you ruin your life. I'm going to save you whether you want me to or not."

The bells of San Felipe washed like waves of a gentle tide against the heavy walls on this Sunday morning.

The lieutenant laid down point after point.

"Because the first thing hate destroys is the hater. You're not the same person I met a few weeks ago. If you go on this way, there soon won't be anything human, anything good left in you. I don't say you're wrong about what you're feeling. But at this moment, I say, feel for yourself! Live with the injustice!"

They were moving past huge piles of material, ready and waiting for Monday's use, bags of cement and sand, lime and gypsum, cartons of fiberglass reinforcements, acoustical ceiling board, and flush-fit light fixtures. Everything that would be needed was ready, waiting. The wealth of the nation had been brought here, from both coasts and from the great industrial complexes of the middle land. America's power was at the disposal of the builders of this place.

"Michael, you could be anything, do anything. This country—all you have to do is make up your mind to be part of it. It's waiting for kids like you to run it, maybe to save it. If you walk away from it now, goddamn you, Michael—pay attention!"

Disturbed by the visitors, a pair of pigeons—did they have a nest somewhere in all that concrete?—flapped awkwardly through a metal door left open so that the young concrete would dry. Inside, plastic sheeting had been stretched over the fresh-poured barriers and edgings of the amphitheater; they stirred when the easy breeze got under their length; they bellied and lifted and made a long eerie rustle that mixed with the footsteps of the two men.

"They're looking for you now, yes, but you're innocent and we'll prove it. You don't want to live as a fugitive. What you did was bring an empty suitcase to the room of a boy who pissed his life away in a meaningless, useless act of—"

They were now in the inmost chambers, those of the courts. Here there was no stir in the air. There were no windows. These halls of justice would get their supply of air from the vast conduits still exposed overhead. Silence was the design here. These were to be places for reflection and decision, for judgments made and sentences pronounced.

Alan handed Michael the card.

"You can get him there—" he pointed, "at night, and here—" again he pointed, "during the day. Call collect, he said. You'll be surprised—if you let yourself be—how intelligent and decent he is. I was. He doesn't mean you anything but good. He is much more sympathetic than you could possibly—"

"Did you tell him you were seeing me this morning?"

"Yes," Alan said, "I did. I told him—"

"When?"

"Just before I came to meet you. I woke him, he didn't mind. He said I should tell you he wanted to help you in every—"

"Did you tell him where you were going to meet me?"

"No."

Alan was looking at the ceiling where a great central fixture of lights was being hung.

"I've often wished I'd become an architect," he said.

Alan turned toward the door.

It was the end of the tour.

"Incidentally," Alan said, "where're you living now?"

Michael turned his head away, didn't answer.

"Michael—"

"Who wants to know?"

"He does. So he can get in touch and—"

It was then that Michael moved toward Alan.

He looked into the eyes of the rabbit.

Then he embraced the man who knew what was best for him.

The watchman, on that Sunday morning, had come in at dawn to spell his fellow who'd passed an uneventful night in their trailer. The day man had immediately fallen down on the same cot to sleep off his night's pleasures.

But if he had been awake and as alert as a catbird, he would not have heard anything that happened in those chambers, certainly not a single sharp sound muffled in cloth. Nor—if he had seen two men walk in and only one walk out and stroll over to the place where the fence had been flattened by the Big Macks and enter a waiting VW— if he'd seen it all, every move, which he didn't, he'd have thought nothing of it.

――――――――――――――――――――

They hadn't gone a block before Michael told Wally to stop, got out of the car, and walked into a phone booth, stood inside with the door closed, but not making a call. A piss, Wally guessed, a piss relieved fear; every soldier knows that.

Then Michael came out and stood in the clear sunlight, watching the straggling line of straights going to early mass in San Felipe. Wally put his head out the window and called, but Michael didn't hear him, followed a family, walked with them into the church.

Wally was not easily worried, but he decided he'd better get Michael. He found him in an altar opposite the nave door, looking at a banner of velvet on which had been inscribed in gold thread, "Unless a man be born again."

"Let's go, Michael," Wally said.

Michael seemed reluctant to leave not only the people in the church but the city itself. Even after Wally had him back in the car, he wanted to stop and watch the social security freaks playing shuffleboard in the park.

At last they were on the long ramp that fed the throughway west.

Michael slept.

Two hours later, Wally skirted Tucson City and turned onto the International Border Friendship Highway, striking south, straight as an arrow, through the empty desert and toward the mountains which had once been the stronghold of the Cochise, where once Geronimo had struck, hidden, struck again.

Michael woke. "I'd like some ice cream," he said.

"There's a Stuckey's at Benson. I'll wake you."

"Okay. We'll get some pecan delight, too."

When Michael woke next they'd been in and out of Benson, were approaching Tombstone. A Junior C. of C. sign quoted Tombstone's old-time boast: "Too tough to die!"

"How are you?" Wally asked.

"I don't know. I never saw a dead man before. I'm trying to—now, it's hard to believe I did that." Wally didn't answer. "You know," Michael said, "it was easy. So quick! It takes a second."

Wally turned on the news. There was nothing special.

Tombstone was for tourists. Old men in baseball caps, oddly inappropriate over their fuzzy gray growth or their clean baby scalps, shod in sandals or shoes of leather soft and loose enough to give for their arthritic nobs, and with them their ladies in hair nets or eyeshades, in cotton and bobby socks and sneakers, these old pairs padded along the ground where Doc Holliday and the Earps had once strutted in their spurred boots, stopped to peek into the saloon, not daring even now to go in where once Old Man Clanton had sat with the brothers McCleary and his son Bobby and there planned the action that was to cost them their lives in the O.K. Corral.

Michael insisted they go into the museum, where they saw Doc Holliday's snub-barrel gun and read the names of the men it had killed.

On the highway to Bisbee they listened to the news again; there was nothing special.

"We forgot Stuckey's," Michael said.

"We'll get something in Bisbee." Wally had passed it by, intent on getting Michael over the border.

A distinguished liberal senator from Florida was quoted on the air saying that while dissent was part of the American system, violence was not. Michael turned to Mexican music—they were getting closer—and that was soothing. Again he fell asleep.

Coming into Bisbee, the defiles narrow and the hills crowd the road. Wally stopped before a statue apparently made of solid copper and dedicated "to those virile men, the copper miners of Bisbee, whose contribution to the State has been magnificent!" The garage man who filled their tank told them the hills had once been all rich ore, that there were fifty miles of tunnels under the town and twenty thousand men had once worked them. But the mines were played out, he said, and what little ore was still taken wasn't worth the expense; Phelps Dodge, which had taken out the copper, was about to close up and move. Bisbee was becoming a ghost town, the man offered with their change.

Michael wanted to hear more, but Wally took the change and slammed off.

Inside the city, Michael became even more the casual visitor with nothing on his mind but the time on his hands. He insisted they park and walk around. The Pythian Castle was closed, but the Copper Queen Hotel, once known—a sign so informed them—as the finest hotel between Dallas and San Francisco, was open or half open, and there they had coffee and Michael a slice of chocolate-cream pie, then another. After this he wanted to walk around.

He got into a long conversation with an old man on the street, a man in his eighties with a tooth and a half in his

mouth and no end of chatter. Wally began to get nervous
again. "Come on, Michael," he said, "let's go!"

"I want to talk to this old man, Wally," Michael said
in his softest voice. "I'm never going to see this old man
again, Wally, ever, Wally, so I'm not going to hurry now."

The old fellow, it turned out, was a scholar of ancient
Greece—what the hell was he doing there? He smiled wick-
edly as he praised Sappho above all other poets of Hellas,
breaking, there in Bisbee, with critical tradition. Yes, she
was greater than Sophocles, even greater than Homer. What
business was it of anyone's that she was a lesbian? he challenged Wally. Then he spoke of Ovid's attacking Sappho
on the grounds that she was black, an "Ethiopian," Ovid
had called her. The old man grinned maliciously as he cut
Ovid down with the faintest praise. "Ovid," he said, "is
often not factual but always interesting."

Now the old man was inviting Michael to his home, his
room, where he would read from Sappho's verse and convince him of her high historic station. There Wally put his
foot down and said No! they were not going to the man's
place, they were leaving.

At this the old man turned on him and for goodness
knows what reason informed him that Christianity was the
greatest blight that had ever been put on the spirit of man,
had turned us from reason to revelation, and drowned the
spirit of humanity in a tidal wave of Jewish morality, and so
he was off on another subject, one that allowed even more
expansion than Sappho.

Wally finally had to drag Michael away. The last they
saw of the old man he was tottering through the traffic
on the narrow main street, waving his hand and shouting
"Vale!"

As they drove out of town they passed an enormous hole
in the earth, big enough to throw eight or nine towns into,
the place from which Phelps Dodge had taken the copper.
There were miles of fence around the excavation but no
sign. Apparently no one was willing to admit the plunder.
When Michael looked down into the crater, a single bird
was flying across the void.

"Let's get going," he said. "Let's get over the border."

They passed the last of the hills and were onto a plain
facing the first mountain of Mexico. The land got drier and

browner and deader as they drove. Just before the little town of Naco (USA) where they were to cross over to Naco (Mex.), there was a great oasis of green, a golf course. On it were two players.

The American Immigration Service takes no notice of people leaving the country; Mexican Immigration takes no notice of people going either way. Wally had chosen Naco because it was sleepy on both sides.

A tiny brown bureaucrat in a very hot uniform which was causing him no discomfort waved them over.

Mexico! Michael got out and stretched; then he looked around. "This is the state where Cesario Flores was born," he announced. "Sonora."

They were on the Avenida Independencia, between the Servicio Pemex and the Barberia "Zafira." Michael walked slowly down the middle of that welcoming dirt street, past the Sistema de Agua Potable and the Salon de Belleza "Berta," up to the Cine Variedades, closed.

He stood in the middle of that very wide, very dusty street and felt fine.

Looking for a beer, they came onto a district of "clubs" —apparently someone had once had the notion Naco might turn into another Nogales or even a small Tijuana, but such had not been its misfortune. Here were the Casa Rosa Club Nocturno, closed, the Casa Blanca, closed, the Arco Iris, closed, the Blue Moon, closed, behind them, empty, their "pony stables," where brown girls once entertained.

The Crystal Palace they found open, there were even a couple of girls leaning over a fence and another, very well slung, walking slowly along the row of bins. She stopped to inspect the men as they did her. Wally was for lingering, but Michael was shy, and, for once, practical. "Let's check out the railroad station," he said, "see when there's a train where."

The train was waiting. "I must have good karma," Michael said. He went in and bought a ticket to Guadalajara, its final destination. In some kind of Spanish he asked the man behind the grille when the train would be leaving and the man answered in English, "Pretty soon, pretty soon."

Now they were on the Calle Morelos. Across the street was the La Reguladera Café, and there they sat, ordering Dos Xs to drink while they kept their eyes on the train.

"You okay?" Wally asked.

"I don't know yet how I feel."

"Don't feel bad about it. It doesn't make any difference."

"If I thought that—that it wouldn't make any difference—I would feel bad," Michael said. "I did it because—" He stopped and looked at the train; a few people were getting on. "I didn't have anything against him," Michael said. "I always liked him. I liked him better than the others."

"I thought I was blown-out!" Wally said. "But you!" He shook his head, took a long swallow of the beer. Then he said, "You optimists, you believe things can get better, you're the dangerous ones. A freak like me, I don't think anything will ever change."

There was a bustle around the train. The diesel gave voice.

Wally looked at Michael carefully; he had the distinct feeling he was looking at a madman. He wanted distance between them. "Better go," he said, and stood up.

Michael left some money on the table, then walked toward the train. It was made up of a Segunda, a Servicio Postal Mexicano, an express, ten freight cars, and a caboose. A man wearing the uniform of the Ferrocarril del Pacifico came out of the station with a sack of mail—almost nothing —and threw it into the Servicio Postal.

This seemed to be a signal. Friends were saying goodbye, relatives embracing each other.

In that last instant, just before the train began to move, Michael said, "It will be remembered for a while—Wally, it won't be forgotten for a while, will it?"

"Don't ask me," Wally said.

He offered his hand, but Michael embraced him Mexican style.

Then he got on the train.

CHAPTER TEN

The body of Alan Kidd was discovered at dusk that Sunday afternoon by the watchman making his single off-day round.

There was no evidence of a struggle.

The police, finding powder burns on the uniform, concluded that the single shot through the heart had been exploded when two bodies were in some kind of embrace.

Chief Burns, on a pleasure boat in the middle of Lake Mead, was reached by short wave. Key men had to be fetched from where they'd been hunting deer on the cool slopes of sierras. On Monday morning, the chief, having driven most of the night, took personal charge of the investigation. There was a flurry of activity. Word was sent to a federal investigative body, all-points bulletins released, border crossings alerted.

But the information sent out was scatter shot.

The confusion increased when a report from ballistics declared the murder weapon service issue.

There were eighteen thousand men on the base to question.

The airman from whom Wally had borrowed the pistol preferred to remain silent. Soured by combat, he was indifferent to death.

On Tuesday morning, Alan was honored by an editorial, its tone of regret tinctured with a few drops of satisfaction. As the owner-editor who wrote the piece said more plainly

372

in private, "The time's past when a man can sit on both sides of the fence."

For what the summer had left of the university's intellectual community, Alan was the topic of the day. Professor Hough was quoted quoting "You're part of the problem of you're part of the solution."

But it was Sergeant Jones's wife who expressed the precise feeling of the rest of the community: "Serves him right for messing with those hippies."

On the base, the person who knew Alan best had nothing to say to her consolers. Dry-eyed, Marian Kidd sat all the day through in a corner of her small living room. When the sympathetic and the curious had left, Muriel and Colonel Dowd got up. "Why don't you come spend the night with us?" her father suggested.

Marian kissed him. "That's not necessary, daddy."

Dowd went to get the car while his wife waited. It was to Muriel, as they touched cheeks, that Marian whispered the conclusion she'd reached.

"He wanted it."

To Marian's surprise, Alan had left what amounted to a will, a short letter addressed to her. He requested that his body be given to a medical school specializing in neurological studies and his worldly goods to Michael Winter.

"Never!" Marian screamed in her empty house.

She tore the letter to shreds. After all, it wasn't legally valid, hadn't been witnessed or properly filed.

Nevertheless, she disposed of the body as Alan had requested. Young medical students found it a perfect specimen.

There was no one for the police to work over. The students were away till fall; the hippies had left the area; most of the known criminals, operating as respectable businessmen, sold olive oil.

Donna, found poolside at her mother's condominium in North Hollywood, was no help.

A week passed.

A communication finally came in from Police H.Q., N.Y, N.Y. A department search had turned up nothing on Michael Winter. Between the lines was: Christ, haven't we enough trouble of our own?

Another week passed.

The heavy heat came down. No one went out of homes or offices in the middle of the day. Even the rattlers stayed in their holes and hunted by night.

It became apparent that the police investigation would be measured in months.

There was no pressure from the community. It wanted quiet.

Then came the public announcement: A twenty-five-thousand dollar reward had been offered for information leading to the capture of the murderer.

With justice a paying proposition, a new impetus was felt. Who put up the money was not revealed.

Mr. Don Wheeler had a couple of weeks to kill before his safari date. He spent some days in New York, walked Fifth Avenue in highly polished cowboy boots, so declaring his scorn for that place and its people. Then he flew to London, engaged a small suite in Claridge's, and decided to wait there.

His first outing was to Grosvenor Square. His mail had been sent to the American Embassy in care of a friend who worked there. It was while he was sitting in this man's office, reading Gavin's letter about Alan Kidd and looking at the newspaper clippings, that the demonstration broke outside.

Over a thousand young men and women stormed the American Embassy and screamed their hatred. Buckets of red paint—"blood"—were thrown on the sides of the building.

Wheeler watched the demonstrators from a second-story window and he knew who'd killed Alan Kidd. When the bobbies had finished breaking up the crowd of young militants, he wired Gavin instructions to offer a twenty-five-thousand-dollar reward for—so he believed—Michael Winter.

Clifford Winter considered engaging the private investigators recommended by his company's labor-relations department. What made him decide not to was the fact he finally faced: If they found Michael, the first thing he'd have to do after kissing him was turn him over to the authorities.

Art Greenbaum was home for the summer. He questioned his father at length about Michael Winter, finally admitted he was writing a long piece about the trial.

The thing that astonished Judge Breen—and made him uneasy—was that while the police had not been able to tag the man responsible for the lieutenant's murder, his son took it for granted that it was Michael, and for some reason Breen didn't understand, Michael was Art's hero.

"What do you mean he made good on it?" Breen demanded of his son.

Art smiled his Greenbaum smile and didn't answer.

"He means," Sarah told him later, "that while you were all exonerating a murderer, young Mr. Winter conducted his own trial, and imposed his own sentence."

"But Sare, he shot an innocent man!"

"Apparently he didn't think so," she said.

Many people, including Judge Breen, Gavin McAndrews, even Cy Walker, benefited from their public exposure at the trial, but none so quickly and dramatically as Irene Connor.

The bar where Irene worked had become the most popular place in town. The lady had a great flow of anecdotes and was shameless in self-revelation. To be at a barside table with her was like being on stage with a great actress through her most emotional performance.

Hal saw the possibility, talked to a few of the affluent regulars, and quickly raised the money to open a bar of their own: *Irene's*.

The symbolic heart of the place is the large tinted picture over the bar, that of the house god, the owner's only son, Vincent.

For reasons open to superstition, photographs of dead men fade. Irene had seen her son only once since he was full grown, and on that occasion she was loaded. So now, when she looks at the fading eyes of the face over her bar, she replaces them with the living eyes of that other boy, the one who helped her bury her son. Sometimes they seem to reproach her, suggest she's getting rich at the expense of the dead.

There are days when Irene is possessed by this irrational

guilt, and on those days she's been known to stop kids on the street and ask them if they've heard anything about Michael, what's happened to him, where he is, what's he doing?

There wasn't a human being to be seen on the plains of Serengeti except the white hunter, a young Englishman who called Mr. Don Wheeler "sir," and the five blacks who called him "master."

But the land was the last of it—unimproved by man.

The lions were so easy to kill with his Mannlicher 243 and its Krollscope that Wheeler stopped shooting them. He remembered the words of his dead wife and ordered that he be driven close to where he could watch the affectionate family play of these beautiful animals. In his Land Rover, it seemed he didn't exist for the lions. He sat by the hour watching one pride; sleeping, yawning, stretching, cuffing their young, licking each other, fondling, fornicating, taking their dust baths.

Wheeler felt he could spend the rest of his life on the plains of Tanzania.

He became particularly fond of a lioness and her three cubs, spent days watching them. They became his family.

One morning he observed the lioness carefully hide her babies under a bush and set out to hunt a meal. As she walked off, another lion moved in, an old male, who killed the three cubs ate one, walked off with the body of another to eat later. On his way he met a larger, younger male who took the dead cub away and ate it himself.

Wheeler determined to see the episode through, waited for the lioness to come back. He wanted to see where she would direct her rage.

Finally she returned, found only the one cub, dead, looked at it for a while then ate it.

Wheeler didn't take time to change clothes, had himself driven to Nairobi, making it in a day and a night's forced journey Then he took the VC-10 to London.

Remembering Grosvenor Square, he didn't leave London Airport caught the first plane to Amsterdam.

He found the Dutch disgustingly overfed, their streets and public places full of hippies. They were everywhere, sitting on the ground—he had to walk through and over their bodies when he crossed the central square. At night when he walked along the canals, he saw couples making love openly. When they looked up at him, it wasn't with antagonism, but rather as the lions had. He didn't exist for them.

He flew to Paris. There was a letter from Gavin with the news that no one had been picked up on the Kidd murder. Perhaps because this news depressed him, perhaps because he was oddly stimulated by what he'd seen in Amsterdam, Wheeler asked the hall porter of his hotel to get him a woman.

She was very young, moved with professional dispatch, getting it over with. Wheeler came before he was in her. While she dressed, he realized he was in a state of tension, near panic. In the hall waiting for the girl was a very thin man who reminded Wheeler of someone he'd seen in the back of a courtroom. He looked at Wheeler murderously until he closed the door.

Wheeler couldn't sleep, got up twice to check that the door was locked, then lay awake considering where he might live the rest of his days in peace.

He recalled a cape buffalo he'd seen in Africa, an old bull in exile from the herd, standing knee-deep at the edge of a swamp between the crocs and the hyenas; a mean-looking old beast, his once-proud hump now withering, his legs thinner than they'd been in their prime and slightly bowed, his head hanging heavy and low as he looked around at the waiting predators.

They knew, those crocs, those hyenas, that all they had to do was wait.

"You've got a long wait, buddy," Wheeler said aloud.

At breakfast an advertisement in the Sunday London *Times* gave him a solution. He'd sell his place on the mountain, and buy an island in the Bahamas, a whole island, live there safe and alone for the rest of his life.

Waiting for the plane home were hundreds of young people, all, it seemed to Wheeler, freely consorting, all it also seemed, waiting to take over the earth when he let go.

Before he boarded the plane he cabled Gavin to raise the reward to fifty thousand dollars.

It was Cesario Flores who first went to the police and

tried to claim the money. He said he knew for sure it was Michael Winter, that he could even tell them where to find the boy. But he wanted the money in his pocket first.

Cesario had become bitter and what had made him so was the inconsistency of the human race. He wasn't a hero to the men at the plant where he worked, he was a pest. They complained that one way or another he brought the case into every conversation, went over and over it like it was the 1962 World Series. "Who cares?" they'd say. "So what?" they'd say. "Forget it!" There were fistfights. "Sooner or later, somebody's going to kill that guy," they'd say.

The police told Cesario they'd have to have the culprit in custody and convicted before any reward could be paid.

Anyway, why don't you tell us where he is—if you're on the level?"

Cesario sneered. "You're just like the rest," he said.

The door to the squad room head was open, and as Cesario walked into it he took a postcard out of his back pocket, tore it into little squares, and flushed it away.

So Juana never saw the postcard.

Addressed to her at the base, its postmark had been Jojutla, Morelos, Mexico. In the space opposite her name there was a drawing of two fingers in the peace sign and, underneath, "V for Vinnie."

When a friend back from a vacation in Mexico said he'd had a glimpse of Michael there, Clifford decided to fly down.

He walked around and talked to the kids. There were hundreds.

A boy knew a girl who claimed she'd taught Michael a song. But whether this proved he'd been there or she somewhere else, Clifford couldn't make out.

There was a persistent if secondhand rumor that Michael used to sit with a small, rather dumpy girl in the plaza of Cuernavaca—or was it Cuautla?—and that he favored enchiladas suizas and Cerveza Dos Xs. Not that these facts would have any particular significance, but Clifford tracked them down in both places. A waiter in Cuautla did remember the couple, but all he could recall was that the girl paid the checks.

On his last night in Mexico City, Clifford ran into some

kids who'd actually talked to Michael some months ago. They said his memory seemed to be affected—well, no, not that exactly, but his mind kept wandering, wouldn't stay on the subject. But a lot of the kids were that way now.

Anyway, they told him, he'd left Mexico.

Now Wheeler had what he wanted, an entire island, no one else on it except a couple to take care of his house and cook his meals, and a man for the boats.

Every morning a gang of blacks arrived in a little gray sloop with a purple sail. Wheeler didn't need a foreman; he knew where he wanted paths cut through the bush, new areas cleared, banana trees planted. Like a stone crab he clambered over the coral, shouting orders, driving the men, his enormous energy compressed like an explosive.

On the day he decided the place was beginning to look like something he invited Gavin.

Gavin was heavier, softer. Wheeler teased him about that penalty of success. It was obvious that he would never be a great legal mind, but he knew by instinct how to deal in influence, its arrangement and exertion, how to compromise issues and put together combines, all the behind-the-scenes work where the big loot lay.

He told Wheeler about his decision to open a branch in the state's capital, and Wheeler listened as if what happened in that world had never interested him any more than it did now.

"I've got Cy Walker working for me up there," Gavin said.

"One of the few pleasures of success," Wheeler observed, "is helping those less successful than yourself, especially if they happen to be old adversaries." Then he was on his feet again, shouting at Russel, the boatman on the dock below, warning him to be sure to have the boat with the 50 horsepower outboard ready at six the next morning, not at seven-thirty!

Gavin was proud of his father but a little worried. The old man was like a heavyweight champion of the world with midgets for sparring partners.

On the last day of Gavin's visit they had a great day bone fishing on the marl flats of an unoccupied island, two down the Exuma line. Gavin tied into several five- and six-pounders, but Wheeler boated a nine-pound beauty.

Later Russel, now wearing a white coat over his khaki top and shorts, served them rum drinks on the terrace. "There's still a sense of order here," Wheeler said. "Compare these blacks with ours. They're not only contented, they're proud of what they do, am I right, Russel?"

"Yes, master," Russel said.

Wheeler laughed. "Russel hasn't even heard that he's not supposed to call a white man 'master' any more."

As Gavin was putting his bags on the small seaplane that was to carry him back to Nassau and the big carriers, he said, "I'm going to lift that fifty-thousand-dollar reward. No one's been able to find that boy. The police believe he's dead. Okay?"

When Donna heard the reward had been withdrawn she took a vacation in Costa Rica. Actually she was prepared not to come back. But she did. She seemed disappointed in her trip, wouldn't talk about what had happened.

Even to Wally, who passed through on the way to L.A., all she would say was that Michael had become sort of strange, "bombed out," permanently tripping.

A few weeks after her return Donna gave up. She decided to move to the state's capital where Cy Walker had moved and accept the offer he'd made her.

It was the commonsense thing to do, but as she spoke to Cy on the phone, saying, yes, she'd take the job, sure, she'd be glad to see him again, it seemed to him she was crying.

Bulletins from the New York underground do not come in on the police teletype. Students of the University of Puerto Rico who came to New York to meet with the Young Lords party spoke with the greatest admiration of this strange *gringito* who'd taken part in the action that burned down the ROTC building on their campus in Rio Piedras, but they also said he was bitter and, when turned on, scoffed at what they were doing, saying that there was only one kind of action that counted now. They were glad to see him go.

One of the kids who'd gone to Cuba to assist in the

sugar harvest reported he'd seen Michael there, cutting cane. This other kid had seen Michael in the square the night of Castro's self-denunciation, and he said that on that night he heard a rumor that Michael had been invited to leave Cuba.

Finally, Clifford got a letter from Algiers. Michael was demanding money, as if asking to be refused. Clifford seriously considered flying to Algiers, even had his secretary look into plane schedules, but unfortunately it was at precisely this time that his company was reorganizing.

So Clifford sent a money order and a loving letter, begging for more news. "What I keep wondering," he said, "is how you get along without money. So I'm going to send you that lousy seventy-five every month whether you want it or not." And so on.

On every fourth weekend Mr. Don Wheeler's cook and butler took off in the twenty-four-footer to visit their home and children in Georgetown across the Inside Water. Before they left they stopped for a moment with Russel, who was working on the 50 h.p. outboard motor. They warned him to reassemble the pieces at once: the master wanted to go fishing and Russel might catch hell again.

What they didn't tell Russel was that Mr. Wheeler had asked them to look for a replacement. What had offended Mr. Don was the discovery that his cinnamon-skinned boatman had brought two young females to the island, they'd been living in the boathouse with him. They seldom came out of the little hut into the heat of the sun, but at night Mr. Wheeler could hear them, all three, whispering and laughing and playing together.

When the couple returned Monday morning, they found the outboard still disassembled on the dock. Near the piece of old tarp on which the parts were spread, there was a wash of blood. On the sand under the shore end of the pier was a knife Russel used to clean fish. It had fallen through the planks and was marked with blood.

The dory was gone, the auxiliary 5 h.p. outboard was gone, Russel was gone—and whoever had been living with him.

Before the couple went back to Georgetown to notify the

police they scrubbed the dock, cleaned the knife. As they left the island, they noticed an unusual show of shark in the bay. When they told the district captain that Russel had disappeared, he observed that the Caribbean is a very large area.

Early the next year, an officer in the air force, retired, shot and killed a longhair who'd been running around with his daughter. Defense counsel did not think it necessary to plead temporary insanity.

Months later, Clifford's letter with the money came back. Time passed.

If Michael had a reason for living, it didn't express itself in any action, at least not that anyone knew about.

For a time people still wondered, asked each other where he was, he was somewhere for sure, he must be somewhere. And they'd answer Yes, of course, he had to be somewhere.

Then it was another season and another year and they forgot him.

The story of Vinnie's funeral became a legend. There were exaggerated accounts of what had been thrown into the grave; it was inevitable that sooner or later someone would go down with a shovel and see what of value might be recovered.

People who'd attended the funeral were recruited, probes were made in several places. None succeeded. The wind and the desert had confused surface evidence, obliterated identifying signs.

The body disintegrates in peace. The bones powder, become part of the sand.

The third largest air force in the world sits idle on the sand of the Military Storage and Disposition Center of the Davis-Monthan Air Force Base just outside Tucson, Arizona.

Why there?

Because the weather is dry, and the soil contains very little acid. A plane not used will disintegrate, but here it will disintegrate more slowly.

So here they stand, the might of America, our answer to

the challenge of history, our pride, our image, our identity, our names.

The A-1E Sky Raider, the A-3 Sky Warrior, the A-4 Sky Hawk, the A-7A Corsair, the B-26 Invader, the B-29 Superfortress, the B-52 Stratofortress, the B-66 Destroyer—
   And more.

The C-46 Commando, the C-54 Sky Master, the C-117 Lift Master, the C-124 Globe Master, the C-133 Cargo Master—
   And more.

The F-8 Crusader, the F-9 Cougar, the F-11 Tiger, the F-24 Thunderstreak, the F-86 Saberjet, the F-89 Scorpion, the F-94 Star Fighter—
   And more.

More Outstanding Fiction
from Fawcett Crest

RABBIT REDUX Q1753 $1.50
by John Updike

A big new bestseller that vividly brings to life Harry "Rabbit" Angstrom, grown conservative and middle-aged in his thirties. "By far the most audacious and successful book Updike has yet written." —**New York Times Book Review**

ANGLE OF REPOSE Q1768 $1.50
by Wallace Stegner

Winner of the 1971 Pulitzer Prize in Fiction. A sweeping novel covering the exciting age of discovery and expansion on the 19th-century American frontier, **Angle of Repose** chronicles the life of Susan Burling and her husband, Oliver Ward.

THE PEACEABLE KINGDOM C1773 $1.95
by Jan de Hartog

The story of the passionate, flesh-and-blood men and women who began the Quaker movement in England in the 17th century and of those who settled in Philadelphia one hundred years later. "A feast of solid, rousing fiction—tremendously impressive." —**The New York Times**

FAWCETT WORLD LIBRARY

WHEREVER PAPERBACKS ARE SOLD

If your bookdealer is sold out, send cover price plus 15¢ each for postage and handling to Mail Order Service, Fawcett Publications, Inc., Greenwich, Connecticut 06830. Please order by number and title. Orders accepted only for United States and Possessions. A free catalog of Fawcett Crest, Gold Medal, and Premier Books is available upon request.